The Wolf At Large

Terry Cloutier

Dedication

I'm lucky enough to not only have a wonderful mother in my life, but a great friend as well. This one is for you, Mom!

Character List By Order Of Appearance

Hadrack: The Wolf of Corwick
Hughe: Hadrack's eldest son
Lairn: Captain of the guards
Gernie: Innkeeper
Jan of Limeview: Minstrel
Tern: Lady Demay's servant
Peren: Pith youth
Baine: Hadrack's friend
Einhard: The Sword of the King
Alesia: Wife of Einhard
Jebido: Hadrack's friend and mentor
Carbet: Cardian
Shana: Lady Demay
Carspen Tuft: Slaver
Josphet: Steward of Gasterny Garrison
Eriz: Pith warrior
Betania: Female Gander slave and healer
Ania: Pith archer
Clendon the Peacemaker: Pith king
Danfor the Lighthearted: The Shield of the King
Flinhard the Eager: The Ear of the King
Larles the Unlucky: The Eye of the King
Talai: Female Gander slave

Son Oriell: Priest
Klesp: Pith warrior
Daughter Gernet: Priestess
Jin: Daughter-In-Waiting
Orfen: Pith warrior
Lale: Pith warrior
Lord Corwick: Lord of Corwick Castle
Lord Demay: Lord of Calban Castle
Quant Ranes: Leader of the nine
Padrea: Pith archer
Gadest: Pith warrior
Prince Tyrale: Son of King Jorquin. Heir to the throne.
Hanley of Laskerly: Gander peasant
Jamet: Pith warrior
Faldir: Ganderman
Malo: House Agent
Daest: Gatekeeper
Finol: Steward of Witbridge Manor
Hasther: Haverty's servant
Haverty: Apothecary and healer
Gris: Malo's servant
Skind Kurko: Ferryman
Sim: Outlaw
Bridy: Ruffian
Nigan: Watchman
Flora: Whore
Aenor: Whore

Linny Plost: Ganderman
Margot: Whore
Hape: One of the nine
Tyris: Archer and deserter
Black Thomin: Outlaw leader
Putt: Outlaw
Anson: Outlaw
Cain: Outlaw
Niko: Outlaw
Alga the Merchant: Gander merchant
Duin: Mute villager
Kylan: Steward of Calban Castle
Larstin: Lord Demay's advisor and confidant

CONTENTS

PROLOGUE

I can't sleep tonight. Just like every other night before it in my recent memory. I toss and turn, willing my mind into blackness, but no matter how I lie, I can't seem to find comfort. My pain-wracked body screams at me with every move, a constant and unsympathetic reminder of the past that I've lived. The room is silent and cold, the stillness broken only by the creak of the bed and my groans as I fidget constantly. The mattress beneath me feels like a hard-oak board against my back and the pillow an unforgiving brick against my head. I snort out loud in frustration and try not to think, willing sleep to overcome me even as I know I'm destined to fail. My body may be broken and wasted, but the mind that controls it is not, and I can't stop it from brooding about the past. Perhaps I should never have started writing about my life? Perhaps writing of my father and sister and Einhard and all the others had been a mistake? After all, what good can dredging up forgotten memories and faces of those long gone from this world do me now anyway.

Finally, I give up with a curse and fling the covers off my skinny legs. There will be no sleep for me this night. I sit up and rest my feet on the floor and slowly rub my scarred face with my hands. Who would have thought that after all I'd been through in my life, that sleep would turn out to be my greatest enemy? The glow from the moon coming in through the window bathes me in faint light and I stare down at my crushed and misshapen left foot with distaste.

"I truly am my father's son," I mutter.

I catch a gleam of gold from beneath the bed and grimace even as I feel a growing pressure coming from my bladder. I slide the chamber pot out with my good foot, not worried in the least that the contents inside might spill. The few sad little drops that I'd offered up before I'd gotten into bed wouldn't have been enough for even a flea to drown in. I stand above the bowl and lift my nightshirt and my manhood and the chamber pot stare at each other with mutual distrust. It is an all-too-familiar standoff. I close my eyes and concentrate, feeling the overwhelming need for release and suppressing the urge to curse out loud as I wait impatiently. Finally, victory arrives in a small, insignificant stream that dribbles half-heartedly into the pot. It wasn't much, but I sigh in relief anyway and then limp over to the fireplace. I use the poker lying beside the hearth and stir the coals until they begin to smoke and glow, then I throw several logs on. Satisfied, I step back to stare up at my sword, Wolf's Head, where it sits regally above the mantle watching me. The wood begins to crackle and smoke on the coals and then, with a faint puff, a flame erupts, quickly gaining strength. The sword's judgmental ruby eyes glitter back at me from the shadows and I look at it guiltily. How long has it been since I'd taken it down? I wonder.

"What are you looking at?" I finally growl in irritation as I shift my gaze away.

Beside Wolf's Head hangs my father's great axe, lost to me more than once, but still with me after all these years. And beside that, Boar's Tooth, the short sword given to me long ago by Malo. Exactly how long has it been since I'd held any of my weapons in my hands? I wonder as I stroke my white beard. Surely no more than a month or so? I pick up a taper from the mantle and light it in the now roaring fire, then turn away. I make my way to the sprawling oak table where I do my writing and light several fat candles that sit on the table. Then I turn back in surprise, staring up at the weapons. I hadn't taken them down since I'd begun writing, I realize. I sit heavily in my chair and fight to focus. When was that? It had been early spring, I think, feeling a thud in my gut as I realize that had been almost a year ago. Where had the time gone?

I remember I'd left Corwick Castle in a bit of a rage just after sundown. My eldest son, Hughe, was entertaining several of his endless whores and he'd even had the audacity to offer one of them to me. As if tossing me a pox-ridden trollop as an afterthought would somehow make up for all the trouble he'd caused me over the years. A trollop, I might add, who'd been paid for with my gold. Needless to say, I do not react well to charity and we'd argued, as we always did. Hughe didn't understand why I was so angry, nor could I tell him that just waking my cock up long enough to piss was torture, let alone asking it to do anything else. That was an unfortunate truth that I didn't care to dwell on back then. Or even now for that matter. I remember I'd belted Wolf's Head around my waist and then stalked away from Hughe before I did something I'd regret later and I headed for the stables feeling meaner than a bear with a thorn in its paw. Lairn, the captain of my guards, saw me come out of the keep and he hurried toward me.

"My lord, what can I do for you?" he asked me.

"You can leave me alone!" I growled back at him as I entered the stable.

Lairn looked confused as I saddled my horse. "Are we going somewhere, my lord?" he asked tentatively. Lairn had been in my employ for almost ten years. He was a good lad and a fine soldier, but he'd learned early on to tread lightly when I was in one of my moods.

"We are not," I said bluntly. "I am." I struggled to get my bad foot into the stirrup and mount my horse. Lairn dutifully moved to help me and I glared at him in warning. "Don't!" I hissed. I ignored the searing pain in my foot and forced myself onto the horse's back, where I sat uncomfortably looking down at Lairn. I still hated being on a horse, even after all the years I'd been riding.

"May I ask where you are going, lord?" Lairn asked me. He slowly stroked my horse's muzzle and I didn't fail to notice that he wrapped his fingers around its noseband.

"Captain," I said, trying to control the rage I felt.

"Yes, my lord?"

"I am an old man." I put my hand on the hilt of my sword. "But not so old and doddering yet that I need permission from you to go where I please."

"But Lord Hughe said that..."

"Who is the Lord of Corwick!?" I snapped, cutting him off. "Is it me or is it my son?"

"You are, lord," Lairn said as he dropped his eyes from mine.

"Then you will obey me and mind your own business! Or you can turn in your sword right now!"

Lairn looked up and met my eyes, then I saw his gaze shift uncertainly to the great hall behind me before he focused back on me. Finally, he released my horse's bridal and stepped back. "My apologies, my lord."

"Accepted!" I grunted. Lairn was dressed in light armor and wore a brown woolen cloak over top of it. I looked down at my fine clothing and grimaced. "Give me your cloak," I ordered. Lairn hesitated, looking again to the hall and I growled loudly in impatience. Lairn hurried to take off the cloak and he handed it up to me. I put it on in moody silence, then lifted the hood, satisfied that it would hide my face. I kicked my horse into motion and glanced down at Lairn as I passed by him. "Don't breathe a word to anyone about this, understand?"

"Of course, my lord," Lairn said. He cleared his throat nervously. "Will you be back soon, lord?"

"I've no idea," I said. Meaning it.

I struck out along the road to the north, happy that no one was about at this time of night. I needed to be alone. I rode for at least an hour or more, just content to be with my thoughts. I wasn't worried about bandits, as it had been several years since any of them had been seen in Corwick. I'd made an example of the last bunch that had come through my lands raping and stealing, and it seemed that message had been clearly heard. I eventually reached a crossroad and I paused, squinting at the road sign that I could just see in the faint moonlight.

"Hatterdam," I muttered to myself as I read it. "Mother's tit! I remember that place!"

I chuckled and kicked my horse's flanks, guiding it onto the road to Hatterdam. Baine and I had been there once, many, many years ago. I don't remember why we'd gone there, but there had been an inn in the village called The One-Eyed Crow where we'd stopped for a drink. I laughed out loud as I pictured the place, my mood lifting as my horse pricked its ears at me curiously. The inn was rough, I remembered, but the beer had been good, and Baine and I had met several women there. Just girls, really but eager enough, nonetheless. I don't remember my girl's name, but she'd been slim and pretty, I recalled, with a saucy way about her. I slapped my leg with mirth, laughing again as I thought about Baine's girl. She'd been big, that one, with an ugly face, brown teeth and a boil on her nose that looked like a beetle. She must have weighed twice as much as Baine did, but none of that mattered to him in the least. He'd taken one look at her huge tits and that was it, he was in love. Baine tended to fall in love almost as often as he farted.

I reached the outskirts of the village and I paused, assessing it for any potential threats. Never rush into anything, Jebido had told me long ago, and his words of caution had become as natural to me as breathing. I figured I'd lived this long because of Jebido's sage advice, though, if the truth were told, I didn't always follow it when I was a younger man. The village was larger than I remembered, which was hardly surprising. It must have been thirty years ago or more since Baine and I had been there. Hatterdam was part of my fiefdom, I knew, but I'd never felt a reason to return to it, until now. Satisfied that all was well, I urged my horse forward. There were people about, here and there along the streets, though few paused in what they were doing to take notice of me. I was just one lone old man on a horse. Nothing special. I reached the village square and saw the two-story inn right away, dominating the corner of the square just as I remembered. A ratty-looking wooden sign hung above the doorway and was swinging meekly in the light breeze. The sign was in desperate need of paint, I saw, but

13

I could vaguely make out the likeness of a crow perched over the name of the inn. I rode my horse around the back to the stables, where I handed him off to a boy of about nine or so dressed in a muddy tunic over torn trousers.

I limped around to the front of the inn and entered, pausing to let my eyes adjust to the flickering lantern light inside. The floor was laid with cut grey stone that was criss-crossed by random veins of white and black throughout it. I remembered the last time I'd been inside this room there had been nothing on the floor but a mixture of dirt, puke and piss. Rough wooden tables and chairs were strewn about without any order to them that I could see. Perhaps as many as twenty people — both men and women — were sitting at the various tables. Several men sitting together near the stone fireplace at the back of the room were eating and talking quietly, while everyone else seemed to be drinking. I recognized no one, of course, and surprisingly, I felt a sudden pang of loneliness. I squashed it with an angry grunt and selected an unoccupied table near the door. I sat down just as a squat, bald man approached me.

"Evening," the bald man said with a friendly smile. I nodded, saying nothing as I kept my face hidden. "I'm Gernie. What can I get for you? We've got a lovely goose stew. Or if you prefer, fresh herring or..."

"Just beer," I said gruffly, cutting Gernie off.

My good mood was quickly fading and I was starting to think that this had been a mistake. My friends were all dead, I thought bitterly, and coming here this night wouldn't change that no matter how much I wished otherwise. I cursed myself for being an old fool as the innkeeper nodded to me and left. I decided I'd drink my beer as quickly as I could and then head back to the castle and forget all about this place. Within moments, Gernie was back and he placed a foaming mug in front of me. I took out my moneybag and handed the innkeeper a coin and took a sip of beer.

"You're in luck," Gernie said as he hovered near my

table. I grunted in irritation, wishing he'd just go away so I could drain my mug. But the innkeeper stood waiting in anticipation, clearly expecting me to ask why. I glowered at my beer and remained silent and he finally added, "Jan of Limeview is here tonight and he's agreed to perform for us."

"Is that so?" I said, trying to feign interest. I kept my head down as I stared at my beer. I had no idea who Jan of Limeview was, nor did I much care. I'd been to Limeview briefly once as a young man and had found it to be a crawling cesspool filled with greed and malice, so I knew nothing good ever came from Limeview. It didn't look to me like the innkeeper planned to leave me alone anytime soon, so I decided a show of appreciation for whoever this fellow was might be enough to get him to leave. "I hear he's good," I managed to mumble.

"Oh, he's better than good, my friend," Gernie said. He slapped me on the shoulder and I ground my teeth, resisting the urge to draw Wolf's Head and cut the offending hand off. The innkeeper seemed oblivious to my anger and he swept his arm behind him toward the stairwell that led to the rooms on the second floor. "And there he is now."

Despite myself, I looked up as Gernie hurried away and I studied the young man who came down the stairs to a smattering of applause from the other patrons. Jan of Limeview was thin and tall, with long blond hair swept back from his forehead that fell well past his shoulders. He wore a matching green jacket with trousers and carried a polished lute in one hand. A minstrel, I realized with distaste as the blond man took up a position in the center of the room. I groaned inwardly. A minstrel from Limeview! Now I'd seen everything! This night was getting worse by the moment. The minstrel plucked a few cords on the lute, then began to play in earnest as he sang. The song was one I'd heard before. A humorous tale about the accidental death of King Harn, the father of King Jorquin of Ganderland. But the minstrel's voice was like nothing I'd ever heard, and I sat up in surprise. His voice was somehow both soft and firm, with perfect pitch and tone. I couldn't help but sit spellbound as I listened. Finally, something out of Limeview that didn't reek of decadence! Wonders never ceased! The minstrel finished his song and I drained my mug, then stood up and crossed to the door as the singer began to speak behind me.

"Thank you," Jan of Limeview said in that soft, soothing voice of his. "This next song is one I wrote just recently about the fall of Calban and the death of Lord Demay. The events of which were told to me by a man who was there. This will be my first time singing it to an audience and I call it The Wolf and The Lamb."

I froze at the man's words and I turned, my hand automatically falling to the hilt of Wolf's Head as the minstrel began to sing.

The wolf came running to Calban that day
With a pledge and a promise that no one could sway
The odds were against him and his ragged band
The fate of the Lady held within his hand

But the legend was growing for all to see
The death of the nine not certain, but soon to be
Inside the castle was the prize to take
But to get it the wolf had a choice to make

The invaders killed with savage glee
Striking down innocents in their victory
The lord of the castle fought for his bride
But even his great strength couldn't stem the tide

The pack of the wolf committed murder and rape
While the lord's new bride begged for escape
But the wolf just laughed and took the lamb for his own
A crime of passion until today unknown

"Enough!" I cried. Even with my bad foot I was on the minstrel in a heartbeat as I drew Wolf's Head from its scabbard. I could feel the old rage pulsing in my veins as I leveled the tip of my sword at the terrified singer's throat. "How dare you!" I growled.

"Please! Please!" Gernie moaned as he ran to us. "There is no call for this! It's just a song, good friend."

"Just a song!?" I snarled at him as Wolf's Head tickled the minstrel's soft white throat. Around us the other patrons were deathly still, staring at us in morbid fascination. "It's a lie!" I shouted. "A filthy lie, and I'll not hear it again from this whoreson's lips!"

"It's not a lie!" the minstrel said, surprising me.

"It is a lie!" I spat back. "And you'll never sing it again. If you do, I'll feed your balls to the dogs!"

"But it was told to me by someone who was there," the minstrel insisted with a slight whine in his voice now.

"Who?" I demanded.

"I...I...don't know his name," Jan of Limeview said. "He was just a boy then. But he swears he was there and saw what happened."

"Well," I said, drawing back the tip of Wolf's Head from the man's throat. I had my anger under control now. "I was there, too, minstrel," I said calmly. "And I promise you, it's a lie." I sheathed my sword and pulled back the hood of my cloak while around me people gasped.

"Lord Hadrack!" Gernie whispered as he and everyone else in the inn dropped to one knee.

When I'd returned to the castle later that night, I'd made my way to my rooms, thankful that I hadn't bumped into my son or any of his whores. I remember hanging up Wolf's Head and pledging to myself that I wouldn't do anything like that again. Then I'd sat down at my table, thinking of my friends and all that I'd lost. That's when I saw the quill and paper and I knew what I had to do. I didn't know then — any more than I know now — how long I had left in this world, but after what I'd heard that night in Hatterdam, I knew that I needed the truth to be out there before I died. And so, I'd started writing.

Now, almost a year later, I was still sitting at the same table with paper and quill in front of me. I thought of that minstrel from Limeview and the song that he'd sung that night and I shook my head. Not all of it had been wrong, of course. But I'd never forced myself on The Lamb as the singer had claimed. I smiled sadly as I thought about her. No, I'd not forced her. The Lamb had come to my bed willingly.

I picked up the quill, dipped it in ink and began to write. I still had so much more to tell.

1: THE LAMB

The man had died a very hard death. It was still early morning and already getting warm as I halted my patrol somewhere northwest of Gasterny Garrison. The sprawling forest behind the garrison lay silent and peaceful and might even have been a pleasant place, if not for all the blood and buzzing flies. That blood was still wet, I saw, and I knew that the poor fellow suspended in front of me hadn't been dead for long. I searched the forest with my eyes for threats, but my gut told me that whoever had done this thing was gone by now. At eighteen I was already a hardened veteran of battle, though I looked much older than my years with my scarred face, thick beard and heavy build. The Pith sitting his horse to my right abruptly hunched over in his saddle and puked out his breakfast of bread and ale. I noticed absently that the flies were already beginning to land on the growing puddle of slime pooling at his horse's feet. The Pith's name was Peren, a boy of no more than fifteen or so, and he was on his first patrol with us that morning. Unlucky for him, I thought. I adjusted my father's axe that lay in its sheath across my back, then lowered my hand to the hilt of Wolf's Head. I studied the dead man's naked, mutilated body where it hung by its wrists between two trees and shook my head slowly at the savageness of what had been done to him.

"Why the spear, Hadrack?" Baine asked from my left.

"What?" I said absently, turning to glance at him.

"Up the ass," Baine said, making a face. "Why shove it up his ass like that? It's just not right."

I shrugged. "I think the spear was the least of his worries." I glanced at Peren. "Do you recognize him?"

Peren wiped his mouth with the back of his hand and

shook his head weakly. "I don't know, brother." He looked at me uncertainly. "It's hard to tell with most of his face gone like that."

"What about you?" I asked Baine. My friend, as usual, was dressed in black leather armor and he just shook his head, staring at the body.

"Well, whoever he was," I muttered, "his troubles are over now."

Whoever had killed this man had taken their time with him, I realized. Clearly, he'd had information that they'd wanted. Information which the dead man hadn't wanted to give up. The question was, what was it they wanted to know and who were 'they'? I stared at the dark red blood that stained the shrubs, leaves and twigs that littered the ground beneath the dead man's feet. Even the trunks to either side of the body were sprayed with blood.

"How far do you think we are from the garrison?" I finally asked.

Baine shrugged. "Three or four miles, I'd say."

I nodded, thinking the same thing. "So, well inside the perimeter then?"

"It would seem so," Baine agreed. "Do you think Ganders would be stupid enough to do this?"

I snorted. "And risk the consequences? I don't think so."

The Bridge Battle, as we liked to call it, had happened over a year ago. Not only had the Ganders lost a humiliating battle to us, they'd lost their prince as well. Prince Tyro, eldest son to King Jorquin and heir to the throne, had spent the last year locked up in Gasterny under the Piths watchful eyes. Einhard's terms to King Jorquin had been simple. If even one Ganderman was seen anywhere within a five-mile radius of the garrison, the prince's severed head would be displayed on the walls for all of Ganderland to see. The king had raged when he'd heard our terms, but in the end his love for his son was stronger than his rage and he'd reluctantly agreed. Now we were at an impasse. The Ganders were effectively stymied from attacking us, but we couldn't attack them either until we received word from the Master to invade. That didn't stop accidents from happening, of course, and over the last year there had been multiple skirmishes between the two forces. Many of which I'd been involved in.

I glanced at Peren where he sat his horse. The boy's face was deathly white and he was trying hard to look anywhere but at the corpse. He was young and inexperienced, I knew, but he was still a Pith and I had no doubt he'd be fine. I looked at the small horn Peren had strapped over his shoulder and considered having him blow it. Then I decided against it. No sense in having a hundred war-hungry Piths crashing down on us through the trees until we knew exactly what we were dealing with.

"Peren, ride back to the garrison and tell Einhard what you've seen here," I finally said. "Baine and I will try to figure this thing out while you're gone."

"I'd rather stay with you, brother," Peren said bravely. "I'm all right now."

"Of course you're all right!" I snapped in irritation. "Why wouldn't you be? I just need someone to tell Einhard about this, and that someone is going to be you. Understand?"

"Yes, brother," Peren said, looking dejected. He unstrapped the horn and held it out to me, but I just shook my head and gestured that Baine should take it.

"Let Einhard know we don't think it's Gandermen," I added as Peren brought his horse about. The boy nodded his understanding and then headed off through the trees.

"So now what?" Baine asked me once Peren was gone.

"Now we figure it out," I said with a grin as I swung my leg over my horse and dropped to the ground.

Baine hooked the horn over his saddle and adjusted the bow across his back, then he sighed loudly and dismounted to follow me as I approached the body.

"What did they do with his...uh...you know?" Baine whispered with distaste as we drew closer.

I glanced at the gaping, oozing hole where the corpse's manhood used to be, then up to his distorted mouth and the bits of torn flesh hanging out of it. "Probably in there," I said grimly. Baine made a face and nodded as we stopped about three feet from the body. I crouched down, looking at the ground for tracks. "Looks like there were three of them," I said, pointing to the various depressions in the undergrowth made from booted feet. There was a good impression of one of them from the heel to the toe in the wet blood and I frowned as I studied it.

"What is it?" Baine asked.

"Look at this," I said, pointing to the track.

Baine knelt beside me and stared at it, then shrugged. "It's a footprint."

"You don't say?" I said sarcastically. "I know it's a footprint." I motioned to the front of the print. "But look at the toe. It's pointed." I glanced down at my rounded, hobnailed boots that I'd taken from a dead Ganderman. "Who wears pointed boots?"

Baine stood up and glanced around. "Nobody that I've ever seen." He motioned past the dangling corpse. "But whoever they are, it looks like they went that way."

Baine nocked an arrow to his bow and together we followed the pointed tracks through the dense brush.

"Blood," Baine said almost immediately, motioning down to the ground where small droplets of red glistened like tiny rubies along the undergrowth. "A straight trail going west."

"Or coming from there," I muttered to myself.

We came to a small clearing of sandy soil surrounded by towering poplars and the trail of blood abruptly stopped. Hoofprints littered the clearing and I noticed some of the lower branches on the poplars had been stripped of leaves in quite a few places.

"Looks like they tied their horses here," I said, motioning to the bare branches.

Baine nodded and quickly crossed the clearing, then stooped down to examine the ground near the treeline. I paused to study the different hoofprints left by the horses where they'd stood chewing on the leaves. One of the horses had an obvious split hoof and a pile of horse dung sat near the treeline. I took off my mailed glove and squatted down and poked a finger into it.

"They headed that way," Baine said, hooking a thumb over his shoulder to the west. "They left a clear trail behind."

I nodded to him and gestured down at the dung with my chin. "The horse shit is still warm."

"How long do you think they've been gone?"

I wiped my finger off in the sand, then replaced my glove and stood up as I glanced to the west. "Not long," I said confidently. "If we hurry, we can catch them."

"And then what?" Baine asked as we returned for our horses.

I untied my horse's reins from the branch I'd hooked it to and grinned at Baine as I swung up into the saddle. I motioned to the mutilated corpse. "We ask them politely why they killed that poor bastard over there."

The brush to the west behind the dead man was too dense for horses, which was probably why the men with the pointed boots had left theirs behind. We skirted around it to the north, then backtracked to the clearing and headed west. I took the lead, moving quickly as the trail of crushed grass and broken undergrowth was easy to follow. The men we were pursuing had ridden away in single file, and they'd made no effort to cover their tracks. Something had been nagging at the back of my mind for a while now and I frowned in puzzlement as I finally realized was it was.

"There's something not right here," I said to Baine as he caught up to me.

"Oh?" Baine said, raising an eyebrow. "And what's that?"

I looked back over my shoulder at the way we'd come. "Three men killed that poor bastard, then went back to the clearing to get their horses."

"Yes," Baine agreed. "It sure looks that way."

I held up three fingers. "Three men, right?"

Baine nodded. "Yes, you just said that."

"But the tracks in the clearing were made by five horses."

Baine glanced at the trail stretching out in front of us, but with the undergrowth here it was impossible to tell exactly how many horses might have passed. "You're sure about that?" he asked, looking doubtful.

"Yes," I nodded.

"Maybe there were five of them and two stayed behind with the horses?"

"Then why tie them up?" I asked. "Why not just hold them and wait for the others to return?"

"Good point," Baine conceded. "Maybe the extra two were pack horses?"

"Maybe," I said doubtfully. "Or maybe one of those horses belonged to our dead friend. He had to have gotten here somehow."

Baine nodded. "Could be. But if that's true, then who was riding the fifth horse?"

"Good question," I muttered.

We followed the trail through the forest for another half hour or so until we came to a stream that cut directly across our path. The water was shallow; no more than three or four inches, but it moved quickly as it swept over and around slick stones and the tops of rotted tree limbs lodged beneath the surface. The bank of the stream closest to us was torn up and muddy and I assumed our quarry had paused there to let their horses drink.

"You're right, Hadrack," Baine said as he studied the ground. "I count five sets of prints."

I pointed to a deep impression at the edge of the stream left by the horse with the split hoof. It was slowly filling up with water. "Looks like we're right behind them," I said with a grin.

We guided our horses across the stream and within minutes reached a steep incline peppered with stunted pine trees. I looked down and then gestured to the incline. "They went up there."

The horses labored up the slope and at the top we found ourselves at the forest's edge looking out onto a narrow dirt road that split off in two directions. One section disappeared north along the forest, heading back to Gasterny, the other headed west along the ridge of a valley that seemed to run on for miles. Baine took the western road and I took the northern, looking for any sign of our quarry in the dirt.

"Here!" Baine finally called out as he pointed down. "The split hoof. Looks like they went this way."

I kicked my horse into motion and Baine and I headed west at full gallop. We rode for ten minutes or so as I constantly scanned the road for any glimpse of the men with the pointed boots. The land along the ridge of the valley had flattened out now and I could see clearly for at least several miles or more. I frowned with growing annoyance. I should be able to see some sign of them by now, I knew, but there was nothing ahead but empty road.

Baine glanced over at me and I could tell he was thinking the same thing I was. "Where'd they go!?" he shouted as he saw my eyes on him.

I took one more look down the empty road, then cursed out loud. We'd missed something. I slowed my horse and looked back over my shoulder in puzzlement. Baine circled to come back as I studied the green-shrouded valley far below us. The valley was deep, with treacherous looking slopes that would give even the most accomplished horsemen pause for thought, but it seemed the only answer.

"What is it?" Baine asked me.

I didn't answer as I trotted back the way we'd come, studying the grass along the side of the road. Finally, I grunted in satisfaction as I saw where the horses had left the road, tearing up the grass before disappearing over the edge of the valley. I paused my horse and looked down over the crest. I grimaced, not liking what I saw in the least. Great grooves had been dug into the side of the hill as the horses of our quarry fought to keep their balance going down. Small, shale-like rock lay loosely on the surface in sections and had been dislodged by the passage of the animals. It would be a hard, uncomfortable ride down, I knew, not relishing it.

Baine rode up to me and I gestured to the valley. "Looks like they went down here for some reason."

"Why?" Baine asked in surprise as he studied the deep furrows. "Are they insane or just stupid?"

"Maybe both," I said. "Either that or they just gave up looking for a better route."

"So, what do we do now?" Baine asked. I just looked at him and he sighed at the look of determination on my face. "You know we're well outside the perimeter, right?"

"I'm aware of that," I grunted as I stared back down into the valley.

"Einhard won't be happy about this, Hadrack."

I snorted. "You let me handle, Einhard."

"Like you did last night?" Baine asked innocently.

I looked at my friend in irritation even as I thought of the heated argument from the night before. Einhard had been an ass, I thought grumpily, and not for the first time either. The disagreement between us had become an all-too-familiar one and it was beginning to strain our friendship. As far as I was concerned, the request I'd made to Einhard should have been granted long ago. But each time I'd asked it in the last year, I'd received the same, stubborn, uncompromising answer.

"No!" Einhard had shouted, slamming his fist down on the desk where he sat.

"No?" I'd said right back to him as I stood in front of him. "Is that the only word you know now?"

We were in one of the rooms in the great hall that the Ganders had used for weapons storage. Einhard had converted it into his office and liked to conduct the daily business of running the garrison from there. He said he preferred it to the great hall with all its gold-plated furniture, rich tapestries and polished wood. Alesia was sitting against the back wall at a table fletching arrows with goose feathers. Her belly was swollen enormously with child and she placed her hand on the roundness of it as she glanced up at Einhard's angry tone. She shrugged and smiled at me in resignation before turning back to her work. Jebido and Baine fidgeted uncomfortably to either side of me and I studiously ignored Jebido as he gave me a warning look. Einhard seemed to have forgotten all about us as he stared down at a map that lay across his desk while he tapped his fingers on the desktop.

"Well?" I finally said in irritation.

Einhard looked back up at me. "Well what, Hadrack?"

"Is the word, no, the only word you use now?" I repeated.

Einhard sighed and put both his hands palm down on top of the map. "No is a small word, Hadrack. Yet, despite that fact, it still manages to convey a very clear message that can't possibly be misunderstood." He stared at me and his green eyes hardened. "At least it should be clear."

"Tell me why you keep saying no," I said as I tried to contain my anger. "It's not like you need me here right now. Nothing ever happens."

"I don't have time for this," Einhard said with a grunt. "The king will be here in two days and the Ganders a week after that. I have to prepare for their arrival."

The king of the Piths had finally decided to come and inspect Gasterny and the entire garrison was buzzing about his pending arrival. The Ganders, on the other hand, had become a common sight each month as they came to ensure that Prince Tyro was well.

"Make time!" I growled. "Why do you keep telling me no?"

"Because, despite what you believe, I do need you here,"

27

Einhard said in a quiet voice. "That should be good enough for you."

"Well, it's not good enough!" I shouted. I could feel the familiar white-hot anger starting to get the best of me. Jebido cleared his throat beside me and I ignored him as I pointed a finger at Einhard. "I made a vow to my family and you're the only thing keeping me from fulfilling it!"

Einhard jumped to his feet and his chair scraped harshly across the stone floor. I could see the anger in his eyes now as he leaned forward on his desk and glared right back at me. Behind him Alesia's eyes were round with worry. "You also made a vow to me," Einhard said tightly. "Have you forgotten that?"

"Hadrack," Jebido whispered out of the side of his mouth in warning.

"I know, I know," I said, turning to my friend. I took a deep breath, trying to calm myself as I gestured vaguely behind me. "Einhard, somewhere out there are seven men who are walking around right now, free to do as they please while I sit here helpless to do anything about it. It's not fair."

"I know how frustrating this must be for you," Einhard said as the anger slowly left his eyes. He exhaled loudly. "I'm not without sympathy, Hadrack, but we're fighting a war here." He frowned. "At least we will be once the Master is willing. A war against an enemy with three times our number and as motivated as we are. When it starts, I'll need all the good men I can get." He looked at Jebido, Baine, and then me. "Good men just like you three." Einhard ran his fingers through his long blond hair. "The Pathfinders could get the word anytime now. And when they do, we have to be ready. That's why I can't have you riding all over Ganderland trying to settle a personal vendetta. Not yet, anyway. That's just the way it has to be right now." I stood there in silence, knowing there wasn't anything that I could say that would change the Pith leader's mind. Once again, I'd lost the argument. "Your time to honor your vow will come, Hadrack," Einhard said gently as he retrieved his chair and sat back down. "But you need to wait and try to be patient."

I snorted sarcastically. "Be patient? You want me to be patient? Every day that goes by those bastards get to breathe while I sit here in chains. They get to eat, they get to drink, and they get to rut, all without a care in the world. Yet my father and sister and all those people from Corwick are nothing now. Nothing but stinking, rotted bits of flesh and wasted bone." I took a deep breath, trying to control my shaking limbs. "You gave our lives back to us," I said, indicating Baine and Jebido. "And because of that we pledged our swords to you that night at Father's Arse." I paused and spread my arms. "I owe you a life, Einhard. So, I'll do as you command, and I'll wait." I leaned forward with my hands on the desk. "But remember this. I'm the only one left alive who will stand up for the people of Corwick. Nobody else gives a shit about what happened to them. Including you. So, you can order me to wait, and I will, but trust me when I tell you I'll never be patient doing it!"

I was brought back to the present by Baine, who'd just kicked my leg roughly with the toe of his boot. "What?" I demanded.

Baine pointed. "I told you three times that I just saw mounted men come out of that stand of trees down there and ride into the woods. But you just sat there with that mean look on your face."

I grunted and glanced at the sprawling woodlands Baine was pointing to. "I don't see anything."

"Maybe if you hadn't been daydreaming you would have," Baine said with a sniff.

"You sure about this?"

Baine rolled his eyes. "I'm not blind, Hadrack. It was them."

"Then I guess there's only one thing to do," I said as I guided my horse over the lip of the valley.

Baine followed close behind me, with both of our horses crisscrossing back and forth down the slick grass and shale. I leaned back as far as I could in the saddle as we des-

29

cended, trying not to think about what would happen if we fell. At one point my horse's back hooves slid out from under it and I felt my heart leap in my throat, certain that we were done. But the sturdy horse somehow managed to right itself and continue downward without further incident. I was greatly relieved when we finally made it to the valley floor and we paused to let the horses catch their breath.

"Let's not do that again anytime soon," Baine muttered as he patted his horse on the neck.

I glanced up at the towering wall of the valley and nodded my agreement, then gestured us onward. We galloped across the rich flowing grass that lined the valley floor, diverting around several groves of tall cedars and pine trees. We reached a thin stream where we startled a doe and her fawn that had paused to drink and we leaped over the water without slowing as they bounded away. I wasn't wearing a helmet or a coif that morning and the wind was rushing through my hair and beard and whipping my black cape wildly around my shoulders. I breathed in deeply, feeling the excitement of the chase building in me as we approached the woods where Baine had seen our quarry disappear. The treeline was dotted with brilliant white trunks of twisted birch trees that grew almost like weeds beneath and around the thicker bodies of taller ash and oak trees. I held up my hand and we paused near the treeline, searching for tracks.

"They went in here!" Baine finally called out as he pointed first to the ground, then to the trees.

I rode over to join Baine and I studied the tracks he'd found. The split-hoof track was plain to see amongst the others and I nodded. We'd found them all right. A muted crash sounded from within the woods just then, followed quickly by a woman's startled scream. I cursed and drew Wolf's Head and spurred my horse into the woods in the direction I'd heard the scream. In less than a minute, I burst through the trees into a small open area dominated by a weathered, two-story building of cracked and chipped limestone. I paused and looked around cautiously. The building had seen better days, I saw, with heavy vines growing all along the walls and reaching up and over the vaulted roof. Open windows faced me from the second floor and the thick vines had pushed their way through them to disappear inside the building. Five horses still slick with sweat stood tethered to a sun-bleached hitching post in front of the stone structure. I knew that we'd found the men with the pointed boots. I jumped from my horse and left the reins trailing on the ground as Baine trotted up beside me and dismounted.

"Anything?" Baine asked as he unhooked his bow and nocked an arrow.

I shook my head and pointed to the front of the building where the shattered front door still swung back and forth slowly on twisted hinges. "Looks like they're inside."

Baine nodded and I advanced on the structure while my friend followed two paces behind me with his bow aimed at the doorway. We reached the crumbling stone steps and I paused to look down at the three sets of pointed-toe footprints in the dirt. I shared a look with Baine, then glanced up at the faded Blazing Sun emblem that sat above the door. Beneath the Blazing Sun emblem was a second, smaller emblem depicting two open hands beneath a small sun. We were at an abandoned Daughters-In-Waiting abbey, I realized.

"Get back!" a women's voice shouted from inside. "I'm warning you!"

I stepped inside the building and paused, taking in the situation with a single glance. A young girl wearing a long red cloak with the hood down stood with her back against the far wall of the room. She was holding a sword with both hands while three men with drawn swords stood around her watching her warily. The men were dressed in dusty mail and wore black pointed boots that reached well past their knees. Each man had a bright red cape thrown over his shoulders and wore a strange conical helmet that curled upward along the edges. The girl glanced at us in surprise and I hesitated, shocked by her almost ethereal beauty. I heard Baine gasp behind me, and I knew he had been affected by her too.

The girl was my age or a little younger and was slightly built. I figured if she stood next to me she might stand as tall as my shoulder, but certainly no more than that. Her eyes were a spectacular shade of blue and her shimmering black hair fell straight as an arrow almost to her belted waist. For just a moment I felt a pang deep in my chest, thinking that this might have been what my sister would have looked like, had she lived. The moment was broken almost immediately, however, as the three men turned their heads and saw us. They whirled and charged just as one of them cried out, twirling and dropping with an arrow lodged in his chest. Baine nocked a second arrow and let fly, then cursed as his target narrowly dodged aside at the last moment. The arrow impacted the far wall of the abbey, just missing the girl before careening away.

"I've got this!" I shouted to Baine. "Get her out of here!"

Baine nodded and he darted forward, rolling to escape a vicious cut from one of our assailants. He regained his feet nimbly and then swung backward with his bow, catching his attacker across the face and splitting open the man's cheek. The other man, who was heavily bearded and almost as tall as I was, cursed me loudly as he swung his sword at my midriff. I twisted away from him and as his blade swished past me harmlessly, I swung back, crashing my armored elbow into his face and pulping his nose. The big man cried out in shock and dropped his sword as he stumbled backward, gasping and spluttering blood.

"Hadrack!" Baine shouted in warning.

I whirled, ducking a wild swing from the second man. "No, you don't, you bastard!" I growled as I feinted toward him.

My opponent jumped back and he stumbled. I wasn't sure if it was a ruse or he'd just slipped on the bloody floor, but either way, it was enough. I leaped forward and swung Wolf's Head high, forcing him to either block it or lose his head. Blood was pouring from the wounded man's cheek and I smiled at him as our swords clashed, then I took my right foot and hooked it against the heel of his pointed boot. I swept his leg out from under him and as he started to fall, I grabbed his throat with my left hand and smashed his head hard against the floor of the abbey. The wounded man's helmet cracked like an egg and then rolled away, but he still struggled weakly in my grasp, so I lifted him again and smashed him down a second time. I felt the man go limp this time as his eyes rolled up inside his head while dark red blood started to pool beneath him. I stood up and glared at the bearded man with the bloodied nose, who was making no effort to retrieve his fallen sword as he watched me warily. Baine stood beside the girl with an arrow drawn in his bow and aimed at the big man. I slowly relaxed.

"Are you all right?" I asked, glancing at the girl.

"I think so, yes," she said after a moment. Her voice was surprisingly deep for such a small person. "Thank you," she added. She glanced at Baine. "Thank you both."

I gestured to the bearded man. "Do you know this bastard?"

"His name is Carbet!" she said, spitting the name out with distaste. "He's a Cardian and works for my husband."

"I see," I said, not really seeing at all. I had no idea what a Cardian was. "And who might your husband be?" I asked.

"Lord Demay," the girl answered. "The Lord of Calban."

I looked at Baine, who just shrugged as he kept his bow aimed at Carbet. "Well, Lady Demay," I said, bowing my head slightly. "My name is Hadrack, and that handsome fellow with the bow beside you is Baine."

And that's how I came to meet my future wife, the girl known as The Lamb.

2: THE RETURN OF CARSPEN TUFT

Lady Demay decided to let Carbet go. We learned that she'd fled her abusive husband several days ago and that Carbet and the other Cardians had been sent to bring her back. She decided she wanted to send the Lord of Calban a message by having Carbet return to him empty-handed. My first thought had been that I should slit the man's throat anyway and be done with it, but I decided to keep those thoughts to myself. After all, who was I to question a Lady's wishes? In hindsight, I wish I had gone with my instincts and killed the bastard, as it would have saved us all a lot of grief in the end.

The three of us stood on the cracked steps of the abbey as Carbet vaulted up onto the back of a magnificent black stallion. We'd taken his weapons and armor and all he had on were his pointed boots, a thin tunic, and light trousers.

"He'll come after you," Carbet said as the big horse snorted and fidgeted beneath him. Carbet's nose was swollen to almost twice its normal size and was still bleeding, but he ignored it as he glared at her. "You know what he's like, and it won't matter if you go to your brother. He'll find you wherever you try to hide."

"Let him come," Lady Demay said with contempt. "But make sure you tell him that the next time I see him my knife will go into his heart instead of his shoulder!"

Carbet reddened. "I'll tell him," he said angrily. He glanced at me. "I won't forget your ugly face anytime soon. We'll meet again, you and I."

"I'll be sure to watch my back, then," I said. We locked eyes for a moment and then he savagely pulled on the reins of his horse, turning sharply before galloping away. "A pleasant fellow," I muttered as we watched him go.

"And a dangerous one," Lady Demay said. She glanced up at me and absently put her hand on my arm and I felt an instant jolt rush through my body at her touch. "Maybe I shouldn't have let him go?" she said, looking regretful. "You've just made an enemy because of me."

I swallowed, trying not to show how deeply affected I was by this slight, beautiful girl that I stood towering over. "I've made enemies before and I'm still here to talk about it, my lady," I finally managed to say. I was dismayed by the awkward-sounding quiver in my voice. Beside me Baine smirked, but I ignored him and patted her hand reassuringly. "Don't worry about it. I know his type. He's more bark than bite."

Lady Demay nodded and she dropped her hand from my arm. She looked at the remaining horses and I saw her expression sadden. "You're certain my servant is dead?"

I hesitated, not sure how much more I should say about the dead man in the woods. We'd told her about the body we'd found and how it had led us to the abbey, but not much else about what had happened.

"I'm afraid so," I finally said.

"But why did they have to kill him?" Lady Demay asked. "Tern was just watching out for me."

Baine and I shared a glance. "They needed to find out where you were hidden," I said carefully, "and he was the only one who knew." I glanced back at the vine-covered abbey to escape those sad blue eyes of hers. "I'm assuming he hid you here and then took the horses, trying to draw them away from you?"

"Yes," Lady Demay nodded. Her eyes were beginning to fill with tears now and she dabbed at them with a kerchief she'd pulled from her clothing. "We'd become disorientated and had no idea where we were. I didn't want us to separate, but once we found the abbey, Tern insisted on it. He left me here and took my horse, hoping to fool them into thinking we were together." She sniffed loudly. "Tern hurt his head helping me escape from Calban and it had begun bleeding again. It was making him feel sick and dizzy, but I couldn't talk him out of leaving no matter what I said."

"It was a good ploy," Baine said. "If he'd gotten farther into the trees, he might have lost them."

Lady Demay nodded. "That was his plan. He was going to circle around once he lost them and come back for me."

"And then what?" Baine asked. "Where were you going?"

Lady Demay shrugged and dabbed at her eyes. "I don't know. We hadn't thought that far ahead."

"Carbet mentioned you have a brother," I said. "If he's highborn, why not ask him for protection?"

Lady Demay snorted. "The only man I despise more than my husband is my half brother." Her face hardened and her eyes glittered with anger. "That bastard as much as sold me to Lord Demay. He treated me like I was one of his possessions, like a horse or a stupid ox. No, I won't be going to my brother for protection. I promise you that!"

"What will you do now, Lady Demay?" Baine asked.

"Please, both of you call me Shana," she said. She returned her kerchief to her clothing and glanced from Baine to me. "Just hearing that name makes me feel ill." Baine and I nodded uncomfortably as she continued, "If you would be kind enough to escort me to the nearest town, I'd be most grateful. I'll decide what to do once I get there." Baine and I shared a look and I cleared my throat uncomfortably, not sure what to say. "What is it?" Shana asked. She looked at me, frowned, then looked at Baine. "What is it you're not telling me?"

"We're actually garrisoned nearby and shouldn't really be here," Baine finally said. "We had strict orders to stay close to the garrison, but we came across your servant and...uh...well...uh." Baine trailed off and looked down at the ground before glancing at me and shrugging helplessly.

"And you're afraid your commander will reprimand you, is that it?" Shana asked. Neither Baine nor I said anything and she snorted. "Take me to your garrison and I'll explain the entire thing. Your commander should be rewarding you for your bravery, not punishing you." Baine and I shared another look. I tried to will my mind to work, to think of something that would satisfy Lady Demay, but I felt tongue-tied and just stood there staring at her miserably. "Enough of this!" Shana finally snapped. She stamped her foot on the ground angrily and I thought she looked magnificent with her eyes flashing and her face flushed as she glared at us. "What is it you two are trying hard not to tell me? Are you deserters? Is that what this is about?"

"We're not deserters," I said. I ran my fingers through my hair, then sighed in resignation. I'd have to tell her, I knew. "We're stationed at Gasterny Garrison," I said, holding my breath as I waited for her reaction.

Shana put her hands on her hips and then nodded, clearly coming to a decision. "Then that's where we'll go, and when we get there, I'll talk..." She trailed off and her mouth opened slightly in a circle of surprise. "You said Gasterny," she said to me almost accusingly.

I nodded. "Yes."

"But I heard Gasterny is held by the Piths," Shana said. "So how can you be stationed there if the Piths hold it?" She stared at us as we stood silently beneath her puzzled glare. I could see her mind turning over the problem and then her eyes widened. "No!" she gasped.

"Yes," I repeated.

Shana turned to look at Baine and he nodded reluctantly, unable to meet her eyes. "You're them," Shana finally said. "The traitors' everyone has been talking about for the last year." She looked at me. "Isn't that right?"

I grinned weakly. "Well, I'm not fond of the word traitor, but yes, that's us."

Shana looked thoughtful and I was surprised by how

calmly she was taking the news. "There's supposed to be three of you," she said as she glanced around the clearing.

"Jebido wasn't assigned to patrol duty this morning," Baine said. He grinned. "Lucky for him, I guess."

Shana nodded absently. "Is it true you murder any Gander women and children you can find and drink their blood from their skulls?"

"What!?" I exploded. "Whoever told you that is a liar!"

"The entire kingdom has heard tell of it," Shana said. "The king has even put a bounty on your heads."

"Really?" Baine said, looking intrigued. "How much?"

"Who cares how much!" I snapped at Baine. I turned to Shana. "Lady Demay, it's been an honor and a privilege to meet you, but we have to be going." I pointed through the trees to the north. "Up that way you'll find a road leading to the west. If you follow it, I'm sure sooner or later it'll lead you to someone who can help you. Good day." I gave her an awkward bow and gestured to Baine to follow me as I turned to go.

"No!" Shana said loudly.

I turned back to her in surprise. "No?" I repeated.

"No," Shana said firmly. "I'm going with you to Gasterny." She walked past Baine and me where we stood with identical stunned looks on our faces before she untied one of the horses from the hitching post and nimbly mounted it. She turned to look down at us. "Well? Are you two coming or not?"

I was to learn over time that Shana had a stubborn streak of epic proportions, and rarely, if ever, would she back down from a disagreement. Today was the first lesson in my education. One of many more such to come. After at least ten long minutes of protests and arguing, I finally had to throw my hands up in defeat and agree to let her accompany us. I'd tried to explain to her that the Piths would be completely unimpressed with her highborn status. I'd warned her that they would probably force her into slavery as they had the other Ganders at the garrison, but if it concerned her at all, she hid it well. Her reply to my arguments had been frustrating, but difficult for me to dispute.

"My husband has treated me like chattel for the last year," she had said. "And this garrison of yours is the one place he can't find me. As far as I'm concerned, I was already a slave in Calban, worse even, so there's nothing these Piths can do to me that hasn't already been done."

And so, unable to counter that argument, I had relented and allowed her to join us, though I was far from happy about it.

"If you thought Einhard was going to be mad at us before," Baine whispered to me out of the side of his mouth as the three of us rode away from the abbey. "Just you wait until he sees her."

I grimaced and didn't bother replying as I tugged moodily on the reins of the extra horses trotting behind me. We made our way out of the woods and then paused, staring up at the valley wall that loomed above us. The incline was too steep to climb here, I knew, and I directed my horse forward, looking for a better path. I knew Shana's servant, Tern, must have found an easier way up somewhere, we'd just have to find it. I stole a glance at Shana and she smiled sweetly at me and I quickly looked away.

"It would seem my presence continues to distress your companion," Lady Demay said to Baine behind me with a musical chuckle.

My friend smiled charmingly. "Don't take it personally, my lady. Hadrack can be something of a bear at times." I glowered at Baine, hoping that he could read my thoughts about what I'd do to him when we were finally alone, but he just grinned widely back at me. "He's not all bad, though, once you get to know him," Baine said. He leaned closer to Shana. "He's grouchy sometimes, but you won't find a better man when there's danger around."

Lady Demay glanced at me appraisingly with her big blue eyes. "So I've come to learn."

I ignored them both after that and I led them eastward along the valley floor, continuing to look for an easier ascent up to the road. For their part, Lady Demay and Baine chattered on incessantly behind me, their conversation interrupted repeatedly by the Lady's amused laughter. My friend was riding as close to her as he possibly could, I saw, and at one point I turned and glared back at them as they laughed with their heads almost touching each other. They both fell silent when they saw my face, until Baine finally said something out of the side of his mouth, which caused them to burst out laughing again. I turned away and clenched my jaw, determined not to look back at them again. Baine was like a younger brother to me, and for the entire time we knew each other, I considered it my duty to protect and take care of him. That morning in the valley with Shana was probably the closest I'd ever come to hating Baine. Jealousy will do that to a man.

We eventually reached an area where the hill wasn't quite as steep and, tired of looking for a better route, I headed upward without saying anything to my companions as I tugged behind me on the reins of the extra horses. My horse got about a quarter of the way up the incline and then stopped, its enthusiasm for the climb waning. I cursed the beast under my breath and kicked my heels repeatedly into its flanks, but the stubborn creature refused to budge.

"See you at the top, Hadrack!" Baine shouted with a laugh as his horse passed mine and continued up the slope without hesitation.

Baine was followed immediately by Lady Demay, who rode her horse like an expert and appeared to be thoroughly enjoying herself.

"Mother's tit!" I grumbled under my breath. I looked back at the extra horses, who all stood staring at me dumbly, obviously waiting for my horse to move first. "Thanks for nothing," I said to them bitterly. I kicked my heels against my horse's flanks again, but it still refused to move. I cursed louder this time and leaned down close to the beast's ears. "Get a move on you mangy, good-for-nothing sack of bones, or so help me I'll skin you alive and wear your stinking pelt as a coat!" The horse twitched its ears at me, but other than that seemed completely unimpressed by my threat.

"Hadrack!" Baine shouted. I saw he and Lady Demay had reached the summit by now and they were peering back down at me from the lip of the valley. "Quit fooling around down there! We need to get back!"

I ground my teeth and pointed up at him, about to fire off an angry retort when my horse chose that moment to lurch forward. I had to scramble desperately with one hand for the reins, fighting to stay in the saddle and keep my grip on the extra horses, while from above me laughter floated down. I finally reached the top of the valley and I paused as the horses and I all regained our breaths. Baine and Lady Demay were both sitting their horses near the road and I trotted over to them, intent on letting Baine know exactly what I thought of him at that moment. Baine wasn't paying any attention to me, however, but was instead looking down the road to the west with an odd expression on his face. I turned to see what had caught his attention, my hand already crossing to the hilt of my sword. Then I paused in surprise. A rickety old wagon drawn by two mules was slowly approaching us. I saw that the driver was small and bald and grinning in our direction with a pleasant, welcoming face. It was Carspen Tuft!

"It can't be!" Baine whispered.

"Oh, but it is," I said, barely able to believe it myself.

Baine's face hardened in hatred and he started to un-hook his bow. I quickly held up my hand, stopping him as I shook my head.

"But it's Carspen Tuft, Hadrack!" Baine protested.

"I know," I said. "But an arrow is too good for that bastard. I have a better idea." I handed the reins of the extra horses to Shana, who sat her horse looking completely confused by the turn of events.

"What's going on?" Lady Demay asked me as she glanced at the approaching wagon.

"We're just taking a moment to say hello to an old friend," I said.

I trotted my horse out onto the road and lifted my hand in greeting as Tuft's wagon drew closer.

"Whoa!" Tuft called out, hauling back on the reins and slowing the mules down. "Whoa there my sweet girls! Whoa!" The wagon finally came to a halt about ten feet from me. I leaned forward with my hands braced on the pommel of my saddle as I stared across at the little man who'd brought such misery to so many people. Tuft's face was flushed red and was a lot more weathered than it had been ten years ago, with deep creases all along the cheeks and across his forehead. His wispy beard and the little hair he had left were both pure white now like freshly fallen snow. His eyes were the same as I remembered, however, their rat-hardness focusing on me warily as he smiled in a friendly greeting. "A good day to you, sir!" Tuft said to me. "And to you, lady and sir," he said, bowing his head to both Shana and Baine. I saw Shana incline her head politely to the little man, but Baine just glared at Tuft with deadly hatred. My friend was not someone who angered or hated easily, but when he did, the transformation from a happy-go-lucky, pleasant boy into a deadly killer was breathtaking to behold. Tuft seemed unaware of Baine's animosity, however, and he turned his focus back to me.

"Where's your wife?" I said, startling Tuft with my bluntness.

"My wife?" Tuft replied, blinking at me in confusion. He studied my face carefully and I could see caution starting to take hold in his rat eyes. Caution, and I was pleased to see, the first glimmerings of fear. "You knew my wife, did you sir?" Tuft asked.

"Just briefly," I said. "But just the same she left an impression that I'll not soon forget."

"Of course, of course," Tuft said, nodding his head repeatedly. He paused to use the sleeve of his worn tunic to dab at his eyes. "Hielda was like that, she was. A rare creature that was put on this earth by The Mother and The Father to help others. She considered it her life's work, you know." He covered one nostril with his knuckle and blew snot on the ground, then did the same for the other nostril before turning back to me.

"She died, then?" I asked.

"Sadly, yes," Tuft sniffed. "The Mother needed her by Her side and took her almost two years ago now. I console myself with the knowledge that Hielda was too pure to remain in this world and is even now continuing to do good for others elsewhere." Baine snorted at that last bit and Tuft glanced at him, his red face beginning to lose its rosy color, as this time he saw the naked look of hatred on Baine's face.

"What's in the wagon?" I asked. I reached over my shoulder and grabbed the shaft of my father's axe, smiling at the look of alarm on Tuft's face before I shifted the weapon in its sheath and then brought my hand back down to my lap.

Tuft dabbed at his forehead nervously and shrugged. "Just some cargo I've been contracted to transport."

"What kind of cargo?" I asked. I flipped a leg over my saddle and jumped to the ground, then crossed over to the wagon and looked up at Tuft, who stared down at me with his mouth hanging open. I noticed a small dribble of slime roll from the corner of his mouth and trickle down the side of his chin, but Tuft seemed unaware of it. "I asked you what kind of cargo?" I repeated. I put my hand on the polished hilt of Wolf's Head. A move that Carspen Tuft did not fail to notice.

"I'm transporting some young ruffians to Tannet's Find to work in the quarry," Tuft said as he nervously fumbled in his trousers. "I assure you, good sir, it's all perfectly legal and has been fully sanctioned by the quarrymaster there."

Tuft pulled out a worn sheet of yellowed paper and he held it up for me to see. I glanced at it, just able to make out some of the words. One of the only positive things about sitting in Gasterny this past year waiting for the war to begin was that I'd started to learn to read and write. The Gander garrison commander had a keen interest in books, and though he had died at the Bridge Battle, his steward, a tiny little man named Josphet, had not, and he was teaching me. The Piths had killed all the soldiers that had surrendered after the battle, of course, but they'd allowed the Ganders in the garrison to live on as their slaves. Even the officers' wives and the highborn were cast down, as I'd warned Shana. Baine and Jebido had thought my interest in reading and writing to be nothing short of perverse, but surprisingly, it seemed I had a talent for it. I still had a long way to go, of course, but I knew enough now to realize that Carspen Tuft was telling me the truth. Not that I cared about it one way or the other.

"So, you see," Tuft continued as he snapped the letter closed and replaced it in his trousers. "I'm on official business." He looked down at me and waggled a tiny finger. "Interfering with an agent of the crown is a serious offense, my friend, so I suggest you remove your big body from my path and let me be!"

I smiled up at Tuft and I saw his body start to relax in relief. That's when I reached up with my left hand, grabbed him by the tunic and pulled him off the wagon into the air. Then I threw him as far as I could. Tuft let out a pitiful wail, his little arms and legs flailing helplessly before he landed heavily on the ground about ten feet from me. He rolled over several times before finally coming to a stop in a heap on the dusty road.

"Get the key," I said to Baine as I turned and headed to the back of the wagon.

I heard Tuft protesting loudly and then a sharp smack, followed by a cry of pain before Baine appeared by my side holding the key.

"Would you like to do the honors?" Baine asked me as he offered the ring of heavy iron keys to me.

The Wolf At Large

I shook my head. "You did it last time, you might as well do it this time too."

Baine nodded and he quickly unlocked the door, then swung it open. We stood there staring in at four, filth-encrusted boys who blinked back at us. I sighed in disgust and closed my eyes, remembering my fateful trip in that hated wagon from years before. Baine immediately got into the wagon, ignoring the filth as he gently unlocked the boys' bonds. I turned away and went to fetch Tuft, while behind me I could hear sobs coming from the wagon along with Baine's soothing voice. Tuft was on his knees when I came around the wagon and he looked up at me in terror as I approached him. I glanced at Shana where she still sat her horse watching with a neutral face. She didn't seem all that upset about what was happening and I was grateful for that. I didn't need a hysterical woman on my hands while I dealt with Tuft.

"On your feet, you heartless bastard!" I said to Tuft.

I grabbed him by the beard and dragged him to his feet as he gasped in pain. Blood pooled on the top of his bald head and I saw that he had a nasty cut all along the top of it. I knew it would be the least of his problems shortly. Baine came around the side of the wagon with the four boys and when Tuft saw them, he started to struggle in my grasp.

"That's my property!" he shouted up at me. "They're criminals! You have no right to free them!"

"Right!?" I snapped at him. "I don't have the right?" I shook him by the beard, rattling him like a child's toy. "Don't talk to me about rights, you petty little man!" I glanced at Baine. "Cut the mules free and let the boys have them." Baine nodded and went to do as I said as Tuft began to whimper.

"Not my girls!" Tuft cried. "Please, don't let them take my girls! They're all I have left in this world!"

"You won't be needing them where you're going," I growled at Tuft as I dragged him to the back of the wagon. I dropped him in a heap on the ground by the door, then pointed inside at the piss and shit-stained floor. "Get in."

Terry Cloutier

Tuft blanched and looked up into the wagon, then shook his head. "Never!"

I drew Wolf's Head and placed the blade close to his throat. "Get in the wagon or I'll start cutting little bits and pieces off of you until there's nothing left."

"Please, good sir, please!" Tuft cried. He got on his knees and clasped his hands in front of him, peering up at me desperately. "Please don't do this! I don't deserve this!" Baine came around the wagon to stand beside me and Tuft glanced at him, then back to me. "I'm an innocent old man just doing his job! What have I ever done to you?"

I grinned at Tuft and hooked a thumb at Baine. "He and I were once guests of yours in that little wagon years ago. You and your ugly fat wife." Tuft's terrified face turned to horror and I breathed in deeply as I looked up at the sky, then turned to look at Baine. "The Mother has given us a gift today."

"That She has," Baine said softy.

I turned back to Tuft. "Get in the wagon."

"I have gold!" Tuft said in a shaking voice. "Lots of gold. You can have all of it. Both of you, if you just let me live!"

"All the gold in King Jorquin's castle wouldn't be enough to pay for your sins," I growled. "Now get in that wagon!" Tuft dropped his head and began to cry, then slowly, painfully, he got to his feet. He pulled himself up into the wagon and turned to face us with tears pouring down his cheeks. I noticed absently that his head wasn't even touching the roof of the wagon as I pointed to the floor. "Sit there, in that shit, and put on the shackles."

Tuft meekly did what he was told, and when he'd locked the first ring around his wrist, he looked up at me helplessly. "I can't lock the other one by myself."

"It won't matter," I said. I leaned into the wagon, ignoring the stench as I held Tuft's eyes with mine. "The Father will have to spend a lot of time with you," I said. "He's had two years already with that bitch of a wife of yours, and I think it'll take many more years for Him to burn the evil from the both

46

of you."

"No!" Tuft shouted at me as spittle flew from his mouth. "I'm a good man and my wife is a good woman. We will both sit by The Mother's side for all eternity!"

I grinned at Tuft. "Well, either way, you're about to find out!"

I slammed the door shut, ignoring Tuft's screams from inside as I locked the door. Then Baine and I headed to the front of the wagon, where he and I turned the tongue so that the wheels were pointed off the road. We returned to the back of the wagon and pushed, heaving against the weight until it started to roll. The tongue slid over the grass without resistance and we picked up speed as we got closer to the valley rim, then at a shout from me, we jumped back, watching as the wagon hit the rim. It wobbled slightly at the top, then teetered over and started to roll down. Baine and I ran to the top of the valley, watching as the wagon began to gain speed. The tongue was bouncing madly from side to side, then it gouged into the hillside, spraying dirt in all directions, before with a crack, it snapped in half. We could hear Tuft wailing from inside as the wagon skittered back and forth, almost tipping over twice, before finally the right front wheel hit a deep depression and the wagon somersaulted onto its back. After that it started to flip wildly end over end as chunks of wood and debris were scattered in all directions. We could hear Tuft screaming in pain and terror from inside, then his cries suddenly ended as what was left of the wagon finally came to a shuddering stop in a cloud of dust on the valley floor. Baine and I shared a long look of satisfaction, then we turned back to get our horses.

After that, Baine, Lady Demay and I headed east along the road to Gasterny, the three of us riding side by side. There was no more talking or laughing now, and we traveled in silence, as Tuft's death seemed to have sobered us all up. Shana was riding in the middle, with Baine on her left and me on her right leading the extra horses.

Finally, after almost half an hour of silence, Lady Demay cleared her throat and glanced at us. "So, is anyone going to tell me what that was all about?"

"Just a minor disagreement," Baine said. He grinned at her, the old Baine returning.

Shana grinned back. "I'd hate to see what you would do if you had a major disagreement, then," she said. Baine laughed and I chuckled, starting to feel my black mood lifting. There's nothing like a little revenge to brighten your day, I thought, picturing Tuft's terrified face. "No, really," Shana continued. "What was that all about?"

Baine and I shared a glance and then we began to talk, sharing the story as we went back and forth telling her our tales about how we'd come to meet Tuft and escape Father's Arse with the Piths.

Lady Demay had become silent and stiff as she'd listened to us, and when we were done, she shook her head in disbelief. I could see the anger flickering brightly in her eyes and was surprised by it. What had happened to us had happened long ago, and I didn't see why it was affecting her so.

"That bastard!" Shana finally said.

"Yes," I agreed. "He was that, but he can't hurt anyone else ever again."

"No, not that bastard," Lady Demay said. "I mean my half brother." She looked into my eyes and held them. "Hadrack, my half brother is the Lord of Corwick."

3: THE KING OF THE PITHS

We finally reached Gasterny about an hour later and barely had time to cross the drawbridge and dismount in the outer bailey before Jebido hurried over to us.

"Now you've done it!" Jebido said, looking worried. He glanced at Shana in puzzlement, then gestured to Baine and me. "Einhard wants to see you in his office. Be warned, he's spitting mad at you two."

"For what?" I asked as a Pith youth approached and led the horses away.

"What do you think?" Jebido said with a snort. "For leaving the perimeter, of course!"

"We had a good reason," Baine said. He gestured to Shana. "This is Lady Demay. She was being chased by these three..."

Jebido held up a hand, stopping Baine as he turned to Shana. "A pleasure to meet you, my lady," he said with a slight bow. "I'm glad Hadrack and Baine were able to assist you. But, as much as I'd like to hear what happened, the Sword of the King needs to speak with these two immediately." Jebido glanced at me and the worried look returned to his face as he ushered us toward the keep. "I don't think you understand just how upset he is right now. I've never seen him this angry before."

"Didn't Peren tell him what we found?" I asked as we walked.

"Of course he did," Jebido said. "Einhard even rode out to see that poor bastard for himself." Jebido looked embarrassed and he glanced at Shana. "Forgive my crudeness, my lady."

"It's all right," Shana said. She touched Jebido's arm lightly. "I remember you."

We paused as we passed through the gates to the inner bailey and Jebido turned to face her. "I don't understand, my lady."

"As soon as I saw you, I recognized you. You worked for Lord Corwick years ago."

Jebido's eyebrows rose in surprise and he turned to me with a question on his face. I just shrugged back at him. I hadn't mentioned anything about it. I was looking forward to telling Jebido about Carspen Tuft, but that would have to wait until Einhard was done shouting at us.

"I did work for him," Jebido said thoughtfully. He indicated Baine and me. "Did they tell you that?"

Shana shook her head. "No. I was just a little girl when we knew each other." She smiled and her eyes twinkled. "Even as young as I was, I couldn't forget that magnificent nose of yours. You were kind to me, remember? I didn't even know your name, but you'd stop and talk to me and even talk to my pet lamb sometimes."

"That's right!" Jebido said, snapping his fingers. "You're Shana, Lord Corwick's little sister."

"Half-sister, actually," Shana said as her expression clouded for a moment.

"And the lamb was named, Twilly," Jebido said with a smile. "I remember it followed you around wherever you went for a while and people started calling you, The Lamb."

"They still do," Shana said with a laugh. "I'm amazed you remember that. It was so long ago."

"There aren't many things about Corwick Castle that I look back fondly on," Jebido said. "But you and your little lamb are one of them."

Lady Demay bowed her head. "Thank you."

"What's taking so long?" Eriz barked from the top of the ramp that led to the keep. "The Sword said now!"

"We better go," Jebido whispered, ushering us upward.

We made our way past Eriz as he stood with his huge arms folded over his chest. The big Pith looked irritated and he scowled at me as we entered the keep and walked into the great hall. Inside, ten Ganderwomen were cleaning and polishing the room as they prepared it for the King of the Pith's visit in the morning. The hall was magnificent and it never failed to take my breath away. Highly-polished wooden planks lined the floor, some of which were covered by thick red carpets. Gold-plated tables and chairs sat in two long lines down the middle of the room and a high-vaulted ceiling rose above our heads, supported by darkly-stained wooden beams thicker than my waist. The Piths didn't have much use for gold, preferring silver, and so they had left the gold in the furniture alone, at least for the time being. Light streamed in from the east through several large windows and it fell on a chair that had been placed on a dais near the back where the king would sit. The great hall seemed to me overly luxurious for a garrison and more suited to a lord's castle. But apparently the Gander commander had been consumed by his importance and had commissioned and paid for the modifications himself.

I saw that one of the Gander slaves polishing the floor was Betania, the girl that had tended to my wounds a year ago. Betania and I had become good friends over the months, and when she saw me her face broke out into a wide grin. She sat up and started to wave to me, then she saw Shana and her expression clouded as she studied her suspiciously.

"Is that your girl, Hadrack?" Shana asked curiously as we hurried past her.

"What!?" I said, genuinely surprised by the question. I laughed. "Of course not. She's just a child. We're good friends, that's all."

Shana glanced over her shoulder as we turned into the corridor that led to Einhard's office. "Does she know that?" she asked softly.

We approached the open door to Einhard's office and

Jebido leaned in close to me. "Try not to say anything stupid," he whispered. "Just keep your mouth shut and nod your head a lot. He's going to yell anyway, so just let him yell and be done with it."

I patted Jebido on the back. "When have you ever known me to say anything stupid?" I asked as we stepped into the room.

"Finally!" Einhard growled. He'd been pacing back and forth behind his desk and now he turned to face us. Einhard put his hands on his hips and studied us silently as we stood in a line in front of him. Alesia was sitting at the back of the room at the same table as the night before, though this time she wasn't fletching arrows. She looked at me and I could read the look of warning in her eyes. "Who is this?" Einhard finally demanded, gesturing to Shana. His eyes looked red, angry and puffy, and I noticed an empty flask sitting on the desk.

"Lady Demay," I said. I turned to Shana. "My lady, this is Einhard, Sword of the King and ruler of Gasterny."

Lady Demay bowed her head. "It's a great pleasure to meet you."

Einhard barely acknowledged her as he glared at Baine. "Did you warn him about leaving the perimeter?"

"We didn't realize we'd gone outside of it," Baine said with a blank face.

"Don't play the simpleton with me!" Einhard snapped. He started to pace back and forth again. "I gave express orders that no one was to step outside our boundaries!" He glanced at me. "Do you remember me saying that, Hadrack?"

"Of course, I do," I said. "But this..."

"And do you know why?" Einhard grunted, cutting me off.

I sighed and nodded. "Because we're not allowed to engage with the enemy unless there is absolutely no choice." I thought about telling him that I didn't think there had been a choice, but I knew how that argument would go, so I said nothing and just waited.

"Exactly," Einhard said. "The last thing I need is you stirring up trouble with the Ganders the day before the king arrives."

"What was I supposed to do?" I muttered. "Just ignore what we found?"

"No," Einhard said. "You were not supposed to just ignore it. You were supposed to come to me and let me decide what to do. That's what good soldiers do."

"I sent Peren," I protested.

"And then you should have waited until we got there," Einhard replied.

"If we had waited those men would have taken Lady Demay back to her husband," I said stubbornly.

"I don't care what the story is!" Einhard snapped. "All I know is the two of you put this garrison at risk because of your recklessness!"

"There wasn't any risk to the garrison!" I retorted. "We saved Lady Demay and everything turned out just fine."

"You think disobeying my orders is fine!?" Einhard shouted.

"Your men were being heroic," Shana interrupted bravely as Einhard and I glared at each other. "They risked their lives to save mine and they should be commended for it."

"Your life means nothing to me!" Einhard grunted. "Nor does your opinion. Don't speak to me again until I say you can." Shana's face grew pale and she stared at Einhard coldly as he pointed at my chest. "As for you. This may be a game to you, but the rest of us are taking it seriously. The Master will soon give us the word and..."

"The word!" I scoffed, cutting him off. I lifted my hands in the air in frustration. "I'm so sick and tired of hearing about the Master and the word! We've been waiting for that word for over a year now, and where is it?"

"It will come," Einhard growled at me, his eyes flashing in warning.

"You were waiting for the word before we even met!" I

said with a snort. "I'm amazed you were allowed to attack the quarry at all." I shook my head and swung my arms around the room. "Sometimes I think you've forgotten our situation, Einhard. The garrison is weak. The Ganders could overwhelm us in a day if they wanted to."

"Then their prince will die," Einhard said.

"And so will we right afterward," I replied. "That might not bother you much, but my vow is more important to me than dying on these walls for no good reason." I sighed and took a deep breath. "Don't you see, Einhard? We need to take the fight to them while they're indecisive and weak. We have the advantage right now, but if we keep sitting here with our thumbs up our arses waiting for your fickle Master to give us the word, that advantage will be lost!"

"That's enough, Hadrack!" Jebido hissed.

Einhard smashed his fist down on the desktop, startling Shana, who jumped beside me. "We are done with this!" He pointed a finger at me. "Say another word against the Master and I swear I'll have you flogged in the bailey in front of the entire garrison!" I opened my mouth to say something and Einhard smacked the table again, this time with his open palm. "I said not a word, Hadrack! I've been lenient with you for too long now! That ends today!" He pointed to the door. "Get out of here! I don't want to see your face again until you know your place!"

Einhard and I glared at each other in the sudden silence. I could feel my pulse pounding in my ears and I fought to control it. Baine and Jebido were both standing like statues staring hard at something on the floor, but I knew this was all about me and that Einhard's fury would fizzle once I was gone. I snorted and shook my head, then spun on my heel and headed for the door.

"Not you," Einhard said gruffly as Shana turned to follow. "I still haven't figured out what I'm going to do with you yet."

I strode out of the office and angrily made my way

down the corridor into the great hall. Behind me I heard rapid footsteps echoing in pursuit, but I ignored them. I wasn't in the mood to talk to anyone right now.

"Hadrack, wait!" Alesia called from behind me.

"Not now!" I grunted over my shoulder as I kept going.

"I said wait, Ganderman!" Alesia shouted.

I sighed and turned, waiting as Alesia hurried toward me as fast as the growing babe in her belly would let her. "What is it?" I asked, unable to hide my sullenness.

Alesia put her hand on my arm and I could see the concern in her eyes. "Are you all right?"

"Of course," I grunted moodily, feeling my anger start to wane at her expression. I pointed back down the corridor. "Your husband is being an ass!"

"You're both being asses!" Alesia said bluntly.

I studied the woman before me, marveling at the change in her. Alesia seemed calmer now, happier than at any other time that I'd seen her. The fire of mischief that had smoldered inside her when we first met had turned into a deep contentment and serenity. I suspected that change was mainly due to the baby growing inside her, but either way, she seemed like a completely different person now. Alesia's face and body had rounded in recent weeks as her birthing date approached, but if possible, she was even more beautiful like this than before. I had a sudden vision of her naked and writhing on top of me during the Ascension Ceremony last year and I thrust it from my mind.

"Is that what you ran out here to tell me?" I finally asked sarcastically. "That I'm being an ass?"

"No, of course not," Alesia said.

Around us the women continued to work cleaning the hall, though I could tell by their postures that they were listening intently. I caught Betania's eye and she gave me a weak smile of encouragement.

"What I came to say, Hadrack," Alesia continued, "is that you need to stop this thing with Einhard. The pressure on him is enormous right now. Running this garrison is no easy task for him, nor would it be for any Pith. You know as well as I do that we're just not designed for this kind of life. And now with the king coming tomorrow," she put her hands around her belly, "not to mention his child soon, it's just becoming too much." She sighed and looked away. "He loves you like a brother, but right now the last thing he needs is you disobeying him on top of everything else."

I lifted my hands in the air helplessly. "But he won't listen to me, Alesia. No matter how hard I try to get through to him, all he ever does is go on and on about the word of the Master. It's almost like he's using it as an excuse to sit here and do nothing."

Alesia blinked in surprise. "Do you truly believe that?"

I nodded. "I do." I motioned around the room. "As long as we hold the prince, we're safe here. We have plenty to eat, plenty to drink, and luxuries like most of us have never known." I pointed back along the corridor. "He's becoming soft, Alesia. More interested in drinking beer than killing Gandermen."

"You couldn't be more wrong," Alesia said, shaking her head.

I could see a hint of anger building up in her and I folded my arms over my chest. "I don't think so," I said.

"Do you think Einhard enjoys this?" Alesia asked. She snorted. "My husband is a warrior, Hadrack." She waved a hand. "Can't you tell he hates this place?"

"He sure doesn't show it," I grumbled.

"What do you expect him to do?" Alesia demanded. "Mope around and pout like a child? The king ordered him to hold this garrison, so that's what he'll do. Einhard is just doing his duty, much as he detests it, and so should you."

"And what duty is that?" I asked scornfully. "What is my purpose in all of this?"

"To serve the will of the Master," Alesia replied. "It's the only one that matters."

"And that's the problem," I said. "I don't serve the Master and I never will. So, where does that leave me? Einhard says I have to wait and be patient to get what I want, but every day that goes by here feels like a lifetime to me."

"You swore an oath to serve my husband," Alesia said. She tapped me on the chest with her finger. "And that means you serve the king and the Master as well, whether you like it or not."

"I also swore an oath to my murdered sister and father," I replied bitterly. I gestured to the corridor. "If he were me, which oath do you think he would follow?"

"That's just it, Hadrack," Alesia said. "You're more alike than you know."

I frowned. "What do you mean by that?"

"Einhard made a similar oath to his family when the Ganders first came to our land. He was just a boy then, not much older than you were when your family died. The Ganders attacked his camp without warning and killed many, including Einhard's mother and father and younger brother." I looked at Alesia in surprise and she nodded. "So, you see, there is nothing Einhard desires more than to shed Gander blood, but his oath to his family must wait, just as yours must too."

We stood facing each other in silence for a time, before finally Alesia sighed and looked behind her. "The Gander girl is beautiful," she said thoughtfully. I nodded, not sure how to respond. "Do you care for her?"

"What kind of question is that?" I asked, caught off-guard and feeling my face redden. "I just met her a couple of hours ago."

"What does time have to do with anything?" Alesia said with a smile. She put her hand on my arm again. "Promise me you'll stop arguing with my husband and I'll make sure that your girl stays safe."

"Safe?" I said, perplexed. "Why wouldn't she be safe?"

Alesia chuckled. "Because she's now a slave in Gasterny, Hadrack. A young, beautiful Gander slave that every one of our brothers in this garrison is going to want to bed, that's why." She winked at me and I saw the old Alesia return for a moment. "And probably many of my sisters as well."

I looked at Alesia in alarm, realizing that she was right. I'd warned Shana that the Piths would be unimpressed with her highborn blood and that they would cast her down as a slave. But I hadn't thought completely through what that would mean once she got here. I cursed myself for being a fool. The Piths considered the Ganders to be beneath them and not only forced them into labor, they used them for pleasure whenever they wished. To be honest, the male Gander slaves didn't seem all that upset about being forced into bed with the Pith women. But there were only a few Gander women in the garrison of an age and look that appealed to the Pith men. These women were in constant demand and found themselves being passed around from warrior to warrior like a jug of wine. Several times already I'd had to come to Betania's defense and fend off a Pith who'd become interested in her.

The thought of Shana undergoing that kind of treatment made my blood boil and I put my hand on the hilt of Wolf's Head. "If anyone touches her, I swear on The Mother and The Father that I'll kill them!" I said hotly.

"I know that," Alesia said soothingly. She put both hands on my chest and stared up at me. "And if you do that, Einhard will have no choice but to kill you. I don't want that, Hadrack. Give me your word you'll obey Einhard from now on and won't mention your vow to your family to him again. Do those things, and in return I promise no one will touch your girl. Do we have a bargain?"

I knew there wasn't much choice if I wanted to keep the Piths away from Shana, so I slowly swallowed my anger and nodded. "You have my word."

The day the Pith king was set to arrive began cold and

miserable, with a bone-chilling drizzle that fell almost side-ways as a brisk northwest wind whipped it around. But, des-pite the disheartening weather, many of us still chose to line up on the roof of the keep well before the great man arrived, hoping for the first glimpse of him. Baine, Jebido and I were standing together along the northern battlements and I stared down at the sodden inner bailey below me. The bailey lay muck-ridden and abandoned, save for one miserable-looking hound sniffing hopefully for food around the well near the keep. Those who had chosen not to watch from the keep, were either watching from the outer walls of the garrison or had wisely hidden inside from the frigid rain. I turned my gaze away and leaned my forearms against the dripping stone of the battlements, looking northward to where the bridge and gatehouses lay. Droplets bounced off my helmet like angry bees as I studied the terrain where I knew the Pith king would eventually appear. I squinted against the rain splashing off the stone, but I could barely make out the trees along the river, let alone anything else. Einhard had made sure to add the river-bank when he'd given his terms to King Jorquin, including in it a corridor that started from the bridge and reached to the ford and the pass several miles to the east. With the garrison as a base and the bridge and corridor open and unchallenged, it gave the Pith forces a well-defended gateway into the heart of Ganderland. Assuming the Master ever decided to use it, of course.

The Ganders were massed in force all around us, but they were taking no chances with the prince's life and were careful to stay well clear of the garrison and the corridor. They were still close enough that they could attack us with short notice, however, should the need or opportunity arise. I glanced down at the wooden walls facing east and north, unconsciously comparing them to their much sturdier stone cousins to the west and south. I frowned, knowing that should an attack ever come, those walls would be our weak spot. The irony that the Piths themselves were the ones responsible for that weakness had not failed to escape any of us. The north wall was less a problem, I believed, as it faced the river and would be tough to assault. I glanced northward and studied the rain-bloated moat that wound its way around the outer northern wall. Beyond the stretch of muddy water lay a flat tract of land no more than ten feet wide, then the ground dipped dramatically toward the river. A narrow road the Ganders had used to transport stone blocks from barges rose from the river, but it snaked away from the garrison to eventually join the main road at the bridge. Any attacker who decided to try the north wall would be forced to ascend a steep, rock-strewn riverbank while archers poured arrows down on them with virtual impunity. Not impossible, I knew, but certainly far from the first choice I would make, were I the one attacking.

As for the eastern wall, Einhard and the Piths had strengthened it as best they could, though none here were experienced builders or engineers, so it had been no easy task. On a suggestion from Jebido, Einhard had ordered the moat redirected away from the eastern wall so that a second, shorter wall of timber could be built about thirty feet out from where the moat had been. The moat had then been repositioned in front of the new wall and then refilled. The Piths added a wide parapet along the new wall, but instead of stairs or ladders to access them, they set ramps down that spanned the gap from the inner wall to the shorter outer one. That short wall was an easy climb with ladders or grappling hooks and would make an irresistible target, which I knew Einhard was counting on. Spears with cut shafts were thrust into the muck of the killing ground between the inner and outer walls and were covered up with a thick layer of straw. Once the attackers crossed the moat and scaled that short eastern wall, the Piths planned to remove the ramps, forcing the invaders to jump to the ground from the ramparts directly onto the waiting spears. I looked down at the wet and filthy straw that hid the killing grounds deadly secret and I pictured the devastation that might occur.

Hopefully it wouldn't be needed, I thought.

"I still can't believe Carspen Tuft is dead!" Jebido muttered, cutting into my thoughts.

My friend was still unhappy that he'd missed out on Tuft's death. Jebido shook his head sadly and pulled his cloak tighter about himself in a futile attempt to stay dry. Above us the rain began to fall even heavier.

"Believe it!" Baine nodded happily beside him. "One of the best days of my life," he added, pausing to wink. "So far." Baine wiped the water from his eyes, then squinted up at the sky and frowned as the wind began to pick up. "The king could have picked a better day for this."

"I don't think even a king has a say in what the weather does," I said with a chuckle.

"Did Tuft scream, at least?" Jebido demanded just as thunder suddenly boomed above us.   A small group of Gander women and children who'd been allowed to come up to the roof with us cried out in terror at the ear-shattering crash. I felt the stone beneath my feet tremble and watched with amusement as the Ganders turned and ran back down into the keep to escape the storm. I saw Ania standing and talking amidst a small group of Pith women and they paused in their conversation to laugh at the Ganders. I managed to catch Ania's eye and I made a crude gesture at her with my hands. She winked and nodded back to me and I grinned. I knew where I'd be sleeping that night.

"What did you say?" Baine finally asked Jebido as the thunder slowly faded away to the south.

"Tuft," Jebido repeated, leaning closer. "Did that little bastard scream when he died?"

Baine and I looked at each other and we smiled at the same time.

"Like a babe hungry for its mother's milk," Baine said with a laugh.

Jebido grinned. "That's something, at least."

"By the way," I said to Jebido. "I've been meaning to ask

you. What's a Cardian?"

Jebido spit sideways and then looked at me with distaste. "Turds with legs, that's what they are. Where'd you hear about them?"

"That's who was chasing Lady Demay," Baine said. "She called them Cardians."

"They come from across the western sea," Jebido said. "Some people call them sellswords."

"Sellswords?" I said.

Jebido nodded. "Pay them enough and they'd slit their own mother's throat without a second thought."

People began to cheer along the wall and we turned toward the bridge. The king had finally arrived, I saw. Above us, the rain abruptly subsided and a weak sun appeared, sliding out from behind the clouds. I frowned, studying the long procession of mounted men that was winding its way along the riverbank. Maybe this king could control the rain, I thought idly. The King of the Piths was called Clendon the Peacemaker, and somehow he had managed in just ten short years to unite the Piths and transform them from a loose band of war-like, nomadic tribes that constantly fought amongst themselves into a nation. A nation with only one goal; the destruction of the Ganders and the First Pair along with them. I thought about that goal and I felt a lurch in my stomach, wondering for the thousandth time what I was doing here with these Piths. I had no love for the Gandermen, and rarely, if ever did I consider myself one of them, but I also knew that I wasn't a Pith either. Trying to justify going against Mother Above and Father Below was something I couldn't do, and, as with every other time I'd thought about it, I quickly thrust the problem from my mind. I liked to console myself with the belief that Jebido was right and that the First Pair had sent the three of us to the Piths for a reason. It was the only thing that kept my conscience clear. Someday I hoped to understand what that reason was, but as I watched the first riders reach the far gatehouse, I knew that today was not going to be that day.

"Do you see him yet?" Baine asked as he peered over the wall eagerly.

"That might be him near the front," Jebido said doubtfully as the back doors to the gatehouse slowly opened.

Above us the skies continued to clear and the breeze fell, the frigid air quickly turning hot and humid as we started to bake in our armor beneath the hot sun. Einhard had insisted that the entire garrison be dressed in our finest for the visit, and while I understood his reasoning, I was quickly beginning to regret it. The head of the king's procession passed through the gatehouse and then made its way along the bridge, stopping for a moment as they reached the gatehouse on our side of the riverbank. I whistled, realizing the end of the column was still out of view along the other side of the river.

"How many men does he have?" Baine asked in wonder.

Jebido shrugged. "Five, maybe six hundred, it looks like."

"I guess he's not taking any chances," I said.

I thought about the Ganders massed around us and knew they were undoubtedly watching the king's arrival from some hidden vantage point. The chance of capturing or even killing the Pith king might have been a temptation even the Ganders couldn't resist, if not for the sizable force he'd brought with him.

"Let's get down there," Jebido said. "Einhard wants to introduce us to the king."

I held back as my friends headed for the stairs and they paused, turning to look at me.

"What?" Jebido asked.

"Maybe you two should go on without me," I said. I thought back to Einhard's last words to me yesterday and I shrugged. "I don't think Einhard wants me around right now."

"Don't be an idiot!" Jebido chided me as he waved his hand dismissively. "That was all just for show. Don't worry about it."

"It didn't look like a show to me," I said.

"Me neither," Baine agreed. "It looked like his eyeballs were going to pop out of his head for a while there."

"Like I said, just for show," Jebido explained. He pointed at me. "If he let you get away with breaking the rules all the time, he'd look weak. Everyone in the garrison knows Einhard has a soft spot for you, Hadrack. This time you put him in a difficult position." Jebido made a face. "I thought you were going to be stupid and force him to have you whipped at one point. You're lucky you shut your mouth when you did."

"Maybe Einhard should start listening to his men a little more," I grumbled as I reluctantly followed my friends.

Jebido sighed and glanced over his shoulder at me as we took the stairs. "That's what you don't get, Hadrack. A man in Einhard's position doesn't have to listen to you, or me, or anyone else other than his god and his king. That's something you'd best get through your thick skull."

We descended the rest of the way in silence and followed the corridor that led to the great hall, then passed through it and out the doors to the inner bailey. Einhard and Alesia were waiting at the top of the ramp and the rest of the Piths were standing ankle-deep in puddles in front of the buildings that lined the eastern and western curtain walls.

"Ah," Einhard said with a smile when he saw us. He beamed and gestured to his right. "Please, my friends, stand here next to us."

Ania and the last of the Piths who'd been on the roof came out right behind us and they dispersed into the crowd. A great cheer rang out moments later and the king appeared riding a muscular white stallion through the gates. The Piths, including Einhard and Alesia, dropped to one knee in a single motion.

"Down," Jebido whispered, motioning for to us to kneel.

I studied the man I'd heard so much about curiously as I dropped to one knee. The king wasn't a big man, I saw, but even from where I knelt, I could tell that he was wide-shouldered and heavily built. The king's beard was cropped close and was dirty blond in color, though it was shot through here and there with grey on the chin. He wasn't wearing a helmet and his hair was short and greying rapidly and when he turned his head, I saw that it was beginning to thin at the crown. Three men rode with the king, one to either side of him and one behind, and behind them rode a group of five Pathfinders, recognizable by their purple cloaks. I'd met the man sitting to the king's right almost a year ago after the Bridge Battle and knew his name was Danfor the Lighthearted, the Shield of the King. To the king's left sat a squat, bull of a man with long greasy hair and a pointed beard. Einhard had described him to me and I knew he was named Flinhard the Eager, the Ear of the King. The man riding behind the king was thin for a Pith, with a nervous-looking face and one eye socket scarred and hollow. I had to suppress a grin at the irony of it, as I knew this man was named Larles the Unlucky, the Eye of the King.

"Rise," the king said as he motioned with his hand. "Please, my brothers and sisters, rise."

The king dismounted and strode up the ramp to Einhard as we rose to our feet and he embraced him warmly.

"It's good to see you, Highness," Einhard said.

"And you, my friend," the king said. He stood back and studied Einhard critically. "You're getting fat, brother."

Einhard laughed and gestured to Alesia. "I'm just trying to compete with my wife, Highness."

Alesia wrapped her hands around her huge swollen belly and smiled. "And failing miserably at it, husband."

The king bellowed with laughter at that before he turned to gently embrace Alesia. "I've missed you, child."

"And I've missed you, father," Alesia said.

Baine, Jebido and I shared a look of surprise as Einhard gestured to us. "And these are the Gandermen you've heard so much about."

"Ah," the king said with a smile. In three quick strides, he was in front of me, staring up at me with sharp, intelligent eyes. "This big one is the wolf, I take it?" he said to Einhard.

"Yes," Einhard agreed. "Hadrack of Corwick. A terror on the battlefield, Highness."

The king looked me up and down thoughtfully. "I've no doubt, brother."

"I'm honored to meet you, Highness," I managed to say.

We locked forearms and he patted my shoulder. "If even half of what Einhard tells me about you is true, then the honor is mine. I look forward to speaking with you when time permits." I nodded and he moved on to Baine, saying a few words, then to Jebido before he turned to Einhard and gestured to the keep. "Come, my friend, we have much to discuss, you and I." He leaned close to Einhard and whispered something in his ear and I saw the Pith leader's green eyes light up.

Einhard immediately gestured to Eriz. "Everyone is to remain here until our return," he ordered. "No exceptions." He deliberately looked over at me as he said those last words and I kept my face as impassive as I could.

"Of course, brother," Eriz rumbled.

Einhard motioned that the king should lead them into the keep before falling into step behind him. Alesia, the Shield, the Eye, the Ear, and the five pathfinders followed them and then the doors were closed firmly.

"What was that all about?" I asked Jebido when they were gone.

He shrugged. "I guess we'll just have to wait and see."

An hour went by, then another one while we stood in the open bailey at the mercy of the beating sun. Jebido and Baine and I talked for a while, but there's only so much talking a man can do and eventually I fell silent. I crossed my arms over my chest and leaned my ass against the stone wall along the ramp, barely listening to my friends as they continued the conversation without me. I removed my helmet and ran my fingers through my sweat-soaked hair and let my gaze roam over the Piths. There were close to two hundred of them crowded into the courtyard, with maybe fifty or so of them women. The Piths seemed perfectly happy to stand and wait all day if need be, and I tried to suppress the annoyance I felt. I'd begun reading a book about military tactics that Josphet had given me and I'd become completely engrossed in it and was anxious to get back to it. The doors to the hall suddenly swung open and Einhard appeared with a brilliant smile on his face.

I hastily stood up and replaced my helmet as all conversation in the courtyard ceased.

"Brothers and sisters!" Einhard cried. He drew his sword and held it in the air. "We have the word!"

The war had finally begun.

4: DECEPTION

The celebration that followed Einhard's announcement lasted all afternoon and well into the night. But despite the Pith king's words to me when I'd first met him, he and I never did get a chance to talk. I wasn't all that disappointed, truth be told, since I was still mired in the black mood that had wrapped itself around me ever since Einhard and I had argued. Einhard and Alesia were set to leave the next morning with the king and his men, though that had not stopped Einhard from getting drunker than I'd ever seen him. Which, when you think about it, is saying a lot. Einhard was returning home to help coordinate the coming offensive against the Ganders and he decided to take Alesia along with him. Alesia was due to give birth sometime within the next two weeks and the garrison facilities were less than ideal for a childbirth. Everyone agreed going home was a wise choice, as Alesia would be better off in the land of the Piths where they had experienced birthers to assist her.

Einhard chose Eriz to command the garrison in his absence, which surprised no one at all, and he promised to return once the baby was born. Einhard and I hadn't spoken much since our falling out, other than a few polite greetings when we bumped into each other. I was just as excited and relieved as everyone else that the war was finally here, but I still couldn't bring myself to talk to Einhard after what he'd said to me. Jebido said I was sulking and acting like a child for no good reason. He was probably right about that.

"There you are, Hadrack," Einhard said the next morning. He'd found me on top of the keep along the eastern wall brooding as I watched the sun come up. Einhard came to stand beside me and we watched the pink sky grow richer together for a time in silence. "I'm getting set to leave with the king," Einhard finally said. "I didn't want to go without seeing you."

I didn't say anything and Einhard sighed. "Are you still angry with me about the other day?" I stared up at the cloudless sky above us. I knew I was being silly, but even so, I wasn't ready to forgive him yet. Einhard crossed his hands behind his back. "I can't say that I blame you for being mad," he said. "A lesser man would have left me long ago."

I glanced at him in surprise. "Lesser?" I managed to mumble.

"Of course," Einhard said. "I know how hard it's been for you to stay here, believe me." Einhard put his hands on the battlements and leaned on it. "Sometimes I forget how young you are, Hadrack." I opened my mouth to point out that he was only a few years older than me, but he held up his hand, stopping me. "Let me finish. There are those among us who think I favor you too much." His green eyes twinkled with mirth in the morning light. "And they would be right about that. Even though turd-sucking Gander blood flows through your veins, I feel we have a connection that goes beyond what race we are born of and which gods we worship."

I turned to face Einhard. "Alesia told me about your family."

"Ah," Einhard nodded, not looking surprised.

"Why didn't you tell me?"

"Would it have mattered?" Einhard asked with one eyebrow raised. "Would it have made you obey me more if I had?"

I thought about that and then slowly shook my head. "No."

Einhard laughed. "I didn't think so." He turned and leaned his back against the ramparts as he crossed his arms over his chest. "What am I going to do with you, Hadrack?" I didn't have an answer to that and we both just stood there in silence again. "Do you remember the day we met?" Einhard finally asked.

"How could I forget?" I said.

"The puppy with teeth," Einhard said with a chuckle. He smacked his fist into his palm. "I'd never seen anything like it! You stood up to that Ganderman like a veteran of fifty battles, not some starving kid with snot running down his nose fresh from the mines."

"I was lucky," I said, thinking back to my first battle. Fanch had been good, and if not for the fact that he'd underestimated me badly, I would almost certainly have died that day.

Einhard rubbed his chin, still chuckling lightly as he shrugged. "Sometimes luck is all we have." He glanced at me, his face turning serious. "Do you remember I told you later that honor makes men weak, and that the only thing they respect is strength?"

"I do," I said.

"Do you remember what you said to that?"

I nodded, thinking back to the celebration the night the Piths had defeated the Gandermen at the quarry. I'd thought the Piths to be nothing but savages back then. Savage perverts who'd kill you just as soon as look at you without any shred of dignity or decency about them. I'd come to realize over the last year that I'd been completely wrong about them. There was no denying that the Piths were different, but they were a decent, loving people, though even today I still found myself feeling uncomfortable with some of their stranger perversions. I looked at Einhard. "I said that honor defined a man and made him stronger, not weaker." I felt my face break out in a grin despite myself. "I thought you were drunk and weren't listening when I said that."

"I was drunk," Einhard said with a snort. "But I always listen." He turned to face me and he put a hand on each of my shoulders. "I was wrong, and you were right. You've served me with both strength and honor and proved your words, despite how unhappy you've been this last year. I know, as you do, what carrying the guilt of a vow left unfulfilled feels like as it eats away at your gut day after day." He stepped back and looked at the sky and sighed loudly. "Before you answer my next question, I want you to think long and hard on it. I want you to think back on all the days you've waited, torn by your vow to your family and your oath to me, and how close we both are to finally getting a chance for vengeance."

"Einhard," I said with a frown. "What are you talking about?"

"Do you want me to absolve you of your oath and set you free, Hadrack?"

"What?" I gasped, caught by surprise. Of all the things I'd imagined Einhard would say, being released from my oath was the last thing I expected.

"Just say the word and I will," Einhard said. He stared at me and waited with a blank face, though I could see what I thought was worry hidden deep in his green eyes.

"Why now?" I asked, confused. After arguing with Einhard for a year to be allowed to go after the rest of the nine, here it was, offered up to me on a platter. All I needed to do was reach out and take it. I felt a tingling of eagerness running down my limbs at the thought and I hesitated, feeling sudden doubt. Being free to fulfill my vow had dominated every moment of my life since I was a boy, but I knew by doing so it would mean I'd have to leave the Piths and Shana and all my friends behind. I shook my head at my sudden indecision, angry that for the first time in my life I was unsure of myself. "Why couldn't you have asked me this six months ago?" I finally demanded bitterly. "Or even two days ago?" I put one hand on the ramparts and leaned on it, staring at the stone beneath my feet as I thought. I could feel the pounding of my heart roaring in my ears as I wrestled with the choice.

"Because we didn't have the word then," Einhard simply said.

"You bastard!" I grunted.

Einhard shrugged. "True, but bastard or not, I still need to know where you stand."

"Where I stand with what?"

"This war will not be pretty, and it will not be quick, Hadrack," Einhard said. "If you stay, I need to know that if a time comes on the battlefield to choose, you will choose the path the Master has set for us. Even if it means not getting what you want most."

"I swore my sword to you!" I spat at him. "Isn't that enough?"

"No," Einhard said with a quick shake of his head. "It's not enough."

I threw my hands up in disgust. "What else do you want from me then?"

"Your sword and your heart," Einhard said. "With both of those by my side, nothing can stop us." He put his hand on my shoulder. "Stay with me and give me all you have, and I promise we'll find every one of those bastards once we've crushed the Ganders." He grinned at me. "We'll scour the entire kingdom of Ganderland if we have to until we've flushed them out." He raised an eyebrow. "What do you say?"

Einhard was an incredibly charming and charismatic man, and few, if any could say no to him. I thought again of Jebido and Baine, Ania, Eriz, and Alesia. I pictured Shana with her deep blue eyes and shimmering hair and I felt a lump rise in my throat. Could I really leave people behind who'd come to mean so much to me? I took a deep breath, wavering back and forth before a sudden stark vision appeared in my mind. I saw a young boy, his face wet with tears as he carried a girl's dead body across a freshly turned field. I saw him kneeling by two graves, one hand on each and heard him speak a vow of vengeance. I knew then without a doubt what I had to do. I straightened my shoulders and stared back at Einhard and I knew he could read the answer in my eyes. He slowly pulled his hand from my shoulder.

"So be it," Einhard said sadly. "I release you from your vow." He shook his head and then wrapped his arms around me in one of his crushing embraces and whispered in my ear, "You have no idea what you are yet, Hadrack, but someday you will, and on that day the world itself will tremble." He broke the embrace. "I will miss you," he said. I nodded, unable to find the words and he sighed and turned to go, then glanced back at me. "Promise me you'll wait until my return before you go."

"I'll wait," I managed to say.

I don't know how long I stood leaning against the ramparts after Einhard left, brooding about my choice and staring down into the inner bailey as the king and his entourage prepared to leave. Finally, I saw Einhard appear and mount his horse and I watched as the procession trotted out of the garrison, heading for the bridge. At one point I saw Einhard riding beside Alesia turn in his saddle and look back up at the keep. I lifted a hand to him and the Sword of the King waved back in farewell. I had no idea that moment would be the last time I'd see Einhard for years to come.

Life in the garrison returned to normal after that. A week went by with nothing out of the ordinary occurring other than one of the Gander slaves falling into the White Rock River and being whisked away. Her name was Talai, and she, along with Lady Demay and several other women, had been washing clothing on the dock overlooking the river when she'd slipped on the slick wood. Talai and Shana had become close in the few days they'd known each other, and she had been devastated by the woman's death. Shana recounted bitterly to me that their Pith guards had done nothing but watch and laugh as Talai cried desperately for help. She'd struggled hard against the fast-flowing current, and at one-point Shana had thought she might even make it to the bank. But twenty feet from the shoreline a sudden surge pulled her under and then she was gone. Shana's hatred for the Piths knew no bounds after that and I had to constantly beg her not to say or do anything that might anger them. Many of the Piths were my friends, but in the end, they were still Piths and could be greatly unpredictable. Thankfully, the bargain that I'd struck with Alesia had worked and Shana had been left strictly alone, though more than one of the Pith warriors — both male and female — had tried to legitimately entice her into their beds. All were politely refused, however, which I was hugely relieved about.

Lady Demay, being highborn, was even more accomplished at both reading and writing than Josphet. It became a normal routine for us to meet in one of the many rooms on the second floor of the keep, where she would instruct me. Eriz had graciously allowed us two hours every morning between nine and eleven for the lessons, which seemed an unusual kindness coming from him. I can only guess that Ania had something to do with it, as she was well aware of my passion for reading. After the loss of Talai, Betania and Shana had surprisingly become friends and quite often the younger girl would join us so that Shana could instruct her as well. Betania was smart and a quick study, and to my chagrin, was rapidly catching up to me in ability.

I'm not exactly sure when it was that I fell in love with Lady Demay. Baine believed it happened the moment we walked into that old abandoned abbey, but I'm not convinced of that. I think it was more likely during those morning writing sessions at Gasterny. Not that it mattered one way or the other, as in the end I was smitten either way. I couldn't bear to tell anyone that I'd be leaving soon, especially Shana, and so I'd only told Jebido and Baine and sworn them both to secrecy. My friends had immediately pledged to go with me, assuming, of course, that Einhard would also release them from their oaths. I'd accepted and tried to hide the fact that I was greatly relieved by their decision, but I don't think I was fooling anyone.

The Ganders arrived for their monthly visit on a Tuesday morning a week after Einhard left. A morning that still haunts my dreams to this day. The visits over the past year had become completely routine for the garrison, and they were barely even acknowledged now. But today's visit, as time would eventually prove, would be anything but routine. Son Oriell — who had survived the Bridge Battle by unashamedly fleeing into the forest behind the garrison — would arrive once a month before nine in the morning with several well-armed men wearing the Rock of Life emblem on their surcoats. He usually spent about an hour with the prince taking confession and ensuring that he was in good health and spirits. Baine had already left on patrol by nine and the priest still hadn't arrived, so Jebido and I decided to spar in the outer courtyard near the stables while we waited. Several Piths, including Eriz, were also training nearby.

"Mother's tit, Hadrack!" Jebido shouted after about ten minutes of swordplay. He took two quick steps back and then glared at me. His chest was heaving and sweat was pouring down his face in rivulets as he pointed his sword at me accusingly. "You're going easy on me!"

"I am not!" I protested.

I was going easy on him, of course, but I was determined not to let him know that. Jebido was getting old, at least in my view, and in the last year he'd begun to slow down quite a bit. The difference was marginal at first, and most people might not have noticed, but I'd been crossing swords with Jebido for many years now and I could tell. We were at a point that I could disarm him whenever I chose, but I knew my friend took tremendous pride in his swordsmanship and I just couldn't bring myself to do it. The problem was it was getting harder and harder to hide that fact from him.

"You're full of shit!" Jebido said as he fought to catch his breath. "Are you telling me you didn't see that opening I left you?"

"Of course I did," I said. "But you covered it too fast for me to do anything about it." I shook my head. "You have no idea how quick on your feet you still are, Jebido."

Jebido studied me suspiciously and I stared right back

at him, trying to look innocent, until finally he nodded and accepted the lie. "Well, miss chances like that on the battlefield too often and your opponent will cut your balls off for you," he grumbled.

"I'll keep that in mind," I said with a laugh. I raised an eyebrow and brought my sword up. "Again?"

Jebido started to advance on me and then he stopped, frowning as a Pith came barrelling over the drawbridge and through the barbican to come to a dusty halt in the bailey. The Pith's name was Klesp, one of the guards posted to the bridge's northern gatehouse. Klesp looked agitated, but I didn't see any cause for alarm as the horn hadn't been blown and the lookouts on the watchtowers above me appeared relaxed and, if anything, bored.

"Brother!" Klesp said as he hurried to Eriz.

Eriz paused in his sparring and grunted. "What?"

"The Ganders have arrived, brother."

Eriz nodded and flicked his eyes to Klesp's warhorse, which was breathing heavily and slick with sweat. "And you chose to ride your horse almost to death just to tell me about something I already knew would happen?"

"There's a problem," Klesp said. "There's more of the dogs than usual, brother."

"More?" Eriz said with a frown. "How many more?"

"Two wagons full of their priests and priestesses," Klesp spat with disdain. "And twelve swordsmen."

"Well, that's interesting," Eriz said. He shrugged and then turned back to his sparring. "They know the rules. Only the ugly priest and his men come in. No one else."

Klesp nodded. "That's what I told them, brother. But they became quite upset about it." He pulled off his mailed glove and held out a folded piece of parchment that he'd stuffed inside. "They gave me this."

Eriz sheathed his sword with a sigh and took the parchment and unfolded it, then frowned in bewilderment as he stared at it. "What is this supposed to mean?" he finally asked.

Klesp shrugged. "I don't know. The ugly priest told me to find a Gander that can read and get them to explain how important it is."

Eriz flicked his eyes at me and motioned me closer. "I've heard you can read, brother." He held the parchment out. "Tell me what these scribbles mean."

Jebido came to stand beside me as I scanned the writing. I mouthed the words slowly, fighting to understand them all. There were words written down that I'd never seen before, but eventually I realized what it was the Ganders were asking for and I shook my head in puzzlement.

"What is it?" Jebido asked.

"They want to perform a cleansing on the prince," I said.

Jebido's eyebrows rose in surprise. "You're joking?"

I shook my head as Eriz looked at me in exasperation. "Which means what, exactly?" he asked.

Jebido answered for me, "Sometimes when a highborn has committed a sin that's above the ability of the confessional to absolve, a cleansing of the soul is used to try to save them from The Father's wrath." Eriz frowned, looking completely confused. "Only a sin-free soul can sit by The Mother's side when we die," Jebido explained. "Which is the ultimate goal for all, whether they be a king or the lowest commoner." Jebido grimaced. "The problem is, trying to find a sinless man is like trying to find a whore with a heart. That's why we go to confession from time to time, to get absolution for those sins and keep our souls clean."

"That's all this is?" Eriz asked, looking irritated. "A confession?"

"Sort of," Jebido said. "A commoner can go to any Holy House to offer their confession, which is usually pardoned with a few words from a Son or Daughter. But a cleansing is complicated and usually involves senior Sons and Daughters." Jebido pursed his lips as he thought. "Cleansings are rare and only performed for the highborn, so, whatever the prince did, it has to be bad for them to come here like this."

"Sins!" Eriz said with a snort. "You Ganders and your gods are such fools!" He shook his head. "Why worry about things that we're supposed to do anyway? The Master created us to live like men, not frightened children sucking on thumbs and hiding beneath the bedding."

Jebido grinned. "Perhaps the Master is more tolerant than the First Pair. But for us, if judgment day arrives and we're sent to The Father, it means many years of painful burning before our souls are cleared and we're sent back to try again."

"Sent back?" Eriz grunted. "You mean here, to this world?"

"Yes," Einhard nodded. "Over and over again if needed."

"But why would the Ganders think Prince Tyro needs a cleansing?" I asked, wondering out loud as I rubbed my chin. "I mean, what possible sin could he have done here that warrants something as drastic as that?"

"Maybe it wasn't done here," Jebido said with a shrug. "Maybe the sin happened before we captured him." He looked at Eriz. "Either way, what makes this really strange is a cleansing is usually only used as a last resort when death is approaching."

Eriz looked alarmed at that. "He's dying?"

Jebido shook his head. "I doubt it. He's still a young man in the prime of his life. Unless there's something about his health that we don't know about, then I'd say they need to do this for some other reason." He glanced at Eriz. "Just the same, you might want to send that girl," he flicked his eyes to me, "what's her name?"

"Betania," I said.

"Right," Jebido nodded. "You might want to send Betania to look the prince over and make sure he's all right."

Eriz grunted his agreement and turned to the Pith he'd been sparring with. "Go find the Gander girl that heals and tell her to check over the prince for any signs of illness."

"Of course, brother," the Pith said.

"What would happen if I just say no?" Eriz asked, turning back to us.

"That could be a problem," I said, holding up the parchment. "According to Einhard's terms, the Ganders say he promised to keep the prince healthy and well cared for. If we deny the request, they'll consider those terms breached."

"But if I say no and they attack us, they know we'll kill him," Eriz muttered. He shook his head. "It makes no sense."

"Maybe they don't care anymore," I said. I glanced at my companions. "Maybe their patience has run out and they're going to attack us regardless of what we do."

"I doubt it," Eriz said. "Their king is terrified he'll lose his son. Einhard assured me of that."

Jebido took his helmet off and wiped the sweat from his greying hair. "Well, something doesn't add up, that's for certain."

"What do you think we should do?" Eriz asked him.

Jebido spread his arms. "I don't think we have any choice but to let them in. Einhard might not be back for another week. We don't want to start this war off by losing the garrison." He glanced at me and I unconsciously nodded, thinking the same thing. "But just to be safe, we should pull in the patrols and double the guards on the walls and at the bridge. If there's some kind of trickery involved here, we need to be ready for it."

"Do you really think this is some kind of scheme to rescue the prince?" I asked.

Jebido snorted. "No, not unless they can fashion wings and fly him out of here! I just think we need to be prepared for any situation."

"I agree," Eriz said with a grunt. "We'll let the Ganders in and double the guards as you suggest." He glanced at Klesp. "Tell the turd-suckers they can enter and perform this cleansing, but only half of their swordsmen can ride in with them. The others can wait at the bridge."

"And if they don't agree to that?" Klesp asked.

"Then tell them to come back next week and Einhard will deal with them then!" Eriz snapped crossly.

"It will be done, brother," Klesp said.

Klesp started to walk away and Eriz called him back. "Make sure you search the wagons before you let them pass."

Klesp nodded and vaulted onto the back of his horse and headed back to the bridge while Eriz, Jebido and I went over every possible scenario we could think of. Nothing about what was happening made any sense, but short of a full-scale invasion, which we were certain wasn't about to happen, there didn't seem to be anything to be all that concerned about. We were still discussing the unusual Gander request when Betania arrived to report her findings on the prince.

"Well?" Eriz growled at her. "Is the man dying?"

I could tell that Betania was terrified of Eriz and she shook her head, staring up at him with big eyes. "No, my lord. I've never seen a man in better health. He's a little underweight, but other than that, he seems perfectly fine."

"Good," Eriz grunted. He waved his hand dismissively. "You can go back to whatever you were doing."

Betania bowed her head, looking relieved. "Yes, my lord." She paused as Eriz turned and took several steps away. "Shana is waiting in the writing room," Betania said to me in a whisper. She glanced at Eriz cautiously, but the big Pith had his back to us as he began to shout out orders to his men. "Do you think you can come, my lord?"

I grinned and nodded. "I should be there in an hour or so, as soon as the Ganders have gone."

Betania smiled happily. "I look forward to it, my lord."

Betania hurried away and Jebido and I moved closer to the gates. I was awaiting the arrival of the Ganders with more than just a little curiosity. More guards were appearing along the walls above us as fifty warriors hurriedly saddled their horses, then trotted past us on their way down to reinforce the bridge. Klesp was already heading back to the garrison leading two wagons that I knew housed the Sons and Daughters and I could see the Pith warriors staring at the wagons suspiciously as they passed each other. Klesp was well ahead of the Ganders by the time they reached the drawbridge and he crossed it first, passing beneath the barbican and through the gates as he halted his horse near Eriz.

"All well?" Eriz asked as Klesp dismounted in front of him.

"Yes, brother," Klesp said. "Four priests in one wagon. Four priestesses in the other. Six guards behind."

"Very good," Eriz nodded as the first wagon pulled by matching white horses arrived.

The driver of that wagon was a thin man with a long nose and droopy eyes, and he looked up at the parapets nervously as both male and female archers stared down at him silently. The driver halted the wagon beside Eriz and I heard the big Pith order him to continue across the bailey and then on through the inner gates to the keep. I turned my attention to the wagon, which was unlike anything I'd ever seen before.

Jebido whistled in appreciation beside me. "I've heard about these, but this is the first time I've seen one." He looked at me knowingly as the second wagon reached the drawbridge. "They're called carriages."

The first wagon, or carriage, had to be at least twenty-feet long I figured. The droopy-eyed driver sat perched on a wooden bench built on top of two small, wooden-spoked wheels with metal plating over them. He rested his feet on a wide toe board of solid oak. Thick leather straps hung from the bench and passed under the front of the deeply-curved belly of the wagon body, supporting its weight along the flat base before rising at the rear to attach to two support beams that sat above the much larger back wheels.

"What are those for?" I asked Jebido as I pointed to the leather straps.

"Suspension," Jebido explained. He grinned at me. "The highborn have soft bottoms and prefer to float over the ground, rather than feel every rut and stone like the rest of us do."

The exterior walls of the carriage body were built of carved mahogany, with a finely cut door and several windows facing us. Those windows were covered at the moment with plush red curtains that hid the interior from our eyes. The roof was high and peaked at the center and at the tip of that peak sat an oversized Rock of Life that I figured had to be almost as big as my head. I nudged Jebido, about to point it out when one of the curtains moved aside and a pale face peered out at us. For just a moment I found myself looking straight into the disdainful eyes of Son Oriell, then the carriage continued past us into the inner bailey and he was gone. The second carriage entered the outer bailey sporting a bright yellow Blazing Sun emblem on the roof. I knew that this one contained the Daughters. The wagon body was a lighter shade of wood than the first carriage, and to my eye didn't seem as deep at the bottom nor as wide across. The Daughters' carriage also had a door and several windows, but the curtains were open halfway. I could see several priestesses dressed in yellow robes looking back at us from the shadows inside.

Six men rode behind the Daughters' carriage in two lines and I studied them curiously. The three men riding to the left of the carriage wore a red surcoat over heavy mail and in the center of the surcoat sat a gleaming Blazing Sun emblem. The men riding to the right wore heavy mail as well, but instead of red, they wore a white surcoat with the dark Rock of Life emblem on their chests. These men were dressed identical to those that had accompanied Son Oriell on all his other trips into Gasterny. All six men were thick-bodied and had heavy beards that jutted out from gleaming helms that covered their faces except for their eyes and a small portion of their mouths.

"House Agents," Jebido whispered as they trotted by without looking at us. "Highly trained and as tough as they come." He glanced at me. "Only one in a thousand are accepted to train to become a House Agent, and even fewer make it."

Jebido and I followed the small procession through the gates into the inner bailey, where the two carriages had pulled up in front of the imposing bulk of the square keep that sat near the back curtain wall. I could smell the faint odor of cooking bread coming from the squat cookhouse that was attached to the keep and my stomach growled hungrily at the smell, rivaling the sounds of a blacksmith pounding away at his anvil somewhere behind me. I looked up at the thick walls of the keep that loomed over us and I paused to glance at the bearded figure watching intently from a barred window on the top floor.

"The prince seems eager for his cleansing," I said to Jebido as I gestured upward.

Jebido looked up and grinned. "Let's hope the Sons and Daughters are in bad form today and the cleansing fails. Burning would be too good for that bastard."

I chuckled at that and Jebido and I moved to the eastern curtain wall to lean against it in the shade and watch. The door to the priest carriage swung open and Son Oriell appeared. He paused with a look of distaste on his face as he bunched up the skirts of his black robe and then gingerly stepped over a scattered pile of horse dung that littered the ground in front of him. Son Oriell was quickly followed by another priest, who was short with a ponderous belly and startlingly white hair. Behind the short priest came two Sons-In-Waiting with their identical shaven heads and long brown robes. I shifted my gaze to the priestess carriage, where two women in bright yellow robes emerged, blinking repeatedly in the dazzling sunlight. One of the women appeared to be about thirty-years-old and had a thin, plain appearance, with a long nose and a weak chin that reminded me of a stray dog we'd sometimes fed at the farm when I was a boy. Her face was set in a permanent scowl as she stared around the bailey and she nervously fingered the Blazing Sun pendant that lay against her flat chest. I noticed her brown hair was braided and piled high on her head and then fanned out at the top in the proper Daughter fashion.

I turned my gaze to the other Daughter, who looked to be much older than the first. Her hair wasn't piled as high as the long-nosed priestess, but it had a wider fan at the top and was grey, with here and there the odd black streak showing through. I guessed her to be about fifty-years-old. She saw Jebido and me leaning against the wall and she studied us intently, shading her eyes from the sun to see better. I turned my attention away from her as two Daughters-In-Waiting stepped down tentatively from the carriage. The girls were both dressed in long grey robes and couldn't have been more than thirteen-years-old as they held hands, looking terrified as they moved to stand behind the Daughters.

Eriz walked over to Son Oriell, while behind him the six House Agents stopped their horses near the well and sat watching silently. I saw several of the Agents glance up at the archers on the walls and I grinned. Just try something, you bastards, I thought, knowing they'd be dead before their swords cleared their scabbards.

"How long will this take?" Eriz demanded.

Son Oriell peered down his nose at the big Pith with distaste. "The cleansing cannot be rushed, heathen," he said. "It will take as long as necessary. No more and no less."

"You have one hour," Eriz said bluntly.

"That's not enough time!" Son Oriell protested.

"Maybe, maybe not," Eriz said with a shrug. "Either way, that's what you have."

"I demand to speak to the Sword!" Son Oriell cried. "We must have more time!"

Eriz stared at the priest, and though his face betrayed nothing, I knew that it was all he could do to stop himself from twisting Son Oriell's head off his skinny neck. "The Sword has no interest in speaking with you," he said gruffly. "You have one hour to do this thing, less the time you've wasted standing here flapping your lips. Take it or leave it."

Son Oriell glared at the Pith and opened his mouth to

say something, then he seemed to think better of it and he clamped his lips shut into an angry line. "Very well," he finally said in agreement. "It will have to do." He turned and looked up at his driver. "Move the carriages into the shade over there," he said, motioning absently to the gap between the western curtain wall and the keep. "And give the horses water. We'll be back as soon as possible."

"Very good, Son," the driver nodded.

The Ganders moved aside as the wagons pulled away, then they began to bunch together at the bottom of the ramp as six Piths emerged from the keep and stood waiting on either side of the door.

"Follow me and stay close," Eriz said as he strode up the ramp. The big Pith looked angry, I thought. Angry at these Ganders and their rituals, and undoubtedly angry at Einhard for leaving him to deal with it. "If any of my men see you lagging behind, you can expect the tip of a sword up your arse!" Eriz growled over his shoulder.

I saw the older Daughter start to ascend the ramp with the others, then she paused to say something urgently to her sour-faced companion. Despite the younger woman's look of surprise and horror, the grey-haired priestess then turned on her heel and headed toward Jebido and me in a determined walk. She was followed closely by one of the Daughters-In-Waiting.

"Daughter Gernet!" I heard Son Oriell squeal. I glanced his way, and despite myself, I smiled at the look of outrage on his ugly face. "What are you doing? There is no time!"

But Daughter Gernet ignored the priest and instead she fixed her eyes on mine as she quickly crossed the courtyard. Eyes, I saw as she drew nearer, that were not just wise with age, but also cold and calculating.

"Uh oh!" I heard Jebido whisper out of the side of his mouth.

We both pushed ourselves away from the wall and stood up straight as the priestess halted in front of us. I flicked my eyes past her to Eriz, where he stood with his hands on his hips and a look of utter annoyance on his face. I shrugged at him. What could I do?

"You are from Corwick, are you not?" Daughter Gernet asked me. Her voice was low and husky, surprising me. I glanced at her Daughter-In-Waiting, who stood behind the priestess with her hands clasped in front of her and her big blue eyes wide and focused on me in fascination. Her blonde hair was braided and piled high and fanned with a single curled ringlet left loose on each side of her temple to signify her apprenticeship. Poor child is terrified of me, I thought, imagining what I must look like to her with my scarred face, dented armor and weapons. "Well?" the priestess demanded impatiently.

"I am, Daughter," I said.

"I thought as much," the woman muttered. "What is your name?"

"Hadrack, Daughter."

Daughter Gernet's eyes widened in surprise before she quickly recovered and glanced harshly at my friend. "And you would be?"

"Jebido, Daughter," Jebido said. I saw him flush as he met her judgmental gaze and he quickly looked to the ground.

"Where is the third one?"

I assumed she meant Baine and I shrugged. "Out on patrol."

"Very well," Daughter Gernet said with a sniff. She glared at me, then Jebido. "Have you forsaken The Mother and The Father to run with heathens?" she demanded.

Both Jebido and I shook our heads at the same time. "No," I replied. I lifted the Pair Stone from where it hung around my neck. "The First Pair are always close to us."

"So you say," Daughter Gernet said, looking unconvinced. She waved her hand around the courtyard. "And yet you choose to remain with these heathens and risk The Father's anger." Her eyes flashed at me and she waggled a finger under my nose. "Tell me, Hadrack of Corwick, why have you chosen to betray your own kind?"

I thought about that for a moment, wondering what to say to mollify her. Then I decided on the truth. "Because they betrayed me first, Daughter."

"Ah," Daughter Gernet said. She studied me intently. "You were there, weren't you?"

"Where, Daughter?" I asked, uncomfortable under her stern gaze.

"Corwick," she said, her eyes gleaming. "During the massacre. You were there and you saw it all, didn't you?"

Now it was my turn to look at her in surprise. "You know about that?"

"I know what I've been told," Daughter Gernet said. "But sometimes we're told the truth, and sometimes we're told what others wish us to believe is the truth." She looked at me thoughtfully. "The trick is trying to determine which is which. What truth do you offer me?"

"The only truth there is," I said.

"Which is what?" Daughter Gernet asked. "That the heathens slaughtered everyone?"

I looked at the priestess, wondering what it was she was looking for. Did she want to hear me accuse Lord Corwick? It didn't seem likely, yet she kept pressing me in that direction. "Do you really think I would have joined them if they had?" I finally asked.

Daughter Gernet shrugged. "I don't know. Men have done far worse things in this world."

"Well I wouldn't have!" I responded hotly.

"Perhaps," Daughter Gernet said. "But if not the Piths, then who could have done such a horrific thing?"

I decided there was no point in dancing around it any longer. "It was that bastard Lord Corwick and his men. That's the truth, whether you like it or not!"

"You're saying Pernissy did it?" Daughter Gernet said with one eyebrow raised.

"Pernissy?" I muttered in confusion. "Who is that?"

Daughter Gernet smiled and shook her head. "Forgive me. I still think of him with that name. Pernissy is Lord Corwick." She chuckled dryly. "He changed it when King Jorquin gave him Corwick. Lord Pernissy doesn't have quite the same ring to it." Daughter Gernet looked up at me and her eyes shone with interest. "So, you claim Pernissy ordered the massacre at Corwick. Is that correct?"

"Yes," I said firmly. "I heard him do it."

"Yet the Lord of Corwick has sworn to the king himself that it was the Piths," she said. I realized Daughter Gernet didn't look surprised at my accusation. If anything, she appeared relieved. "So, tell me, Hadrack of Corwick. Why should I believe you, a commoner and a traitor to his people, over a man such as Lord Corwick?"

I took a deep breath, then shrugged and replied, "Have you met him?"

Daughter Gernet's lips twitched in amusement and she glanced back at her Daughter-In-Waiting before turning to me. "I have," she said, bowing her head slightly. "And it's a point well taken."

"Daughter Gernet!" Son Oriell cried from the top of the ramp. "We are running out of time!"

The priestess sighed and looked up at me. "We will speak of Corwick another day, you and I."

"I doubt that, Daughter," I said, thinking of the coming Pith invasion. I had no idea how wrong I'd be about that.

Daughter Gernet just smiled. "There are things afoot that you can't possibly understand yet, Hadrack of Corwick. But hopefully in time you will." She held my eyes for a moment and then lifted the hem of her robe and turned away, heading back across the bailey with her young charge in tow.

"Whew!" Jebido said as he collapsed back against the curtain wall. He took off his helmet and rubbed his scalp roughly. "I almost shit myself there! That woman has eyes that stare right through a man!"

I nodded my agreement and watched as Daughter Gernet and the others filed into the keep. What had she meant by there were things afoot that I didn't understand? I wondered. What things? And how did she even know about what had really happened at Corwick?

I looked at Jebido in confusion. "Any idea what that was all about?"

"No," Jebido muttered. "But something tells me we will someday, and that day will not be a happy one." He glanced past me through the open gate. "Ah, the patrols are back."

I turned and watched as Baine and the others trotted through the barbican. Once Baine had taken care of his horse, we filled him in on all that had happened.

"A cleansing!" Baine said in disbelief when we were finished. He looked up at the keep. "Here? In Gasterny? Have they lost their minds?"

"It would seem so," I grunted. I too looked up and studied the barred window, then checked the position of the sun. "They've been up there a long time," I muttered.

"It's been a while," Jebido agreed. He glanced at the six House Agents who still sat silently on their horses. "I keep forgetting those bastards are even there. They never move."

"It's not natural," Baine said.

The doors to the keep abruptly opened and Eriz appeared, followed closely by the short priest, the two priestesses, and the four apprentices. I looked for Son Oriell, but he was nowhere to be seen. The short priest looked angry, I realized as he stomped down the ramp and waved impatiently to the House Agents. Behind him, the two Sons-In-Waiting looked unhappy as well. One of the Agents whistled to get the drivers' attention, signaling for them to bring the carriages around.

I nudged Jebido in the ribs with my elbow. "Son Oriell hasn't come out yet, and look at him," I said, gesturing to the priest. "The man's practically frothing at the mouth, he's so upset."

"So he is," Jebido said. "I wonder what's got him so riled up?"

"Forget about him," Baine said as the carriages approached. He pointed. "Look at them."

I turned my attention to the women and girls, who were all grinning from ear to ear as their carriage pulled up. I just had enough time to see the two Daughters hug each other happily before my view was hidden by the horses and their carriage. Jebido, Baine and I shared a confused look as Eriz strode over to us.

"What happened up there?" Jebido asked the big Pith.

"Not much," Eriz said with a shrug. "All they did was stand around and whisper the entire time."

"What about Son Oriell?" I asked, feeling uneasy. Eriz's description of the cleansing didn't sound like what I'd been taught would occur. "Where is he?"

"He asked to speak with the prince privately," Eriz said. "He'll be down in a moment."

I looked up at the top floor window. "You didn't leave him alone, did you?"

Eriz snorted. "Of course not." He looked at me. "Do you think me a fool, Hadrack? The priest may be old and weak, but even so, I don't take chances. Orfen and Lale are watching him." Eriz glanced back over his shoulder. "And there the ugly bastard is now," he said, jerking his thumb toward the keep as Son Oriell appeared flanked by two Piths. I studied the priest's face intently as he hurried down the ramp and entered the carriage, but there was no sign of anger there. If anything, Son Oriell looked content and at peace with himself.

"All well, Lale?" Eriz asked as Son Oriell's guards approached us.

Lale was young and tall, with a braided beard and a slight limp from a pike wound he'd received during the Bridge Battle. "All well, brother," Lale nodded. "They just sat together and talked for a few minutes. That was it."

"And the prince?" Eriz asked.

Lale shrugged. "Sleeping now, brother."

"Fair enough," Eriz grunted. "Escort the Ganders to the bridge and send them on their way. It'll be good to be done with the bastards."

"Yes, brother," Lale said.

The carriages pulled away and passed through the inner gates, then the barbican, followed closely by the House Agents. We watched them in silence until the Ganders rolled over the drawbridge and finally disappeared down the road.

"I guess there was nothing to worry about after all," I said to my friends with a shrug as the drawbridge slowly rose. I turned away and headed for the keep.

"Where are you going?" Baine demanded.

"Lessons!" I shouted over my shoulder, already looking forward to an hour in Shana's company.

I entered the great hall and took the stairs to the second floor as quickly as I could. The reading room, as we liked to call it, was at the far end of the corridor on the left. I headed that way, feeling my spirits soar in anticipation as my booted feet clomped loudly against the stone. I passed through the doorway, a smile already breaking out on my face, then I froze in mid-step as I stared down at the floor in shock.

"Hadrack!" Betania called to me in a pitiful voice from where she lay sprawled on top of scattered books and broken furniture.

"Mother Above!" I whispered, horrified at the spreading pool of blood that stained Betania's cotton dress. I dropped to my knees and lifted her gently in my arms. "What happened?" I asked. Betania struggled to speak and I could see tiny air bubbles popping on both sides of her mouth. My heart sank as I stared at the deep puncture wounds in her chest, knowing that she had but moments to live.

"He...he..." Betania fought to say.

"It's all right," I whispered gently. "Take your time."

"He...took...her," she managed to gasp. "Shana...he..."

Trickles of blood were running down the sides of Betania's mouth and I bowed my head and held her close as I whispered in her ear, "Who took Shana, Betania. Who?"

"She called...him...Carbet!" Betania gasped. She looked up at me, desperately trying to say something else, but all she could manage was a garble before she went limp and died in my arms.

I sat back, stunned, my mind unable to grasp what had happened. How? How could Carbet have gotten into the compound? I heard shouts coming from the great hall, then the pounding of running feet along the staircase. I gently lowered Betania to the floor and kneeled beside her. Nothing on this earth would protect Carbet from my wrath once I found him, I vowed.

"Hadrack?" I heard Jebido call out.

"Here!" I responded, my voice catching in my throat. I stared down at Betania's blood-soaked body and I slowly removed her wimple, then gently stroked her light-brown hair. She looked so innocent, I thought with sadness. I remembered kneeling beside my sister in much the same way so many years ago and my hands started to shake with the need to feel Carbet's throat beneath my fingers.

"Mother Above!" Baine whispered as he and Jebido appeared in the doorway. "What happened?"

I looked up at my friends. "Carbet killed her and he has Shana!" I growled. I stood up. "We're going to turn this garrison upside down until we find that whore-son, and when we do, I'm going to kill him!"

"Hadrack," Jebido said. He took a deep breath. "Prince Tyro is dead!" I looked at him in shock and he added, "Somebody slit his throat!"

5: GASTERNY

In the end, it was Jebido who figured out how they'd managed it. After spending several hours searching the garrison from one end to the other, we reluctantly concluded that somehow Carbet had gotten away without a trace. A feat made even more impressive since he'd had either an unconscious or very unwilling prisoner in Lady Demay along with him.

"He must have used the carriages," Jebido muttered as he, Baine, Eriz and I gathered in the inner bailey near the keep. "It's the only way."

"Impossible!" Eriz snorted. "Klesp searched them. He swears there was nobody else inside but those eight Ganders."

"Maybe when they came in," I said. "But what if Carbet scaled the outer wall somehow, grabbed Shana, then hid her in the carriage after they were already here? Nobody thought to check when they left."

"Why would we?" Eriz grunted. "The prince was safe and asleep in his room." He shook his head. "Or so we thought. As for scaling the walls, I don't think so. There wasn't an inch of wall that wasn't constantly in the guards' view. There's no way anyone could have approached, let alone climbed them without us knowing about it."

"Besides," Baine added. "Carbet had no way to know for sure that we wouldn't check the carriages on the way out as well."

"Carbet was in Son Oriell's carriage when they entered the garrison, and when they left," Jebido said confidently.

"But how?" I protested. "Eriz just said Klesp checked."

"I'm sure he did," Jebido said with a sigh. "But Son Oriell's carriage was wider at the bottom, remember?" He looked at us. "I'm sure if we got young Klesp up here and asked him if he checked the floor, he'd say no."

"Mother's tit!" Baine whispered. "It had a false bottom?"

Jebido nodded. "That's my guess." He looked at Eriz, whose face had hardened in anger. "Don't blame Klesp. What's done is done. I doubt any of us would have thought to look there either." Jebido gestured to the western wall. "The carriages were parked out of sight over there, so it would have been an easy matter for Carbet to get out unseen."

"The guards would have noticed him," I pointed out.

Jebido shook his head. "Not if you timed it right. The guards were looking out most of the time, not in. I imagine the drivers helped Carbet with that part."

"Maybe," I said. "But that doesn't explain how he knew where Shana would be or how he got in the keep. We had our eyes on the door the entire time."

Jebido started walking away, looking thoughtful. "I don't know how he knew she'd be there," he said over his shoulder. "But somehow he did, and I'm willing to bet he scaled the wall up to the second floor to get to her." We followed Jebido around the keep and then stopped, staring up at the open window twelve feet above our heads and the clearly seen scuff marks below it. Sometimes the heavy shutters on the windows were closed and locked at night, but the evening had been warm the night before, so they'd been left open. "He probably used a grappling hook of some kind," Jebido explained. "Then pulled himself up, stabbed Betania and lowered Shana back down to the ground."

"It makes sense," Baine said. "But how did he manage to kill the prince?"

"I don't know how he did that," Jebido admitted. "But an even bigger question is, why did he do it?"

I looked up at the barred top floor windows where the prince had been kept and suddenly I knew. "Carbet didn't kill him," I said.

"Then who did?" Baine asked.

"Son Oriell," I answered, knowing in my gut that it was true. It was the only thing that made sense.

"What!?" Baine gasped, looking horrified. "You think a priest murdered the prince? Why would he do that?"

"I have no idea," I grunted. "But the windows are barred and there were guards at the prince's door. No matter how slippery Carbet is, there's no way he could have done it."

"And the priest was the only one who stayed behind," Eriz said, nodding his head.

"Yes," I agreed. "Remember Lale told us Son Oriell and Prince Tyro sat together and talked for a time?" I glanced at my companions. "My guess is Son Oriell must have slit the prince's throat when no one was watching, then lay him on his bed in such a way as to make the guards think he was sleeping." I thought about what Daughter Gernet had said to me, that things were afoot that I had no idea about. Had she meant this? I wondered. Had she been in on Shana's abduction and Prince Tyro's murder? And why had the short priest been so angry and the priestesses so happy? I shook my head, trying to get a grasp on it, but I couldn't wrap my mind around it.

"So, what do we do now?" Baine asked, breaking the silence.

Eriz shrugged. "We wait for Einhard to get back. He'll know what to do."

Jebido made a face. "I doubt we'll have that much time."

"Why not?" Eriz asked.

Jebido gestured upward to the barred window above us. "With the death of Prince Tyro, our leverage over the Ganders just ended." He grimaced. "Which it looks like they wanted all along. They'll be coming."

"Mother Above!" Baine grumbled. He ran his fingers through his long black hair. "How long do you think we have?"

Jebido shrugged. "This was well planned, so maybe a day or two. Certainly no more than that."

Eriz took a deep breath and then nodded, accepting Jebido's assessment. "I'll send young Peren to go fetch Einhard and the king." He stared up at the garrison walls, looking worried for the first time since I'd met him. "In the meantime, we better start preparing for a siege."

And of course, the Ganders came the next morning.

The first horns began to blow faintly from the bridge at dawn, followed almost immediately by the louder horns along the northern garrison walls. I sat up quickly in bed, blinking in the half-light, while beside me, Ania grumbled groggily.

"What's going on?" she mumbled.

"Looks like we have visitors," I said as I flung back the furs and hurried to get dressed.

I grabbed my father's axe and set it in its sheath across my back, then belted Wolf's Head around my waist while Ania slipped naked out of bed and rapidly dressed beside me. Neither one of us said anything as we headed up to the roof of the keep to join Eriz and Jebido, who were waiting for us along the northern wall. Torches still lit the outer walls of the garrison and the keep rooftop, though the horizon was just beginning to glow pink and orange now, enabling us to see faintly. A low mumble of anticipation mixed with dread seemed to ripple back and forth across the garrison as Pith warriors ran for the walls. Many of them were still pulling on their clothing and armor as they clambered up the ladders to the ramparts. The Piths lined the wooden parapets facing to the north and east, jockeying amongst themselves to get a better view. Beneath them in the courtyard, Gander children hustled the few stray chickens, pigs and geese that had escaped slaughter into pens. The adults, in the meantime, worked at carrying bundles of over-stuffed sheaths of arrows up to the waiting Piths on the battlements or filling whatever container could be found with water from the well. We all knew that fire was going to be our enemy, and to that end we'd slaughtered anything we couldn't ride the night before so that we could drape the wooden northern and eastern walls with their hides. The water would be applied during the coming battle to keep the hides wet and slick, and hopefully stop fire arrows from setting the walls ablaze.

"Ganders?" I asked Eriz, already knowing the answer.

Eriz just nodded silently and pointed to the north, where hundreds of torches carried by foot soldiers, archers and cavalry lit up the field along the forest edge. A horn blared from the corner tower to the west and we turned in surprise as more men on foot broke the horizon and appeared in a solid wall along the road. They looked to be at least a half a mile away still, but even so, we could already hear the faint crunching of their booted feet as they trudged toward us.

"More coming from the trees!" a lookout cried as he pointed to the shadowy figures that slipped in and out of the darkness beneath the branches of the forest behind us like wraiths.

"Motherless bastards!" Baine cursed he appeared beside me with his bow clutched in his hand. "How many of them are there?"

"Way too many," Jebido grunted.

The army to the west of us began to move off the road, skirting around the garrison well out of bow range as they headed for the open eastern fields as the sky above them quickly began to brighten. Once there, they began to form into barely organized lined ranks as sergeants wearing heavy armor bellowed in frustration at them to tighten up. I noticed perhaps a hundred archers dressed in bright red surcoats march quickly to the rear of these men to form into a disciplined unit. Most of the foot soldiers wore well-worn leather armor and were armed with swords and rectangular shields. Many in the first four ranks held long pikes, which they awkwardly held in their right hands with the butts braced on the ground. I knew most of the men facing us were probably just simple, inexperienced peasants like I had been, but even so, what they most likely lacked in ability would be more than made up for in numbers. I tried not to think of those numbers swarming over our puny walls like angry ants. Instead, I turned my attention back to the road, where men-at-arms, archers, and lancers dressed in light armor appeared trotting three abreast. I guessed there had to be perhaps four hundred of them, maybe more. Each lancer wore a full visor and held a nine-foot spear in their right arm and a triangular shield that tapered to a point at the bottom on their left. Red pennants with a coiled-snake emblem fluttered in the heavy breeze at the end of the spears. The lancers reached the bend in the road and they spurred their horses around the massing foot soldiers, taking up a position blocking the road between us and the bridge. Jebido and I shared a look. The Piths in the gatehouses were effectively cut off from any chance at escape now.

A horn sounded a single, strident note that echoed up to us from somewhere deep within the massed army to the north. The call was immediately answered by cheers and the clanging of weapons on shields from the Ganders. The soldiers on foot began to form into a rough wedge aimed straight at the gatehouse before coming to a halt just out of arrow range, while behind them the cavalry swerved a hundred yards to the right and then formed into a line three deep. Another horn sounded, this one blunt and precise and the foot soldiers instantly parted in the center, revealing an eight-wheeled wooden monstrosity the likes of which I'd never seen before. I figured it had to be at least two-stories high and thirty feet long, with a slanted roof that looked as though it might be covered in scales like a snake.

"What in the name of The Mother is that?" I whispered in awe.

"A tortoise," Jebido grunted beside me. We leaned out over the wall to watch the wooden beast as it slowly crawled across the ground. Even from this far away I could hear the high-pitched squeak of its axles as the wheels turned. Jebido pointed. "Underneath that shell is a battering ram hanging from the roof by chains and capped with a metal head. The men inside are shielded from the Pith arrows by the roof and the side walls. Once they get to the gate, they'll be able to smash away at it with little fear of the Pith archers."

I couldn't see or hear any arrows striking the tortoise from here, but I knew that the Piths were peppering it with bolts anyway, looking for a weakness.

"Why not just set it on fire?" Ania asked.

Jebido shook his head. "They've covered it with metal plating."

"So what can they do then?" Baine asked.

Jebido didn't say anything, which said a lot, while beside him Eriz just shrugged. "They are Piths. They will fight and they will die, but not before taking as many of those turd-suckers as they can with them."

Eriz was right, the Piths at the bridge did fight, and they did die, right down to the last man. The battle for the bridge took several long hours of vicious hand to hand fighting, punctuated by the never-ending screams and clash of weapons that drifted up to us from the river. During that entire time, the Ganders surrounding the garrison just waited and watched, some of them occasionally waving their weapons up at us and daring us to come out. I imagine they were hoping we'd be foolish enough to ride out and try to help our brothers, which would save the Gandermen the trouble of having to come over the walls to get to us. Eriz just watched the battle solemnly with his great hands braced on the battlements as Ania stood beside him with her arm around his waist.

"We should do something!" Baine said at one point as the Ganders finally cleared the first gatehouse and advanced on the second.

"What would you suggest?" Jebido asked. He gestured over the walls to the east. "There are at least a thousand men out there. And just as many at the bridge. We'd be slaughtered before we even got there."

"I know," Baine grumbled. He turned his back to the bridge and leaned against the ramparts. "It's just a hard thing to watch, is all."

Jebido nodded his agreement and squeezed Baine's shoulder as we continued to wait, knowing that once they'd secured the bridge, the Ganders would turn their full attention to us. Finally, after the tortoise had done its work on the second gatehouse and the Piths had been overwhelmed, the victorious army crossed the bridge and joined with the others waiting in the fields. Jebido, Baine and I moved from the roof of the keep to join the Piths lined along the ramparts of the shorter outer wall. We watched silently as the Gandermen set up several large tents behind the massed soldiers, where I imagined their leaders would soon be plotting how to assault us. The cavalry, now swollen to almost a thousand riders, had picketed their horses and set up camp to the right of the tents, while more foot soldiers continued to arrive from the north. These men trudged past us in long lines, many of them glancing up at our walls as they passed before taking up a position in the southern field that faced the drawbridge. I'd been enraged to see that they flew the Lord of Corwick's dragon banner, and it took a lot of talking from Jebido to get me to calm down and think rationally. Jebido probably believed I might jump over the walls at any time and go looking for Lord Corwick, which I have to say had occurred to me the moment I'd seen that hated banner. I had to promise repeatedly that I was in control of myself, until finally Jebido left me alone to brood by myself. I constantly looked from Lord Corwick's men to the tents, and then back again, hoping to see the man who'd brought such misery to my life. I saw that one tent now flew the coiled-snake banner, while the other flew Lord Corwick's dragon banner. I promised myself that whatever happened this day, I'd find that bastard and take his head off with my father's axe.

"Don't worry about them," Jebido finally said to me when he saw me look to the south for the hundredth time.

"They're not going to attack anywhere but here," he said confidently, slapping the wall with his palm. I looked down over the foul-smelling hides tacked to the wood to the sloping ground that led to the moat. The wall was fifteen-feet tall, no more, and I knew a man could scamper up a scaling ladder and be over it in seconds. The moat would give them trouble, though. It was twenty-five feet wide and twelve feet deep in the middle. Jebido had promised the Ganders would use wooden ramps to cross it and I had no reason to doubt him, but even so, their paths would be limited to those ramps and they'd be at the mercy of the Pith archers. A horn suddenly blew from the eastern fields and the massed Gander army began to cheer as five men emerged from Lord Corwick's tent. The last man out was dressed in black robes and I knew in my gut that it had to be Son Oriell. The other four men were dressed in armor and I studied them as they mounted their horses, trying to determine which one was Lord Corwick.

"Took them long enough," Eriz grunted as he came to stand beside us.

A strong breeze was blowing that morning from west to east as the mounted men spurred their horses across the long, swaying grass of the fields toward the road that led to the garrison. Many of Lord Corwick's men waiting to the south were sitting or lying on the ground, having grown weary of standing in the hot sun. They began to stand up and cheer as Lord Corwick, Son Oriell and the other three men approached. Finally the riders came to a halt twenty paces in front of the cheering soldiers, where they sat their horses and stared up at our walls. I recognized Lord Corwick sitting astride a gleaming black warhorse and I could almost taste the hatred I felt for him as my hand tightened on Wolf's Head. Two men in full armor and open helms sat to Lord Corwick's left, while Son Oriell and the fourth soldier, who wore a full helm with a slit for the eyes, sat to his right. This man rode a white horse with a grey patch on its chest, and at a word from Lord Corwick, he raised a branch with a white rag tied to it. The rag snapped madly in the breeze as the Gander began to swing the branch back and forth to get our attention.

"Looks like they want to talk," Jebido said.

Eriz hacked contemptuously and then spit over the side of the wall. "I have nothing to say to them!" He drew his sword and waved it in the air. "Get on with it, you shit-eating cowards!" he shouted.

The Piths along the ramparts erupted in cheers at his words, smashing their swords against their shields or banging their bows against the walls. The Gander holding the parlay branch hesitated in mid-wave, then slowly lowered it. He turned to talk with his companions and I took the time to study Lord Corwick's soldiers, knowing that if not for a twist of fate, I could easily have been one of them. I realized that if anything, these men were even less well-armed than the foot soldiers waiting in the eastern field. Though there had to be close to five hundred of them, few wore any armor at all. Each man carried a battered sword and shield of some kind, but as far as I could tell, none carried spears or pikes. There were archers among them, I saw, but not many, and as I glanced to the east at the unmounted cavalry an idea began to form in my mind. I nudged Jebido in the ribs and quickly explained my thoughts, while around us the Piths continued to cheer, urging the Ganders to attack.

"That, my boy, is one very good idea," Jebido said with a wide grin once I was finished. He turned and explained it to Eriz and I saw the big Pith's eyes light up with interest.

Eriz stared out over the battlements at Lord Corwick's men, studying them critically, then he glanced to the east before nodding in decision. "I like it."

At Eriz's command, Jebido had one of the slaves fetch us a white tunic, which he waved to the Ganders, signaling that we were ready to talk. Meanwhile, Eriz had set the Piths into motion, and within minutes, fifty eager warriors were mounted and ready, poised behind the bulk of the Holy House and the smaller buildings that ran along the eastern curtain wall. The drawbridge slowly lowered with a rattling of chains as Eriz, Jebido, Baine, Ania and I mounted our horses.

"Don't do anything stupid!" Eriz growled as he looked at me darkly.

I just grimaced at him and nodded, having already had to promise both he and Jebido repeatedly that no matter what happened, I would control myself. It was either that or not go at all, so it was an easy promise to make. I just hoped that when I looked Lord Corwick in the eye that I could follow it. We passed through the heavy barbican and crossed the draw-bridge, taking our time as we rode out to meet the waiting Ganders. The massed foot soldiers began to jeer at us, hurling insults our way, until finally we stopped our horses about half-way from them and the garrison. We sat and waited as Lord Corwick and Son Oriell spoke animatedly together. I could see the ugly priest shaking his head repeatedly, obviously point-ing out that they'd be at the outer range of our arrows if they rode to meet us. Lord Corwick finally waved his arm at the priest dismissively and said something that silenced him, then he nudged his horse toward us. The three armored men joined him, while Son Oriell, looking at us sullenly, finally fol-lowed along behind.

"Hadrack!" Baine whispered beside me. He motioned with his chin to the big man on Lord Corwick's far-left wear-ing gleaming, black pointed boots and riding a huge, familiar-looking black stallion with a flowing mane.

I felt instant anger explode in my chest and I ground my teeth, saying nothing as I stared into the amused eyes of Carbet. My hand instinctively began to fall to my sword and I forced it away, determined to control myself no matter what happened. If things went as planned, I knew there was a good chance I might get to Carbet, I just needed to be patient. I took a deep breath, forcing all thoughts of Carbet and Shana from my mind. I glanced at the man sitting a spotted mare beside the Cardian. This man was almost as big as Carbet, but with wider shoulders and a massive head sitting on top of a bull-like neck. What little of his face I could see beneath the nose guard of his helm and his long grey beard was cold and determined-looking. His helm was polished silver and had pointed horns jutting out on each side, with a long wolf's tail hanging down the back. I had no idea who he was, nor did I care much. I turned to focus on Lord Corwick, who nodded his head to us and smiled as he halted his horse five paces away.

"I appreciate that you chose to parlay with us like gentlemen," Lord Corwick said. "Perhaps you're not quite the heathens Son Oriell has portrayed you to be." The lord had aged somewhat since the last time I'd seen him as a boy. His blond beard was now sprinkled with white hairs and he had a scar shaped in a star pattern beneath his right eye, which tended to droop a little when he looked at you. "You would be the Sword of the King, I imagine?" Lord Corwick said to Eriz.

"He is not!" Son Oriell piped in shrilly. The ugly priest halted his horse beside Lord Corwick and waved his hand. "He's just an underling of no great importance."

"Ah," Lord Corwick said with a frown.

"Einhard is not a trusting man," Eriz rumbled as he shrugged his shoulders, "so he sent us to hear your terms."

"Trust no one," Lord Corwick said with a grin. "A man after my own heart." He glanced at Jebido where he sat his horse beside Eriz and smiled coldly in recognition. "It's been a long time, Captain."

I looked at Jebido in surprise. I'd always thought he'd been a simple man-at-arms, not a soldier of rank.

"Not long enough!" Jebido grunted.

Lord Corwick chuckled and bowed his head. "I suppose I deserve that. But, believe it or not, I've always felt bad about how we parted, and I wondered from time to time what had become of you."

"Felt bad?" Jebido said with a snort, shaking his head in disbelief. "I guess shame and guilt will do that eventually to even the worst of men."

Lord Corwick grinned. "Oh, I don't have any shame or

guilt, old friend. You can trust me on that." He stared at Jebido with hard eyes. "You got away from me once, Captain. I promise you, that won't happen again."

"Can we get on with this?" the grey-bearded man growled impatiently.

"Ah, of course," Lord Corwick said, breaking eye contact with Jebido. "Forgive me, Lord Demay. I forget myself sometimes when meeting old friends." I stared at Shana's husband in surprise, while beside him Carbet grinned mockingly at me. Lord Corwick swung his arm behind him. "As you can see, we have you outnumbered ten to one. Surrender now and save us the trouble of a siege, and we'll be lenient with the children inside and some of your more attractive women." He glanced at Ania, pausing to stare in appreciation at her breasts before adding, "I have little doubt my affection-starved men would enjoy using your women as camp whores." He looked up and pointed past us. "Refuse, and we'll kill every last person inside that garrison."

Eriz laughed deeply and he let his eyes roam over the foot soldiers. "You think you can defeat Piths with this rabble?" He spit on the ground. "Try to come over our walls and my sisters will skewer them before they even get halfway across this field."

"The only thing your sisters are good for, you piss drinker," Lord Demay sneered, "is lying flat on their backs moaning as they serve Gandermen!"

I barely saw Ania move, but somehow her bow was off her shoulders and she nocked an arrow, then let fly. The warrior holding the parlay branch had propped the base of it on his saddle while we talked, and he abruptly cried out as the arrowhead struck the wood an inch above his hand, snapping the branch with a crack, sending the top careening backward. The massed soldiers behind Lord Corwick muttered amongst themselves uneasily as Ania quickly and efficiently hooked her bow back over her shoulders.

"Well," Lord Corwick said after a moment. He nodded

his head to Ania. "That was impressive."

"I'm just one of many," Ania said grimly. "Send your men against me and my sisters and you'll find out what we can do."

"Actually, I'm looking forward to it," Lord Corwick said. He shifted his gaze over our shoulders to the garrison. "I see that you've diverted the moat and built a secondary wall." He glanced at Jebido. "Not too tall, either. Very tempting. Your doing, I expect?" Jebido didn't say anything and Lord Corwick just grinned and then shrugged. "No matter. I imagine you've got a nasty little surprise waiting for us over there. Am I right?" He chuckled at the looks on our faces and then waved his arm behind him. "I was expecting something like this. That's why I brought these hardy young men with me." He grinned and winked. "Hardy and strong, but not all that bright. Why lose perfectly good fighting men when there are so many cattle such as these to be sacrificed?"

"And I'm sure you'll be at the back!" I spat at him, unable to contain myself any longer. "Hiding like the coward you've always been!"

Lord Corwick glanced at me dismissively and then shifted his gaze back to Eriz. "You should train your dog to keep its mouth shut. All that yapping is annoying and could get it killed."

"Just try it, you bastard!" I snarled. "I know what you did at Corwick!"

Lord Corwick's eyebrows rose. "Do you now?" he said. "And what exactly might that be?"

"It wasn't the Piths that slaughtered the villagers!" I growled. "It was you and your men!"

I saw Son Oriell's eyes widen in surprise as Lord Corwick glanced at Jebido. "Have you been spreading lies about me, Captain?" Before Jebido could respond, Lord Corwick turned back to me. "The man's a deserter and a known liar, so why would anyone believe a word he says?"

"He didn't tell me anything," I said. I carefully put my

hands on the pommel of my saddle, afraid I'd lose control of myself and go for Wolf's Head. "He didn't have to. I was there that day, you spineless, sniveling coward! My father was Alwin of Corwick!"

I saw Lord Corwick's head snap back as if he'd been slapped and he stared at me in surprise. "You're lying," he finally said.

I shook my head. "I'm not lying. I was there and I'm going to make sure you and your men pay for what you did!"

"Enough of this!" Son Oriell snapped. He pointed at Eriz. "You and the Sword brought this down upon yourselves, heathen. Surrender now and we will be merciful."

Eriz just chuckled and leaned forward. "And how did we do that, priest?" he demanded.

"You murdered the prince," Son Oriell said primly. "Did you think we wouldn't find out?"

"You're the one who killed him!" I growled, pointing a finger at the ugly priest. I gestured to Carbet with contempt. "And this bastard took Shana and murdered an innocent child!"

"Shana, is it?" Lord Demay said with an angry grunt. "Learn you're place when referring to my wife, you filthy scum!" He gestured to the Cardian. "I owe this man a great debt for rescuing my beloved from you heathens."

Baine snorted and rolled his eyes. "Who are you trying to fool? She hates you, you big ugly bastard!"

Lord Demay started to reply angrily, but Lord Corwick put his hand on his arm, stalling him. "As enjoyable as this conversation continues to be," Lord Corwick said as he looked up at the sun overhead. "I would very much like to start the killing before nightfall. Judging by the pace of the negotiations, there appears to be a real danger of that not happening." He grinned and looked at Eriz. "So, I apologize for my rudeness, but I need your answer to our terms now or we'll just kill you right here and take our chances on the walls."

Eriz glared back at Lord Corwick's smiling face and I

tensed as the big Pith's hand dropped to the hilt of his sword.

"We'll take your terms back to Einhard," Jebido said quickly. He glanced at Eriz. "You'll have his answer within minutes."

"Good," Lord Corwick said with a curt nod. "But before you go, I have a gift for you." He glanced at Carbet, who grinned and unhooked a burlap bag from his saddle and then dumped the contents onto the ground. "He died well," Lord Corwick added as we stared down at Peren's blood-soaked, decapitated head. "But sadly, he won't be able to bring any reinforcements to save you." Lord Corwick smiled. "Sorry about that."

Eriz glared at Lord Corwick and I was convinced that despite our plans, the big Pith was going to charge him. I dropped my hand to my sword, already planning my first swing when Eriz finally swung his horse around angrily. "Back to the garrison!" he commanded us gruffly.

"I'll see you soon," Lord Corwick promised me with a grin.

"I look forward to it," I replied.

"And I'm looking forward to hearing you moan, little one!" Lord Demay sneered at Ania as we turned away.

"You first, ugly man," Ania replied over her shoulder. "I'll be sure to kill you nice and slow." She held her horse in check and looked Lord Demay up and down with contempt, then added, "An arrow through each shoulder and knee and one between the legs should do it."

With that we headed back to the garrison at full gallop, while behind us the soldiers continued to laugh and jeer at us as they waved their swords at our backs. I was looking forward to ruining their good mood and turning their laughter into fear and horror. The five of us pounded across the drawbridge and galloped through the barbican. The moment we were through the gates, Jebido, Eriz and I wheeled our horses about, while Baine and Ania dismounted and ran for the ramparts.

"Remember," Eriz said to me as he drew his sword. "The moment you hear the horn you break off and return to the garrison like we planned, no matter what. Understood?"

I nodded and drew Wolf's Head as my pulse began to ring in my ears. "No matter what," I promised.

"Good," Eriz growled as the mounted Piths massed behind us. "Now, let's go have some fun!" He pointed his sword toward the open gate, then kicked his heels hard into his horse's flanks. "Kill the Ganders! Kill them all!" he cried.

We swept back out through the barbican and down the drawbridge at full gallop. Fifty-three throats were screaming a bloody promise of death and destruction at the Ganders, who stood staring at us in shock as we bore down on them. I could see the cavalry in the eastern fields making a mad dash for their tethered horses, but they were too far away to do anything and I quickly forgot about them.

"Here's our answer, you turd-sucker!" Eriz cried, pointing his sword at Lord Corwick as we thundered toward him.

Son Oriell seemed to finally get over the shock of seeing us at the sound of Eriz's voice. He squealed like a frightened pig and slapped his horse's flank desperately as he dashed away to the east and the safety of the Gander lines. Lord Corwick and the others, to their credit, held their ground for a moment longer as we bore down on them. I thought maybe I'd get my chance after all, before a sharp word from Lord Demay caused them to turn and race after the ugly priest.

"Cowards!" I screamed at their retreating backs as I watched them go. I was disappointed, but hardly surprised. Only a madman would have tried to stand against us in that situation.

I turned my thoughts away from Lord Corwick and Carbet and I screamed in joy as we smashed into the front ranks of the Gander footmen like a giant, unstoppable wave. I howled at the sky, feeling the need to kill taking over me as I let Wolf's Head have free rein, cutting and hacking down at the horrified Gandermen that scurried before me like terrified rats.

"Kill them!" I screamed. "Kill the Ganders!"

The Piths took up the chant, moving with deadly precision as we plunged three, four, then five ranks deep into the Ganders. Blood sprayed and men screamed and dropped as our warhorses barrelled into them without slowing. Many of the terrified Ganders tried to run, but they were brought down almost immediately by our horses' heavy hooves, which trampled them mercilessly into shattered, unrecognizable chunks of meat and bone. The red-smeared blades of the Piths rose and fell over and over again, chopping down and slaughtering anyone who got in the way as we pushed our way further into the swirling mass of men. A tall boy of no more than fifteen, with just a few wispy black hairs growing on his chin, appeared at my horse's head. He grabbed its bridle and screamed something unintelligible at me and then swung his sword wildly at my head. I easily blocked his blade with my shield, then flicked Wolf's Head downward, chopping off the Gander's hand. The boy screamed in agony and I absently noticed that his severed hand stayed hooked to my horse's bridle, flopping there almost obscenely. I grinned down at his horrified face as he continued to scream wildly, then I thrust the tip of Wolf's Head into his right eye, silencing him. I moved on, urging my horse forward over the many sprawled and disfigured bodies.

"Kill! I screamed. "Kill!"

The Gandermen were now in full-out retreat, many of them having thrown down their weapons as they tried to flee from our blades in a mindless, panic-stricken frenzy. The Piths, Jebido and I continued to lay waste around us, but, even as I chased down a sobbing Ganderman and severed his bald head from his shoulders, I felt the killing heat that had overwhelmed me since we'd spurred out of the garrison starting to leave. I began to use Wolf's Head half-heartedly, my mood turning from one of elation to one of contemplation. There's nothing easier than killing a man from on top of a horse when he's running away from you, but, at the same time, there's not much sport in it either. To each side of me the Piths carried on, whooping with delight as they cut down the fleeing Gandermen without a hint of remorse or mercy. Finally I halted my horse, breathing heavily as I held Wolf's Head across my saddle and sat and watched the slaughter.

"What's the matter?" Jebido asked as he guided his horse alongside mine. "Are you injured?"

I shook my head, not saying anything. Jebido's armor was splattered with blood and I saw that his helmet had a good-sized dent in it. I gestured to the dent. "You let a farmer do that to you?"

Jebido grinned. "Well, to be fair, he was an awfully big farmer."

I chuckled and gestured to the jubilant Piths. "Can't say I'm enjoying this part."

Jebido nodded and we both turned to watch as Eriz grabbed a scrawny boy with a blood-smeared leg by the back of the neck and lifted him single-handedly into the air. The big Pith laughed with delight as the boy struggled helplessly and squawked in terror. Eriz shook the boy like a child's doll, then cut his throat with a quick slash of his sword and tossed the corpse aside before he lifted his head to the sky and howled. The big Pith looked almost unrecognizable to me, covered in blood like he was, and I realized that only moments before I'd looked just like him.

"Killing is never an easy thing, Hadrack," Jebido said. "But this time it's necessary."

"I know," I agreed.

Jebido was right, of course. Every dead Gander in this field was one less that would be coming over our walls later. I knew that as well as anybody. It had been my plan, after all. But even so, I couldn't help but feel sorry now for these simple men as I watched them die. This fight wasn't their fight, it was Lord Corwick's, and the men and boys we'd just killed were only players in his twisted game.

"Ah," Jebido muttered as a horn blasted urgently from the garrison. He glanced to the east, where the Gander cavalry, led by the lancers, were charging across the field toward us. "Time to go."

I nodded and he and I turned back toward the garrison. Behind us the Piths had heard the signal as well and they wheeled around, ignoring the fleeing Gandermen now as they headed back. Jebido and I waited for them to join us and we fell in beside Eriz.

"Patience now!" Eriz growled as he led us at a tightly controlled trot toward the garrison.

We moved across the ground in a compact bunch, riding almost knee to knee and shoulder to shoulder, while constantly turning to watch the progress of the Gander cavalry. I glanced over my shoulder at the approaching dust cloud. The sun was glinting off a hundred lowered spear tips aimed at our backs as the lancers raced across the field after us. Behind them rode more men-at-arms and archers and I felt the first stirrings of doubt rise in my chest.

"We're cutting it close," I muttered, wishing Eriz would pick up the pace.

"Soon," Jebido grunted beside me. He too glanced toward the Ganders and I could see the nervousness on his face as the ground started to rumble beneath the hooves of the descending lancers.

The garrison was a hundred yards away, and the lancers on the fastest horses were maybe two-hundred yards behind us when finally the second horn blew. I breathed a sigh of relief and kicked my heels against my horse's sides, giving it its head as the Piths broke into a full gallop, heading straight for the drawbridge. Behind us I could hear the excited cries of the Gandermen as they followed in pursuit and I chanced a look back. Twenty lancers, perhaps more, were right on our tails, with their great spears eagerly reaching out for our vulnerable backs. We pounded up to the drawbridge and Eriz shouted a command as we started to cross. Five Piths immediately broke off from the back of the formation and turned, guarding our rear. The Ganders bore down on them at full speed with lances lowered and I knew the Piths small round shields couldn't withstand an impact from those wicked points. I glanced up at the empty ramparts above me and the arrow slots along the barbican. Where were they? I wondered. That's when the third horn blew, and suddenly the ramparts were filled with archers.

"Nock! Pull! Loose!" I heard Ania cry. Scores of arrows with armor-piercing barbs smashed into the lead lancers, hurling them effortlessly from their saddles as the air filled with their screams. "Nock! Pull! Loose!" Ania shouted again just as Eriz, Jebido and I pounded through the barbican.

"Lift the drawbridge!" Eriz commanded even as the last of the Piths began to clatter across it.

Somehow six lancers had made it through the rain of arrows, and these men followed the Piths across the drawbridge and through the gate. The bloodlust of the Gandermen had clearly overcome their common sense, and now they hesitated, pulling up on the reins of their horses. The lead lancer looked back over his shoulder at the rising drawbridge and he bowed his head for a moment, obviously knowing death had arrived. I could see him almost shrug to himself in acceptance, then he shouted a war cry and bolted his horse toward me with his lance aimed at my chest. I twisted sideways in the saddle at the last moment and the wicked point of his spear hissed past my ear. Then I reached out with my left hand and grabbed the heavy ash shaft and yanked the lancer out of his saddle onto the waiting tip of Wolf's Head. My blade easily sliced into his neck and punched out the back with a soft plopping sound. The Ganderman gurgled blood and shuddered and I let him go as he sagged limply to the ground. Around me the Piths pounced on the other five Ganders, making short work of them as they hacked away from all sides.

From above us, Ania's voice rang out repeatedly, "Nock! Pull! Loose! Nock! Pull! Loose!"

6: LORD CORWICK'S LINE

My father used to play a game called chatrang with the Reeve of Corwick. Not that ugly, whore-son of a reeve I'd killed with my father's axe, of course, but the one before him, who was a good and fair-minded man. Even though the reeve was well educated and highly respected by everyone in the village, my father never lost to him in all the times that I'd watched them play. I'd asked my father once why he always beat the reeve, and his answer had puzzled me greatly.

"Because he only plans in a straight line," my father had said. "And when you force him to move from that line, he becomes confused and makes mistakes." He'd looked at me and smiled and then put his big hand on my shoulder. "Every man's line has a weakness, Hadrack, you just have to look for it."

My father's words had made no sense to me at the time, since there were multiple game pieces set up within a grid in chatrang that could be moved in almost any direction possible. The goal was to capture your opponent's mounted king, while avoiding having your king captured first. There were peasants, called pawns, and horsemen and archers on the board, as well as warriors and priests and priestesses that you used to block your opponent and try to ensnare his king with. I'd watched them many times and had a fair idea of how the game was played, but no matter how hard I studied the reeve's moves, I'd never seen the line my father spoke of. As I stared out over the battlements of Gasterny at the seething mass of confused and dying men outside our walls, I finally understood why my father had won all those games.

Lord Corwick had a plan, and in his mind that plan was a

straight line that began with the assault on the bridge, then to the massing of his army around the garrison, until eventually ending in the capture and probable deaths of everyone inside. But, for that plan to work the way that he'd wanted it to, it had meant sending those poor peasants over our weakest walls first, where he would gladly sacrifice them in a bid to wear us and our defenses down. Then, once his pawns had done their work, he'd planned on sending in his more seasoned warriors and archers to finish us off. It was a good plan that might have worked, had we not attacked them first. By doing so, we'd broken Lord Corwick's line, and it appeared, at least for the moment, that just like the reeve, Lord Corwick had no answer to it. That first battle at Gasterny was a learning experience for me, and from then on, whenever I could, I always tried to anticipate my opponents' plans first and then move against them to break their line.

"Have you ever seen anything like this?" I whispered to Jebido in awe as I watched the devastation.

"Never," Jebido said in wonder as he shook his head. "It's like watching pigs at slaughter!"

The Gander lancers who'd led the charge against us were pressed tightly along the banks of the moat, trapped between the water and the hundreds of mounted men-at-arms and archers pushing at them from behind. With no way out, the cornered lancers could only curse and lash out at each other in panic, while from above their heads the Piths poured wave after wave of arrows down into their ranks with devastating effect. Horses screamed in terror and men yelled in confusion and died, but no horns blew the retreat, no commands were shouted, and incredibly, it appeared that no one seemed to know what to do or where to go. I looked for Lord Corwick or Lord Demay, but if they were somewhere down in that disorganized mass, I couldn't see them.

Beneath us, lancers, archers and men-at-arms continued to die by the twos and threes, while above them, Ania called out over and over again in a voice ringing with pure joy, "Nock!

Pull! Loose!"

A hundred Piths bent their bows and let fly with each command as dark shafts of steel-tipped ash fletched with white goose feathers hissed and whistled as they cut through the air. I saw Baine standing beside Ania, matching her arrow for arrow and he paused to glance at me and grin before turning away and aiming downward.

"Shit!" Jebido said as he gestured to the east. "Here they come!"

The peasant army waiting in the eastern fields had begun running toward us in a disorganized rabble, swinging their swords and waving their spears. I could hear their faint battle cries rolling over the fields as they approached, while amongst them mounted sergeants laid about with the flats of their swords, urging them to greater speed. The horde was almost out of control with battle rage, but even so there had to be close to a thousand of them sprinting toward the garrison. Many of the peasants in the first few ranks were working in twos and threes as they balanced long wooden ramps across their backs or scaling ladders over their shoulders. We'd heard the ringing of carpenters' hammers all morning long and knew what they were up to, so seeing the ramps and ladders came as no surprise to any of us.

"Eriz!" I shouted, pointing at the approaching peasants in warning.

The big Pith was looking over the battlements impassively with his great arms folded across his chest and ignoring the odd arrow shot from below while he studied the struggling Ganders beneath us. He glanced to the east and nodded when he saw the foot soldiers.

"Follow the plan," Eriz called out calmly. He pointed to the approaching peasants. "Keep them back as long as you can." He slapped the battlements. "As soon as they start to get over the wall, the archers will fall back." Eriz drew his sword and smiled. "The rest of us will deal with those turd-suckers!"

The Piths cheered his words just as a horn sounded

below. The piercing note was urgent and demanding, rising from somewhere deep within the mass of men trapped along the moat. Then, after a short pause, it rang out again, longer this time, and if anything, even more demanding. The mounted archers and men-at-arms on the perimeter finally seemed to come to their senses at the sound of the second horn and they began to turn their horses away from the Pith arrows to flee to the east. The lancers trapped along the moat needed no urging once they saw open land appear and they bolted after them in pursuit. I saw many riderless horses in amongst the fleeing Ganders and they quickly surged ahead of their weighted-down cousins as they headed straight for the screaming mass of men approaching on foot. I realized the Gander riders behind couldn't see what was going on in front of them with all the swirling grass and dust and I started to grin, hardly able to believe what was about to happen. The enraged peasants didn't recognize the danger they were in either until it was much too late. The panicked horses bore down on the men with mindless terror, not slowing as they smashed into them with a bone-crunching crash as the first three ranks of the footmen fell screaming in horror beneath the horses' hooves.

"Hold!" Eriz cried, lifting an arm to stop the barrage of arrows. He looked just as surprised as I felt at what we were seeing. I stared across the walls in fascinated silence as cries and screams began to ring out from the men lying crushed and destroyed in droves along the open field. The riderless horses and mounted men continued, however, heedless of the devastation they were causing as they pounded through and over the terrified peasants. Eriz glanced at me and then grinned as he lifted his sword to the sky. "The Master is with us!" he cried. "Death to the Ganders!"

"Death to the Ganders!" the Piths screamed back, taking up the chant.

It was well past noon before the Gander army had recovered enough to organize itself into some semblance of order again. Hundreds of peasants had already died or been injured, but despite the losses, there appeared to be no shortage of them as they regrouped beneath the stern gazes of their sergeants. The lancers, archers and mounted men-at-arms had suffered losses as well, but nothing in comparison to the peasants. I estimated there might still be six or seven-hundred horsemen left that could fight, even though a hundred or so had ridden away around noon, heading over the bridge to the north. I had no idea where they were going or what they were doing, but as far as I was concerned they were going in the right direction, so I considered it good riddance. Even with their departure and the men the Ganders had already lost, however, we were still dearly outnumbered by at least eight to one. Despite that fact I grinned to myself, imagining the look on Lord Corwick's face as he sat inside his tent brooding in humiliation. After what had happened that morning, he and Lord Demay had to know that we were laughing at them from behind our walls, which, I have to say, was hugely gratifying.

Dead lancers, archers and men-at-arms lay scattered across the blood-soaked grass around the garrison. But the bulk of the corpses lay in crumpled piles two or even three deep along the sloping banks of the moat where the Piths had concentrated their arrows. Some of the dead had rolled down the banks and into the murky water, where they now floated almost fully submerged within its depths, slowly being dragged down by the weight of their armor. More bodies lay in distorted heaps to the south where we'd attacked Lord Corwick's men, and also to the east where the peasants had been trampled to death. The Ganders had ignored their fallen comrades completely when they'd retreated, leaving the dead and soon to be dead behind for the ravens and other scavengers to feed upon. Eriz ordered several Piths to silence anything on the battlefield that was in range and moved, and every so often we'd hear the thrum of a bowstring as some poor bastard was put out of his misery. Eriz didn't offer these men a quick death out of the goodness of his heart, however, as he found their constant moaning and cries for help to be hugely annoying. I knew Eriz wasn't worried about our arrow supply either, since we'd spent the better part of the last year making and stockpiling them in preparation for the coming war. We had enough arrows in Gasterny to last for a months-long siege if need be, but none of us expected they'd be needed, as we expected Einhard to return soon with the Pith army at his back. All we had to do was survive until then.

Most of us were in a jubilant mood after the battle, laughing and joking amongst ourselves as we sat resting in the outer bailey while we waited for the slaves to bring us something to eat. With some skill on our part, and a great deal of luck, hundreds of Ganders had died without the Piths taking even a single casualty. Which, when you think about it, was nothing short of remarkable. Baine, Jebido and I were sitting on the stairs that led up to the Holy House, which Einhard had converted last year into additional barracks for the men. Einhard had been adamant that the Blazing Sun and Rock of Life above the door be destroyed, along with anything else inside that made any reference to the First Pair. I can't say I wasn't angered by his decision, but it hadn't come as a great surprise either. I prayed to both The Mother and The Father every night for a month afterward asking Them to forgive the Piths for their ignorance.

Eriz and Ania walked over to join us just as a line of female slaves appeared through the inner gates carrying trays of wooden bowls filled with hot broth made from a mixture of chicken innards, peas and onions. This was a standard fare in the garrison, and I knew that a small chunk of dark, freshly-baked barley bread would be floating on top of each bowl. The slaves were led by Josphet, my friend and tutor, and when he saw Eriz standing with us he headed the slaves our way with a curt command. Three young boys followed behind the women; their faces set in almost comical concentration as they each pulled a small cart lined with tin mugs brimming with beer that had been chilled in the well. Josphet offered the food and beer to Eriz first, then to the rest of us and I accepted mine gratefully, realizing that I was suddenly starving. Once Josphet was finished handing out the food, he came to stand beside me, and though I was sitting and he standing, he was so short that we still looked at each other in the eye.

"The Lord of Corwick will not be happy after this," Josphet said softly, looking worried. He flicked his eyes nervously to Eriz, but the big Pith was intent on his broth and paid the little man no mind.

"No," I agreed as I fished the bread out of my bowl. "I expect not." I felt that Josphet and the rest of the Ganders had a right to know what was going on, so as I ate I quickly told him of Lord Corwick's terms and that everyone in Gasterny would be put to the sword if we lost. Including the slaves.

The little man looked crestfallen as he digested the news and he sighed loudly and removed his battered hat before bowing to me. "Thank you for telling me, lord. I will inform the others. Hearing this should convince them to help you fight in whatever manner they can." He turned to go and then paused and looked back at me. "They hate the Piths, but I imagine the fear of imminent death will be a great motivator to help them overcome that hate."

I grinned, knowing the little man was probably right about that.

"That was smart, Hadrack," Jebido said, looking at me in admiration as Josphet left.

"What was?" I asked, genuinely confused.

"You guaranteed the slaves loyalty to us with just a few words," Jebido said as he raised his mug to me. "If anyone else here had told Josphet what Lord Corwick had said, he might not have believed it." Jebido grinned. "But he likes and trusts you, so now we don't have to worry about any kind of rebellion from them when the fighting gets tough. Well done."

"Ah," I said. I nodded and looked down at my bowl. It hadn't been my intent to gain the slaves' loyalty when I'd told Josphet, I'd just wanted to be honest with him, that was all. But, looking at it after the fact, I saw what Jebido meant and I had to admit that I was secretly pleased by his praise.

"So, what do you think the Ganders will do now?" Baine asked Jebido.

"Probably nothing," Jebido said around a mouthful of wet bread. "After that shambles of an attack, I'm willing to bet they'll try to regroup and come at us again in the morning."

"Let's hope not!" Eriz boomed as he approached us. He set his empty bowl on the step and took a long drink of beer, then wiped the foam from his beard and mustache with the back of his hand. "There's still plenty of daylight left to kill a few more of those bastards." He looked down at Jebido and lifted an eyebrow. "How much?" Jebido looked at him in confusion and Eriz snorted. "You mentioned a bet. I'll put three fingers against yours."

"Same," Ania grunted before she lifted her bowl to her lips and slurped hungrily.

Baine and I grinned at each other and I decided to get in on it. Having spent more than a year in the company of the Piths, I'd come to enjoy gambling almost as much as they did. "Six fingers against," I said.

"Seven," Baine chipped in with a laugh.

"So, let me see if I understand this," Jebido said with a perplexed shake of his head. "You're all betting against me, hoping they'll attack again? Is that right?"

"Yes," Baine agreed. "That pretty much sums it up."

"Fair enough," Jebido chuckled as he set his bowl down. "I'll take that bet." He counted off on his fingers. "So, that's three for Eriz. Three for Ania. Six from Hadrack, and seven from Baine." He looked at us and grinned. "Nineteen fingers to me if they don't attack again today, right?"

"Right," Eriz grunted.

"Mother's tit!" Jebido said as he picked up his bowl. "I'm

going to be rich!"

The five of us all laughed at that and I glanced up at the sun as it slowly slipped behind a thick cloud that looked vaguely like a five-legged horse. I frowned as the stairs fell into deep shadow, noting the solid wall of cloud cover quickly coming up behind the horse cloud from the north. If there was rain in those clouds, Jebido might win his wager after all. We finished eating and Ania and Eriz wandered off toward the keep arm in arm, while Padrea, the girl Baine had been seeing this past week, sauntered over to us. Padrea had come with the king's forces and had asked to stay to replace Alesia, which had been just fine with both Einhard and Eriz. Padrea was a large, confident and stocky woman, with surprisingly perfect teeth, a flat nose with a small, hook-shaped scar on the tip, and very large breasts. I had secretly doubted she could even pull the string back on a bow with those huge breasts in the way, but from what I'd seen that morning, my doubts were now put to rest. Padrea walked halfway up the stairs and then paused to look down at Baine. She raised an eyebrow and then gestured to the building with her head before stepping past us and going inside.

"Well," Baine said as he jumped to his feet. "I'd love to sit here with the two of you doing nothing all afternoon, but," he glanced at the door and grinned, "duty calls."

"You sure you know what to do in there?" Jebido asked with a straight face as Baine hurried past him.

Baine just snorted. "When you hear her moans, you'll have your answer."

Jebido and I talked for a while after that, until finally, Baine re-emerged about a half an hour or so later with a big grin on his face. To be fair to my friend, both Jebido and I were forced to agree that he did seem to know what he was doing, judging by the sounds we'd heard coming from inside.

Another hour went by while we sat and waited, with no serious movement coming from the Gander camp. At one point the Gandermen sent out some peasants to retrieve the fallen ramps and ladders that were still usable, but they were too far away for our arrows to be even remotely effective. The Ganders had also made sure to send horsemen to guard the peasants, just in case we decided to try a quick sortie against them. Everyone inside the garrison was on edge to some degree as we waited, but few showed it. One of the things I'd learned about the Piths early on was that they rarely worried about things out of their control. We had lookouts in each of the watchtowers, so there was no chance of being caught unawares by a surprise attack, so why worry? The Ganders would attack, or they would not attack, it was as simple as that. But, until they did, the Piths would continue to live life the way they always had. Some preferred to play games in the inner or outer baileys and gamble on the outcome, or drink beer and swap outrageous lies. While others, like Padrea, preferred to rut to take the edge off. Which, I have to admit as I thought about it, did tend to ease tension quite a bit.

"Well," Jebido finally said as he glanced upward. The thick cloud cover from earlier had blown away on the wind, taking any chance of rain with it as the sun slowly made its way westward. "Only a few more hours of daylight left. If they're going to do anything, it'll have to be soon."

I stood up and stretched, bending my right leg back and forth to get the kink out. The Pith arrow that I'd taken in the thigh last year had healed long ago, but occasionally when I sat too long my leg tended to stiffen up. I was starting to think that Jebido might be right after all and the Ganders wouldn't attack, but part of me wished they would just for something to do. At least Baine had Padrea to distract him for a little while, I thought glumly. I had a sudden vision of Ania writhing in my bed and I quickly brushed the image away. She'd been very clear to me about her wishes that morning. Until this was over, she planned on being with her husband, she'd told me, and while I wasn't all that happy about her decision, I certainly couldn't fault her on it. She was his wife after all. I knew of several single Pith women who'd shown an interest

in me, but I didn't feel like trudging around the garrison looking for them like some love-starved puppy. Besides, knowing
Piths the way that I did, they were probably already occupied
anyway.

I moved away from the stairs into the shade of the
circular stone watchtower that intersected the inner eastern
wall and the heavy rock of the southern wall and I leaned
against it. The Gander builders had just enough stone left to
finish the watchtower, though the battlements hadn't been
added to it, which left the lookout vulnerable to arrows. The
builders had only managed to get a quarter of the eastern and
northern walls laid out before the Piths had stopped the flow
of stones from Father's Arse. Not having many options, they'd
begun building walls of heavy oak on top of the stone instead,
using the blocks as a foundation. We'd spent the last year finishing that wall and building the secondary one, which connected to the watchtower and then headed east before curling
back against the northeastern watchtower.

A Pith appeared above me, leaning over the wall as he
peered down and he whistled to get my attention. His name
was Gadest, one of the warriors who'd come with the Shield to
find Einhard a year ago. Gadest, like most Piths, was a big man
and heavily bearded. He had a twisted sense of humor, I found,
made even worse when he was drinking, which was often.

Gadest cupped his hands to his mouth. "Hadrack,
where's Eriz? Something might be happening in the Gander
camp!"

I stepped back into the sunlight and looked up. "Gone
to the keep with Ania!" I shouted. "What do you see?"

Gadest shrugged. "I'm not sure if it's anything, but some
Gandermen just came out of the tent with the dragon banner."
He paused and glanced over his shoulder, then shielded his
eyes with his hand. I heard him curse before he turned back.
"They're on the move! I'm blowing the horn!"

"Ah, shit!" Jebido grunted bitterly from the stairs as he
looked upward almost accusingly.

Baine chuckled as he and Jebido got to their feet. "So much for being rich, my friend."

Jebido rolled his eyes. "I was so close," he grumbled.

Gadest blew the horn just as I reached the ladder that led up to the parapet of the inner wall. I started to climb with my two friends following close behind me as Piths ran to man the southern and eastern walls. The Gander slaves had restocked the arrows along the ramparts after the battle that morning, so we were as ready for the coming attack as we were ever going to be. I carefully crossed the ramp that led down to the secondary wall and glanced at the straw and dried mud beneath me that hid the spears. I involuntarily shuddered, unable to imagine the horror of falling in there.

I reached the outer parapet and leaned against the crudely-cut pointed battlements as I stared out over the field littered with dead men. The Gander camp was alive with motion as the sounds of horns slowly drifted across the fields to our walls. Lancers, archers and men-at-arms all began to mount their horses and move toward us in a solid mass that I guessed had to be easily two-hundred feet across. I saw two riders at the head of the group holding long pointed banners that fluttered and snapped in the wind. I didn't need to see the banners to know that one bore the dragon symbol of Lord Corwick, and the other the coiled snake of Lord Demay. The peasants were quickly forming up into ranked squares of about a hundred men in each, their discipline the exact opposite of what we'd seen that morning. Even from where I stood, I could hear the harsh bellowing of orders echoing over the fields as several of the squares turned smartly and began marching toward the southern road. Meanwhile, the rest of the footmen started to advance at a steady pace toward our eastern wall as the mounted horsemen fell in behind them. It looked to me like Lord Corwick was going back to his original plan.

"They're not going to make that mistake again," Jebido said as at least a hundred mounted men led by the rider with the coiled-snake banner turned to follow the peasants heading south.

Eriz arrived with Ania and he studied the Gander movements with a critical eye. "They're going to come at us from three directions," he finally said to no one in particular.

"That would be my guess, too," Jebido agreed. He gestured to the south and then the west. "Sending men against those walls will drain away some of our defenses while they concentrate their main force against us here."

I nodded my head, having come to much the same conclusion. "And with cavalry to support them, we won't be able to repeat what we did the first time."

"No, we won't," Jebido said. He frowned as he looked out over the wall, then turned to glance at Eriz. "Better get the slaves ready with the water." He pointed to the eastern field. "They're going to start this thing with fire."

The Gandermen had just lit three bonfires about two-hundred yards or so away from us and had spaced them twenty-feet apart. The peasant army came to a halt behind the flames while ten of the archers wearing red surcoats that I'd seen that morning approached the fires.

"Cardians!" Jebido grunted in disgust when he saw them. He spit over the wall in their direction. "They'd sell their own mother for a loaf of bread. But the bastards can shoot, I'll grant them that."

"They're too far away and the wind is blowing in their faces!" Baine protested as Eriz shouted at the slaves to get ready. "They'll never hit us from that distance."

Jebido shrugged. "Maybe, maybe not, but we make a big target, so you never know. They don't have to be accurate, either. All they have to do is get those arrows over our walls." He gestured behind him. "Loft enough of them onto the roofs of some of those buildings back there and we're going to be in big trouble."

Most of the buildings in the garrison had stones walls but, other than the keep, the roofs were all made of wooden shingles and were vulnerable to fire.

Jebido pointed to the Cardian archers. "See there, just below the arrowheads? Those are flax tows that they've soaked in resin. Once it gets going it's hard to put out, wind or not."

Being a farmer, I knew tows were long stringy fibers extracted from flax, hemp, or jute that burned fiercely and smelled horrible. I just nodded to Jebido as I watched the Cardians closely. I noticed the bows they held were taller than the men themselves, taller actually than anything I'd seen before. I started to get an uneasy feeling just as Gander slaves began to form a human chain in the bailey behind us. The slaves started to pass wooden buckets slopping with water up to the inner ramparts, where a Pith met them at the top of one of the ladders. The Pith then handed the buckets off to other warriors, who crossed the ramps and poured the water down the skinned hides hanging on the outer wall before returning for more. Within minutes the foul-smelling hides were drenched, glistening wetly as rivulets of water rolled down them to the ground and then trickled in small streams into the moat. The Piths then headed to the inner wall, where they repeated the process all over again on the hides hanging there.

"Start throwing water on the rooftops when you're done!" Eriz commanded gruffly. "I want every inch of those shingles soaked through." He turned and looked back over the battlements, then glanced at Ania. "Do you think you can hit those shit-eaters from here?"

Ania studied the Cardians thoughtfully and then shrugged. "We can only try. It's a long way, but we have the height and the wind at our backs, which will help." She grinned. "One or two arrows probably won't do much, but if you throw a single rock at a bird, the chances are you'll miss it."

"But if you throw a handful, you just might knock it out of the air," Eriz finished for her.

"Exactly," Ania said with a smile. "Archers!" she cried, her face turning serious. "Nock!"

There had to be thirty or so archers along the outer eastern wall and they moved in unison, fixing arrows to their bows.

"You going to get in on this?" I asked Baine as he stood beside me making no effort to unhook his bow from where it rested across his shoulders.

"Not a chance!" Baine snorted with a shake of his head. "Give me a target inside of seventy-five yards and I'll hit it every time." He gestured over the wall. "That's just a waste of good arrows."

"Ania thinks it can be done," I pointed out.

"That's because she's too stubborn to admit it can't be," Baine grunted. "You'll see."

"Five fingers to the warrior that brings down one of those bastards!" Ania cried as she pointed to the Cardians. "Pull!" Thirty bows creaked as the Piths pulled the arrow nocks to their right ears and aimed toward the sky. Across from us the enemy archers nocked their arrows and then held the tips over the flames until the tows caught and began burning. "Loose!" Ania cried.

The sound of the Pith bows all releasing at the same moment echoed over the ramparts. I watched as a black cloud of spinning shafts flew straight up, seeming to climb forever until they were almost out of sight before finally, they began to angle back downward again. The man I'd seen that morning carrying the parlay branch appeared on horseback and he dismounted near the Cardians. He strode confidently at least ten feet in front of the bonfires, where he stopped and studied the arrows coming toward him. He didn't appear concerned at all as he watched the arrows in flight, and eventually he turned his back on them and drew his sword and held it in the air. Despite myself I was impressed by his courage. The Cardians pulled back on their bows and aimed the burning arrows high into the air toward us before the soldier swept his sword downward. The bowmen immediately loosed their shafts, which arched upward, flaming and smoking as they fought the wind just as the swarm of Pith arrows slapped into the ground in a ragged arc twenty feet away from where the man-at-arms stood. The Ganderman didn't even bother to look behind him as the shafts fell.

"Told you," Baine said out of the side of his mouth while the Piths around us muttered in grudging admiration at the Gander's steely nerves. Baine took a deep breath and glanced at me. "The only good news is at least they can't hit us either."

I watched the heavy arrow shafts wrapped in smoking, sputtering flame as they drew closer, unconsciously holding my breath and hoping that Baine was right. The arrows continued, rising impossibly high into the air until they were just mere specks of flickering light before they began to arc down toward our walls.

"Impossible!" Baine gasped. "What kind of a bow can do that?"

I felt his hand on my forearm and he squeezed it in disbelief as a flaming arrow smacked with a thunk into the outside of the wall four-feet below where we stood. The arrow hissed and smoked feebly against the wet hide, then went out just as more shafts hit the wall. They too smoked and flickered, burning weakly. The air immediately filled with the stench of singed fur as a female Pith near the northeastern watchtower cried out in surprise and stumbled backward with an arrow embedded in her shoulder. She dropped her bow and slapped madly at the burning shaft in panic before howling in dismay as she lost her footing and tipped over the edge of the parapet. If not for the quick thinking of the Pith warrior beside her, who grabbed her by the neck of her leather armor and hauled her back, the wounded Pith would have fallen onto the deadly spears waiting in the killing grounds.

More flaming arrows were on the way, and this time the Cardians had stepped forward ten paces. Behind them, more of the red-clad archers were bunching in tight ranks where the first line of Cardians had stood. The flight of burning arrows reached our walls and I looked up as they hissed one by one over our heads like hungry hawks seeking prey while trailing black smoke and tendrils of flame behind them. Several arrows dropped into the killing ground, where they smoldered harmlessly in the mud-packed straw, but most kept going over the inner wall to drop out of sight into the bailey. I heard surprised shouts and cries of alarm echoing up from below and knew that at least one of those arrows had managed to do some damage. The Cardians sent off another volley of flaming arrows, while behind them the second line of archers released a host of barbed shafts just as billowing black smoke began to rise from somewhere inside the bailey.

"Get down!" Ania cried in warning.

I pressed myself tightly against the wood, with Jebido and Baine on either side of me as arrows thudded all along the ramparts and battlements.

"Should we go help put out the flames?" Baine asked as curling black smoke swept over us.

Jebido coughed and shook his head. "No, we stay here." He gestured to the wall. "That's what those bastards want." He cautiously stood up and peered out over the fields, then hawked deeply before spitting over the battlements. Baine and I joined him and I saw that Ania, Eriz and most of the Piths were also standing as they stared across at our adversaries. Many of the Piths had their round shields lifted and ready in anticipation of another volley and I copied them, wondering idly if our shields could withstand the heavy Cardian arrows. "You'll hear the horns in another minute or two and then they'll charge," Jebido said confidently.

As if on cue, horns began to sound, first from the east, then from the west, and then the south. Eriz had placed warriors on the western and southern ramparts, but the bulk of our meager forces were concentrated on the inner and outer eastern walls and watchtowers to either side, where we knew the fighting would be the fiercest. Whatever happened on those other walls was up to the Piths there to contain, as we would surely have our hands full where we were. More flaming arrows arced over our heads as the Cardians continued the assault, while from behind them the second rank of bowmen sent another volley of dark-spinning shafts toward the battlements. I peered through the notch of sharpened stakes in front of me at the massed peasant army, which had begun banging their swords and spears against their shields as the mounted sergeants worked them into a frenzy. Then the horn blew again, three sharp blasts this time, and the sergeants pointed their swords at our walls and let the enraged foot soldiers loose.

I guessed at least six-hundred men were bearing down on us across the grass, with many of the leaders quickly coming into bow range as they ran waving their weapons and screaming their war cries. All along the ramparts the Pith bowstrings started to thrum as peasants were snatched backward or fell twisting and writhing along the ragged front line. I looked up at the watchtower above me as Gadest shook his battle-axe at the sky and screamed curses at the Gandermen. Beside him, the packed mass of Pith archers shot quickly and calmly down into the peasant ranks.

"Hadrack, Baine," Jebido said. He turned his back on the approaching horde and placed a hand on each of our forearms. An arrow whacked into the tip of the battlement behind him, sending several large splinters exploding outward over our heads, but my friend didn't even flinch. "I've known you both since you were little brats picking the snot from your noses and laughing as you flicked it at each other." He chuckled and shook his head. "I remember I used to ask the First Pair every night what sin I could have committed that warranted having to watch over a couple of dumb asses like you two." Baine and I shared a glance and we both smiled at the same time. "But," Jebido said, "The Mother and The Father always know what's best for us, even if we don't realize it ourselves." Jebido cleared his throat, ignoring the battle raging below us as he squeezed our arms. "I'm proud of you both. It's been an honor and a privilege to have been a part of your lives."

"Mother's tit!" Baine said gruffly as he rolled his eyes and looked away. I couldn't help but notice just a hint of wetness in those eyes as he turned back. "You're talking like a silly old man who's ready to lie down and die."

Jebido shrugged and gestured with his head behind us. "There's too many of them. Any fool can see that. I'm just saying what I want to say before I can't, that's all."

"You always told us as long as there's strength in your sword arm and breath in your body, then there's hope," I said, feeling a lump rise in my throat.

"I did," Jebido nodded. "And it's still true. I'm not giving up. We'll fight those bastards, and, in the end, we'll win, or we won't, but either way I'll have said what I wanted to say to you."

It seems odd now, writing this so many years later, but up until that exact moment with arrows whizzing past our heads, the thought of dying on the walls of Gasterny — or anywhere else for that matter — had barely even occurred to me. I just assumed we'd find a way to win, or, if not that, then Einhard would return to save us like the Shield had a year ago. I was only eighteen-years-old back then, young, strong, and full of life, and I rarely if ever thought about death. It just seemed like something that happened to other people.

I glanced over the wall after listening to Jebido's words, looking this time with fresh eyes. I saw that the peasant army had already reached the moat and were throwing down the ramps to cross it. Pith arrows were causing huge losses in their ranks, but for every man that fell and dropped a ramp or ladder, another took his place. Along the parapet the enemy arrows were taking their toll as well, as I saw gaps here and there where Pith warriors had fallen. Hundreds and hundreds of men swarmed toward us, with mounted men-at-arms waiting in reserve, while archers loosed waves of arrows at any of us that showed our faces. I knew the same thing was happening along the western and southern walls as well and I prayed that the Piths there could hold them back. I could make out individual faces in the mass of peasants below me now and could read the mixture of fear and hatred they felt for us on their faces. That's the moment when I finally understood what Jebido was talking about. There were less than two hundred of us trying to defend a weak garrison against well over a thousand Ganders thirsty for our blood. These men wouldn't stop for any reason, and Einhard wasn't coming to save us. That much I now understood. The death Jebido spoke of would be coming over our walls soon in the form of vengeful Gandermen and I knew there wasn't much time left before the ladders went up. I turned back to Jebido, wanting him to know what he'd meant to me all these years.

I put my hand on his arm and fought for the words, until finally I simply said, "Thank you for everything."

It wasn't much, not even close to what I would have liked to say, but even so, Jebido seemed moved by it and he nodded. "You've been like a son to me, Hadrack." He glanced at Baine. "The both of you have." He cleared his throat. "So enough of this chattering like old women. We've got a job to do." He pointed his finger at my chest, then to Baine's. "Just remember this, all men have to die sometime. The only question has always been when and how." Jebido drew his sword. "Well, we know the answer to when, and all that's left now is the how. Fight well, my friends, and make sure those turd-suckers out there pay for our blood with their own before you fall!"

Jebido turned away and I glanced at Baine, who stood uncertainly beside me. I put my hand on his shoulder and squeezed it like my father used to do to me. "It's going to be all right," I said. "Now get that bow of yours off your shoulders and show those Gander bastards what you can do!"

Baine nodded and his face turned grim, his eyes darkening in that look I'd come to know. He unhooked his bow and moved toward a gap in the battlements and began to shoot downward into the mass of Gandermen below us with cold precision. I drew Wolf's Head with my right hand and grabbed my Pair Stone with my left and kissed its smooth surface as I said a quick prayer. Then I headed for the wall just as the top of a ladder landed with a thump against the wood in front of me. A bearded face with wild eyes immediately appeared over the battlements and I instinctively lifted my shield as the man screamed gibberish at me and swung his battered-looking sword down at my head. Spittle was spraying wetly from the man's mouth in a wide arc as I deflected his weak blow with my shield, sending his blade to the side where it got wedged into a chink in the wall. The bearded man's eyes widened in fear as he tugged at his weapon, but it was held fast and wouldn't budge. I grinned at him, hesitating as I let him see his death reflected in my eyes before I stabbed hard with Wolf's Head right between the gap that separated the sharpened points of the wall. My blade took the peasant in the chest, piercing easily through his thin leather armor and his ribs before bursting out his back with a wet-sounding crunch. The Ganderman cried out and released the hilt of his sword before he tumbled sideways off the ladder and disappeared from view.

I felt the familiar joy of the killing-blood roaring in my ears and I howled a challenge as I peered down over the wall. The lifeless body of the man I'd just killed crumpled against the ground at the base of the wall and then rolled slowly into the moat as two more peasants climbed the ladder above him. I sheathed Wolf's Head, knowing that I had time as the peasants had paused to stare down at the dead man floating in the moat face down with blood pooling around him. I placed a hand on each of the side rails of the ladder and then started to push it outward. Beneath me the Gandermen cried out in dismay, and the one in the lead, a blond boy around my age, cursed me and all my ancestors as he tried to scurry up the rungs. I laughed down at him and then shoved with all my strength. The ladder seemed to hang balanced in the air for a moment, perfectly straight with the two Gandermen clinging to it in terror, before it finally tipped backward and collapsed with a splash into the moat. I didn't have time to enjoy my triumph, however, as more and more ladders were being thrown up all along the entire length of the wall.

"Archers!" I heard Ania cry from somewhere to my left. "Fall back! Fall back!"

I knew that signal meant that the Gandermen had gotten a foothold on the parapet, and now it was up to Eriz, Jebido and the rest of us to try to push them back with swords, axes and war hammers. The archers scurried backward across the ramps, still shooting arrows at the screaming peasants that clawed and fought to get over the battlements. Two Ganderman came over the wall in front of me at the same time and I rushed at them, easily ducking under the wild swing of the gap-toothed, grinning peasant on my left. I shoved my shoulder into his chest as hard as I could, knocking him stumbling backward while blocking the other peasant's two-handed swipe with my sword. The man I'd hit with my shoulder crashed into the inside of the wall, where he fell to one knee, clearly stunned. Jebido was fighting along the parapet several paces from me and he paused in his battle with a fierce-looking peasant with flaming red hair to slash across the stunned man's chest. Blood spurted and the man dropped as Jebido turned back to his adversary. I glared at the peasant in front of me, who was just a boy much younger even than Baine. The young peasant had long black hair and pleasant features, though at the moment they were twisted ugly with fear. He held his sword nervously in both his hands and kept glancing sideways over the wall, obviously hoping for some help. I growled and advanced several paces on him, then paused as the boy's sword started to shake uncontrollably in his hands.

"What's your name!?" I barked.

"Hanley of Laskerly, lord," the boy said, his voice cracking. "Please, I don't want to die!"

I sighed, suddenly reluctant to kill another of Lord Corwick's unknowing pawns. I nodded and gestured to the wall with my sword. "Then go back the way you came and run as far away from here as you can. Do you understand?"

Hanley nodded just as more men appeared on the ladders behind him. I assumed this would give the boy the courage to fight, but the young peasant surprised me and without another word he flung his sword aside and then leaped awkwardly over the wall. I didn't know it at the time, of course, but one day in the not too distant future, Hanley and I would be destined to meet again. I barely gave the frightened peasant another thought at that moment, however, as more and more Gandermen continued to stream over our walls. Though the peasants were untrained with sword and spear, Jebido and I were still hard-pressed to keep them back as they surged around us. The Pith archers along the inner wall and above on the watchtowers were loosing arrows into the struggling throng of men as fast as they could, but it seemed like there was no end to them regardless of how many fell. The peasants finally managed to push us back against the southeastern watchtower just by sheer weight of numbers alone, until Jebido and I were fighting alone shoulder to shoulder in an improvised shield wall with another Pith named Jamet. Behind us, Baine — who'd stubbornly refused to leave with the other archers — shot calmly and efficiently over our shoulders.

"Pull the ramps!" I heard Eriz's booming command rise from somewhere behind the peasants facing us.

Pith warriors were being mobbed all along the parapet, the pressed bodies of the enraged peasants making it almost impossible for the embattled Piths to swing a sword effectively. I saw Eriz standing alone and isolated near the northeastern watchtower as he bellowed in defiance at the Gandermen trying to pull him down. He cursed loudly as he flung a peasant over the parapet into the killing grounds before he shouted once again for Ania to pull the ramps away. The big Pith had lost his sword, I saw, and he swung madly in all directions with a war hammer, crushing and cutting down Gander after Gander. But, for every man he crunched aside, two more jumped over the battlements to replace him. A straggly-bearded peasant appeared over the wall behind Eriz and before I could shout a warning, he jabbed the point of his spear into the back of Eriz's neck. The big Pith cried out and staggered, then fell as triumphant peasants swarmed him as they swung their swords or stabbed downward with their spears. I cursed under my breath and glanced to my left, where Ania had finally commanded the Piths to remove the ramps. I shared a look with Jebido, knowing that our time had come as well.

The four of us were all that was left of the Piths along the outer wall and the peasants began to converge on us with hate-filled eyes. Behind these men, more Ganders were hopping over the wall in droves, until finally there wasn't enough room left for all of them to stand on the walkway. The peasants on the outer edges began to fall off into the killing grounds, pushed by the pressing bodies arriving behind them. We waited, wedged in tight against the wall of the watch-tower as the screams began below us where the peasants had fallen in amongst the spears. There was only enough room on the parapet for two or three men to come at us at a time and the Gandermen facing us held back, clearly working up the courage to rush us. The Pith arrows were dropping the peasants all along the rim of the ramparts as Baine continued to shoot into their midst from behind us, yet still they hesitated to attack us. I took the brief respite to think of my sister and father and I felt my heart sink, knowing that I wouldn't be able to uphold my vow to them. I cursed the nine for what they'd done, then I cursed Einhard for not letting me go after them when I'd had the chance. I took a deep breath, trying to think like a Pith and accept what I could not change. I sheathed Wolf's Head and stared across at the wall of dirty, blood-stained peasants massed along the walkway. Jebido looked at me questioningly and I just smiled at him as I drew my father's axe from my back. If I was going to die, it would be with Alwin of Corwick as close to me as possible.

"Are you sure?" Jebido asked me.

I nodded and glanced at Baine one last time before turning back to Jebido. "I'm sure." I tossed my shield aside into the killing grounds and strode forward three paces. I spread my arms and held my father's axe with its carved handle up for them to see. "I am Hadrack!" I shouted as I shook the axe at them. "The Wolf of Corwick! And your lives belong to me now!" And then I charged.

I felt no fear or regret at that moment, only an all-encompassing rage that seemed to explode outward from every part of my body. The faces in front of me weren't those of ill-fed peasants now. Instead, they'd somehow changed, transforming into those of the nine right before my eyes. Quant Ranes was there, and Heavy Beard, Hape and all the others. Even the two I'd managed to kill, Searl Merk — who I knew as Crooked Nose — and the youth, Calen, were there as I charged across the wooden parapet. I smashed into the Gandermen like a half-crazed bull, swinging my father's axe and screaming my hatred of the nine as I slaughtered men left and right. I think I lost my mind for a time, as I don't recall much of what happened after my initial charge. Jebido told me later that he'd never seen anything like it, and I've never forgotten the look of pure awe on his face when he'd told me what I'd done. When it was over, the peasants that had filled the parapet lay dead and dying or writhing below in the killing grounds, impaled by the spear points. Those that had been coming over the ladders hung back fearfully, refusing to jump down and fight an obvious madman. The entire eastern side of the garrison lay in shocked silence, with only the sounds of the ongoing battles still raging along the western and southern walls marring the eerie stillness. Finally, Ania barked a command, breaking the spell of amazement affecting everyone and the Piths hurried to throw one of the ramps across the killing grounds for us. Jebido, Baine and Jamet led me stunned and shaking across the ramp, while behind us the Gandermen just stared in fascinated awe and let us go.

"Hadrack!" Baine said to me in wonder as he helped me

climb down onto the parapet of the inner wall. "You killed them all!"

Around me the Piths began to cheer wildly, calling out my name and banging their weapons against their shields. I was covered in blood; none of it my own, surprisingly, and I clasped both Baine and Jebido on the shoulders and grinned as I swayed on my feet like a drunken man. Ania flung her arms around me as she kissed me hard on the lips, while all along the parapet the Piths whistled their appreciation.

"I'm sorry about Eriz," I said when she finally broke the kiss.

Ania's smile faltered. "He died like the true warrior he was," she finally said. "It was a glorious death befitting him."

Ania turned abruptly away and began barking orders to the jubilant Piths, focusing their attention back on the peasants, who were regaining their courage and coming over the walls again. Despite our losses, we were brimming with optimism now, and as the sun began to set behind us, it was beginning to look like we'd win the day. But, unfortunately, that optimism would be short-lived, as things were about to change drastically. As it turned out, we hadn't broken Lord Corwick's line after all like I had initially thought. In fact, in the end, it was he who'd broken ours instead. Because we hadn't anticipated the limits of Lord Corwick's cunning and willingness to sacrifice lives, the miscalculation ended up costing everyone in the garrison dearly.

The secondary wall was only fifteen-feet tall and easily scaled, but our inner wall was almost double that, and with the ramps pulled back the peasants were in a quandary. None of them wanted to jump down into the killing grounds, for obvious reasons, so on their sergeants' orders they began hauling some of the long ramps that had spanned the moat up the ladders to bridge the gap between the lower and higher walls. This proved to be a near-impossible task, however, which left the peasants vulnerable as they worked and ridiculously easy targets for the Pith archers.

Terry Cloutier

I began to recover my strength quickly as I watched the peasants struggling and dying in the futile attempt and I thought about what Lord Corwick had said about cattle and sacrifice. I began to get an uneasy feeling that something was wrong and I looked behind me, then froze in shock. Gander-men were pouring over the northern wall in a horde, while beneath them slaves throwing water along the rooftops cried out in fear as they dropped their buckets and leaped to the ground to escape. These men weren't simple peasants like we were fighting on the eastern wall, but instead were heavily-armored men-at-arms and red-clad archers clutching their long-bows. We didn't have any of our men on the northern walls to stop them either, since we hadn't expected an attack coming from the riverbank. I didn't learn until much later that the Ganders we'd seen ride away around noon that day had followed the river to the west, then doubled back to a spot where they couldn't be seen. They'd then fashioned rafts from the trees nearby and waited until the attack on our walls had begun. Once our attention was elsewhere, the Ganders had floated down the river to the dock, where the Cardian archers had shot ropes tied to arrows into the tops of the battlements. The attackers then pulled themselves up the steep bank and over the wall. It had been flawlessly planned and executed, and if I hadn't hated Lord Corwick as much as I did, I might have even admired him for its pure perfection.

"To the rear!" I shouted in warning.

It had only been several seconds since I'd become aware of the danger behind us, but in that time the northern parapets had already filled with enemy soldiers. I glanced to the far northwestern watchtower overlooking the river, but there was no sign of any of the Piths stationed there. Either they'd left their post to join the fighting or the Cardian archers had managed to silence them without anyone noticing. Some of the Gander men-at-arms dashed down the ladders to the inner bailey, or jumped nimbly down onto the wet rooftops, while others ran along the parapet, heading for the northeastern watchtower that intersected our two walls. The Cardian archers knelt in a tight, disciplined formation along the parapet facing us, while the men-at-arms barrelled around the curve of the watchtower, shouting in triumph as they descended on the Piths. The Ganders didn't hesitate as they plowed into the Pith archers lining the wall, many of whom hadn't heard my warning and were still focused on the peasants in front of them and unaware of the threat from behind. Blades flashed and blood splattered wetly against the wooden walls as Pith men and women were cut down mercilessly, while from behind Cardian arrows flicked past and over the attacking Ganders to strike at warriors all along the parapet.

Piths were falling from the watchtowers and along the walkway, while across the killing grounds the peasants cheered as they labored to maneuver the ramps into position now that they were free from the Pith arrows. The Piths quickly got over their initial surprise at the sudden attack and rebounded, fighting back with desperate ferocity as they pushed the Ganders back against the watchtower. The Ganders wore heavy plate armor and fought with great longswords or more maneuverable short swords, while the Piths fought back with battle-axes, swords and war-hammers. Some of the female archers only had knives along with their short bows and they lashed out with these, heedless of the heavy Gander armor and rectangular shields opposing them. Both sides cursed the other as they pounded away at each other in disorganized shield walls as the screaming mass of struggling Gandermen and Piths surged forward and back beneath the northeastern watchtower, with neither side able to take the advantage.

Jebido and I shared a look and he gestured with his round shield toward the fighting, his face set in a grim mask of grey. I nodded back and hefted my father's blood-stained axe as we pushed our way through the Pith archers, who'd begun targeting the Cardian bowmen along the northern parapets. Baine joined the Piths, his black-leather armor and thin frame unmistakable among them as he calmly loosed arrow after arrow. I saw red-clad archers twisting and writhing as they fell beneath the deadly barrage of Pith arrows and I grinned. If it came down to a test of marksmanship, I'd pick Baine and the Piths over the Cardians and their heavier bows every time.

The smell of fresh blood, sweat and shit competed for attention across the ramparts as men and women cried out and died all around me. I stepped over a fallen Pith with a surprised look on her face and an arrow lodged in her temple just as something careened wildly off the side of my helmet, stunning me. I stumbled and dropped to one knee beside the body of the Pith as my vision blurred.

Jebido hurried back and put his hand on my shoulder as he leaned over me. "Are you all right?" he asked anxiously.

I nodded and opened my mouth to reply just as another arrow hissed through the air past my face, tickling my beard with its feathers before sneaking over the top of Jebido's lowered shield and burying itself in his armpit.

"No!" I screamed as Jebido grunted in surprise and stumbled.

I could hear Ania shouting at the Piths to kill the Ganders from somewhere nearby as she rallied them, but all I could focus on was my friend. I gently eased Jebido down to the parapet as Cardian arrows buzzed through the air like angry wasps all around us. Another dead Pith lay close by and I realized absently that it was Jamet. I pulled his heavy body toward me before propping it up sideways to provide my wounded friend some cover. Jebido's eyes were half-closed as he stared up at me, and I saw with dread that dark red blood was already pooling beneath him on the wood.

"Now I know the how," Jebido said weakly.

I shook my head, refusing to believe it. "You're not done yet!" I said.

Jebido just snorted, then groaned as he closed his eyes.

"How bad is he?" Baine asked anxiously as he dropped to his knees alongside me. An arrow thudded into the walkway in front of us, quivering as it buried itself in the wood, but neither Baine nor I even flinched.

"Bad!" I grunted. I hefted the axe in my hand and glared at Baine. "Take care of him!"

Baine nodded as I started running toward the entrenched battle at the end of the parapet. I bellowed and raised my father's axe, swinging it in a tight arc toward a big Ganderman who'd just cut down a female Pith with his red-stained sword. The Gander stood above the Pith grinning down at her like a fool, until something made him look up and he saw me. Then his eyes widened in fear just as my axe caught him squarely in the stomach. I didn't wait to see what effect my blow had, I just wrenched the axe head from his flesh and continued running. Below me I heard cheers ring out, followed by the unmistakable sounds of chains rattling. My heart sank, knowing that somehow the Ganders had gotten to the drawbridge. I thrust it from my mind, trying to fight rising panic as mounted Gandermen pounded through the barbican and into the outer bailey. To my right, the peasants were crossing the ramps and swarming over the walls, while across the bailey I saw men-at-arms and Piths desperately fighting all along the western and southern parapets.

A red-faced Ganderman appeared in front of me and I twisted aside as he thrust his short sword at my belly. I lashed out with my foot as the blade hissed past me, cracking his shin before swinging the butt of my axe hard against his cheek. The Ganderman bellowed in pain and then tumbled over the parapet and crashed through the roof of the smithy below us. I could see Ania fighting alongside Lale and several other Piths near the base of the northeastern watchtower and I fought my way through the packed, cursing and screaming bodies toward her. I felt a blow land on my right shoulder as a sword slashed down against the steel pauldrons there, but the overlapping plates withstood the jolt, though I felt my arm go numb for a moment. I cursed the wielder of the sword, who had turned away from me to hack at the vulnerable back of a Pith. I lashed out at him, severing the man's shield arm at the elbow. The Ganderman screamed and fell writhing and I stepped over him as a Pith female pounced on the man and began stabbing at his eyes with a knife.

I don't know what made me turn just then, but something did and I looked back and down, freezing as my eyes met those of the Lord of Corwick. He was sitting his horse in the outer bailey watching the fierce battle raging along the ramparts. He grinned when he saw me and even had the nerve to wave to me. My head exploded with rage at the mockery on his face and I instantly forgot about Jebido and Baine and the Piths and everything else. I wanted Lord Corwick's head! I glanced down to the roof of the smithy, gauging the distance, then I jumped, making sure to avoid the hole where the Ganderman had fallen through. I landed with my booted feet on each side of the peak of the roof where the wood was strongest, then I knelt and slid down the shingles on my rear before flipping off the edge to the dusty ground. I landed hard, wobbling, but just managed to stay on my feet. Lord Corwick sat his horse no more than forty feet away from me and he stared at me in obvious surprise. I glared at him and twirled my father's axe in my hand. Son Oriell, Lord Demay, and the man-at-arms with the full helm sat their horses beside Lord Corwick, but I only had eyes for him.

I pointed the axe. "You and me!" I shouted.

Lord Corwick leaned on the pommel of his saddle, looking amused as four Cardian archers moved into position thirty feet from me. "You're not worth the effort," Lord Corwick said with a chuckle. He gestured to Lord Demay. "Besides, I've promised you and your friends to Lord Demay and his Cardians, so, as much as I'd enjoy killing you myself, I'll leave you to them."

"You coward!" I screamed.

I raised my father's axe over my head and rushed toward Lord Corwick. My mind turned back ten years to another place and time when I'd done the same thing and I cursed the reeve who'd raped my sister and started all this. The Cardian archers raised their bows and I bellowed out my defiance, knowing what was coming just as Lord Demay gave a sharp command. The first arrow hit me in the shoulder, crashing into my armor with a thud and a jolt that spun me completely around, followed by another that impacted the back of my knee. I cried out and fell as two more arrows thudded into my back, one after the other like giant hammer blows. My hands weakened around the shaft of my father's axe and I felt it slide from my grip as I landed heavily face down in the dirt. My helmet flew off from the impact and I cursed, raging at the unfairness of it all as I struggled to push myself upright. The coppery taste of blood filled my mouth and I spit red wetness onto the ground, then turned and glanced back at Lord Corwick with hatred just as something hard and unyielding exploded against my temple. Then everything went black.

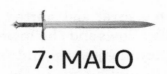

7: MALO

When I awoke, I found myself propped up with my back against the well in the inner bailey. Gandermen stood in a crowd near the cookhouse attached to the keep, where they milled about drinking from mugs as they cheered and laughed. Many of the men held torches in their hands, as darkness must have fallen at some point while I'd been unconscious. A Ganderman with a black beard and angry-looking face stood thirty feet from me holding a long spike in his right hand with a rectangular shield on his left arm. I blinked at him in confusion and he stared back at me for a moment, then looked away to peer over his shoulder at the throng of shouting men. Twisted shadows flitted across the rough, fire-lit stone of the keep above the heads of the Gandermen, and occasionally I caught a glimpse of stark white flesh struggling within their pressed ranks. I heard a feminine scream of anguish rise up from somewhere inside the group and I ground my teeth, pretty certain I knew what was happening. My head ached beyond belief and I shifted position, realizing that both my hands and feet were shackled with heavy irons attached to chains. I could move around if I chose, but bound the way I was, I probably wouldn't have been able to even walk upright, let alone do much else. I blinked repeatedly as I tried to focus, surprised that I was even alive at all.

"Thank The Mother, you're awake!" Baine said beside me with obvious relief. "I thought they'd killed you."

I glanced at my friend and saw that he was shackled like I was, though his right wrist looked swollen and bloody where the skin pushed against the rusted iron band holding him. Baine's legs were thrust out in front of him and I could see wetness shining all along his left trouser leg. Bits of stark white bone gleamed at me like twisted bloody teeth through a long tear in the cloth.

"What happened?" I managed to croak out. I shifted my body again against the well and then groaned as stabbing pain arced across my forehead.

"We lost," Baine replied, looking exhausted and deflated. He sighed heavily and then shrugged. "There were too many of the bastards, just like Jebido said."

I could hear the pain in Baine's voice and I nodded, not surprised by the answer. "Is Jebido all right?" I asked, afraid of the response.

"He's alive," Baine muttered, not sounding encouraged. He gestured to the other side of the well with his head. "He's lying here beside me. His eyes are closed and I can't get him to talk, but I can see his chest moving." Baine pointed to our guard with a finger from his good hand. "I asked that bastard over there to help him, but the stupid ox never talks or moves."

I lay my head back against the rough stone of the well in relief. I had truly feared Jebido was dead. The pain across my forehead continued to pound away relentlessly and I could feel the same pain coming from both my knee and my back where I'd been struck. I frowned as I pictured the four Cardian archers drawing their bows and aiming at me. Though the areas where I'd been hit were painful, I knew from experience that metal barbs tearing through flesh and bone should feel ten times worse than what I was feeling now. I wondered how I was even alive at all, considering the last blow I'd taken to my temple.

"They used blunts," Baine said as if reading my thoughts. "They wanted us alive."

"Ah," I replied, understanding now.

Blunts were round, heavy wooden balls fitted to the shafts of arrows for use during practice or for striking down small game. Accuracy could sometimes be an issue with blunts, but a target that was only thirty feet away like I had been would be well within their effective range. I realized that the short distance would also explain why the impact had been so devastating, despite my armor.

Smoke was rising in lazy tendrils from several of the buildings along the curtain walls, though the flames had been extinguished some time ago. Lifeless bodies lay strewn all about the bailey and I realized that many of the corpses were headless. I glanced up, feeling sick to my stomach as I saw a long line of shadowy severed heads jammed onto the pointed battlements of the northern wall. Even in the semi-darkness I recognized Eriz and Gadest and many of the other Piths that I'd come to know in the last year. I saw old Josphet's head and some of the Gander slaves as well and I looked away bitterly.

There was a sudden break in the crowd of men in front of me, momentarily revealing four naked women tied face down over a line of barrels. One of the women was Padrea and I hissed in anger as the opening in the throng abruptly closed, hiding the women from my view. A long wail of pain rose from within the crowded men and I shuddered, wondering what could make a Pith make that terrible sound. Throughout my life, one constant that has stuck with me is my absolute loathing of anyone who would commit the sin of rape, be they Piths, Gandermen, or anyone else. There is nothing more vile or repugnant than a man taking that which is not offered.

"I'll kill the bastards!" Baine hissed beside me. He wrestled with the bonds around his wrists, crying out at the pain but tugging at them anyway with a fierce look of determination on his face. Our guard didn't seem overly alarmed by Baine's actions and finally he grunted and gestured at Baine with his pike to stop what he was doing. Baine quit struggling and he glowered at the guard as he fell back against the well with his chest heaving.

"They'll pay for this," I said softly as I tried to console my friend. Our silent guard turned his attention back to the action behind him and I met Baine's eyes. "The Mother and The Father will see to that. Mark my words."

Baine slowly shook his head. Deep black circles of pain

The Wolf At Large

stained the skin beneath his eyes and I could see despair welling up within their depths. "I don't think They're on our side anymore, Hadrack," he whispered.

The doors to the keep swung open just then and Lord Corwick appeared, followed by another man with long grey hair tied back and a thick grey beard that covered most of his cheeks. I could hear laughter and singing coming through the open doors from inside the great hall as I studied the two men. The bearded man wore full armor and had a full-faced helmet tucked under his arm. I saw that my father's axe was lying across his back and I growled in anger as Lord Corwick walked down the ramp toward us. The lord was wearing dark leather boots with metal clasps down each side. He'd removed his armor and helmet at some point, wearing only a fine leather jerkin over a rich tunic. A long sword was belted around his waist and I saw when he turned to nod a greeting to our guard that the head of a short sword lay sheathed at the small of his back. Lord Corwick stopped several feet in front of me and stroked his blond beard as he studied me, then finally grunted and knelt on his haunches. He casually picked up a small stone from the ground and began to flick it from one hand to the other while the bearded man stood behind him watching.

"That was rather foolish, charging at us like that," Lord Corwick said. He held the rock up and studied it critically in the torchlight for a moment, then turned his eyes to me. "What exactly was the point of that?"

"The point was to kill you, you bastard," I replied.

Lord Corwick chuckled. "Yes, well, that didn't exactly turn out as planned, now did it?"

"Because you're a coward," I grunted at him with disgust. "You always get others to do your dirty work for you."

"Sometimes it's better that way," Lord Corwick said with a shrug. He didn't seem bothered in the least by my insult. "Actually, you should be thanking me. If I'd taken you up on your offer, you'd be dead right now, rather than," he paused and smiled humorlessly, "soon to be dead." Lord Corwick glanced briefly at Baine, then turned back to me. "So tell me, are you really Alwin of Corwick's son?"

"This again?" I snorted as I looked to the darkened sky. "Why would I lie about it?" I fixed my gaze on the lord, feeling my features twist with loathing and contempt for him. "Does it frighten you that much that I know what kind of man you really are?"

"Hardly," Lord Corwick said. "But just the same, I'm curious to know if you speak the truth about who you are." He leaned forward. "So humor me, if you will. If you are truly the son of Alwin, then you were in Corwick and will know how he died."

"I do," I said tightly, trying not to let my anger get the best of me.

"So how did he die?" Lord Corwick prompted.

"You already know that, you bastard!" I spit back. "You were there!"

"Yes," Lord Corwick agreed. "I was. But Jebido was there too, so he could have told you about certain things." Lord Corwick flicked the stone in the air casually and then caught it. "But he didn't see everything. So, if you are who you say, then you will know what he does not." He leaned forward and his eyes shone with interest and, I was surprised to see, perhaps a shade of worry. "Tell me exactly what happened to your father."

I had no idea why Lord Corwick seemed so threatened by me. After all, even if I had been there, from his point of view I was still just a peasant and nothing I could ever say against him would be believed by anyone who mattered. I thought of Daughter Gernet and her obvious interest in me and felt a sudden doubt rise in me. Maybe there was more to this than I realized? But, even if there were, I decided I wanted Lord Corwick to know the truth, if for no other reason than it seemed to make him uncomfortable.

I cleared my throat, collecting my thoughts as I tried to ignore my aching head. "After you came back from seeing the reeve's body," I paused and looked mockingly at Lord Corwick. "I mean, your brother's body." I saw Lord Corwick's eyes turn hard with anger and I grinned, pleased that I'd gotten to him. "After you saw your brother lying dead in the mud, my father tried to speak with you. Searl Merk and Hape were on either side of him and Merk told my father to be quiet and go join the other villagers. When my father refused, Merk killed him."

"How?" Lord Corwick growled at me. "How did he die?"

My grin faltered and I looked down at the ground, swallowing bitterly as I pictured the day again in my mind. "The bastard chopped his head off," I whispered. I looked up at Lord Corwick in defiance. "I watched everything from the bog and hid there all night, waiting for your men to leave. When I came out the next morning, I found someone had stuck my father's head on a fence board. I was just a boy, and because of you I had to bury my sister and my father that day. None of those people in Corwick had done anything wrong, but you didn't care." I took a deep breath, then let it out loudly. "I made a vow to my family that I'd avenge them for what your men did in Corwick, and I won't rest until that vow has been honored!"

"Well," Lord Corwick finally said when I'd finished. "Those are mighty brave words coming from someone in your unenviable position." He flicked the stone in his hand aside and then grinned at me. "I guess that settles it then. You are Alwin's son." He glanced over his shoulder to his companion. "The Mother and The Father must have a sense of humor, eh old friend?"

"Indeed They do," the bearded man said in a voice that I will never forget as long as I live. He moved forward and stared down at me with a look of contempt covering his ugly features. "I stuck your father's head on that board myself, and I would have enjoyed adding yours. You're lucky you got away from us."

My skin went cold as I looked up into the eyes of Quant Ranes, the leader of the nine. He looked different with the beard and long hair, but his voice and eyes were impossible to forget. My mind went blank and I roared with rage as I went for Ranes' throat, forgetting everything but the need to kill him. Lord Corwick flinched in surprise and fell backward as I jumped to my feet, but I ignored the fallen lord and reached for Ranes with my hands hooked like claws. I saw the guard's jaw drop open in shock, but he was too far away to do anything but watch. The shackles around my ankles were separated by a chain no more than four inches long, which was then connected to the shackles around my wrists. As I rushed forward and tried to lift my arms, the chains pulled on each other and I immediately tripped, losing my balance before falling hard on my face. I spit dirt out of my mouth, cursing Ranes as I struggled to my knees just as I felt the sharp, almost gentle touch of an axe blade at the back of my neck. I froze, breathing heavily with pain and anger.

"I always wanted this axe," Ranes hissed in my ear. I could smell his fetid breath wafting around me as he chuckled. "I never should have allowed Merk to keep it, but I got sick of listening to his whining and finally let him have it." He ran the blade gently along the skin of my neck. "So tell me, son of Alwin, how exactly did you manage to steal it from him?"

I didn't answer and Ranes pressed down harder with the axe. I could feel the steel biting into my flesh, drawing blood, and I had a sudden vision of the fight with Searl Merk during the Bridge Battle. I'd come close to dying that day, but in the end, I'd lived and Merk had not. I focused on that. Somehow, I'd find a way to get out of this, and when I did, Quant Ranes would pay just like Merk had.

"I didn't steal it," I finally said, ignoring the cold blade now as I glared up at Ranes. "I killed the bastard and took it from him! Just like I'm going to do to you, too!"

Quant Ranes' eyebrows rose and he grinned yellow teeth at me through his beard. "Is that so?" he said. "So you snuck up on Searl in some trash-filled alley and stabbed him in the back, did you?" I didn't bother to respond. Let the bastard think what he wanted to. "No matter," Ranes said as he lifted the head of the axe away from my neck. "He was a drunken fool most of the time anyway." Ranes laughed and put his booted foot on my shoulder and shoved hard, knocking me from my knees to the ground. "Crawl back to where you came from, worm."

I dragged myself across the ground back to the well, then pushed myself up against it beside Baine. My friend and I shared a long look and I could see the anger and frustration brimming in his dark eyes.

"So," Lord Corwick said as he again knelt in front of me. This time he held his short sword in his right hand, which he made sure to show me. He pointed the tip of it toward Baine. "Do that again and I'll cut your friend's nose off. Understand?" I took a deep breath, then nodded. "Very good," the lord said as he sheathed his sword behind his back. "Let's try to be civil, shall we?" He studied me for a time, then shook his head. "Your being alive complicates things." He sighed and ran his fingers through his thick blond hair. "I really should just kill you and be done with it, you know."

"Why don't you then!?" I snapped angrily.

Lord Corwick spread his hands out to either side. "Because I made a deal with Lord Demay and his Cardians," he said, "and, as you've no doubt heard, I'm an honorable man." I just snorted at that and Lord Corwick grinned lopsidedly at me. "Of course, at the time of the bargain I just thought I was giving up the king's reward for you three to get the Cardians valuable assistance. Had I known the son of Alwin was one of the traitors in Gasterny, I would never have agreed to it."

"We should slit his throat now while we have the chance," Ranes growled as he looked over his shoulder at the guard. "The Cardians might be mad as hornets at first, but they'll get over it."

"While I do tend to agree with your assessment, dear Quant," Lord Corwick said, "the fact of the matter is I still need Demay and his Cardians and have no desire to anger them right now."

"Then cover the reward," Ranes said with a shrug, "and kill them all and be done with it."

Lord Corwick chuckled. "And halve my treasury over it? I have a war to fight, as you might recall, and the reward for these three is quite substantial. The Cardians smell opportunity and money like a dog smells a rat, and I have no doubt they'd expect me to pay even more for the traitors once they realize my interest." Lord Corwick shook his head. "No, that won't do."

"Then just pay the reward for him and let the Cardians collect on the other two. They mean nothing."

"Not true," Lord Corwick said as he rubbed his chin thoughtfully. "The captain was there as well, as you recall."

Ranes sighed in frustration and flicked his eyes to the far side of the well where Jebido lay, then he glanced back. "By the looks of him, I doubt he'll even make it past tonight anyway."

"Why don't you take these off me and let the two of us decide this," I growled as I shook my bound hands and gestured at Ranes with my chin. "If he wins, your problem is solved. If I win, you let us go."

Lord Corwick laughed deeply, looking genuinely amused. "You are a game one, son of Alwin. I'll grant you that." He stood up and put his hands on his hips. "But I think after today the Cardians have earned the right to claim the full reward." He glanced at Ranes. "Even if the boy talks and Jebido lives to back up his story, no one will believe a peasant and a deserter anyway."

Ranes shrugged. "If that is your will, my lord, then so be it." He gestured to me with the axe. "But you have enemies that would jump at the chance to use him to discredit you."

Lord Corwick patted Ranes on the shoulder. "I'm quite sure I'm aware of that, my friend. The risk is minimal at best. My enemies have nothing but suspicions and whispered rumors and the boy's presence here will add nothing to any of it.

In a few days his neck will be stretched by a rope and the matter will be settled. So, until then, why don't you stick to doing what you do best, which is killing, and I'll stick to doing what I do best, which is everything else."

"Of course, my lord," Ranes said as his face clouded.

The doors to the keep crashed open again and this time Lord Demay walked through, stopping and swaying drunkenly at the top of the ramp. "Here's another one for the walls!" he shouted as he held up a severed head by its long blonde hair. He shook it for the massed men to see, then tossed it dismissively onto the ramp. "She moaned like a whore the entire time!"

The crowd of Gandermen cheered as the head began to roll down the incline of the ramp and I had a sudden, sickening feeling I knew who it belonged to. Lord Demay lifted a mug in salute to his men, then drained it and belched loudly before he turned and walked unsteadily back into the keep. The bloodied blonde head twirled and bounced wetly along the stone as it came spinning down the ramp. Finally it smacked into the base of the wall near the bottom and then rolled out onto the dusty ground, stopping five feet from where Baine and I sat in horrified silence. I stared at Ania's slack face and dead eyes, having known in my gut that it would be her, but hoping somehow that I would be proved wrong. I looked away and stared at my feet bitterly as Lord Corwick knelt in front of me again.

"You should have stayed in that bog," he said to me with a wink. He shrugged and stood up. "Too late now."

Lord Corwick turned and he and Quant strode up the ramp and disappeared inside the keep as despair welled up inside me. Seeing Ania's head thrown aside like rubbish had taken what little strength and hope I had left inside me and squashed it. I turned at the sound of riders and watched with an almost morbid detachment as Carbet and four other Cardians appeared through the inner gate. An open wagon pulled by two matching black horses and driven by a fat man with a bushy black beard and bored, compassionless eyes followed the Cardians through the gate. The wagon stopped ten feet from where we lay by the well and Carbet smirked down at me from his big horse. I didn't fail to notice that he had my sword strapped around his waist.

"On your feet, maggots!" the Cardian finally grunted.

I glared up at Carbet and cautiously stood up, then turned and helped Baine to his feet, taking as much of my friend's weight as I possibly could. Several of the Cardians dismounted at a gesture from Carbet and they cut Baine's and my armor and clothing away from us with their short swords. Once we were naked and shivering in the cool evening air, they took our shackles off, ignoring Baine's gasp of pain as they prodded us toward the wagon with the tips of their swords. Three flat cages sat lined up in a row on the floor of the wagon directly behind the fat driver.

I glanced at Ania's head lying discarded in the dirt, feeling a deep sadness overcome me when I realized her greatest fear had just come to pass. She, like all the Piths who'd died in Gasterny, would not have a Pathfinder to help them ascend to the Master now. They would be condemned to spend all of eternity searching for the right path on their own. I cradled the Pair Stone in my hand and prayed to the First Pair to let the Sword of the King return quickly and avenge them. A Cardian with bushy eyebrows and a pock-marked face poked me in the back with his sword and growled at me to get moving. I glared at the man and considered taking his sword from him and shoving it up his ass, but I knew if I did that Baine and Jebido would pay for it along with me. I turned away reluctantly and helped Baine up into the bed of the wagon, lifting him as gently as I could. I tried not to focus on his deathly white face as an ugly Cardian with the tip of his nose missing indicated the middle cage. I lifted the cage door open and helped Baine lie down inside it as he hissed air between his teeth in pain.

The Cardian locked Baine inside the cage, then gestured to me. "Now you," he said gruffly as he pointed to the cage beside Baine's.

I squeezed myself in, lying on my side as I tried to fight my growing fear and hopelessness and failing miserably at it as the Cardian locked me in. The Cardians then went to fetch Jebido and they stripped his limp body before dragging him moaning to the wagon, where they tossed him inside the last cage.

"Let's move!" Carbet ordered once the Cardians had re-mounted.

The fat driver whistled at his horses and I heard a whip hiss through the air as it snapped harshly against flesh. We began to move, while behind me I could still hear the cheers coming from the victorious Gandermen and the occasional cries of pain coming from the female Piths being raped. I thought of Ania and Eriz and all the others who'd died and I closed my eyes as a single tear trickled slowly down my cheek. I felt a sudden, overwhelming need to scream my rage and anguish at the sky and I clamped my hand over my mouth, suppressing it. Baine was listening beside me, I knew, and I couldn't let him hear me. I would be strong for him and Jebido, I vowed to myself. I clung to that vow desperately as we passed beneath the ravaged walls of the defeated garrison, through the barbican, and finally crossed over the drawbridge into open country. No matter what happened, I had to be strong.

I guessed the iron cage I was crammed into was no more than two-and-a-half-feet high, three feet wide, and perhaps four feet long. I believe it had at one time been intended to transport chickens, but now had a much more sinister purpose. Today was the third day of our imprisonment, and in all that time I had barely been able to move a muscle. Because of my size, I was forced to lie on my side with my knees bent to my chest and my right shoulder jammed painfully into the top of the cage. The three of us were being transported northwest to Calban Castle in the open wagon, which had sun-bleached floorboards, crooked sidewalls, and a squeaky back wheel that was maddening in its repetition. My cage sat against the right sidewall of the wagon and I lay facing away from my friends, unable to even turn my head to check on them. All I could see were the faded and scuffed planks in front of me and blurred flashes of green through a knothole in one of the boards. I could hear Baine moaning softly to himself behind me from time to time, but I could only lie there in silence and listen helplessly to his pain. The Cardians were riding on either side of the wagon watching us and they would get quite angry if we spoke.

I was naked, filthy, thirsty, and hungry, but despite my situation, all I could think about were my friends. Baine had a broken leg, and possibly a broken wrist, judging by the swelling I'd seen at Gasterny. But it was Jebido that I was the most concerned about. The Cardians usually left us to ourselves after we made camp and Baine had managed to get a few words out of Jebido that first night, but he'd been silent ever since then. Jebido's wound had been bound by the Cardians, which I was grateful for, but none of us had been given any water or food since the journey had begun. I had pleaded with Carbet more than once to at least give Jebido some water, but the Cardian refused each time. Carbet had described it as a waste of resources, since, according to him, Baine, Jebido and I only had to be breathing, even if just a little, for them to claim the reward for us. I had pointed out that without water, the chances were good that Jebido would die well before then, but Carbet had seemed unimpressed.

It was well past noon on our third day of travel and above me the skies were becoming grey and threatening, with a cold wind blowing from the north that left me shivering uncontrollably. Carbet rode in the lead and the other four Cardians — each of whom had the same polished pointy boots and churlish attitude as their leader — continued to ride beside the wagon. I was quickly beginning to understand Jebido's disdain for the Cardians and I wondered if their women were just as unpleasant as the men. The fat driver, whose name was Faldir, and who never seemed to speak, guided the wagon northwest along dusty roads, forest lanes and open fields. Somewhere along the coast lay Calban Castle, where, Carbet had told me, we'd be stopping for a short time before heading north to Gandertown and a date with the king's executioner. I thought of Shana and how she'd been abducted from the garrison right under our noses and I wondered if she would be at the castle when we arrived. Part of me was hoping she would be so I could at least see her one last time, but another part of me hoped she wouldn't, as I didn't want her to see me in this state.

I prayed to Mother Above for rain as we plodded onward beneath the threatening skies, willing to put up with cold rain in exchange for easing my swollen lips, dry mouth and ravaged throat. I managed to clasp the Pair Stone with my left hand where it lay near my chest on the cage floor and, like I had many times since the journey had begun, I squeezed it as I prayed. Carbet had taken my sword for his own, but he had surprisingly left the Pair Stone around my neck, which was the only kindness I'd ever get from that bastard. A fat, cold droplet of rain splattered against my forehead and I blinked up at the sky as several more drops fell on my face. I groaned in anticipation as I eagerly tipped my head back as far as I could against the top of the cage, then opened my mouth and extended my swollen tongue. The rain began to fall heavier, soaking me and I started to laugh like a drunken fool; though the laughter came out as more of a croak than anything else. The rain soon coated the numb dryness of my mouth and throat and for the first time in days, I felt some sense of strength and even hope returning to me. I heard Faldir curse under his breath at the cold rain, the first words I'd heard from the man. I ignored him and greedily sucked in as much of the life-giving water as I could while fat, heavy drops plopped wetly against the wood around me.

The sky continued to grow darker and the wind began to pick up as the rain started coming down almost sideways, driven along by the strengthening gale. I turned my head away from the rain, my thirst sated now as I clasped my arms around my chest as best I could, trying to protect myself against the driving water that pounded and stung my flesh. Lightning flashed overhead, cutting through the thick black cloud cover that roiled above me as a mighty boom of thunder crashed, shaking the ground. Leaves, small twigs and even several pine-cones blew against my cage, rattling the bars.

"Faldir!" I heard Carbet shout above the wind. "Pull off the road up ahead!"

Faldir's whip snapped in response and the wagon immediately lurched sideways as we left the road. The cages bounced and shifted crazily with each bump, then we hit a deep rut that lifted my cage five inches off the floorboards before it came back down with a heavy thud. My cage pitched wildly across the planks, then came to a shuddering stop as it crashed hard against Baine's cage. I heard him cry out, whether in fear or pain, I couldn't tell.

"Baine!" I shouted as I lifted my head, ignoring the rain that pelted my unprotected face. "Are you all right?"

"Never better!" came back the weak reply. "But it's getting hard to sleep with all this commotion!"

I grinned despite myself and wrapped my hands around the iron bars tightly as our cages continued to bounce and slide wildly against each other. More lightning flashed above me just as something small and hard cracked painfully against my thigh. I grunted in surprise, then gasped as something caromed painfully off the bridge of my nose before dropping to the floor. I peered down at the small, frozen ball of ice lying near my face.

"Hail!" I whispered in awe.

My mother had told me about hail once, so I knew what it was, though, truth be told I'd thought she'd made it up as

I'd never actually seen it until now. I glanced upward unconsciously, realizing too late that it was a mistake as more hail fell, clattering loudly against the floorboards and striking my flesh with meaty smacks. I turned away and covered my head with my hands as best I could, helpless to do anything else but try to wait it out. I could hear the Cardians shouting to each other above the shrieking wind as my cage continued to slide back and forth inside the wagon. The hail began to subside just as we reached the protection of some trees, though the wind still raged and the rain continued unabated. I cautiously lifted my hands from my head and looked around.

"Baine?" I called.

"Still here!"

"Jebido?" I asked.

"All right as far as I can tell!" Baine shouted back just as thunder erupted above us, rocking the wagon.

The Cardians had found a good-sized woodland, which offered us some protection from the raging storm, though even the branches of the trees over our heads were not enough to shield us completely from the driving rain. We plodded along for several minutes through semi-darkness before finally we came to a halt beneath a network of gloomy, widespread branches supported by a gnarled, moss-covered trunk of an ancient oak tree. I was cold and miserable and could feel tiny welts rising all along the top of my body and across the back of my head and face. I was beginning to regret my earlier wish for rain as my teeth chattered and I shivered uncontrollably. Carbet shouted at his men to make camp as thunder continued to rumble around us, shaking the ground. Though it was still dark outside from the storm, I knew it was only a little past mid-day and I was surprised that we were stopping for the day rather than sitting and waiting out the weather.

Faldir noisily unhooked the horses from the wagon and then guided them away from us while above me the branches were suddenly lit up by a flash of lightning, casting peculiar-looking shadows that danced and twisted among the leaves.

For the moment we were left alone and even though I had tried many times before and knew it was hopeless, I pushed hard against the top of the cage with my shoulder, ignoring the discomfort as the bars pressed against the welts on my flesh. The cage lock, though rusty in places, was made of forged iron and was shaped like a heart, with a thick, u-shaped shackle that passed through a plate that connected the door to the cage. The lock and plate screeched in protest as I pushed, but like every other time before it, it refused to budge. I cursed under my breath, about to try a second time when I suddenly froze. A man wearing a dark green cloak with the hood pulled low over his face and dripping rainwater was peering down at me from over the sidewall of the wagon. His features were cast in deep shadow from the darkness enveloping us and all I could see of him was a bushy, wet black beard and thin lips pressed tightly together. I opened my mouth to say something and the man shook his head and put a finger to his mouth just as thunder boomed again above us. The hooded man took a quick glance over his shoulder, then he turned back to me with a short sword held in his right hand.

"What are you doing?" I whispered as the thunder rolled away, not sure if I should feel afraid or hopeful at the man's presence.

"What does it look like?" the man muttered back in a gruff voice.

The hooded man lifted the sword and stuck the point in the keyhole of the lock, turning it back and forth for at least a minute — a minute that seemed an eternity to me — before, with a sudden click, the shackle snapped open. Rain continued to fall on us as the hooded man fumbled with the wet lock, before finally he got it off and tossed it aside. He carefully lifted the door of my cage open, then lowered it down gently until it lay on top of Baine's cage.

"Hadrack, what's going on?" Baine hissed from behind me.

I ignored my friend and stared at the hooded man, still

trying to comprehend what was happening. I fought to pull myself to a sitting position, but I'd been lying the same way for almost three days and my limbs wouldn't cooperate. Finally I gave up and fell back weakly in the cage as huge raindrops rolling off the leaves above my head struck me repeatedly in the face.

"Take a moment," the hooded man told me. "Your muscles are all seized up. They'll return once the blood flow starts again." He balanced the short sword across the top of my cage within easy reach of my hand. "When you're ready to fight, come and join me." He removed his hood for just a moment, revealing a handsome face of thirty or so with a finely chiseled nose, thick, curly black hair and dark-brown eyes. He grinned at me as he replaced the hood. "Assuming of course there are any of them left to fight."

The hooded man turned to go and I called out, "Wait! Who are you?" I struggled to lift my arms and grasp the top of the cage as the man came back.

"The name is Malo," he replied. A shout of discovery rose from the Cardians and Malo looked over his shoulder, then turned back to me, looking remarkably relaxed. "All you need to know right now is that I work for a friend of yours." Malo drew his long sword and placed the hilt against his lips and kissed it before he whirled around and disappeared from my view.

"Hadrack!" Baine called. "What's happening? Who was that?"

"A friend here to help, I think," I said as I concentrated on making my body move.

I clamped my teeth together and forced first one hand, then the other onto the frame at the top of the cage, then groaning with effort, I pulled my body up to a sitting position. I sat there for a moment, fighting to regain my breath as fire swept all along my limbs. Finally I turned my head to look at Baine and my breath caught in my throat. My friend had always been slight, but now he looked as thin and shriveled as a corpse left out in the sun except for his left leg, which was black and swollen to three times its normal size. I felt a thud in my gut when I saw thick green and yellow mucus oozing from his shin. Our eyes met and Baine must have seen the shock in my eyes, because he just shrugged and smiled weakly.

"Mother Above!" I said. "Why didn't you tell me?"

"What could you have done?"

I grasped the short sword and pulled myself up to my knees. "I'm getting you out of there!"

Baine waved his good arm to his right. "Jebido first. He's worse than me."

I nodded and glanced at Jebido's cage. My friend was lying on his back with his eyes closed and I could see hundreds of welts crisscrossing his flesh. The Cardians had wound cloth around Jebido's chest not long after we'd left Gasterny, but part of it had come loose, revealing a swathe of red, angry-looking skin surrounding a blood-encrusted hole just below his left nipple. Jebido's chest was still moving, which could only be viewed as some kind of miracle after what he'd been through these last three days. I grasped the Pair Stone around my neck and said a quick prayer of thanks to the First Pair for watching over my friends, while behind me I heard shouts and the clash of metal on metal. Malo was surrounded by the Cardians, I saw as I turned, who were taunting him as first one, then another of them took tentative swipes with their swords at the hooded man. Malo appeared calm and relaxed, and though he was a big man, he seemed to move with the grace and agility of a much smaller person as he easily parried their attempts. For just a moment there I could have even sworn he was smiling beneath his hood. I noticed Faldir stood off to the side watching impassively with the same bored expression he'd had on his face for the last three days as thunder boomed once again above us.

"There's too many of them for just one man," I said to Baine as I struggled to stand upright. "I have to help Malo first."

"Go then," Baine said weakly as he nodded. He wrapped

the fingers of his good hand around one of the cage bars and stared up at me. "Kill the bastards, Hadrack!" he whispered fiercely. "You make sure you kill every one of them, and then you come back for us! You hear me?"

"I hear you!" I growled.

I forced myself to my feet, wobbling uncertainly as I gripped the short sword tightly in my right hand. Then I turned, groaning as I lifted one leg up and over the cage and placed it on the floorboards before I grabbed the sidewall and hauled myself forward. My muscles felt on fire and I could feel a strange tingle all along my limbs, yet despite my need, my body wouldn't do what my mind was telling it to. Instead of standing outside the cage by the sidewall like I'd intended, I found myself suddenly pitching forward, unable to support my weight with my arms. My knees scraped against the heavy planks of the wagon and I cried out helplessly as I flipped over the sidewall and fell heavily to the ground. I landed on my side and felt the wind rush out of my lungs as the short sword went spinning out of my grasp to land three feet in front of me. I stared groggily at the sword lying in the rain-soaked grass, fighting to breathe, then shifted my gaze to Malo and the Cardians.

Two of the Cardians were down, I was shocked to see. I watched in fascinated awe despite my situation as Malo twirled and spun within the surviving Cardians' midst, moving faster than any man I'd ever seen before. The Cardians were shouting at each other in confusion, their voices sounding panicked as they desperately tried to bring the hooded man down. But it seemed wherever the Cardians struck, Malo was gone, only to appear somewhere else and they began to curse in growing frustration. Another Cardian fell to Malo's sword as I weakly pushed myself onto my hands and knees. I saw that only Carbet and the Cardian with the tip of his nose missing were left and I reached for the short sword, cursing my weakness as my arm shook like an old man's. Malo brushed Carbet and the other man back, parrying both their blades in a dizzying display, then whirled and lashed out with his foot, catching Carbet in the stomach and knocking him to the ground. I saw Wolf's Head clutched in Carbet's hand and I growled with hatred for the man as I wrapped my hand around the hilt of the short sword and drew it to me. Malo and the man with the missing nose tip were exchanging blows back and forth across the ground, until finally, the hooded man dropped to one knee to avoid a slash, then lashed out with his sword, hamstringing his opponent. The Cardian wailed in pain just as Malo thrust upwards, punching through armor and impaling the man's chest with his sword. Malo's hood had fallen back and I saw him smile grimly at the man writhing on the end of his sword, while behind him Carbet rose to his feet and stalked toward him.

"Behind you!" I managed to croak in warning.

Malo glanced over his shoulder as he tugged at his sword, then I saw his face fall. His blade was stuck in the Cardian's ribs! Jebido had warned me repeatedly about just this sort of thing happening during a battle, and it's why he'd always advised me to slash with a long sword if you could, rather than stab. Carbet howled in triumph when he realized Malo's predicament and he lashed out with Wolf's Head just as Malo released the hilt of his sword and rolled sideways out of the way. The blade swished harmlessly over Malo's head and Carbet cursed loudly even as he bounded after his opponent. Malo came out of his roll to land on the balls of his feet in a crouch and he waited as Carbet cautiously advanced on him.

"I don't know who you are, you bastard!" Carbet said, breathing heavily as he lifted Wolf's Head and aimed the tip at Malo's throat. "But your head is mine now."

I could still feel weakness in my arms and legs and I knew there was no chance I could make it to Carbet in time. I looked down at the short sword in my hand, then flipped it so I held the point first. Baine had taught me how to throw a knife while in Gasterny, and though I couldn't come close to matching what he could do, I did seem to have a bit of a knack for it.

I'd never tried throwing something as heavy as a short sword, of course, but I knew it was either that or Malo would die. I just hoped the muscles in my right arm wouldn't let me down. I drew back the sword, trying not to think about my shaking arm as it protested, then, saying a silent prayer to the First Pair, I threw. The blade twirled end over end, cutting through the rain as lightning flashed, lighting up the woods. Something must have warned Carbet of his danger, for he turned at the last moment to stare at me in surprise just as the short sword caught him in the left shoulder. Carbet was wearing a breastplate over a mail tunic and the sword sliced easily through the mail, spinning the Cardian around, though he still had the presence of mind to hold onto my sword. Malo instantly dashed forward and snatched Wolf's Head from Carbet's hand, while at the same time kicking the Cardian's feet out from under him. Carbet cried out and fell heavily to the ground as Malo quickly reversed Wolf's Head and stabbed downward into the Cardian's eye. I saw Carbet's body jerk several times as blood sprayed into the air, then he lay still as Malo slowly drew my sword from the dead man and turned to face me. He lifted Wolf's Head to me in salute, then paused to wick rain from his face with the sleeve of his cloak before he bent and wiped the blade clean on Carbet's corpse.

"Stay where you are," Malo said, glancing at Faldir, who hadn't moved or changed his expression during the entire battle. Faldir merely nodded as Malo pulled his short sword from the Cardian's shoulder. He carefully cleaned it, then returned the sword to its sheath as he moved to stand above me. "A fine weapon," Malo said as he held the sword up and examined it. He twirled it in his hand and held it out to me, hilt first. "I believe this belongs to you."

8: HALHAVEN

Seeing that bastard Carbet get what he deserved seemed to snap my muscles out of whatever had been holding them back. Malo was having a tough time getting the other cage locks to open with his blade like he had mine, so at his request, I began searching the bodies of the dead Cardians for the keys. I finally found those keys tucked away in Carbet's pocket and, once we had the locks off, Malo and I lifted Jebido out first, then Baine and we laid them carefully on the floor at the back the wagon. I asked Malo again why he had helped us, but other than repeating that he worked for a friend of mine, he remained tight-lipped about it. For the life of me I couldn't imagine who he could be talking about and the one or two-word answers he offered when I pressed him on it did nothing to help enlighten me. He did tell me that this friend was anxious to see me and that we'd have to travel for the rest of the day and through the night to get there. He also told me that there would be medical help for Baine and Jebido when we arrived, which was all the reason I needed to agree to go with him. I noticed Faldir standing in the rain watching us with his bored, expressionless eyes and I wondered why he hadn't run away by now, or for that matter, been allowed to live at all. Malo ignored the driver, however, and he knelt between Jebido and Baine to examine their wounds while I threw the cages off the wagon and began to fashion a thick bed of soft fir branches in their place.

"Will I lose the leg?" Baine asked, trying to look brave and not quite pulling it off as Malo prodded gently with his fingertip at the foul-smelling limb.

"Don't know," Malo finally said with a shrug. "Time will tell." Malo found some rope in the wagon and got me to hack off two stout branches with my sword, each about two feet in length. He placed the branches and rope beside Baine's broken leg and looked up at me. "I'll need you to hold him," he said. I put my hands on Baine's shoulders uncertainly and Malo shook his head. "Not like that. Put your arms around his chest and pull him into you. Don't let go no matter what." I nodded and did as he said while Malo put both his hands around Baine's foot. "This is going to hurt," he warned. Baine signaled he understood, his face set in a deathly-white mask of dread as Malo took a deep breath, then pulled hard on Baine's foot. My friend screamed and I hugged him to me as he thrashed in agony while Malo turned his foot and pulled his ankle at the same time. Dark green pus and yellow mucus mixed with blood erupted from Baine's shin and I gagged at the fetid odor. Malo didn't seem bothered by the smell, however, and he continued the pressure on Baine's leg as my friend wailed in torment. Finally I saw the shards of white bone that had been jutting out of Baine's leg slowly slip back inside the ravaged skin. "There," Malo said as Baine collapsed against me and sobbed softly in my arms. "Almost over now." Malo looked up at me. "Come here and hold his leg in this position." I gently laid Baine down, then moved to his foot and held it as lightly as I could while Malo quickly and efficiently placed the wood on each side of the break and then tied them securely with the rope. When he was finished, he pointed to Baine's injured wrist. "Now we do that. Can you move your fingers?"

"You're joking, right?" Baine managed to gasp as he blinked away tears. "Can you give me a moment?"

"No," Malo grunted. Baine stared at Malo angrily and then finally snorted as he lifted his injured hand off of his chest. He stared at his hand with a look of intense concentration on his face and I sighed with relief when he finally managed to wiggle his fingers just a little. "Well, that's something at least," Malo muttered. He turned to Jebido. "Now this one." Malo inspected Jebido's wound, pursing his lips as he felt Jebido's forehead, before finally he nodded to me that he'd seen enough. The two of us moved Baine and Jebido onto the bedding I'd made and when we were done, Malo jumped down from the wagon and turned to look up at me. "I'll be back soon." He gestured behind him. "While I'm gone, scavenge what clothing you can from the dead for you and your friends." He glanced at Faldir. "And have him try to find some dry kindling to start a fire with. I'm going to need it." With that, Malo turned and disappeared into the forest.

"You heard the man!" I growled as I glanced over at Faldir, not even trying to hide the contempt I felt for him. "Start a fire."

Faldir wordlessly began searching for dry wood while I moved to the Cardian corpses and stripped them of their armor, clothing and weapons. I threw the items into three separate piles as rain fell on me in heavy drops from the drooping branches above my head. When I was finished, I started going through the wet clothes, selecting the best of the torn and bloody tunics and trousers. All of the soiled garments would be too big for Baine, I knew, but I also knew that oversized clothing was the least of his problems right now. Luckily for me, Carbet was almost as big as I was. Most of what he'd had on fit me, including his boots, though I wasn't overly thrilled about wearing them with their high tops and pointed toes. I dressed quickly, then put on Carbet's mail and armor, and even though I knew I looked like a filthy Cardian now, it still felt wonderful to be wearing armor again, even if the mail was bloodstained and had a slit in the shoulder.

By now Faldir had located enough reasonably dry kindling to get a weak fire going and I watched him as he blew on the flames while the wood smoked and crackled uncertainly. I belted Wolf's Head around my waist, then gathered the rest of the clothing I'd chosen for my friends and made my way over to the wagon. I crouched down beside Jebido and cautiously dressed him, careful not to brush his wounded side. My friend's skin was hot to the touch and he moaned several times while I worked, but as far as I could tell he remained unconscious the entire time. I put my hand on Jebido's shoulder once I was finished and closed my eyes.

"Please Mother, please Father," I whispered as I clutched the Pair Stone in my other hand. "You've kept him alive through so much already. Please don't choose to take him now. Baine and I need him."

"It's all right, Hadrack," Baine said when I was done. "There's nothing to worry about now. The worst is behind us. You'll see."

"Aren't you the optimistic one all of a sudden," I grunted as I moved to help Baine pull the tunic that I'd chosen for him over his head. I glanced at the bloodstained trousers I'd selected, then to Baine's splinted leg. I couldn't imagine trying to pull the trousers over that, even though they were several sizes too big.

"Forget it," Baine said, reading my thoughts. He held up his good hand, waving the sleeve of the tunic at me that extended several inches past his fingertips. "Let's just consider this thing a nightshirt and leave it at that, shall we? Besides, it makes it easier to take a piss."

I grinned at Baine, as always caught by surprise by my friend's good humor and spirit even in the toughest times. Malo reappeared as I helped Baine roll the sleeves of the tunic up leading a pretty brown mare and carrying several thick green plants with odd pointed leaves. Each shoot of the plant had a red berry the size of my thumbnail attached to the top. Malo tied his horse to the wagon and removed a battered tin bowl from his saddlebag, then moved to kneel by the sputtering fire. He removed the berries from one of the plants and dropped them to the ground, then started rolling the plant back and forth between his hands. I could smell a sudden, sharp odor rise up as small clumps of the plant fell into the bowl from between Malo's palms. I noticed the rain was tapering off now as the heavy gloom that had been hanging beneath the trees slowly began to lift.

"I need water," Malo muttered to me over his shoulder.

"What is that?" I asked as I jumped down from the

wagon to stand beside him.

"A poultice for your friends' wounds," he grunted. "Now get me water."

The Cardians had tethered their horses nearby when they'd begun to make camp and I went to them, choosing to search the saddlebags of Carbet's black stallion first. The horse rolled its eyes angrily at me and then pawed the ground, but quickly settled down when he seemed to realize I wasn't interested in riding him. I found several hunks of dried meat in the saddlebags and a waterskin tucked into one of the compartments. I hefted the waterskin, pleased to see that it was almost full as I worked to bite off a chunk of the meat into my suddenly salivating mouth. My stomach rumbled with greed as I chewed and I felt a jolt of energy jump along my limbs as I turned and hurried back to the fire.

"Pour some on top," Malo said without looking up at me as he lifted the bowl.

I pulled out the cork with my teeth and carefully did as he instructed and the plant particles began to instantly dissolve in the water. "What plant is that?" I asked as I spit the cork out. Growing up in Corwick, I'd thought I knew every plant there was, but this one was new to me.

"Goldenseal," Malo replied, sounding distracted. He lifted his hand and waved it abruptly. "That's enough water." Malo used the tip of his short-sword to stir the mixture, then placed the bowl on the ground as close to the fire as he could get it. "Get me some strips of cloth," Malo ordered. "The cleaner the better."

I nodded, still chewing on the tough, salty meat in my mouth as I glanced at the wagon. Baine had pulled himself up with his good arm to watch us and he was staring over the sidewall at me with a strange look on his face. I started guiltily, feeling my face turning red as I realized he was just as hungry as I was. I swallowed the last of what was in my mouth and threw the remaining piece of meat to him underhanded without thinking. I winced the moment I let it go, cursing myself for my stupidity, but Baine just stared up at the meat spinning through the air, then stabbed out with his good hand and snatched it as it started to sail over his head. He grinned and saluted me with the meat, then fell back against the bedding as he started to devour it. I returned to the pile of clothing and routed through it, tearing off a piece here and there until I had six good-sized strips that seemed relatively free of blood and filth.

"Good," Malo said when I offered them to him. He took one of the strips and wound it around his hand, then grabbed the hot bowl and stood up. I glanced in the bowl and wrinkled my nose at the thick green paste that was giving off a noxious odor. "It smells like the inside of a leper's arse," Malo grunted, "but there's nothing better in the world for sucking out infection than goldenseal." He glanced at the cloth in my hands. "Give me those. I'll do what I can for your friends. In the meantime, you and Faldir hook up the horses to the wagon. I want to be on the road as soon as I'm finished binding their wounds."

I glanced at Faldir. "Why do we need him?" I demanded. "That bastard is just as bad as the Cardians and I can drive the wagon."

Malo shrugged. "Undoubtedly true on both counts. But since he's the one who left a trail behind for me to find, I think he deserves a little appreciation for his effort." Malo lifted an eyebrow to me. "Don't you?"

I looked at Faldir in surprise and I could have sworn that for just a moment I saw the fat man's mouth twitch in a faint smile.

"Why would he do that?" I asked, turning back to Malo.

"That's between him and Mother Above," Malo replied. He winked at me. "And our mutual friend, of course."

I didn't bother asking Malo who he was talking about, since I knew he wouldn't tell me anyway, so I just nodded to him and walked away. I helped Faldir hook the horses back up to the wagon and he and I worked silently, though I could tell by the other man's body language that he was amused by what had happened. I was still distrustful of Faldir, but admittedly my animosity toward him had been tempered somewhat by what Malo had just told me. By the time the horses were hooked up to the wagon, Malo had spread the hot goldenseal paste on to three strips of cloth and pressed them against Jebido and Baine's wounds before wrapping them tightly with the remaining strips.

"It's not perfect," Malo told me after he was finished. "I don't have any wheat meal or pig's lard, which would help, but it should be enough to draw out some of the infection until we can get them to the healer."

Malo instructed me to select one of the Cardians' horses for myself and set the others free. I decided that Carbet's big black stallion appeared to be the best horse suited to handle my weight, though the look he gave me whenever I approached him made me a little apprehensive. Faldir and I went through all the saddlebags and we took whatever food and water we could find, then we unsaddled the extra horses and set them free while Malo doused the fire. Once we were ready, Faldir took up his customary position in the wagon and Malo mounted his mare. I approached the stallion and he immediately tossed his head at me and rolled his eyes, but despite his demeanor, the horse allowed me to put a foot in the stirrup and pull myself up.

"You be good to me and I'll be good to you," I said to the stallion once I was in the saddle. "Is it a deal?"

The horse just blew angrily out of his nostrils and swished his tail at me and I shook my head. Even the Cardian horses were ill-tempered, I thought as Malo led us out from the trees and back onto the road. The storm had blown itself out by now, though I could still see a mass of black clouds hovering threateningly far to the south, with the occasional flash of lightning crackling inside them. The sun hung low in the sky to the west of us, but even as dusk approached the air was still filled with the calls of songbirds as they celebrated the passing of the storm. We rode for several hours, not seeing another living soul as darkness slowly descended on the land, until finally we reached a crossroad faintly seen in the weak light of a fresh crescent moon. Malo didn't hesitate at the crossroads and he turned us northeast. We rode for at least another hour after that, until we reached a bend in the road dominated by a long-dead, twisted oak tree shrouded in shadows that stood hanging over the road and looking like it might fall at any moment. Malo guided us off the road with a snap of his fingers, leading us around the dead tree and onto a path so faint that I thought it might be a figment of my imagination. I made sure to check on Baine and Jebido every hour or so, and they both seemed no worse off as far as I could tell, all things considered.

Malo hadn't said a word to anyone since we'd begun our journey and he led us onward with single-minded determination. We traveled over an uneven, meandering path that was strewn with small rocks and tall, prickly weeds that kissed the bottom of my pointed boots as I brought up the rear of our little procession. The big black had turned out to be stubborn and moody and he was already more of a problem than I'd bargained for. It had only taken just a few minutes of uncomfortable riding for both of us to come to the same conclusion. He didn't like me and I didn't like him. I cursed myself for the thousandth time for picking the horse, which tended to stubbornly go right when I indicated left and left when I indicated right. I followed Faldir and the wagon down an incline as the stallion fought the bit and I rolled my eyes. What was it about me that horses didn't like? I wondered. I'd already given the big black a swat on the ass with my hand several times to let him know I was displeased, and I considered doing it again, this time with the flat of Wolf's Head. But each time I'd done it in the past the stallion had snorted and turned its head to look at me with an angry eye and a promise of something else in it that I couldn't quite read. I wasn't sure I wanted to find out what that promise was, so I resisted the temptation to draw

Wolf's Head and decided to try reasoning with the temperamental horse instead.

"You're always angry because of that mean bastard who owned you before, isn't that right?" I said to the big black. "I bet that turd treated you badly, didn't he?" I looked down at the stained armor I wore and made a face. "And I bet you don't like that I have his stink on me, do you? Maybe that's why you're being such a pain in my ass." The horse snorted sullenly and I snorted right back. "Are you ever anything but angry?" The big black swished his tail aggressively and rolled his tongue around the bit as we closely followed behind the wagon. I chuckled and shook my head. "I didn't think so. But I've got some news for you, my big stupid friend. I'm angry most of the time, too. So maybe you and I will make a good pair after all." The horse twitched his ears at me, seeming to be listening now and I grinned in the darkness, starting to gain confidence. "So, if you and I are going to be friends, then we should introduce ourselves properly. I'm Hadrack of Corwick." The stallion didn't seem overly moved by my introduction, but I decided to press on anyway. "And what should I call you? How about Blackie?" The stallion snorted angrily again and I frowned. "You don't like that, huh? Maybe I should just call you, Angry? Would you prefer that?" The big horse turned to look back at me again, but this time the glare in his eye seemed less sullen to me, or maybe it was just wishful thinking on my part. Either way, whether the horse liked the name or not, that's exactly what I decided to call him. It just seemed to fit. I didn't know it that night, riding through almost pitch darkness to an unknown future, but Angry and I would be destined to spend the next twenty-two years together — through all the good times and the bad.

Malo led us onward for the rest of that night, and as the sun finally started to rise in the east, we reached a steep incline that led us upward through a thin pine forest rife with blight. We eventually came out from the trees onto a high rocky knoll that overlooked a heavily fortified town that lay in a valley shrouded in early morning mist. Malo paused at the crest of the knoll as Faldir halted the wagon behind him facing a narrow road that wound its way through sparse trees to the west. I rode Angry to the side of the wagon to check on my friends, having to stop the big horse at the front wheels by yanking as hard as I could on the reins while cursing at him to stop. Both Baine and Jebido lay on the fir boughs on their backs with their eyes closed and for a moment my heart leaped in my throat with dread. But then Baine's eyelids fluttered and opened and he focused on me. My friend's face was still quite pale, but at least I could see a familiar spark lighting up his eyes.

"Well, you look a bit better," I said as I grinned down at him.

"I feel pretty good," Baine said, sounding surprised. He stretched his good arm and looked around. "Where are we?"

I shrugged. "I've no idea, but there's a town close by, so we're going to get you two some help." I glanced at Jebido, pleased to see that he had a little more color in his cheeks. "How is he doing?"

"Still not talking," Baine said. "But I actually got some water into him a few hours ago."

"That's great news!" I said. Angry fidgeted and stamped his feet impatiently and I fought to keep him still. "Do you need anything? More food or water?"

Baine shook his head and he lifted one of the Cardians' waterskins. "No, I still have some." He pushed himself up onto one elbow and studied the big black I rode with admiration. "He's a beauty," he said. I could see the familiar humor dancing in his eyes as he glanced at me. "Looks like he's quite a handful."

"That's the truth," I agreed as Angry shook his ears. "We're still sorting things out."

"He's still very young, so just let him know who's the boss and you'll be fine," Baine advised as he lay back down.

"Oh, that's already been established," I grunted as Malo

waved me over to him. "Just not in my favor." I grinned at Baine and urged Angry forward until I sat beside Malo and his mare overlooking the town. I whistled when I got a good look at the size of it as the mist slowly burned off beneath the sun. "Is this Gandertown?" I asked in wonder.

Malo chuckled and shook his head. "No, this is Halhaven. Gandertown is hundreds of miles from here and five times this size."

I'd heard of Halhaven, of course. Our king had lived in the town before King Jorquin had invaded and destroyed his army during the Border War. I thought of my older brother, who would have been almost thirty-years-old now had he not died in that war and I shook my head at the waste of it all. Everything bad that had happened in my life, starting with the death of my brother, then my sister, father, and all the people in Corwick, had all been a direct result of that war.

I gestured to the town. "Is that where the physician is?"

"No," Malo said with a quick shake of his head. He pointed to the hills that ringed Halhaven to the west. "The healer lives up there. He's an apothecary, actually, who's renowned for his medicines as well as his ability to heal. His name is Haverty. He's a bit of an odd fellow, but there's no one I'd trust more to help your friends. He already knows they're coming and will take good care of them."

"That sounds good," I said with relief. I had no idea how Malo had gotten word to the apothecary, and frankly, I didn't care. All that mattered was someone well versed in healing would be taking care of Baine and Jebido. Despite everything Malo had done for us, there had still been a part of me that had distrusted him. I could feel that distrust begin to dissipate now and I felt a sudden warmth toward my companion. "So, what are we waiting for then? I asked eagerly. "Let's get going."

"There's one other thing," Malo said, not moving. He glanced at me sideways from beneath his hood. "You probably won't like it very much, but it has to be."

"What?" I growled, feeling the warmth evaporate as my

right hand unconsciously moved to Wolf's Head.

Malo looked down at my sword hand and frowned. "Don't be foolish." He motioned to the western road. "Faldir will take your friends to see Haverty, but you and I won't be going with them."

I shook my head as anger exploded in my chest. "That's not going to happen! I go where they go!"

"Not this time," Malo said with an edge to his voice. He gestured to Halhaven. "I told you someone is anxious to see you and that someone is down there right now waiting for you. There's nothing you can do for your friends that Haverty can't do a hundred times better."

"I don't care," I said stubbornly. "I'm not leaving them."

Malo shrugged. "Suit yourself. If you won't do as I say, I'll have Faldir dump your friends on the road and leave the three of you here to rot." He glanced at me in warning. "But keep in mind, Hadrack, that word will spread quickly about your escape. How long do you think you'll last on your own with two badly injured men to care for and two powerful lords breathing down your necks?"

I pursed my lips as I thought, knowing that everything Malo was saying was true. But, even so, just the idea of being separated from Jebido and Baine was making me feel very uneasy. The three of us had been together every day for the last ten years and I couldn't imagine not being with them. I glanced at the wagon, where I could see Baine watching us curiously. Could I trust Malo with their lives?

"Don't be a fool, Hadrack," Malo said gently. "I give you my word no harm will come to them."

"How do I know I can trust you?" I finally asked.

"Who got you out of that cage?" Malo demanded, looking angry now. "I risked my life to do that. Isn't that enough?"

"Normally it would be," I said. I held Malo's eyes. "But when it comes to my friends' lives, I'm a little less trusting than usual."

"Fair enough," Malo said. "I can respect that." He

lowered his hood and undid the silver clasp at the neck of his heavy wool cloak, then drew the cloth aside. "Perhaps this will be enough to earn your trust, then?"

I stared in surprise at the red surcoat Malo wore underneath his cloak with the Blazing Sun emblem in its center. I looked away and glanced down at Halhaven, knowing with certainty now who our mysterious benefactor was. "You're a House Agent," I finally said as I turned back to Malo.

"I am," Malo confirmed as he studied my face. "So now do you understand?"

"I do," I said. I glanced again at Baine and Jebido, then sighed and looked away. I knew I had no choice now but to trust Malo and see where this led.

Malo drew the cloak around him again and fastened it. "So you agree to my terms?"

"Yes," I said as I turned again to gaze at Halhaven. Somewhere down in that sprawling city waited a woman I had met just a few short days ago. A woman with piercing eyes, a husky voice, and possibly intimate knowledge of what had happened to Shana and Prince Tyro in Gasterny. I pointed my finger at Malo and glared at him with a promise in my eyes. "But if anything happens to Baine and Jebido, I'll hold you responsible. Do I make myself clear?"

Malo bowed his head. "Very clear. Your loyalty to your friends is admirable, Hadrack. No harm will come to them. You have the word of a House Agent on that."

I took a few minutes to ride over to the wagon and fill Baine in on what was happening. I was hoping Jebido would awaken so I could say goodbye to him as well, but he didn't, and I finally had to say my farewells to Baine alone. I watched moodily from atop Angry as Faldir slowly guided the wagon away through the trees, heading along the western road that would eventually take them to the waiting apothecary. Baine lifted his good hand to me just before I lost sight of them and I waved back, wondering despite myself if this might be the last time I ever saw my two friends.

Malo and I headed down the knoll after that along a winding path that led to a narrow cobblestone road flanked by squat apricot trees brimming with the ripe-looking fruit. Peasants were harvesting the bright orange apricots and were placing them carefully in worn baskets woven from river rushes. The peasants paused in their labor to stare at us as we guided our horses onto the road and I saw more than one of them make the sign of The Mother when they recognized Malo. A man stood in a field some distance away from the road watching as a little boy ran ahead of him trailing a thin rope attached to a yellow kite that swooped crazily against the wind. I'd heard of kites but had never seen one before and I marveled at it as the man shouted encouragement to the boy as he fought to keep his grip.   We continued until we came to a wooden bridge that spanned a fast-flowing river. The river ebbed from east to west, flowing quickly into a hook-shaped basin to my left where four worn and weathered cargo ships sat rocking on the tide. The water surged out of the basin following a narrow channel that wound its way around the city before continuing and disappearing into a rocky valley far to the west. Red-tiled buildings stood in a neat row in front of the dock where the boats sat and I could see men sitting on barrels along the pier repairing sails. I could even hear their good-natured teasing of one another as they worked. Great winged birds with long beaks, white heads and grey bodies cawed and scolded the men as they flew overhead. The city rose impossibly large ahead of us as we crossed the bridge and headed for the gates and I studied it in fascination. Forty-foot high walls of imposing granite that Malo told me were close to twenty-feet thick encircled the city. The walls were reinforced every fifty feet or so by massive square watchtowers that flew the stag emblem of the king of Ganderland. I could see the gleaming white granite of the great castle where once a king had lived and ruled over his people where it sat perched high on a hill, dominating the city.

"That's the Grand Holy House over there," Malo said,

pointing to four tall, elegant-looking red spires that jutted up over the walls near the eastern corner of the city. "Only the First Holy House in Gandertown is bigger." Malo halted his mare and took off his cloak as I stopped Angry beside him. "Put this on," he said as he held it out to me.

"Why do I need to wear this?" I asked as I drew the cloak about my shoulders.

"Because we have to be careful," Malo said. He glanced at the open gates of the city, which even this early were already bustling with activity as merchants, peddlers, wine and wood sellers, and many more I could not distinguish, passed through the gates with their wares. Malo gave me a look filled with warning. "There are eyes and ears everywhere in Halhaven. I don't want them remembering you."

"No one knows me here," I said with a shrug as I drew the hood over my head. "So who would remember me?"

"They don't know you yet," Malo muttered. "But with your size and face and what's coming, they soon will. I don't want them to connect us when they do."

"What's coming?" I asked, my curiosity piqued by the man's caution.

"That's not for me to say," Malo said. "When the time comes, you'll understand."

I sighed and nodded. More of Malo's secrets, I thought. "So, where to now?" I asked to change the subject.

"The Holy House, of course," Malo said as he kicked his heels against the mare's flanks.

"Is that where Daughter Gernet will be?" I asked.

Malo chuckled and glanced at me out of the side of his eyes as we made our way into the city. "That's where she'll be," he confirmed.

I thought of Daughter Gernet and her assertion when we met that she and I would someday speak of Corwick again. I had secretly scoffed at the idea at the time, never having expected to see her again. But, as we rode through the city streets of Halhaven and made our way to the Grand Holy

House, I realized that she had somehow known that this moment would happen all along. I felt a hardness take over my heart as I thought of Betania. I pictured her on the floor of the keep covered in blood and I vowed that if Daughter Gernet had anything to do with what had happened, then, by The Mother Herself, she'd pay for it with her blood. Daughter or not.

We reached a set of wrought-iron gates set within high stone walls behind the sprawling grandeur of the Holy House and a man appeared when Malo called. The man was completely bald but for a thin band of grey hair around the base of his skull and was dressed in a simple brown tunic and black trousers. He glanced at me appraisingly and I noticed his feet were bare and his toenails were thick, twisted and yellow looking. I guessed him to be about sixty years of age.

"If the face beneath the hood of your companion belongs to who I think, then it would appear The Mother has favored you with success, Agent," the man said as he unlocked and swung open the gates.

"Indeed She has, Daest," Malo replied as we passed into the courtyard. He glanced at the Holy House that towered above us. "Where is she?"

"Pacing back and forth in The Daughter's Tower," Daest said with a snort as he closed and locked the gates behind us. He rolled his eyes. "She's been impossible since you left." Daest glanced at me. "I hope he's worth it."

Malo shrugged and dismounted, handing the reins of his mare to the old man. "Time will tell on that, I expect."

"Indeed," Daest agreed.

"What news of the Son?"

"Gone to see the bailiff," Daest said. "A child was caught yesterday stealing from the merchant Belfoy and he's gone to ask for leniency. He should be away for at least another hour or more."

"Belfoy is an ass," Malo grunted.

"True," Daest agreed. "But he's a very rich and influential ass."

"What about the Sons-In-Waiting?" Malo asked.

"At lessons," the old man replied. "I'll make sure to keep them out of your hair until you're done."

"Good," Malo said.

I had no idea what they were talking about, but finally tired of just sitting there, I swung my leg over Angry and dropped to the ground. "Careful," I warned Daest as I handed him the reins. "He's got a lot of attitude."

"Don't we all," Daest sniffed as he accepted Angry's reins and led the horses away.

The courtyard was only about thirty feet wide, but probably at least fifty feet long. The cobblestones beneath our boots quickly gave way to a well-manicured lawn as Malo led me toward a semi-circular, three-story building with a red-tiled roof that fit neatly into the juncture where the Mother's Nave and Father's Nave intersected each other. All the larger Holy Houses were formed in the shape of an X, with the smaller, more traditional ones like the one in my village built in a rectangle or simple square where the single nave was shared. Four round towers topped by the red spires I'd seen from outside the city were set at each end of the X. I knew that various other buildings, such as the Daughters' and Sons' rectories, apprentices' dormitories, and the servants' quarters, were situated along the other walls of the Holy House.

Malo ushered me up the stairs and into the building and I found myself standing in a room roughly twenty-feet wide furnished with stout-looking benches sitting along both sidewalls. The floor was laid with intricate yellow tiles surrounded by a red banner and shaped in a diamond pattern, with each tile being no bigger than my hand. An arched doorway led to a passageway on my right, with a similar passage leading left. In front of me, high wooden arches gave way to an open cloister brimming with greenery and dominated in the center by a small pond with a gushing fountain. I could see more arches across the cloister, and beyond that the gleaming white-tiled walls of the inner naves. Walkways of multi-colored rocks cut through the cloister, shaped in an X with the fountain at its center. I noticed a Daughter-In-Waiting hurrying around the fountain toward us as she held up her grey robe.

"Malo!" the girl squealed in excitement as she ran.

The apprentice was blonde and pretty and I realized as she drew closer that she was the same young girl who had been with Daughter Gernet in Gasterny.

"Ah, Jin," Malo said, breaking into a smile. "I was hoping I'd get a chance to see you."

"You found him!" Jin said breathlessly as she ran to Malo and embraced him warmly. "You actually found him!"

"Indeed I did," Malo chuckled as he held the girl. The two broke the embrace and Malo stood back with his hands on her slight shoulders. "Had you any doubt, child?"

Jin shook her head, her eyes wide as she stared at me in fascination. "Of course not," she said. She walked over to me and peered up at my face beneath the hood. "I can't believe it's really you," she whispered. I didn't know what to say to that, so rather than sound foolish, I just stood there in Malo's cloak feeling awkward as I shifted from one foot to the other. "You and I are going to be great friends," Jin finally told me, looking quite pleased with the idea as she lay her hand on my arm. "You'll see."

"Daest tells me Daughter Gernet is in the tower," Malo said. "I want Hadrack away from Halhaven as soon as possible, so we'd best be getting to her."

"Of course," Jin agreed. She squeezed my arm and then gestured to the right-hand passage. "I'll take you to her now."

Malo and I walked with Jin and the entire time the girl chattered on excitedly with Malo while I kept my mouth closed and my eyes and ears open. Servants and other Daughters-In-Waiting passed us as we walked and many of them called out a warm greeting to Malo. It was obvious to me that the House Agent was well-liked within the House. Occasionally I got a curious glance, but I kept my head down and no one questioned what I was doing there.

"Was it very difficult?" Jin asked Malo as they walked arm in arm.

"Was what difficult, my dear?"

"Finding him," Jin said. Her face was flushed slightly and her eyes sparkled with excitement. "Did you have to kill anyone?"

I could see Malo struggling with the answer to that, so I cut in, "It wasn't just me he found. He saved my friends as well." I glanced sideways at the House Agent. "I owe Malo a great debt for what he did for the three of us."

"That's right!" Jin said. She put her hand on my arm again. "I forgot about the other two. Are they all right?"

We'd reached a wide stone stairwell that wound its way upward and Malo paused with one foot on the first step. "I sent them to Haverty," he said. "Their wounds are severe, but if anyone can return them to health, it will be him."

"That's true," Jin nodded to me eagerly. "He's the best there is."

Jin, Malo and I climbed the stairs, going around and around so many times I lost track. How tall is this tower? I wondered. We met two House Agents wearing red surcoats with the Blazing Sun on them coming down the stairs and we all paused as they and Malo talked for a moment. Both the agents were big and bearded and they looked at me appraisingly as Malo whispered something under his breath to them. I just stared back at the men, starting to feel annoyed at the delay and wishing to get on with things so I could get back to Baine and Jebido. Finally the agents clapped Malo on the shoulder and we started our climb again, until eventually we came to the top floor with only a narrow, arched passageway in front of us. Malo guided us down the passageway until we came to an open doorway that led into a circular room dominated by a thick oak table surrounded by carved benches. A small desk covered in leather-bound books sat beneath an arched window along the curve of one wall, while a roaring fire snapped and crackled in a fireplace directly opposite me. A woman in a long yellow robe sat in a padded chair close to the flames and I recognized Daughter Gernet immediately as she stood up to greet us.

"So you found him," Daughter Gernet said. I could see her shoulders slump as she spoke, whether from relief, exhaustion, or something else, I couldn't tell. "I was so afraid that you'd return to tell me he'd been killed in the battle."

"No," Malo said. "The Cardians were taking him to Gandertown to claim the king's reward."

"That figures," Daughter Gernet said with distaste. "And the others?"

Malo frowned. "Both alive, but badly injured. I sent them to Haverty."

Daughter Gernet nodded and wrapped her robe tighter about her thin frame, then she focused on me. "Remove your hood, Hadrack, so that I can see your face." I did as she ordered and stood watching her warily as she came to stand in front of me. Daughter Gernet lifted a hand and gently traced the scar that ran down my forehead and cheek and ended in my beard. "You have seen pain," she said, more a statement than a question.

"More than you know, Daughter," I replied. I could see something in her eyes, something different from the last time we'd met. In Gasterny, her eyes had been cold, calculating, and guarded, but here, in this tower, she gazed at me with empathy and an openness that was impossible to ignore. I felt all my doubts about her and Malo and their motives flow out of me at her expression and I put my hand on hers and squeezed it gently. "The scars on my skin tell only a small part of the story."

Daughter Gernet took in a deep breath, nodded and then drew her hand away. "I know some of that story, I think," she said. She gestured to the table and benches. "Please, sit, Hadrack. We have much to talk about."

I hesitated and glanced at Malo and Jin, who stood behind me waiting. "I need something answered first," I said as I turned back to the priestess.

Daughter Gernet bowed her head. "Then ask."

"The last time we talked you spoke of Corwick and asked me what really happened there," I said. "When I told you it was Lord Corwick who ordered the villagers killed, you didn't look surprised at all."

"No, I wasn't," Daughter Gernet said as she pursed her lips.

"Why not?" I asked.

Daughter Gernet moved to the table, indicating again that I should sit. "Please, humor an old woman and sit, Hadrack, and then I will answer your question. My legs are not what they once were." I nodded and sat on a bench opposite her and Malo came to sit beside me, while Jin sat beside the priestess. "I have spent the last ten years trying to prove what happened in Corwick was not the work of the Piths," Daughter Gernet said. She looked down at the table and traced a pattern on the rough wood with her finger that only she could see before she eventually sighed. "But that task has not been an easy one, I'm afraid. Pernissy is a powerful man, and even with my position within the House, no one wants to go against him to speak the truth." She looked back up at me and I was struck again by the searing intelligence in her eyes. "I'd heard rumors over the years that a boy had survived the massacre, but though I searched everywhere, it was in vain and I could not find him." She leaned across the table and put her hand on mine. "Until Gasterny, that is."

"Why do you even care?" I asked, trying to keep the bitterness from my voice and knowing that I was failing. I drew my hand away and crossed my arms, feeling doubt begin to resurface. I thought of Betania and Shana and the betrayal at Gasterny and I felt my heart harden against what I was hearing. "Nobody else has ever cared about Corwick. So why do you?"

Daughter Gernet sat back and placed both her hands on top of Jin's hand and the two shared a look. I was surprised to see that the young girl's eyes were now brimming with tears.

"Because my daughter, Meanda, lived in Corwick," Daughter Gernet said, "and she was murdered by those bastards, just like your sister and father were." I could see tears threatening in the priestess' eyes as well and I stared first at her, then at Jin in shock, knowing what was coming next. "And this delightful child," Daughter Gernet said with a quiver in her voice, pausing to lift the girl's fingers to her lips. "This child, who like you, managed to survive that massacre, is my granddaughter, Jinny."

9: OUTLAW

Little Jinny, I thought in wonder as I stared at the slight blonde girl weeping across the table from me. How was it even possible? My mind turned back to a morning filled with smoke, tears, death, and the overwhelming stench of burning flesh. I remembered seeing Little Jinny among the bodies as I'd searched for my father. She'd been lying with her knees drawn up to her chest and I recall thinking that she could have been sleeping if not for the blood on her dress. I'd been so focused on finding my father, however, that I hadn't even thought to check on her.

I shook my head, feeling unbelievably guilty for abandoning Jinny as I tried to think of something to say. "I'm so sorry," I finally whispered to her. "I didn't know."

Jin blinked at me in confusion through her tears and she sniffed loudly as Daughter Gernet put her arm around the girl to comfort her. "What could you possibly be sorry for?" Jin asked in a tiny voice. "You were just a child like me." She leaned her head on Daughter Gernet's shoulder and stared at me with big eyes. "I'm the lucky one," she said in a voice so low that I unconsciously leaned forward to hear her better. "I was too young to know what was going on and I don't remember any of it." She looked at me in wonder. "But you, Hadrack. You saw everything, didn't you?" I breathed in deeply and nodded, remembering the blood and terrified screams of the men, women and children as the nine slaughtered them mercilessly. "I've spent my entire life wondering what really happened to my mother," Jin said, "and now, thanks to you, I'll finally get to know." Jin sat up, pausing to nod to Daughter Gernet in reassurance before facing me. "Please, don't ever tell me you're sorry for what happened in Corwick, Hadrack." She placed her hands over her heart. "I know in here that none of it was your fault."

Her words hit me like hammer blows, one after the other and I swallowed and looked down at my filthy hands that I'd clasped together on the tabletop. She didn't know what I knew, and when I told her what I'd done, about how it had all begun, then I knew her attitude toward me would change. I'd only known Jin for a short time, but already the idea of seeing this pleasant, sweet young girl viewing me with hatred was almost too much for me to bear. I focused on the small, jagged white scar on the knuckle of my little finger on my right hand and I rubbed it unconsciously as I stared at it. Baine and I had been wrestling down in Father's Arse, I remembered, and my friend had unintentionally butted me in the face with his head. It had been an accident, but even so, I'd become instantly enraged and had swung at him without thinking, chipping one of his teeth and slicing open my hand. All my life I'd always reacted first, without thinking things through, and the little white scar was a glaring reminder of all of my failings. I thought of Corwick, the reeve, and my beloved sister and I shook my head bitterly. If I'd only found another way to deal with that bastard, things might have turned out very differently. I considered for the briefest of moments not telling them about the reeve and what I'd done. But, even as I thought it, I knew I couldn't do it. The story needed to be told in its entirety, no matter how it made me look personally. Daughter Gernet and Jinny deserved that much, I figured, as did Meanda and the Widow Meade and everyone else who'd died in Corwick. I sat back and rubbed my scarred hand over my eyes, then I sighed and stared across the table at Daughter Gernet and Jin.

"You've got it all wrong," I said, determined now to make them understand at all costs. "It really was my fault. If it hadn't been for me and what I did, all those people would never have died." I saw Daughter Gernet's eyebrows rise in surprise and I focused on Jin, who was staring at me with wide

Terry Cloutier

eyes. "Jinny, your mother would probably be with you right now if not for me."

"That can't be true," Jin said, shaking her head adamantly. "You're being too hard on yourself."

"Am I?" I growled. "You said that you were too young to remember what happened." I could hear the tremor in my voice as I added, "But, like you also said, I wasn't too young. I wish I was like you and couldn't remember at all, or if not that, could at least forget sometimes. But I can't no matter how hard I try." I stood up and moved to stare into the fire as I fought emotions I'd thought I'd come to terms with long ago. I could see my home burning in the flames of the fireplace, see again the sty and the chicken coop and the woodshed as the hungry inferno consumed them all. I turned abruptly away to escape the dreadful memory and faced the others. Daughter Gernet, Jin and Malo were all focused on me, staring at me in silence as I started to pace back and forth across the room as I talked. I told them everything, moment by moment, word by word, leaving nothing out and hesitating only twice — once when I spoke of my father's death, and once when I spoke of Meanda, Jinny's mother — who I remembered seeing staked out naked with the other women behind the sty. When I was finished, I stood near the table with my arms crossed over my chest, waiting for, and expecting, their harsh words of judgment. Jin and Daughter Gernet were openly crying, and even Malo seemed strangely moved as the three sat at the table and digested what I'd told them.

"Well," Malo finally said, shifting position on the bench. He flicked his gaze to Daughter Gernet. "I see what you mean, Daughter," he said. "The boy is remarkable."

I blinked in surprise at Malo's words as Jin rose from the table and slowly approached me. Here it comes, I thought, expecting a slap or worse. Jin stopped with her body almost pressed against mine and her hands on my chest as she looked up into my eyes.

"You poor boy," Jin whispered as tears slid unashamedly down her cheeks. "I can't imagine what you have been through."

She wrapped her arms around me as far as they could go and then buried her head in the cloak that I still wore. I felt her body shudder and heard her sobs and I gently put my arms around her, feeling as protective of her as a father to his child. I knew at that moment that I'd just found a friend for life. I held Jinny for what seemed an eternity as the fire crackled behind us and Daughter Gernet and Malo silently waited. I was happy to hold Jin and give her my strength for as long as she needed it and, I realized in surprise, it seemed she was doing the same thing for me. My black mood had lifted while we clung to each other, the bitterness and anger evaporating, leaving behind a deep sense of belonging that I had only ever felt around Jebido and Baine and, for a short time before she'd been taken, Shana.

Finally, Daughter Gernet stood almost reluctantly and came to stand beside us. She gently laid a hand on Jinny's shoulder and stroked it affectionately. "Jin, darling, time runs short and there is still much to discuss with Hadrack."

Jin nodded and sniffed into my chest, then she broke her embrace with me and stood back. She wiped the wetness from her red cheeks and glanced at her grandmother. "Of course, you're right," Jin said. "Forgive my selfishness." She looked up at me almost shyly. "I've been waiting most of my life to meet Hadrack. Now that the time has finally come, I don't want it to end."

"Today is not the end, child," Daughter Gernet said kindly. "Today is only the beginning." She gestured to the table. "Please, both of you sit. I have much more to say." I sat down opposite Malo and Jin sat down beside me as close as she could get. She grabbed my hand in both of hers and squeezed it and I squeezed back as Daughter Gernet cleared her throat and wrapped her robe tighter around herself. "First, I'd like to thank you, Hadrack, for your heartfelt honesty and offer you my condolences for your father and sister. What happened to them, my daughter and you, and everyone in Corwick, is a travesty that cannot go unpunished under the eyes of the First Pair. Justice will be served for the lives stolen that day, mark my words." Daughter Gernet paused and her face clouded as she looked down at the stone floor. "But, though I understand and share your need for justice, Hadrack, it will have to wait. There are more urgent issues that demand our attention first."

"What!?" I demanded in disbelief. I half stood, feeling anger erupt inside me.

Jin fought to pull me back down to a sitting position. "Please, Hadrack!" she pleaded. "You need to listen to her! The fate of the House depends on it!"

I glanced at Jin in confusion as I sat. "The House?" I said, thrown off now. "What does that even mean?"

"It means, Hadrack," Daughter Gernet said, "that a war is coming. A war that has the potential to bring the Holy House to its very knees, and we need your help."

I shook my head and despite myself I laughed out loud. "Do you really think I can stop the Piths? Especially after what happened at Gasterny?" I glanced at Malo, then Jin. "You don't know them. None of you do. Nothing will stop them after that."

Daughter Gernet gave me a strange look, then she flicked her eyes to Malo. "You didn't tell him?"

Malo just shrugged. "The opportunity never arose."

"Tell me what?" I growled suspiciously.

Daughter Gernet looked to the ceiling, then sighed and turned back to me. "Two days after Gasterny fell, Lord Corwick and Lord Demay ambushed the Pith army as they marched through…" She paused and glanced again at Malo.

"They're calling it Victory Pass, now, I believe," Malo said.

"Yes," Daughter Gernet agreed as I stared at her with my mouth hanging open. "Victory Pass. The Piths suspected nothing amiss, as they believed the treaty to still be in effect and marched right into the ambush."

"No!" I whispered in dismay. I remembered Einhard

telling me long ago that the pass was a natural trap and even a small amount of men could keep an army pinned down in it forever.

Daughter Gernet nodded. "Hundreds of Piths died, so I'm told, and it was a resounding victory for Lord Demay and Lord Corwick. The king of the Piths was killed along with most of his top men." Daughter Gernet moved to stand above me as I sat in stupefied silence, still trying to grasp what I'd just been told. "I am sorry, Hadrack. I know these savages meant something to you, but the world is better off without them. Some day you will come to understand that."

"Einhard," I said softly, not listening now as I felt a thud of loss clawing at my gut. I pictured my friend's dancing green eyes and brilliant smile the last time I'd seen him, then the picture changed and I saw his twisted body lying bloodied and broken among the dead in the pass. I closed my eyes, trying to come to terms with the idea that Einhard was no more as Jin put her arm around me and hugged me tightly.

"Actually," Malo said. "I heard that one got away." My eyes snapped open and I glanced over at the House Agent in sudden hope. "The Sword of the King, right?" Malo asked. I nodded breathlessly, not daring to believe it could be true. "He was badly injured, I believe," Malo said, "but even so, he managed to rally some of his troops and fight his way out of the trap back to his lands."

I felt my body sag with relief and I glanced at Jin, who removed her arm from around me and took my hand in hers once again. "This man meant something to you, didn't he?" Jin asked me.

I nodded, caught by the look of kindness emanating from within the depths of her light blue eyes. "Einhard freed me from slavery," I whispered. "I owe him my life."

"Then I will pray to the First Pair every night that he recovers from his wounds and sires many strong sons and lives a long, fruitful life," Jin said as she kissed my knuckles.

I took her hand and squeezed it in silent thanks, feeling

a joy fill my chest where moments ago there had been nothing but sorrow. Einhard was alive! Thank you Mother! Thank you Father! I turned back to Daughter Gernet with renewed vigor. "You said a war was coming," I said, thinking back on what I'd heard. "But if you weren't talking about the Piths, then who did you mean?"

"I meant us," Daughter Gernet simply said. Her jaw was set in a firm line and I glanced at Malo, whose face mirrored that of the Daughter.

"I don't understand," I finally said.

"Do you recall the last time we met?" Daughter Gernet asked. "The reason we were in Gasterny in the first place?"

"For the cleansing," I said, feeling my face tighten in anger as I thought of Shana and Betania.

"Yes," Daughter Gernet said, bowing her head in agreement. "But that was just a ruse to get us inside the garrison. The cleansing never actually occurred. We were there to see Prince Tyro for an entirely different purpose."

"That much I already figured out," I said, having suspected there had been no actual cleansing for some time now. "What about Lady Demay?" I asked. "Did you know what Carbet was going to do?"

Daughter Gernet shook her head firmly. "No, I only learned of it after the fact, once we'd left the garrison."

I glanced around the room, trying to imagine these people conspiring to seize Shana and murder a prince and knowing even as I did so that there was no way they could have been party to it. I decided the best way to get the answers I wanted was to just be blunt and see what happened, so I said, "Why did Son Oriell kill the prince, then?"

I sensed Jin stiffen beside me and felt her fingernails bite painfully into my flesh. Across the room, Daughter Gernet's face turned pale and she stared at me in obvious shock.

"Mother Above!" the priestess whispered, looking as though I'd just slapped her. She wavered weakly in place and Malo jumped to his feet, moving to support her. "I must sit,"

Daughter Gernet said to him. Malo nodded and gently guided the priestess to the table and helped her to sit on the bench opposite me. "Malo," Daughter Gernet said, looking up at the House Agent with haunted eyes. She pointed at me, her finger shaking. "Tell him what we know."

Malo nodded. "We were under the impression that the Piths killed Prince Tyro," he said, looking worried. "Now you claim that is not true and that Son Oriell did it. Do you honestly expect us to believe that a Son of The Father would commit such an unforgivable crime?"

I saw Daughter Gernet visibly wince as she awaited my answer and it suddenly dawned on me that they, like me, had no idea what had really happened in Gasterny. Whatever was going on, it seemed that each of us only held half the picture.

"I promise you in the name of The Mother and The Father that the Piths did not kill the prince," I said. "It was that ugly bastard, Son Oriell. You have my word on that."

Malo and Daughter Gernet shared a long look and I could see some kind of message pass silently between them before Malo turned back to me. "The official story is that several Cardians wandered across the five-mile perimeter and that's why the Piths killed the prince."

"A lie!" I snorted. "There were Cardians near Gasterny," I conceded, "but they were pursuing Lady Demay and didn't know they were that close to us. A few Cardians in the forest is hardly a reason to risk jeopardizing the garrison by killing the prince." I shook my head and grimaced, certain now I knew who had spun the lie. "Lord Corwick told you the Piths killed the prince, didn't he?"

Malo nodded, his eyes burning with anger. "He and Son Oriell, yes."

"Seems like we've heard this kind of lie from him before," I said. "But what I really don't understand is why they killed the prince at all? Surely not even Lord Corwick would be able to corrupt a Son just to attack Gasterny?"

Daughter Gernet sighed, motioning for Malo to sit beside her. "So many games," the priestess muttered. The Daughter looked as though she'd aged ten years in the last minute as she wearily placed her hands palms down on the table and looked at me. "This wasn't about Gasterny at all," she said.

"Well, it couldn't have just been about Shana," I replied.

"It wasn't," Daughter Gernet agreed. "As I mentioned before, Lady Demay's rescue was incidental to the true reason we were there." I bristled at the term 'rescue' and the priestess raised her hand to stall my protest. "Lord Demay was desperate to get his wife back and he devised the scheme to send in that dreadful Cardian to attempt to bring her out."

"How did Carbet even know where she would be?" I asked, remembering Jebido and me and the rest of us puzzling over that very fact.

"Talai," Malo said, answering for Daughter Gernet. I looked at him in puzzlement for a moment until the name finally registered. Talai had been Shana's friend, the girl who had fallen into the river and been swept away. "The Cardians found her half-drowned and washed up on the banks of the White Rock," Malo continued. "She told them she'd been a slave in Gasterny and had slipped and fallen into the river."

"And she also told them about Shana and where she'd be every morning," I said, finishing for him as I thought of our morning reading lessons.

"Yes," Daughter Gernet said. "I assume that's when Lord Demay came up with the plan to use the carriage. We were going into the garrison anyway for the cleansing and he probably decided that would be the best chance to get to Lady Demay while everyone else was focused on the prince. Talai was quite observant in the year the Piths held her, and with her help the Cardians learned all about you; troop strength, morale, weapons, even the lengths of the watches."

"That explains a lot," I said, rubbing my chin as I thought. I remembered the look on Daughter Gernet's face when she'd first emerged from the carriage and had seen me leaning against the curtain wall with Jebido that fateful morning. "Did the Cardians tell you about me as well? Is that why you came over to talk to me?"

"Yes," Daughter Gernet said. "Everyone in the kingdom had heard of the three Gandermen who'd joined the Piths, of course. But it wasn't until one of my operatives overheard a Cardian mention one of them was from Corwick that I realized that person might be the survivor I'd been searching for." Daughter Gernet smiled sadly. "I had great hopes my search had finally come to an end when I met you, but I confess I never expected you would turn out to be the son of my old friend, Alwin."

"You knew my father!?" I said in surprise.

"I did," Daughter Gernet nodded as she avoided my eyes. "I even held you as a newborn." She lifted her hand to stop me before I could say more. "But now is not the time and place to speak of my connection to your family, Hadrack. That was a very long time ago and in another lifetime." She glanced past me out the window. "It's almost mid-day and we're getting off-topic. You wished to know why Prince Tyro was murdered, and that's now an answer that I can tell you with confidence." Daughter Gernet folded her hands one atop the other on the table. "You know of Mount Halas, of course?" she said.

I nodded, brimming with questions about her and my father, but also curious at the shift in the conversation. "Mount Halas is the birthplace of The Mother and The Father," I answered dutifully.

"I'm glad to see you were paying attention during lessons," Daughter Gernet said with a thin smile. "Indeed, as you say, the birthplace of the First Pair." She shifted on the bench, taking a moment to collect her thoughts. "I'll try to keep this as brief and to the point as I can. Earlier this year an ancient codex written entirely on sheepskin was found in the eight-hundred-year-old monastery originally built in the First Pair's honor. The codex was cleverly hidden inside a book about botany, just one book among thousands and on its own, completely unremarkable. Why it was hidden thus, no one can guess. It's possible the codex might never have been found at all, had a curious, and I have to say, disrespectful scholar not overturned the book while using it among others as a stepping stool." I glanced sideways at Jin, wondering where this was all going, but the girl just sat beside me and held my hand, her eyes shining with fervor as she listened. "That codex," Daughter Gernet said, "has challenged everything we have come to know and believe about the role of the First Pair in our lives."

"I don't understand," I said, genuinely confused as I glanced from the priestess to the House Agent, then to Jin again. "What does any of this have to do with Gasterny?"

Daughter Gernet sighed. "I'm getting to that. The codex dates back to the time of Ardena, the First Son, and Dilestra, the First Daughter, who came after The Mother and The Father and, as you know, were charged with being the First Pair's representatives in this world. Most, if not all of this codex was written by Ardena and Dilestra as far as we can tell, with the first entries beginning with their commencement at the age of sixteen, and the last entries being written several months before their deaths. Unfortunately, the pages are so badly decomposed that most are unreadable other than the odd word or two here and there." Daughter Gernet paused and pursed her lips. "Except for the back of one page, that is, which, as fate would have it, has been left entirely intact."

"What does it say?" I asked breathlessly, caught up in the story.

"It says," Daughter Gernet said, "that despite what we've always believed, the First Pair have never been equals, and that the teachings of the Holy House have been wrong for almost eight-hundred years. One of Them sits above the Other!"

I sat back, stunned by the revelation. Everything I'd been taught my entire life hinged on the belief that The Mother and The Father were equal partners, working together in harmony to better all our lives. To hear that one of Them has always been considered higher than the other was information I found almost impossible to comprehend. "Which one?" I finally whispered.

"Ah," Daughter Gernet said, raising a finger. "That is where the crux of the issue lies. The undamaged page tells us how and why one of the First Pair was chosen to lead, but not who, and before either The Mother or The Father is named, that page runs out."

"And the next one is unreadable," I said, realizing with dismay the implications.

"Precisely," Daughter Gernet agreed.

"But why does any of that even matter anymore?" I asked. I thought of Daughter Elias and old Son Fadrian from my village when I was a boy. Though it was true I hadn't liked Son Fadrian very much, I'd never seen any animosity between him and Daughter Elias or, for that matter, between any of the other Sons and Daughters I'd met. I shook my head. "These are just ancient words that mean nothing to us now," I said. "Why break the House apart and start a war over something that no one even needs to know about?"

"Because we are, and have always been, a House divided, Hadrack," Daughter Gernet said. "It's true that we portray unity in front of the masses, but away from unknowing eyes, both sides of the House are hugely distrustful and suspicious of the other. The codex has, for good or bad, become a beacon of hope for both the Sons and the Daughters, with the prize being complete control over the running of the House. For the last year, scholars from the two sides have desperately poured over the codex, with one side insisting there's enough evidence to favor The Father, while the other saying it can only be The Mother. Since no one could agree, it was decided, though reluctantly, that it would be left to the king to interpret the writings himself and then make a decision that would be forever binding."

"King Jorquin!" I said with a snort. "Are you saying that man now holds power over the fate of the House?"

"No," Daughter Gernet said, shaking her head. "The king fell while on the hunt almost a month ago now. He can neither speak nor move, but only lies in his bed staring at the ceiling, mumbling and drooling. The physicians tell us their best guess is he will die within the year. It could be tomorrow, or it could be ten months from now, no one knows for certain. What we do know is the law states that if a king becomes incapacitated and cannot fulfill his duties, then all important decisions regarding the kingdom fall to his heir."

"Prince Tyro!" I grunted, slamming my fist down on the table. Both Daughter Gernet and Jin jumped, while Malo just stared at me blankly with his arms crossed over his chest.

"Now you're beginning to see," Daughter Gernet said. "That's why the Sons and we Daughters went to Gasterny. Each to petition the prince with the known facts, and each with the hope that he would choose us."

I thought back to how angry the Son and Sons-In-Waiting had been when they'd come down from seeing Prince Tyro, and also how happy the Daughters had been and suddenly it all fell into place. "He chose The Mother," I said to Daughter Gernet.

"He did indeed," the priestess nodded. "We left Gasterny ecstatic, only to be told shortly afterward that the Piths had killed Prince Tyro in retaliation for a breach in the treaty." Daughter Gernet shook her head. "Horrible luck, we believed. With Prince Tyro's decision, we would have had the final say on all Holy House matters and even greater influence over whichever king sat on the throne without the need to ever compromise with the Sons." Daughter Gernet's eyes gleamed. "And with that newly found power, I would have had the ability to finally get to the bottom of what had happened in Corwick." She shrugged sadly. "Pernissy has always been favored by the Sons and their unswerving protection of him has stymied my inquiries at every turn. We Daughters were apprehensive when we arrived in Gasterny, but we put our faith in The Mother and The Father and were prepared to accept Prince Tyro's ruling, whichever way it went. It never occurred to any of us that the Sons would think any different."

"But now it all makes sense," I said. "Doesn't it?"

Daughter Gernet looked at me and I could see anger brimming in her eyes. "Indeed, it does."

"So, with Prince Tyro dead and King Jorquin unable to make a decision, where does that leave everyone?" I asked.

"In big trouble," Malo grunted. He glanced at Daughter Gernet and she nodded that he should continue. "There is another heir," Malo said, "or rather, there are two of them."

"Tyden and Tyrale," Daughter Gernet said with a sigh. "Twin boys born minutes apart."

I blinked in surprise, then shrugged. "So, the eldest becomes king and chooses. He might still side with The Mother, so I don't see the problem."

"The problem is both have compelling evidence that they were born first," Malo said with a snort, "and so both lay claim to the throne."

"Tyden supports The Mother's right to lead," Jin added, finally speaking.

"And Tyrale, The Father's," Daughter Gernet finished for her.

I shook my head at the complexity of it all. "So, once King Jorquin finally dies..."

"Civil war comes to Ganderland," Daughter Gernet said bleakly. "With prince fighting against prince and House fighting against House." She tapped her finger on the wood as she stared across the table at me. "Which brings us to you."

"I don't see what I can do to help," I said as I spread my hands in the air.

Daughter Gernet glanced at Malo for a moment, then shifted back to me. "We want you to work with us to weaken Prince Tyrale and his people," she said. "As things stand now, most of the more powerful lords, like Pernissy and Lord Demay, side with him and the Sons. When the war does come, which it will, we'll be hard-pressed to even hold our own, let alone triumph."

"I still don't understand what I can do about it," I said.

Jin put her hand on my arm. "What they are trying to say, Hadrack, is because you're already a known and wanted man, they want you to strike at Prince Tyrale from outside the law. This way no one can accuse Prince Tyden and the Daughters of doing anything."

I snorted. "You want me to become an outlaw? What good will living in the woods and living off berries do your cause? You're talking about powerful men here with armies and castles. How can one man bring them down?"

"You don't need to," Malo said. "You just need to sow confusion and doubt within their ranks and strike at the selected targets we pick for you. There's a vast network of rich merchants, bankers and traders spread out all over the kingdom whose wealth is essential to further Prince Tyrale's plans. We want you to steal that wealth for us to fund our armies and deny it to his."

I frowned. "But unless this prince is a fool, he'll quickly realize what's happening and who's behind it," I said.

"Not at first," Daughter Gernet said. "And maybe not at all. Your targets won't always be Prince Tyrale's people. We'll make sure you go after some who are neutral, and even some known to support Prince Tyden. We'll also have operatives within the towns spreading rumors of your exploits, whether they be true or not. That should throw Prince Tyrale off the scent long enough for us to grow stronger."

"And I'm supposed to do this thing alone, am I?" I asked sarcastically.

"Certainly not," Daughter Gernet said. "I have an estate near the town of Laskerly, a small manor house that I inherited when my brother died almost five years ago now. It's called Witbridge Manor, and though it's in some need of repair, I expect it will do nicely as a base for your operations. I'll send word to my steward there, Finol, that you're coming and instruct him to spread the word that you're my nephew come to take up residence. You'll have to hire men of the unsavory type, I imagine," she added. "Although that shouldn't prove too difficult, as there are many such men willing to do just about anything for gold close by in Laskerly." Daughter Gernet looked at me severely. "Whatever happens, Hadrack, you can't let them or anyone else know what you're up to. Prince Tyrale can never know that you're connected to us, and as far as the men you hire are concerned, you'll just be a simple outlaw out to rob whomever you can."

I frowned, thinking I'd heard the name Laskerly before, but I couldn't remember where and I thrust if from my mind as I stood up and started to pace. My head was beginning to hurt from all the bits of information I'd just taken in, with each one demanding my immediate attention as I tried to focus. I thought of Baine and Jebido, wondering how they were doing under the care of the apothecary. My stomach suddenly lurched unpleasantly when I thought about what would happen to them if I refused to help.

"These targets you speak of," I finally said. "Would Lord Corwick be one of them?"

Daughter Gernet hesitated. "Yes, and no." I frowned at her and she sighed. "Pernissy is a different matter altogether. As much as I despise the man and want retribution for what he's done, his ambition in all this might prove useful to our cause. I know for a fact that he aspires to take the crown for himself, since he is of the royal bloodline, so leaving a snake like that slithering around behind Prince Tyrale's back could further weaken him. For that reason I don't think eliminating Lord Corwick, at least right now, would be wise."

I turned to face her and I propped my fists on my hips. "Why should I care about any of that? You say you want my help, but it sounds to me like I'm just going to be an errand boy at your beck and call with no say in anything. I've already spent over a year waiting to fulfill my vow, and I'm telling you right now that I'm done waiting and taking orders!"

"No one said you have to wait, Hadrack," Daughter Gernet said. "I have something you desperately want, and if you agree to help us, I'll give it to you."

"What?" I growled, feeling suddenly suspicious.

Daughter Gernet stood up and walked over to the desk, where she removed a piece of parchment from a drawer. She held it up. "The names of the nine men who destroyed Corwick," she said.

I snorted and shook my head. "That's it? I already know their names. I've even killed two of the bastards already."

Daughter Gernet blinked at me in surprise and I saw her glance at Malo uncertainly.

"It's not just their names," Malo said. "We also know where most of these men are located." Malo stood up and crossed the room to stand in front of me. "Join with us and we'll give you one of those names right now and where to find him. After you kill him, go to Laskerly and do as we ask. When the time is right, we'll give you another name, and then another one after that, until all of them are dead. Then, when Daughter Gernet feels it's appropriate, you can kill Lord Corwick as well. This way we all win." Malo extended his hand to me. "Is it a deal?"

"You'll continue to care for Jebido and Baine if I do this, even if I'm caught and killed?" I asked, weighing my options.

"As though they were my own family," Malo said. "You have my word. When they're healthy again they can join you in Laskerly."

I thought about my friends and the seven men scattered across the kingdom of Ganderland, knowing how difficult it would be to locate them all on my own. What was happening right now within the House, though upsetting to me, was incidental to my vow and I knew that I might never get a better opportunity than this to fulfill it. I glanced at Jin, who nodded to me, looking hopeful. I sighed and locked arms with the House Agent.

"You have a deal," I said.

10: SIM

The apothecary was odd, just as Malo had warned me he would be. I'd already spent two days in his rambling cottage, which was the best description I could come up with for the highly unusual place. The sprawling, disjointed building looked as though it had been designed by a man that had lost his mind long ago. Additions had been tacked onto the structure with no thought to style, practicality or accessibility. On two occasions I'd come across a door, only to open it and find myself facing a solid wall of yellow brick that Haverty had told me he'd bought from far off Taspania. I can't even begin to guess what the purpose of the bricks might be, as I hadn't seen it used anywhere else in the building except in those doorways. I quickly concluded that while the apothecary was undoubtedly brilliant in the arts of medicine and healing, he seemed to be completely lacking in the ability to do anything else. It became an all-too-common sight to see him having a heated conversation with a wall or a chair, and if not for Hasther, his doting, matron-like servant, I can't imagine the man lasting for more than a day or two on his own up in the hills.

Whatever Haverty's failings outside the realm of healing, however, inside them he was without question unmatched. Jebido was awake and talking now due to the apothecary's skill, and I was relieved to learn that although an arrow had come close to nicking Jebido's heart, he would eventually make a full recovery. Baine would recover completely as well, I was happy to hear, and Haverty assured me he wouldn't lose his leg or any significant loss of movement in his wrist. Baine might have a slight limp when all was said and done, but considering what his leg had looked like when he'd arrived, I think it was safe to say my friend considered it a bargain.

Malo had given me two days to spend with Jebido and Baine and I enjoyed that time with them immensely, though Jebido did become moody and abrupt with me whenever I mentioned leaving. We'd argued more than once already about Malo's plans for me and I knew there would probably be another one coming now that I was finally set to leave. Jebido and Baine were both sitting up on straw-filled mattresses placed side by side in a room shaped like a triangle, with the beds against the plaster wall at the wide end and a thick Afrenian carpet filling most of the floor space. A small, round window let in light from above my friends' heads and a narrow entrance with a wondrous folding door the likes of which I'd never seen before was set at the point of the triangle. That entrance was so small that I had to duck and turn sideways just to pass through it and I was always afraid of getting stuck.

"Why can't this outlaw business wait until we're all ready to travel?" Jebido grumbled as I said my goodbyes.

"Because that's the deal I made with Malo," I replied with a sigh. "We've been over this already."

Jebido stared past his hooked nose at me and I could see the bitterness he felt at being left behind in his eyes as he examined my new armor. "You look ridiculous in that," he grunted. "Like some kind of prancing dandy."

I bit my tongue, knowing Jebido's harsh words were being said out of frustration, though I have to say I was still a little hurt by his criticism. I thought I looked pretty good and had been anxious to show off my new armor. Gris, a servant of Malo's, had arrived an hour ago and he'd brought the specially-made armor with him. The armor had a muted grey finish, with the joints along the pauldrons, breastplate, plackart, and even the gauntlets that I had tucked into my belt, lined with thick black leather padding embossed with a gold border. Even the tasset around my waist, the cuisses for my thighs and the heavy greaves protecting my legs were lined in black and gold. My helmet, which I held under my arm, was shaped like a snarling wolf, with two holes for my eyes, while my mouth was barely visible behind sculpted protruding teeth sharpened to fine points. The helm seemed a little much, I have to admit, but Malo had insisted it was a necessary extravagance to help create the effect they were looking for.

I shifted the heavy black shield on my back that was embossed with a howling wolf overlaid over a white X and I shrugged at Jebido. "Malo wants people to remember and fear me," I said uncertainly.

"Oh, they'll remember you all right!" Jebido snorted. "They'll be pissing themselves laughing so hard they won't be able to even lift a sword to stop you!"

"Don't listen to him, Hadrack," Baine said. "I think you look very fierce." He glanced at Jebido and shook his head. "It was a lot quieter around here when you weren't talking."

Jebido glared back at Baine. "Is that right? Well, it hasn't been all sunshine and roses sitting here listening to you prattle on all day either, you know."

"You don't say!" Baine said angrily. "Maybe we should..."

"Gentlemen," I said, cutting Baine off. "I hate to break this up, but I have to go and I'd prefer knowing that my two friends aren't going to end up on the floor trying to kill each other the moment I'm out the door." I put my free hand on my hip. "You're going to be here together all winter, so I suggest both of you try to get along."

"Of course you're right," Baine said sheepishly. He glanced sideways at Jebido. "Truce?"

Jebido grunted sullenly, barely nodding his head. I sighed inwardly, knowing the only thing that would get Jebido out of his black mood was him getting out of that bed. Unfortunately, that wasn't going to happen any time soon and I decided to change the subject. "I'll be heading to Hillsfort when I leave here," I said, feeling my pulse start to quicken at the thought. I glanced at Jebido. "Do you know it?"

Jebido just shook his head and looked at his hands.

"Are you sure the bastard will be there?" Baine asked.

I shrugged. "Malo's information seems sound. Time will tell."

No one said anything and I stood there awkwardly in the silence, trying to think of something else to say. Finally I nodded. "Well, I hope to see you both at the manor in the spring."

I turned and headed for the door, pausing as Hasther appeared in the doorway with fresh dressings in her hands. The servant was very short and very fat, with a ruddy complexion and thin, greasy-grey hair. She rolled her eyes and groaned out loud as she worked to squeeze her bulk through the opening and I automatically took her arm and helped to pull her in.

"Thank you, Hadrack," Hasther said, out of breath. "I've been after His Lordship for years to make this doorway bigger, but all he ever tells me is I just need to make myself smaller."

"My pleasure, Hasther," I said as I moved aside to make room for her. "And I think you're fine just the way you are," I added with a wink. I gestured to Baine and Jebido with my head. "Careful, they're in fine form today."

Hasther chuckled. "Not to worry. I've found that a good swat across the temple can do wonders for a man's sour disposition."

I grinned, secretly wishing Hasther luck and not liking her chances as I started to leave.

"Hadrack!" Jebido called out to me. I paused and glanced back as he pointed a finger. "You be careful and don't do anything stupid. If you go and get yourself killed before we get there I'm going to be angry with you."

"Same here," Baine said. "You stay alive."

I grinned at my two friends. "I promise I won't let anyone kill me until you arrive in the spring."

I pushed my way through the narrow doorway into a room that I thought of as the map room. Maps of all kinds, shapes and sizes were pinned to the walls and sat in unruly piles atop furniture. Some of the maps were even fastened to the ceiling and others tacked to the floor as carpeting. I was always afraid of tearing the maps with my heavy boots as I walked over them.

"So, you'll be leaving us, then?"

I glanced at Haverty, who stood in the doorway that I knew led to what was once a kitchen, but was now referred to as something called a laboratory. The apothecary spent most of his time mixing his medicines in that room and there were always strange smells coming from inside that turned my stomach. Haverty was incredibly thin and tall, with an egg-shaped, bald head ringed by long strands of white hair that fell almost to his waist. His nose was long, almost rivaling Jebido's, and his beard was shaven down the middle of his chin, leaving two long white strands hanging to either side that dangled like the fancy curtains I'd once seen in the reeve's house in Corwick.

"Yes, it's time for me to go," I said. I hooked a thumb over my shoulder. "I want to thank you for what you've done for them. I'll always be indebted to you."

Haverty waved a hand in the air dismissively. "Think nothing of it, my boy. I enjoy a good challenge." He smiled ruefully. "It's refreshing to get away from my plants and bottles once in a while and feel useful again." Haverty was dressed in a long-flowing green robe, with a Blazing Sun pendant hanging around his neck suspended from a thick gold chain. The thin cloak thrown over his shoulders was bright red and clasped with a small Rock of Life pin, which the apothecary fiddled with constantly as he talked. "It's not often anymore that I get to..." Haverty paused and turned his head sideways, clearly listening before he glanced up at the map-covered ceiling above him. "Not that again!" he grunted. I stared at the man in confusion. "Can't you hear them?" Haverty asked, pointing above his head. "Listen to the little bastards. They've started playing that music again despite their promises. That's the third time this week." Haverty brushed past me, mumbling to himself as he strode across the room and disappeared down a crooked corridor that I knew led to a set of rickety stairs and the second floor. "I hear you!" Haverty shouted as he stomped up the stairs. "You won't get away from me this time!"

I shook my head as I let myself out of the apothecary's residence. I hadn't heard anything from upstairs and as far as I knew, other than Jebido and Baine, Hasther and the old man were the only other people who lived in the rambling building. Gris was waiting for me in the overgrown courtyard outside the cottage when I came out and he nodded to me, looking irritated. Gris was a thin, nervous man with a crooked back, huge overbite, and weak, watery eyes. I glanced at Angry as he shook his ears at me and I sighed, wondering yet again why I hadn't insisted on a different mount. For whatever reason, there was something about this horse, even with its painful stubbornness, that made me reluctant to part with him. A small brown mare laden with heavy saddlebags had her reins fastened to the back of Angry's saddle and I nodded back to Gris that I was ready. I reached out to pat Angry's muzzle, then snapped my hand back as the big black tried to nip at my fingers with his yellow-stained teeth.

"We should have been gone by now," Gris said with a nervous twitch. The servant twitched a lot, I noticed, and he had an odd way of speaking, always drawing out the last word of a sentence for emphasis. I found both things to be hugely annoying. "Malo says you have to wear the cloak until you get across the White Rock," Gris added, gesturing to the saddlebags.

I sighed and walked over to the mare, stowing away the wolf helmet and shield before rummaging around in the bags until I found the heavy green cloak. I put it on as Gris mounted his horse and then sat watching me expressionlessly. I flipped up the hood and turned to glance back at the building, which, truth be told, didn't look nearly as bad from the outside. Thick stone walls, stone chimneys at each end, and a high, tiled gable roof all lent it an air of normalcy, until you started to look closer, that is. The gabled dormer, normally set in the center of a cottage roof, jutted out from above the crooked and slanted porch roof, where it had no business being. Leaded glass windows faced me, one on each side of the doorway, with heavy wooden shutters placed above and below the windows, rather than to the sides. As far as I could tell, the shutters served no practical purpose whatsoever. Wooden corridors on stilts ran off each side of the house, curling back behind it like a bird's wings that lead to a multitude of small, medium and large structures that all connected with the cottage in some way. The sprawling additions only ended when they eventually reached the chiseled rock face of the hillside almost forty yards behind the original structure.

"The man's as mad as a squirrel with one leg," Gris said as he looked at the house. "But there's no face I'd rather see when blood's pouring out of me than his."

I nodded and swung up into the saddle, urging Angry into motion. The packhorse resisted the pull of the reins for a moment, but then fell in behind us in resignation as Angry followed Gris down a steep path overgrown with weeds and clumps of ryegrass. We traveled north for the rest of that morning, keeping off the roads when we could and rarely saying anything to each other. Gris was an unimaginative sort, and with his annoying way of speaking, I was just as happy to spend the journey in silence. We finally came to an escarpment of dark granite shaped vaguely like a bear's head around mid-day and we stopped our horses near the edge, looking out over the countryside to the west. Below us lay a wide valley separated by a river that twisted and turned through fields, woodlands and rolling hills. Far to the north I could see the towering, snow-covered peaks of the Father's Spine mountain range.

"The White Rock," Gris said, pointing to the far-away river. He nodded to the north. "There's a pathway leading down over there about a quarter mile or so. You shouldn't have any trouble finding it."

I looked at the servant in surprise. "You're not coming?"

Gris twitched and then shook his head. "Malo told me to take you here and go no further. You're on your own now." He spit on the ground and wiped his mouth with his knuckles, then pointed. "You see that smoke down there, near where the river almost turns back on itself?" I shaded my eyes, squinting against the mid-day sun until I found the spot he meant, then I nodded. "Good," Gris said. "Make your way there to a place called Limeview. The town is a crawling cesspool, no other word for it. With beer so bad and whores so ugly even the drunkest of men would run from both. But at least they have a ferry that crosses the river. The nearest bridge is a day and a half ride from here, so the ferry is the quickest way to get across. Just make sure you keep that cloak on until you're over the river. Malo doesn't want anyone seeing your face until then. After you get to the other side, it's up to you what you do." Gris squinted up at the sun. "The ferry is run by a mean bastard by the name of Skind Kurko." Gris reached inside his tunic and drew out a small moneybag and offered it to me. I pretended not to notice his hand twitching as he held it out. "This is from Malo. Don't give Kurko more than two Jorqs for passage. Any more than that and he's robbing you."

A Jorq was a gold coin that had the impression of King Jorquin's face stamped on it on both sides. I nodded that I understood as I took the pouch.

Gris looked me up and down. "He's a tricky bastard, Kurko is, but he usually just picks on the weak. You're young, and with your size and look it should give him pause for thought. Whatever you do, don't let him see how much gold you have, and don't let him push you around."

"I'll keep that in mind," I said. I hefted the moneybag and looked at Gris thoughtfully. "What's all this for? Daughter Gernet already gave me money to hire men."

Gris shrugged. "I just do as I'm told, Hadrack." He winked at me. "But where I come from, if somebody wants to hand you a bag full of gold, you take it and keep your mouth shut."

I nodded and tucked the bag under my armor, nestling it against the bulging moneybag Daughter Gernet had already given me. Combined, I had more wealth on me now than I had ever expected to see in a lifetime. "Once I get across the river, how do I find Hillsfort?" I asked.

Gris gestured with his head. "Keep heading west until you pass through those hills over there." I glanced to the west, just able to make out the hazy, rippled backs of forested hills far in the distance. "Hillsfort is on the other side." Gris held out his hand and I locked arms with him as he twitched in my grasp. "Good luck, and may The Mother watch over you."

Finding the pathway down to the valley was as easy as Gris had told me and I let Angry have his head as the big black gingerly picked his way along the rock-strewn trail. Once on level ground, I headed west, cursing the need for the heavy cloak as I sweated in the heat of the sun. It took several hours to reach Limeview, which turned out to be pretty much just as Gris had described it. Other than a tavern clad with faded and warped boards, a tall, rectangular Holy House that I was ashamed to see was almost falling apart, and a squat cookery called Tam's, there wasn't much else to see. There weren't many people moving about the town either, and those that were paused in what they were doing to stare at me suspiciously. There didn't seem to be any purpose for the place being there as far as I could tell, other than perhaps as a staging area for the ferry, I suppose. I made my way along what passed for the main street, with only a thin mongrel for company as it followed behind the mare's heels sniffing hopefully. I quickly made my way out of town, following the directions of a weathered sign tacked to a dead tree that stated Kurko's Cable Ferry was half a mile away to the west. The road led steadily downward, passing through a stunted forest of pine trees, where I paused to dismount and stretch my aching legs and back. I thought of the man I was heading to see in Hillsfort and I closed my eyes, picturing his face in my mind and hearing again his voice calling out to the others to save the women until the end. He was the last of the three who'd chased me into the bog and I relished the thought of finally getting a chance to make him pay.

"It's been ten long years, you bastard!" I said under my breath as I remounted. "But I'm coming for you."

Ten minutes later I found myself looking down at the White Rock from a small grassy knoll covered with a bed of bright yellow cat's ears. I'd left the road several minutes before to avoid a flock of bleating goats that a peasant and his two sons were herding, presumably heading for Limeview. Rather than wait for them to pass, I'd struck out overland until I'd reached the hill. Angry bent his head to nibble at the weeds and I jerked his reins hard, stopping him. I was far from an expert on horses but I suddenly remembered Ania had told me to never let a horse eat cat's ears, as it could give them something called stringhalt. An affliction, she'd told me, that caused the horse to jerk its legs upward, sometimes kicking itself in the belly and occasionally rendering the animal unable to even walk.

"That's not for you," I said, urging Angry forward with my heels.

The big horse snorted and glanced back at me in annoyance and I could tell by the stubborn look in his eye that he was considering taking a swipe at the weeds anyway. I yanked even harder on the reins until he reluctantly gave up and started to move. I looked over my shoulder, ensuring the mare hadn't touched the cat's ears either, then I guided the horses back onto the road that cut between my hill and the one adjacent to it. The road and land sloped down toward the river quickly at this point, and though I knew it was the same river that I'd seen at Gasterny, the two parts of the White Rock couldn't have been more different. In Gasterny, the river had been extremely wide and very wild, the surface foaming and seething as the quick rushing water rolled over hidden rocks, but here the river was perhaps a quarter of the width and was flowing almost serenely. Tranquil green hills lined the far bank of the river and a flat boat with sidewalls made from thin boards tacked to posts floated close to the shore on this side of the riverbank. A huge oak tree rose across the river directly opposite the boat and a thick rope was tied to it. The rope spanned the length of the river, passing through two drilled beams on the ferry, front and back, before ending wrapped securely around a thick post that had been set into the ground and then buttressed from in front by more posts set deeper into the ground. I saw the road ended at the riverbank where the ferry was moored and a small hut stood off to the side perhaps twenty feet from the water's edge. Three men sat around a weak fire and they studied me silently as I approached.

One of the men stood up and took several steps toward me as he pushed back his broad-brimmed straw hat to scratch at his bald head. The man was of medium build, with a closely-cropped grey beard and a spattering of deep pockmarks marring the skin along his cheeks. He regarded me with what I took to be greedy interest, while the other two men, who were both big and brawny wearing knee-length tunics, felt hats and wool trousers, looked away with disinterest.

"You would be Kurko," I said as I halted Angry about five paces from the man with the straw hat.

"That's me," Kurko said. He pointed a thumb toward the ferry. "Need to get across, do you?"

I glanced at the river and nodded. "I do."

"Well, that's what we're here for," Kurko said as he studied me appraisingly.

"How much?" I asked.

"Four Jorqs," Kurko said without hesitating.

I shook my head and peered down at the man from beneath my hood. "I'll give you two. Take it or leave it."

Kurko shrugged. "Then I'll leave it."

I kept my face expressionless, hiding the dismay I felt inside. I was pretty sure the man was bluffing, but if he wasn't, it was going to be a very long ride to that bridge. "Suit yourself," I said. I pulled at Angry's reins to bring him around and head back to Limeview, then I added as an afterthought, "But you and I both know two Jorqs is a fair price, and by the looks of things, you don't appear to be doing a booming business. Good day to you!"

"Hold up there," Kurko called as I guided Angry back down the road. "Did I say four Jorqs?"

"You did," I called over my shoulder.

"Mother's tit!" Kurko muttered as he removed his hat to scratch at his head. "I must be getting old or something. I meant for both ways. Four Jorqs for a trip across and back."

I stopped Angry and turned in the saddle to look back. "Now why would I pay you to take me over there, just to bring me right back?" I asked.

"You wouldn't," Kurko agreed hastily. "Only a fool would do that." He put his hat back on and shrugged. "Sometimes men go across for the day, then return at night. I thought you might be one of those. My mistake. My men and I will gladly take you across for three Jorqs."

I turned Angry back around so we were facing Kurko again. "I think you mean two!" I growled at him.

Kurko's face tightened, then he smiled and bowed dramatically, though his eyes registered no warmth at all as he stood back up. "Yes, of course. That's what I meant to say."

"Very well, then," I said, suppressing a grin of triumph. "On those terms, we have a bargain." I'd had the presence of mind to take three coins from the moneybag Daughter Gernet had given me and slide them alone into an inside pocket in my cloak before I approached the ferry. I fished around for them as Kurko watched me expectantly. I drew one out, flicked it to him, then the other one as Kurko caught them both deftly. I held up the last Jorq for the ferry owner to see. "Which leaves me with one left to get lodging and food tonight in Hillsfort. Is there a place you can recommend?"

Kurko chuckled. "For food and somewhere to sleep, or for something else?" he asked slyly.

I forced a laugh and then shrugged. "Whatever fate brings my way, I suppose."

Kurko turned to the men at the fire and whistled between his teeth. "Bridy, Sim, on your feet, you dogs! We have a paying customer here!" He turned back to me. "I have a friend who runs an establishment in Hillsfort," Kurko said. "Goes by the name of Hape. The place is called The Last Ride. Tell Hape that Skind Kurko sent you and he'll treat you right."

"I'll do that," I said, nodding and keeping my face neutral.

Inside I felt a jolt of elation. Malo's information had been correct after all. I'd found the bastard! I urged Angry and the mare forward eagerly as Kurko, Bridy and Sim jumped the short distance from the shore to the ferry, then maneuvered a wooden platform across the two so that we could board. Angry paused at the wood planks, sniffing the ramp with distrust before he snorted and stepped back. I cursed under my breath, feeling my face redden under the stares of the three men as I kicked the horse with my heels, but Angry refused to move. Finally I dismounted and tugged on the reins, trying to pull him up after me. The big black whinnied angrily and tossed his head, then retreated, pulling me along with him and bumping into the mare, who stood waiting docilely behind him.

"We don't have all day!" Kurko scolded from the ferry. "Get control of your horses!"

"I'm trying!" I grunted as I heaved back on the reins. My booted feet were sliding on the slick ramp as Angry pawed at the shore and snorted in defiance, refusing to budge.

"Sim!" I heard Kurko snap in disgust behind me. "Get those horses aboard!"

"Right away!" Sim shouted as he ran to my side. He lifted a hand to Angry and glanced sideways at me. "You just need to know how to talk to him," he said almost apologetically. Sim was around my age, with brown eyes, thick brown hair that hung over his forehead from beneath a black, pointed felt cap, and a wispy beard. "Horse's are a lot like people," Sim explained. "They just need to understand what's going on, is all." He looked up at Angry. "Easy now, easy. We're just going to take a little ride on a boat. Nobody is going to hurt you." Sim never took his eyes off Angry and I was surprised to see the big black allow the boy to gently stroke his muzzle. I held my breath, expecting Angry to try to bite, but the horse just stood there and twitched his ears happily. "Hand me the reins," Sim said out of the side of his mouth. I did so, then backed up the platform until I was on the ferry. "It's all right," Sim coaxed, taking a step up the ramp. "Just come with me and everything will be fine." Angry took a hesitant step forward, then another until his right front hoof was firmly on the wood of the ramp. "That's good," Sim whispered. "Really good." He took another step back and Angry followed, then another and another until finally the big stallion had made his way up the platform and onto the ferry. "Good boy!" Sim said with a smile as he stroked Angry's muzzle. "What a good boy!"

The mare had automatically followed Angry up onto the ferry and Sim guided the two horses further onto the boat. He tied Angry's reins to the sidewall as Kurko and Bridy worked to pull in the ramp.

"Take us out, Bridy," Kurko commanded once they'd stowed the platform against the sidewall.

Bridy had short black hair, sloping shoulders and a sullen-looking face. He moved to stand with Sim near the rope, which hung about waist height on the right side of the ferry. Together, the two men began pulling the flat boat hand over hand out into the river as Kurko stood against the sidewall facing me with his back against the planks.

"That's quite a horse you have there," Kurko said as he nodded to Angry. I didn't bother answering and just stared out over the water. Kurko crossed his arms over his chest and frowned. "What did you say your name was again?"

I could feel the wind tugging at my hood and cloak as we moved further out onto the river and I shifted my eyes to the ferryman. "I didn't give a name," I said, trying to hide my dislike for the man and failing miserably. "And that's the way it'll stay."

Kurko shrugged his shoulders. "That's your affair, I suppose," he said with a tight smile.

The ferryman glanced over to the mare and the saddlebags across her back and I saw his eyes burn with interest. I sighed inwardly, knowing there was going to be trouble. With some people you could just tell. We'd made it about halfway across the river and Kurko suddenly whistled between his teeth at his men. Both Bridy and Sim stopped pulling on the rope and they turned to watch us with an air of anticipation about them. I saw Bridy bend to pick up a rounded club that lay along the sidewall and I shifted my body so I could keep my eyes on all three men at once.

"The thing is," Kurko said as he tapped his fingers on his elbows while he studied me. "I've decided the deal we made over there," he pointed to the shore we'd just come from with a hooked thumb, "is no longer valid." He grinned widely at me and I was surprised at how small his teeth were. "We're going back to the original deal of four Jorqs."

I nodded, not all that surprised. Gris had warned me about Kurko, after all. "I told you I only have one Jorq left," I said, trying to keep my voice sounding calm and reasonable. "I don't want any trouble. All I want is to get across the river." I shifted my eyes to Bridy, who'd taken two steps closer to me. I noticed Sim hanging back looking reluctant, though the boy now held a club of his own in his hands.

"That's what you said," Kurko agreed. "One Jorq left." He gestured to Angry. "But I find it hard to believe that a man who can afford a horse like that, along with an equally fine mare, would be traveling with only three lonely Jorqs in his pocket." Kurko raised an eyebrow. "Am I wrong?"

Kurko was three paces from me against the railing and Bridy at least six or seven away, with Sim wavering uncertainly behind him. I tried to meet the boy's eyes over Bridy's shoulders, but the moment he saw my gaze on him, Sim quickly looked away. I didn't think the boy was going to be a problem judging by his body language, so I turned my focus back to Kurko and Bridy. Gris had told me Malo's instructions were very clear, wait until I was over the river to remove the cloak, and after that, the choices were mine.

"Would you say, in your expert opinion, that we're more than halfway across the river by now?" I asked Kurko.

The ferryman frowned, caught off-guard by the question. "What does that matter?" he finally asked as he pointed a finger at me. "We're not moving from here until you pay us what you owe!"

I decided halfway across the river was close enough and I pulled my hood back, revealing my scarred face as I smiled at Kurko. "Now we both know it wouldn't matter if I paid you or not," I said. I gestured to Bridy. "You and your man, here, want what's in those saddlebags, don't you? And I imagine you're willing to kill me for it." I'd deliberately left out mentioning Sim, hoping he'd get the message that I didn't consider him a threat.

Kurko grinned his small teeth at me. "Wouldn't be the first time," he said. "Won't be the last, neither."

The ferryman glanced sideways and I saw him nod imperceptibly and I tensed as Bridy bellowed and rushed toward me, already swinging the club for my head. I was expecting just such a move and I ducked, feeling the wind from the club's passage ripple my hair as I punched upward as hard as I could into Bridy's stomach. The big man gasped and shuddered as the wind exploded from his lungs and he fell to his knees, desperately trying to suck in air. I didn't give him time, however, and I kicked upward with my foot, catching him with the hard toe of my boot underneath his chin. Bridy's head snapped back and the club went flying from his nerveless hand as the big man fell limply onto his back and lay still. All of this had taken less than a second or two, and as I stood over the fallen man I glanced first at Kurko, who stood riveted in shock by the sidewall, then to Sim, who was staring at me with big round eyes.

"Get him, you mindless bastard!" Kurko finally screamed at Sim.

Sim hesitated, flicking his eyes first to Kurko, then to me. I could tell he didn't want to attack me, but I could also see fear in his eyes when he looked at Kurko. I decided before the boy did something foolish that now would be a good time to let them know who they were dealing with. I tore the clasp from my cloak, then pulled the garment off my body, revealing the armor underneath as I drew Wolf's Head and held the tip to Kurko's throat.

"You asked my name a moment ago," I growled to the ferryman. "Well it's Hadrack, the Outlaw of Corwick!" I glanced at Sim, then at the club he held and the boy immediately dropped it like it had suddenly become hot. I turned back to Kurko. "And I have to say, Skind Kurko, I'm not happy with your service. I believe I would like my money back."

"But!" Kurko started to protest.

I put pressure on Wolf's Head, cutting into the ferryman's neck. "This isn't a negotiation. Hand it over."

Kurko swallowed noisily and he reached inside his tunic with a shaking hand, drawing out his moneybag.

The ferryman fumbled clumsily with the drawstring and I just smiled at him and shook my head. "No need for that, friend," I said. I snatched the half-full moneybag with my free hand. "I'll take this as compensation for a poor experience and we'll just call it a day. What do you say?" Kurko opened his mouth to say something, then thought better of it and clamped his lips shut. "Good choice," I said. I stepped back, glancing down at Bridy, but the big man still wasn't moving. I gestured to Sim with Wolf's Head. "You, start pulling us across." Sim nodded and hurried to the rope and I turned back Kurko. "Go help him. I want to get away from this stinking boat as quick as I can."

"I can't!" Kurko protested, looking horrified. He held up

his hands, which I hadn't noticed before were red, swollen and deformed looking around the wrists. "Ganglia," the ferryman explained. "I can't pull on the rope. I swear or else I'd gladly help!"

"So you can't pull?" I growled as I sheathed my sword.

"No," Kurko said, shaking his head adamantly.

"Then what good are you?" I asked.

Before the ferryman could say a word, I leaped forward, grabbing him by the neck with my left hand and the crotch with my right. I heaved upward, grunting with effort as I lifted Kurko completely over my head, then leaned out over the railing and threw him into the river. The ferryman cried out in a long sustained shout of fear, which was abruptly cut off as he landed with a heavy splash in the water.

"Be happy I left you with your life!" I called after the man as the ferry slowly pulled away. I could hear Kurko cursing me and splashing around wildly as he tried to stay afloat and I turned my back on him. I heard a subdued chuckle and I glanced at Sim, who I could see was trying to suppress a smile, but not quite pulling it off. "That pleases you, does it?" I asked the boy.

"You can't imagine how much," Sim said as he labored to draw us across the river. He glanced down at Bridy, who I saw was beginning to stir and his face hardened with hatred. He nodded to the fallen man. "I don't suppose you could give that bastard a bath as well?"

I chuckled as Bridy groggily got to his hands and knees and I shoved hard with my foot, knocking him down beneath the lower planks of the sidewall near the edge of the boat. "It's the least I can do for him, I suppose," I said.

I stuck my foot under the sidewall and gave Bridy another shove and the big man slid easily and soundlessly over the edge and disappeared from view into the water. That should get tongues wagging about the Outlaw of Corwick, I thought with satisfaction as I went to help Sim on the rope. I glanced at the broad back of the boy as we worked and

I frowned, realizing the price he'd probably have to pay for what I'd done once he returned with the ferry to Kurko.

"What are you going to do now?" I asked. "I doubt your friends are going to be very happy with you."

"I don't know," Sim said with a shrug as he pulled on the rope. He glanced over his shoulder at me. "I always wondered what it'd be like to be an outlaw, though," he said almost shyly.

And that's how I gained the first member of my soon-to-be notorious outlaw band.

11: HAPE

Angry seemed a different horse now that Sim was riding the mare by my side. For the first time since I'd gotten onto Angry's back, he accepted my guidance without resistance or even a wayward glance. I was well aware, of course, that Angry's new attitude in life had nothing to do with me, and everything to do with Sim. My companion, I quickly realized, had a forthrightness and honesty about him that I found, much like Angry did, strangely comforting and soothing. Sim's story, I learned as we left the ferry behind, was similar to my own; one of hardship and loss, though certainly not to the extent of what I'd been through. I quickly developed a deep feeling of kinship with Sim and listened with interest as he told me of his life growing up on a farm near Limeview. As the hours went by, I told him of my upbringing as well, although I was careful to leave out the part about the massacre at Corwick and let him believe I'd been forced to leave my village to join in the war against the Piths.

"So how is it you became an outlaw, then?" Sim asked me as we paused to let the horses drink from a thin stream cutting through a meadow alive with white clover and buzzing bees. He raised an eyebrow. "Did you run away?"

I glanced at the sun, which was just beginning to kiss the hills that sheltered Hillsfort from my eyes. "Something like that," I said evasively. Sim nodded, accepting that as an answer, though I could see him examining my armor curiously. I knew he was wondering where I'd gotten it and I decided to change the subject before he could ask. "Actually, today is my first day as an outlaw."

Sim looked surprised at that and he leaned down and patted the mare's neck tenderly as she drank. I was struck again by his gentleness as he glanced sideways at me. "So how's it going so far?"

I don't believe my companion had meant it as a joke, but it struck me as incredibly funny anyway. I tilted my head back and laughed deeply from the pit of my stomach. I hadn't laughed like that in a very long time and I fought to gain control of myself while Sim just stared at me in confusion. Finally, still chuckling, I shrugged. "Not too bad, I guess," I managed to say through my mirth. My face slowly hardened, though, as I thought of Kurko. "It would have been a lot worse if I'd let those bastards back there get the better of me like they'd planned."

Sim took in a deep breath and his expression saddened. "I'm sorry about that," he said, sounding genuinely upset. "It wasn't my idea. I hated what they were doing and I tried to run away more than once, but he always found me and brought me back."

"Who, Kurko?" I asked, motioning that we should get moving again.

"Yes," Sim said with a nod.

"Why'd you let him bring you back?" I asked as we splashed through the stream while tiny tadpoles darted around the horses' hooves. "You're twice his size."

Sim made a sour face. "Because he's my uncle and all the family I have left. I wanted to hit him but I just couldn't bring myself to do it. Every time I thought about doing it, I'd see my mother's face and hear her voice pleading me not to." Sim sighed. "She's long gone from this world, but when she was alive she loved him deeply. I'll never understand why."

"Ah," I said, understanding the power of family. I thought about how good it had felt lifting Kurko over my head and hearing his screams of fright as I threw him into the river. I smiled. "Well, he wasn't my uncle."

Sim grinned back at me and I saw his eyes start to twinkle. "No, he wasn't. Thank The Mother and The Father for that!"

We road in silence for a while after that, until finally the sun sank completely behind the hills, casting the valley in a blanket of darkness. "How far is Hillsfort now?" I asked, starting to feel annoyed. It looked to me like we were no closer to the shadowy hills in front of us than we had been several hours ago.

I sensed Sim shrug. "Another eight or nine hours maybe. Should we make camp for the night?"

I shook my head. "No, I've been waiting a long time to get to Hillsfort and I'm tired of waiting. We'll keep riding all night long if need be."

"Fair enough," Sim said, sounding unperturbed by the idea. We rode in silence for several minutes, then he added, "Mind telling me what we're going to be doing when we get there?"

I gestured to the hills, even though I knew Sim couldn't see me. "There's a man up there that's needed killing for ten years now," I said with an edge to my voice. "It's taken me that long to find him and I'm not stopping until he gets what's coming to him."

"He must have done something pretty bad to make you hate him so much," Sim said.

I could hear the question in my companion's voice, but although I'd quickly developed a liking for Sim, I wasn't prepared to tell him everything yet, so I just nodded in the dark and didn't bother to reply. We traveled on for several more hours, heading west as best I could tell, since a fine mist blanketed the ground and the moon and the stars were hidden by a thick layer of cloud cover. Sim assured me more than once that we were heading in the right direction, although I couldn't tell east from west to north in the mist. We reached a dense forest of pine and spruce, which the horses had to slowly and carefully pick their way through in the dark. The going was frustratingly slow and after almost half-an-hour of brushing past and under prickly branches, the land began to rise and the trees thin out. We crested a small knoll and paused just as high-pitched howls began off to our right, echoing eerily through the trees. I could barely believe what I was hearing and I felt the hairs on my arms stand up on end as the strange howls continued for several long minutes while we listened.

"Fortune watches over us tonight," Sim finally whispered as the sounds ended, his voice quivering with awe.

"Indeed," I agreed, knowing that we had just heard the call of a Golden Masked Owl.

The owl was a rarity and was well known to be both The Mother's and The Father's eyes and ears in this world. If you were lucky enough to hear or see one in your lifetime, it meant that one of Them was watching over you and giving you Their blessing. I felt a deep sense of satisfaction well up in my chest, certain that the call of the owl was from The Mother giving me Her support for what I was about to do in Hillsfort. I heard Sim whisper something to himself beside me and his saddle creaked loudly as he dismounted. He appeared at my side and fumbled in the darkness before he took my hand in his.

"I swear before The Mother and The Father that I will serve you with loyalty and honor for all of my days, until my dying breath!" Sim pledged to me.

I sat for a moment in stunned silence, amazed by the emotion in my companion's voice. "What's all this about?" I asked, perplexed by Sim's oath. "You've already agreed to join me."

Sim pressed my hand to his lips and I could feel the wetness of tears on my skin. "That was to be an outlaw," he said. "I joined you because I had nowhere else to go. Now it's different."

"Having nowhere else to go is as good a reason as any," I said, feeling uncomfortable as Sim continued to hold my hand.

"When we set out on this journey together," Sim said. "I asked the First Pair to send me a sign if my destiny was to serve you." He sniffed and kissed my hand again. "The owl's call leaves no doubt. You have my oath and my life, to do with as you please."

I cleared my throat, not sure what I should say. No one had ever given me their oath before and I was uncertain how to proceed. "I accept your oath of service, Sim of Limeview," I finally said formally. "From this day forth you will be known as my sworn man." I pulled my hand away and gestured to the mare. "Now get back on your horse. We still have a long way to go."

Hillsfort, I learned from Sim, was established almost four-hundred years ago when a group of pilgrims heading for Mount Halas became inflicted with the weeping bumps plague, which is more commonly known now as smallpox. As the disease worsened, they finally stopped and settled on a large hill by a branch of the White Rock that broke around the hill on both sides. The splintered river created a natural moat that helped to protect the pilgrims from roving attacks from the Pawantee, who were a savage tribe of flesh-eaters that used to flourish in the area. The pilgrims were convinced they would all perish on that hill, either from disease, starvation, or from the flesh-eaters, and according to Sim, many of them did. But, against all odds, some of them managed to survive, and those that did decided to stay, believing the hill to be blessed by the First Pair. As time went by, more and more people arrived, having heard of the sacred hill, until eventually a town developed.

Now, as I sat on Angry's back and stared at Hillsfort in the early dawn light, I saw that buildings not only dominated the top of the hill, but also everywhere along the sides from top to bottom as well. I tried to count the houses, but there were so many of them that I lost track, thinking idly that they looked like fat, blood-filled leeches clinging to the haunch of a cow.

"I didn't expect it to be so big," I said, wondering how I'd ever find Hape in all of that.

Sim shrugged in the half-light. "They say almost a thousand people live in Hillsfort," he said skeptically. He glanced at me. "I've heard Halhaven has double that, and Gandertown three or four times that amount."

I shook my head, unable to comprehend the idea of that many people living in one place. "There's only one in that thousand I care about," I finally grunted as I urged Angry forward.

A narrow bridge made of stone crossed the river and Sim and I cantered over it, only slowing the horses when we came to a tiny cluster of drab buildings that sat outside the walls that ringed the bottom of the hill. Dogs barked at our arrival and several of the braver ones took turns nipping at the horses' heels as we rode. Angry finally caught one of them on the snout with his back hoof, sending it whimpering away. After that the dogs just watched and barked at us from a respectful distance. We made our way through the huts just as a cock appeared and perched itself on a stump beside the dirt path. It ruffled its feathers and glared at us imperiously as we passed by before it began to crow the start to a new day. A man of about forty appeared naked in the doorway of one of the huts and he shouted at the cock to be quiet, grumbling to himself when the bird ignored him and continued crowing. Both Sim and I smiled at each other as the naked man cursed loudly and then went back inside.

We left the huts, crowing cock, and barking dogs behind and made our way to the city gates, which were surrounded by a fortified gatehouse of breathtaking white stone with tall rounded turrets set on each side of it. I saw with displeasure that the iron gates were closed and barred and I cursed under my breath, not wanting to wait until the sun came up before the gates were officially unlocked and opened to visitors.

"We'll have to wait, I guess," Sim said to me with a

shrug.

"I'm not big on waiting," I grunted as I put two fingers in my mouth and whistled loudly.

A watchman appeared almost immediately at the gates dressed in light armor with a conical helmet on his head and a long pike held in his right hand. An iron key was hooked to a leather belt that encircled his waist. "What you want?" the man asked, looking disinterested as he picked at his teeth with a dirty thumbnail.

"I need to get inside," I said.

The man glanced at the slowly rising sun. "Come back in an hour," he grunted as he turned to leave.

"I need to get in right now," I growled impatiently.

The watchman shrugged. "That's not my problem. Come back in an hour."

I dismounted and crossed to the gates and put my hands around the bars. "I don't have an hour, you imbecile!" The watchman instinctively took a step back and I tried to smooth out my features and make them less threatening. I decided to tell him the truth, or at least the version of it that I thought might get us in, at any rate. "I'm here about a murder! I need to see the town constable right now!"

"A murder!?" the watchman gasped in surprise. "Who's been murdered?"

"No one yet," I said, "but unless you let me in, someone will be soon."

"Who?" the watchman demanded, looking alarmed.

Sim came to stand beside me. "Can you keep a secret?"

"Of course I can," the watchman said eagerly as he leaned toward us to hear better.

"Good," Sim nodded. He looked around. "Who's the most important man in town right now? The one that just arrived recently?"

The watchman furrowed his brow, then I saw his eyes light up. "Do you mean Lord Pandergin?" he asked in wonder.

I gave Sim an approving glance, understanding where

he was going with the question and I nodded to the watchman. "That's the man," I said. "And if you don't let us in, he'll be dead within the hour."

"Mother Above!" the watchman muttered as he rubbed his chin. Finally he gestured behind him. "I'll call out the watch and we'll…"

"No!" I hissed with a quick shake of my head. "If you do that we'll never catch the person who's here to kill him." I tapped my temple with a finger. "We have to be smarter than him, you and me. Let us in, and my man and I will go quietly to see the constable. We'll set a trap for this murderous bastard and when he goes for Lord Pandergin, we'll nab him." I could see the watchman thinking it over and I added, "I've known Lord Pandergin for a long time now. When he learns you were the man smart enough to see the danger and brave enough to do something about it, I guarantee he'll reward you handsomely." I saw the watchman's eyes light up at the mention of a reward and I knew I had him.

"Very well," the watchman hastily agreed. He quickly unlocked the bar and slid it open, ushering us inside. "Quickly now," he said as first Sim, then I led our horses through the gate.

Once we were through, I put my finger to my lips. "Remember, not a word of this to anyone. We don't want the killer to get wind of it."

"Not a word," the watchman agreed. Sim and I mounted our horses and the watchman called after our retreating backs, "The name is Nigan! Nigan of the town's watch!"

I waved over my shoulder to Nigan without looking back as Sim and I hurried the horses through the gatehouse. Several more members of the watch stepped out to regard us with curious eyes and one called out a question, but I ignored him and we kept on riding.

"They'll remember us later," Sim warned as we followed a road upward that cut through a jumble of three-story houses. The buildings were built together so closely that a man would have had to turn sideways just to walk between them.

"By then it won't matter," I said.

I glanced up in annoyance at a woman who'd just thrown the contents of a chamber pot from her top story window, narrowly missing Angry's rump, then stopped a young boy carrying a heavy basket of linen. I asked the boy where I could find The Last Ride and he pointed up the road and told me it was in Upper Town. Sim and I followed a narrow, cobblestone road that wound its way around and around the hill, until we finally reached the gates to the town at the top. These gates were open, I was relieved to see, and Sim and I passed through them without incident. We paused the horses to stare in bewilderment at the already bustling streets.

"So many people," Sim muttered in obvious discomfort.

I saw an old man with a magnificent white beard leaning against the curtain wall near the gatehouse, while a boy no older than eight sat in a small cart laden with turnips in front of him. A goat was harnessed to the cart and the beast gave out a continuous and annoying bleating sound as I headed Angry toward the old man.

"Good morning to you," I said down to the man pleasantly. The bearded man nodded to me cordially, but said nothing. "I'm looking for someone," I said. "Runs a tavern here called The Last Ride, I believe."

"You believe, youngster?" the bearded man asked in a deep voice. "Or you know?"

"I know," I said with a quick nod. "Goes by the name of Hape."

The bearded man's face twisted with distaste and he scratched at his beard. "Is he a friend of yours?"

I snorted and shook my head. "Anything but. The bastard swindled my brother out of some money and I'm here to get it back."

"Ah," the bearded man said with a chuckle. "That

sounds like him." He gestured with his hand. "Three streets over. You can't miss it. Just look for the place with all the bruised whores."

I glanced at the man in surprise, then nodded, trying to keep my face neutral. "Thank you," I said.

The old man studied me thoughtfully as he played with the end of his beard. "Don't hurt the whores when you kill him," he finally said. "Hape beats those poor girls something fierce. They fear and hate him, so I'm betting they won't try to stop you. They're good girls underneath all that powder and fluff. Just had a rough go of it is all."

I paused, blinking at the man in surprise. "How did you know?" I asked.

The old man pointed his fingers at his eyes. "Shows right here, youngster. Death rides with you. It's as plain as the nose on your face."

I nodded, not bothering to try to deny my purpose. "I won't hurt the girls," I promised. "You have my word." The old man bowed his head in acknowledgment and I turned Angry away and headed up the street in the direction I'd been told.

"You find him?" Sim asked as he caught up to me.

"I did," I grunted, feeling a hardness taking over me as we guided the horses through a throng of ox-drawn carts, servants, maids, and harried-looking merchants all preparing for another day in a busy town.

I rested my hand on Wolf's Head as we passed one street, then another, until finally we reached the street the old man had told me about. I guided Angry down it, following behind a two-wheeled cart being pulled by an enormous, black-bearded man, while a small, skinny fellow dressed in a bright red tunic sat in the cart whipping the bigger man with a willow branch and urging him to move faster. I was aware of other people moving in the street as well, but I cared nothing for them. I studied the buildings to either side instead, barely able to control my breathing as I awaited that first glimpse of the place called The Last Ride. It was Sim who saw it first and he whistled to get my attention, then nodded toward a tall building nestled between a tanner's shop and a butcher's shop. I grunted in acknowledgment and headed toward the sprawling, three-story structure with its name painted boldly across the top of the doorway on a slab of rough pine. Sim and I dismounted near the cracked stone steps that led into the building and I handed Angry's reins to my companion.

"Wait here," I said gruffly. I looked up at the scuffed and sun-faded brick of the building and thought of the sins the man inside had committed. "I might be a while."

"I'll be here as long as it takes," Sim said with a nod.

I strode up the stairs and pushed in the doors. Inside, two windows on either side of the door let in weak light that barely cut through the gloom. Fat candles that were burnt down almost to the nub flickered weakly from rough ledges cut into the stone walls. The room was long and narrow, with a low ceiling of what might once have been white plaster that was now stained and cracked throughout. Darkened beams supported by thick posts ran down the center of the room every ten feet or so. A thin woman with brown hair sat hunched over a table near the door snoring loudly with her face pressed into her crossed arms and a low bar ran along one wall. Several stout shelves filled with bottles were attached to the wall behind the bar and a huge cask sat on the floor nearby with a spigot at the bottom dripping the occasional drop of beer into a spreading pool on the stone floor. A man and woman lay stretched out on a table further into the room and I crossed over to them eagerly. I studied the man's face, realizing with disappointment that whoever the sleeping man was, he wasn't Hape. A stairwell led up to the second floor and I heard the steps creak as a woman appeared at the bottom of the stairs.

"Oh!" the woman said when she saw me. "You startled me." She fussed with her hair and studied me, looking me up and down with interest. "We're closed now, but I just might consider making an exception for you," she said with a knowing smile. "I'm Flora, by the way."

Flora was tall and plumb, with blonde hair and ample breasts spilling out from a low-cut dress that left little work for the imagination. She reminded me of Meanda, Daughter Gernet's daughter and Jinny's mother, who'd died in Corwick. I noticed Flora's chin was bruised with a deep cut in its center and her left eye was swollen and puffy. I remembered what the old man had told me about Hape and his bruised whores and I shook my head, knowing instinctively that he had done this to the girl.

"I'm looking for Hape," I said, trying to keep the hostility and disgust I felt for the man from my voice.

"Oh," Flora said, looking disappointed. She waved her hand in the air. "He's gone somewhere to do something. I don't remember what."

I tried not to show my frustration. "Do you know when he'll be back?" I asked.

Flora shrugged and walked over to a table where several tin mugs sat. She grabbed one of the mugs, sniffed the contents, then drank whatever was in it before moving to the cask. "Not long," she said as she got down on all fours and poured some beer into the mug. She looked back at me and wiggled her hips suggestively. "The offer still stands if you want to have some fun before he gets back. It's on the house."

I forced a smile. "Thank you, but as tempting as it is, I'm just here to see Hape."

Flora closed the tap and then got back to her feet. "Suit yourself, handsome." She winked at me and headed to the table where the man and woman slept. "But trust me when I say you haven't been bounced properly until you've been bounced by me." Flora grinned surprisingly white teeth at me, then leaned forward and pushed the sleeping man away from the woman. "On your feet, you lecherous goat!" she shouted. The man rolled sideways, crying out in surprise as he flipped off the edge of the table and fell onto the floor with one of his feet draped awkwardly over the bench that sat near the table.

Terry Cloutier

"Mother's tit, Flora!" the man swore as he fought to extricate himself. "Why'd ya have to go and do that?"

"Don't you curse at me, Linny Plost!" Flora snorted as the woman lying on the table sat up, blinking in confusion. "It's well past closing time and you should be home by now taking care of your wife and the new babe."

Linny glanced to the door, looking crestfallen. "I must have lost track of the time," he muttered as he stood up and gingerly bent his knee back and forth. He turned to the woman sitting up on the table and took her hand in his. "It's been fun, Aenor. Can I see you again tonight?"

"Hape told you last night you get no more credit," Aenor said in a strange accent as Flora helped the girl to her feet. Aenor was perhaps fifteen or sixteen, with long brown hair twisted and piled on her head and darkly tanned skin tarnished by a livid bruise on her chest above a pair of small breasts that poked through her thin, blue cotton dress.

Linny's face fell. "Oh yeah. I forgot about that."

"Go home, Linny," Flora said. "Go home to your wife and stay there and don't come back. You hear me?"

Linny rubbed his hair, which was disheveled and greasy looking as he looked around. "Where's Hape?" he asked. "I'll have a talk with him and we'll come to some kind of agreement." He looked at Aenor and I could see the lust in his eyes. "I can't imagine a night without you, my love."

Flora snorted and rolled her eyes as she set her mug on the table. "Go stick your willy somewhere else, Linny. I told you to leave and not come back and I meant it."

Linny's eyes turned mean and he advanced on Flora. "Who are you to tell me what to do?" he demanded.

I stepped in front of Flora and put my hand on Linny's chest. "The lady asked you to leave. I suggest you do that."

"Lady!" Linny said with a sneer. "She's nothing but a fat whore with a big mouth that's good for only one thing."

I didn't think, I just reacted and I lashed out and up with my fist, catching Linny beneath the jaw and snapping his head

238

up. Linny grunted in surprise, then sagged to his knees as I grabbed him by his tunic and drew my clenched fist back to hit him again.

"No!" Flora cried, grabbing my arm with both her hands. I looked back at her questioningly. "Hape will be furious enough as it is!" she pleaded. "Please, just let him go! He's harmless!" I saw the intense look of fear in both Flora's and Aenor's eyes and I slowly lowered my arm and released my grip on Linny. "Go home, Linny," Flora said, turning to the kneeling man. "Go home and we'll forget this ever happened."

Linny pushed himself to his feet and gingerly felt his jaw as he glared at me, then Flora. "Wait until Hape hears about this, you bitch! He'll tan your hide!"

I took a threatening step toward Linny and he broke and ran for the door, glancing once over his shoulder at Aenor before he flung the door open and disappeared outside. The door slammed shut behind him and the woman sleeping at the table started and sat up in surprise.

"What's going on?" she asked in bewilderment.

"Trouble," Flora said as she grabbed her mug and took a nervous sip. I could see the mug shaking in her hand as the woman at the table stood up and approached us. "This is Margot," Flora said, indicating the woman. Margot was perhaps thirty and looked tired and worn, with huge bags under her eyes and sallow, unhealthy looking skin. Flora quickly explained what had happened and Margot's eyes widened in fear as she listened.

"What are we going to do?" Margot asked with a tremor in her voice. "I can't take another one so soon."

"Another what?" I growled. I was pretty sure I knew what she was talking about.

"Don't worry about it," Flora said, putting her hand on my arm. "It's not your problem."

"He beats us," Margot said. She turned and lifted her dress, showing me her bare backside, which was red with welts and bruised black and yellow. "For even the littlest thing," she added, smoothing out her dress again. "He enjoys it." She shook her head and I could see her fighting tears as both Aenor and Flora rushed to comfort her.

"Are you three the only ones here?" I asked as an idea began to form in my mind.

"Yes," Flora said with a nod. "Basina, our barmaid went home a few hours ago. It's just us."

"Good," I replied. I put my hand on Flora's shoulder. "Don't worry. When I'm done with him, Hape won't be able to hurt anyone ever again."

The eyes of all three women widened in surprise and hope at my words and I held up my hand, stalling any questions. I quickly told them about Corwick and what Hape had done there, then I told them the reason I'd come to Hillsfort. When I was done, they stood in shocked silence as I told them what I had in mind for both Hape, and them, if they were willing.

"So, what do you think?" I finally asked when I'd finished.

Flora shared a look with Aenor and Margot, then she turned back to me and nodded firmly. "We'll do it," she said with a gleam in her eye. "After hearing that story, it's only fitting."

I nodded and searched the room, finally finding what I wanted on the stairs, while the three women sat together at a table and whispered among themselves in excitement. When everything was ready, I hopped onto the bar and sat staring at the door, brooding about the man who would soon walk through it. I thought back to the women of my village who'd been staked out behind the sty in such a callous way, and even after ten years, the horror of what had been done to them still made me shudder. I'd known each of those women well and I instinctively knew that Hape had been instrumental in what had happened to them. The justice that I'd promised those women of Corwick when I was just a boy was finally coming for Hape, and I felt certain that they would approve of what I had decided to do.

I don't know how long I waited staring at that door, but eventually it opened and a medium-sized man with a pointed beard wearing a rich green tunic and blue trousers appeared silhouetted in the light from outside. Even from where I sat with the man's features cast in semi-shadow, I knew instinctively that it was Hape.

"What's this, then?" Hape demanded as he kicked the door closed behind him with his foot. Hape was holding a small crate in his hands and he looked first at me in confusion, then turned his angry stare on the women. "I asked you a question!" Hape snarled as he approached the bar and set the crate down on it. "Get off!" he grunted absently at me.

"Hape, we have a visitor," Flora said, gesturing to me. "This is Hadrack."

I studied the man, picturing his face the last time I'd seen him in the bog. Hape had aged surprisingly well, I saw, with only a few strands of grey peeking through beard and hair to show for ten long years of living with his crimes. Those crimes hadn't weighed on the bastard at all, I thought. I couldn't imagine how he had risen from a simple soldier to an obvious man of means, but knowing Hape, I suspected that it hadn't been done through honest hard work.

"I don't care who you are!" Hape said with a sneer. He put his hands on his hips as he regarded me. "This is my place of business and I told you to get down off my bar!"

"Hadrack from Corwick," Flora added before Hape could say anything more.

Hape hesitated and he flicked his eyes at Flora for a moment and licked his lips before focusing back on me. "Is that supposed to mean something to me?" Hape finally asked.

"Yes," I said, willing myself to remain in control. I jumped down to the floor, standing towering over Hape and fighting the urge to pummel him out of existence.

"Never heard of it," Hape said with dismissive a shrug. He turned to the women, his face red with anger. "How many times have I told you we don't allow guests after hours?"

"I'm not here as a guest," I said softly. I moved so I was blocking the path to the door and lay my hand on Wolf's Head. "I'm here to kill you." Hape gaped at me and I saw his hand fall to his side, where the hilt of a knife jutted out. I leaned closer to him. "You said I was stupid!" I hissed at him. "Remember?"

Hape shook his head, his eyes darting from side to side, looking for a way out. "I don't know what you're talking about," he said. "I've never even met you before."

I laughed. "Oh, but you have, Hape." I put my hand out about chest high. "I was only this big then. A frightened boy hiding in a bog. Remember?"

Hape's eyes widened in understanding and he began to shake his head back and forth. "It can't be!" he whispered.

"It is," I said. "I saw everything you did. You and the others." I nodded my head toward the women. "And now they know what a murderous bastard you are as well."

"Listen," Hape said, wetting his lips. "Maybe you and I..."

Hape suddenly snatched out his knife, moving faster than I would have thought he could and he stabbed wildly at my stomach. How he thought he could puncture my armor with it is a mystery to me. I twisted sideways automatically to avoid the knife and the blade went between my arm and my side. I instantly snapped my arm down, trapping his hand between it and my side as Hape struggled helplessly to turn the knife on me.

"There wasn't any quicksand in the bog," I said with my face mere inches from Hape's. "So who's the stupid one now?"

I could smell the fear coming off of Hape and I smiled, enjoying the moment, then I drew my head back and smashed the top of my skull into the other man's face. Hape cried out in shock, dropping the knife as I released him. He stumbled wildly backward into one of the support beams, then bounced off it and spun away before tripping heavily over one of the table benches. Hape collapsed to the floor on his face and I drew Wolf's Head and stood over him as he rolled himself over and raised his hands to ward me off.

"Please!" Hape pleaded. "I have money!"

I snorted with disgust and flicked out with the sword, cutting deep into Hape's left bicep as he howled in agony. "That's for Meanda," I said in a flat, emotionless tone. I stabbed outward again, this time into Hape's right bicep. "And that's for her daughter, Jinny." Hape screamed a second time and he awkwardly rolled onto his stomach, trying to get away from me. I noticed that he was leaving behind twin red smears of wetness on the stone as he crawled across the floor. Hape began to blubber deliriously and I growled and caught him by a leg as he tried to get under a table. I dragged him back into the open as he wailed in dismay, then I flipped him roughly onto his back. "Were not done yet!" I grunted. "This is for the Widow Meade!" I stabbed deep into Hape's left leg, then stood back, staring down with indifference at the sobbing man by my feet. "And this is for Daughter Elias, you bastard!" I said. I lifted Wolf's Head high in both my hands, then plunged the blade deep into his right leg just above the knee. Blood sprayed and I twisted the blade back and forth savagely as Hape howled and writhed beneath me. When I was satisfied he'd suffered enough, I slowly drew my sword from Hape's flesh and bent and wiped the blade clean on his rich tunic as I whispered into his ear, "I've waited ten years to see you pay for what you did in Corwick." I glanced up at the women, who were watching us with rapt fascination. "And that day has finally come."

"Please! Please!" Hape pleaded with me through his tears. "I'll do anything you ask! Please don't kill me!"

"Too late for that," I growled as I stood up. "You've lived too long as it is." I turned and glanced at the seated women and I nodded that I was ready. "For the women of Corwick," I said.

"For the women of Corwick," Flora repeated as she, Margot and Aenor slowly stood.

Each of the women held a stout baluster in their hands that I'd broken off the stair railing and they slowly approached Hape and surrounded him.

"No!" Hape shouted, looking from one grim-faced woman to another. "You can't do this!"

Flora ignored Hape and looked at Margot. "I think you should go first," she said. "You've had to deal with him the longest."

Margot nodded and drew back the baluster in her skinny arms as Hape screamed and tried to raise his hands to ward off the blow. Margot just laughed as his arms flopped uselessly, then she struck downward with the baluster, catching Hape on the shoulder. Margot was followed immediately by Flora, who hit the helpless man hard in the stomach. Aenor was next and she hit Hape on the right kneecap, causing him to howl in agony as he writhed and tried to roll away. Flora snorted and put her foot on Hape's neck, pinning him down with her weight, then they started all over again. They worked in a steady rhythm after that, gaining confidence while I called out the names of all who'd been murdered in Corwick with each blow. Blood sprayed across the room and ceiling as the names rang out, and after a time Hape's horrified cries began to weaken. Eventually the room fell silent except for the sound of my voice, the meaty thuds of wood on flesh, and the heavy breathing of the women. Finally, when all the names had been called, I took the balusters from the shaking hands of the three women and tossed them aside, then I knelt beside what was left of Hape. Using his knife, I scratched deeply into the battered flesh of his forehead.

I stood up when I was done and tossed the knife aside. "Come, it's time to go," I said, ushering the three women out the door. I paused in the doorway to look back one last time at the shattered corpse and I glanced at the word that I'd cut into his flesh.

CORWICK

I smiled in satisfaction, knowing that the others would understand the message when they heard about Hape's death and would know that I was coming for them too.

12: WITBRIDGE MANOR

Witbridge Manor was more of a letdown than I had been expecting. Daughter Gernet had suggested to me in Halhaven that it might require some repair. But the stark truth, I realized as I sat Angry atop a rock-strewn hill and studied the place, was that it was more in need of knocking down and starting over than anything else.

"That's where we're going to stay?" Sim asked me as the cold morning wind blowing in from the north whipped at his tunic.

Behind us the three women sat their horses that I'd bought with Skind Kurko's money in silence, huddling against the cold breeze as they stared at our destination in obvious disappointment. The decaying walls of the manor sat perched on a high hill choked through with thorny weeds and wild-looking scrub brush, while behind it, I could see the imposing bulk of the Father's Spine mountains rising in the distance. A single raven sat on a rare section of the wall that was still intact and it cawed harshly at us, sounding very much like laughter to me before it sprung in the air and flapped away. I felt a moment of guilt wash over me, having promised the women a better life if they chose to come with me to Witbridge Manor. I was sure at that moment that all three of them were wishing they had stayed behind in Hillsfort.

The manor, as far as I could tell from my vantage point, appeared barren of life other than that single raven. The crumbling buildings and walls overlooked a fast-flowing stream that came from the north and cut directly around the rocky base of the hill. The water continued to flow south over and through the rocks toward us before it finally twisted away to the east and disappeared through a stand of trees almost a mile away. Overgrown fields that might have once been fertile land lay at the southern base of the manor, separated by low walls of different sized stones. I remembered collecting similar stones from the fields around Corwick when I was a boy. Long-abandoned, sagging houses were lined up in a row on both sides of the barely discernible road that eventually broke in two. One section of the road headed up the hill toward the manor, and the other continued on east along the stream, before skirting around the woods.

"Perhaps it's not as bad as it looks," I suggested with an optimistic shrug as I urged Angry down the hill.

"And perhaps the sun is really the moon," Sim muttered under his breath as he and the women followed me.

The cold wind was cut off substantially once we were down in the valley and, as the sun rose and warmed us, we crossed through the overgrown fields and made our way over to the road. I led my little band in single file down the road and past the houses, studying each building curiously as we passed. I saw among the traditional wattle and daub houses an obvious blacksmith shop with the anvil still inside and its entire roof missing. A small bakehouse with its door swinging slightly back and forth lay across the road from the smithy, and a good-sized Holy House with the Blazing Sun and Rock of Life still intact above the door sat at the end of the road. I wondered what had happened to the Daughter and Son as we passed the House and I lifted the Pair Stone from around my neck and kissed it superstitiously.

"Where is everyone?" Aenor asked softly in that strange accent of hers.

Flora had told me Aenor had been stolen by slavers when she was a child from a primitive country called Swailand that was even farther west across the sea than Cardia. Since I had never seen the western sea and had no idea where or how far Cardia was, I had just nodded to Flora and pretended

The Wolf At Large

that I understood.

"Perhaps some kind of disease broke out and everyone left," I said, regretting it the moment I'd uttered the words as we turned at the bend in the road and headed for the manor.

No one responded to that, though I did see my companions exchanging nervous glances with each other. Other than the raven, which I saw was watching us suspiciously as it flew in circles above us, nothing moved as we approached a rounded gatehouse with part of the south-facing roof missing. The entire top of the curtain wall to the left of the gatehouse had collapsed outward onto the ground and lay in a jumbled ruin. I paused ten paces from a narrow wooden gate covered in slick moss that barred our way in and gestured to Sim that he should open it. Sim dismounted and pushed on the gate gingerly, looking as if he expected it to collapse, which, I have to say, wouldn't have surprised me in the least. The gate protested his hand loudly, swinging inward on long-rusted hinges, but though it wobbled threateningly, it remained standing. Sim turned to say something to me, then he froze as the tip of a sword appeared at his throat, held by a shaking hand that I saw was covered in mottled age spots and dark, rope-like veins.

"Another step inside these walls and the next face you see will be that of Father Below!" a voice barked.

"Easy there," Sim said, lifting his hands to show he was unarmed.

"Finol!" I called out, believing that I knew who the sword and hand belonged to. "Lower your weapon! My name is Hadrack of Corwick. I was sent here by Daughter Gernet."

The sword wavered at Sim's throat, then fell away as an old man with a neat grey beard appeared. He was wearing a dirty fur stole of what I took to be fox over top of a faded purple tunic. His face beneath the flat black hat he wore was thin and pinched looking and I noticed he wore tight hose with several holes in them that emphasized how skinny his legs were.

Finol glanced from one face to another, frowning when he saw the women before he bowed to me formally. "I am at your service, my lord," he said. "Forgive my impertinence, but I didn't expect you so soon. A band of brigands has been operating near Laskerly of late and I thought you might be them." He gestured behind him. "I also would like to apologize for the state of the manor, lord. I'm all alone here and the ability to do physical labor passed me by some years ago."

"What happened to all the servants and villagers?" I asked as Finol stepped aside and I guided Angry inside the walls.

"All gone over time, lord," Finol explained with an air of exasperation. "When Lord Canten perished and Lady Jesel left, they felt, quite rightly, that the manor would be forgotten about by Daughter Gernet. One by one, the servants and villagers left to find a better life, until I and the Son and Daughter were the only ones who remained." Finol shrugged. "A House without a flock is not truly a House, as you well know, lord, and not long after that the Daughter and Son left as well."

"The lady of the manor chose not to stay after her husband's death?" I asked, raising an eyebrow.

"Indeed," Finol nodded. "Her continence, I'm sorry to say, was never suited for this life. There was an heir, but he was just a babe at the time. The moment Lord Canten was no more, the lady took him and her servants back to wherever it was she'd come from. I've not seen hide nor hair of her or the babe since."

"I see," I said as I dismounted in the courtyard. Weeds and grass pushed through the cracked and broken cobblestones beneath my feet and I saw that a stable sat to my right, the shingled roof looking surprisingly sound. "Sim," I said, pointing to the stables. "See to the horses." Sim nodded as the women dismounted behind me and I turned to Finol. "Do you have any oats?" I asked, thinking that the animals deserved it after the long trek from Hillsfort.

"Nothing, lord," Finol said with a shake of his head. He

gestured to the stables. "There's a back door that leads out to a small paddock in there. The fences are still in good repair, so you can let the horses graze without fear of them getting out." Finol shrugged. "It's all I can offer, I'm embarrassed to say. Daughter Gernet sends me money when she remembers, but it's been many months since the last time. I have to make do with what I have."

"But she did send a messenger to tell you about my arrival," I noted suspiciously.

Finol wrung his hands together. "Indeed she did, my lord. Gris, who I understand you know, was here several days ago, but no money was sent with him. All he arrived with was word from Daughter Gernet that you'd be coming and a letter for you." I studied Finol with my hands on my hips, wondering if he was lying to me. "I would never steal, my lord," Finol insisted, having read my body language. He spread his arms. "I'm a simple old man who needs very little in life. If she had sent money, I would have used it to provision the manor appropriately for your arrival. It must have slipped her mind."

"How do you survive here without money, then?" I asked. "What do you eat?"

"There's a small garden that I maintain behind the manor house, lord," Finol said. "I have found as I've gotten older that I don't require much in the way of food anymore. The garden provides more than enough to sustain me."

"Very well," I said, deciding the old man was telling me the truth. I glanced at Sim. "Just rub them down for now and then graze them in the paddock. Tomorrow, you and I will go to Laskerly to get supplies. In the meantime, we'll make do with what we brought with us."

Sim nodded and glanced at Finol. "Water?"

"You'll find buckets in the stables," Finol answered. "But you'll have to go down to the stream to fetch the water. The well dried up several years ago."

"Take care of the horses, Sim," Flora said. "Aenor and Margot and I will get the water." Flora glanced at me and smiled. "That will give you time to get acquainted with your steward."

I nodded to Flora gratefully, then followed Finol onto the porch and into the manor house, which was a medium-sized, two-story stone structure with a roof of cracked and weathered-looking wood shingles. Finol led me along the screens passage, noting that the buttery, pantry and kitchen were all located to the west of the screens, and the great hall to the east. I turned east, pausing in the oversized entrance to look around. I was pleased to find that the great hall was fastidiously tidy and well cared for, though I noted there was a suspicious-looking nest almost hidden in the corner of the high ceiling that I thought would need investigating. A wooden dais was built along the north wall, with several large windows sitting above it and framed by rich red curtains that hung down to the platform. A banner depicting a black bear holding a pike over a yellow background hung on the wall above the dais. I noticed a doorway sitting off to one side of the dais that Finol quickly informed me led to the lord's solar, which had been a private room for him and his family. A long, gleaming table with polished benches sat beneath an ornate, brightly lit candelabra that hung from the carved ceiling. I noticed even the oak planks that lined the floor looked liked they'd been scrubbed clean recently.

I nodded my approval to Finol and stepped into the great hall. Two more windows with drapes identical to the ones over the dais let in light on the southern wall, giving me a good view of the manor courtyard.

Straw lay piled in one corner of the room, I saw, with bedding placed neatly on a bench nearby. I turned to Finol in surprise. "You haven't been sleeping in the solar or upstairs in one of the guestrooms?" I asked.

"On no, lord," Finol said, shaking his head animatedly. "I could never do that. My place is here."

I grunted in acknowledgment. My opinion of Finol was rising by the moment, I realized, though I was still uncomfortable with the idea that a man of his stature would refer to me as lord. I comforted myself with the knowledge that I was, in essence, just playing a role devised by Daughter Gernet and that the old steward probably knew that. I walked to the arched fireplace that dominated the eastern wall and warmed my hands above the roaring fire that burned inside. I paused to look closer at a painting over the mantle of a man with a wide chin, pointed nose and piercing eyes sitting astride a white mare.

I gestured to the painting with my head. "Lord Canten, I presume?" I asked.

"Yes, my lord," Finol said as he came to stand beside me and stare up at the portrait. "He was a good man, more or less. It's a pity what happened to him."

"How did he die?"

Finol glanced at me out of the corner of his eyes. "An unknown illness, lord," he said in a subdued tone. He shrugged sadly and turned away to move to the table. "Lord Canten seemed in fine health, then one day he complained of stomach pains. Two days later he was dead."

I faced Finol. "Surely you called for a physician about the pains?"

Finol sat on one of the gleaming benches and sighed wearily. "Naturally we did, lord. But there was nothing he could do." Finol looked down at the table and fidgeted with a scroll of parchment that I assumed was for me that lay on the tabletop tied securely with a white ribbon. "There were some that thought Lord Canten's death was unnatural," he said, pursing his lips, "but the physician said he'd found no evidence of foul play."

"And what do you think?" I asked as I moved to stand over the table.

Finol grimaced. "I have always thought that he was poisoned, my lord."

I nodded, having expected that answer. "By his wife?" I said, more statement than question. Finol nodded silently and I glanced away, looking out through the front windows. I watched through the open gate as the three women came up the hill, each laboring with a slopping bucket of water held in their hands. The women were talking and laughing together and I felt a moment of gladness rise in my chest at the sight. Things might turn out all right for them after all. Finally I turned away once the three had disappeared into the stables. "Well," I said, looking at the old man. "Whatever happened in this place long ago has nothing to do with me." I gestured behind me, deciding that if I was to play this role, then I would act like any lord would who'd just taken over a manor. "Remove the painting," I ordered. "There's a new master of the house now."

"As you wish, my lord," Finol said with a slight bow of his head. He pushed the scroll toward me. "This is for you from Daughter Gernet."

I nodded and picked it up, knowing instinctively that the steward had not looked at it. I undid the ribbon, then unrolled the scroll, which turned out to be two scrolls, one wrapped inside the other. I slowly read Daughter Gernet's words to me, fighting to understand them all. I reread it a second time, certain I understood it now, though perplexed by what it said and surprised by the name invoked boldly in ink on it. I paused to glance at the list of names on the second scroll before looking at Finol. "Can you read?" I asked.

Finol straightened his spine dramatically on the bench, his face turning red. "I am a steward, my lord! The son of a steward, and he also the son of a steward! I could read before I could walk!"

"I meant no disrespect, Finol," I said hurriedly as the old man's face continued to redden alarmingly. "I'm only just learning to read myself." I handed over the scrolls. "Look these over with your more experienced eyes and tell me what you think."

Finol took the scrolls grudgingly and looked at them as his complexion slowly began to return to normal. I walked impatiently around the room with my hands behind my back, thinking about the instructions from Daughter Gernet and the name on the scroll as I waited for him to finish.

"Well," Finol finally said when he was done reading. "That's interesting."

"Will people believe it?" I asked.

Finol shrugged as he handed the scrolls back to me. "I cannot imagine why not. It stands to reason that Daughter Gernet could have had a nephew born with the affliction she proposes in this letter, and that this same nephew would more than likely desire to live out his days in a holding far from the eyes of other men. A holding just like Witbridge Manor."

"But why is that part even necessary?" I asked.

Finol crossed his thin arms over his chest. "I imagine she wants to ensure no one ever connects the lord of Witbridge Manor and the Outlaw of Corwick as being the same man." He glanced at me with a thin smile on his lips. "You do have a face that's hard to forget, my lord."

I frowned and shook my head. "All this secrecy seems ridiculous. Who will see me but my men and the women that I brought with me?"

Finol spread his arms and lifted his palms in the air. "You might be surprised, lord. Once word gets out that a new lord has come to live in Witbridge, then the people will also return. When that happens and they see your face, I do not doubt that tongues will wag. When they do, it won't be long before the king's soldiers are at our gate, looking to string up the Outlaw of Corwick. Better to hide that face and be safe now, rather than not and be sorry later."

"Fair enough," I grunted, not relishing playing the role of invalid that Daughter Gernet had set for me but realizing that Finol had a point. "But what about the name she uses for me?" I asked, watching Finol's face closely. "Why would she choose Lord Alwin of all names?"

"It's as good a name as any other, I suppose," Finol said carefully.

I could tell by the look in the old steward's eyes that he knew something and we stared at each other for a time. "You know who I am, don't you?" I finally asked. Finol nodded cautiously but remained silent. "As a steward, I'd wager you've been around the highborn most of your life," I continued. "Yet you refer to me as lord without a second thought, knowing that I'm not. Why?"

Finol glanced up at the ceiling, then sighed and shrugged. "Because those are my instructions, my lord," he said simply. "And I take them seriously. The matter of your bloodline is inconsequential to me compared to that."

I snorted. "Since when does a steward not look down his nose at a common peasant, regardless of the situation?"

Finol colored slightly and inclined his head. "While I would agree there is some truth to what you say, my lord, in this instance the greater good of what you can accomplish far outweighs your social status. Or, for that matter, the question of morality that arises from you posing as someone far above your class."

I was losing my train of thought beneath Finol's big words and I shook my head, focusing back on what I considered was the most important part of the letters from Daughter Gernet.

"When I mentioned the name Alwin to you earlier, you looked surprised," I said. "As though you'd heard it before." I tried to hold Finol's eyes, but the old steward kept sliding them away. "Did you know my father?" I asked bluntly.

Finol hesitated for a brief moment. I could see him weighing his answer, then he nodded slightly. "I did, my lord. But only in the most circumspect way. We rarely talked, as I recall. It was more chance meetings from time to time as we each went about our business." He looked at me and smiled. "You are the spitting image of him, by the way, my lord. Though I dare say even bigger than he was."

I nodded absently, thinking back to my conversation with Daughter Gernet when she'd told me she'd also known my father. She had been evasive then about how well she'd known him and afterward, before I'd left Halhaven, I'd tried pressing her on it, but again she'd brushed aside my questions and I'd finally given up in frustration. Why she had chosen my father's name for me to use as the master of Witbridge Manor was a mystery for which I had no answer.

"Let me guess," I said as I glanced at the scrolls again. "You're not able to share what you know about my father with me. Is that right?"

Finol looked down at his hands uncomfortably. "I regret to say, my lord, that you are indeed correct on that issue."

"Why?" I demanded, feeling anger rising in my chest. I leaned on the table and glared at the old steward. "As the master of Witbridge Manor, I order you to tell me what Daughter Gernet is hiding from me about my father!"

Finol stood shakily, his face white now as he looked to the floor. "Forgive me, lord. My will regarding this is not my own and I dare not answer. If you wish to terminate my employment, I understand and will be gone within the hour."

"Don't be an old fool!" I growled as I straightened up and threw the scrolls on the table. "Sit down!" Finol obediently sat and I stared at him as I tried to decide what to do. I knew I could continue to demand answers from Finol, but I also knew by the look in his eyes that the stubborn old steward would never give them regardless of how much I threatened. Whatever my father's connection to Daughter Gernet was, it was going to remain a mystery to me, at least for now. So, rather than lose Finol's services for no good purpose, I decided it was best to let the matter drop for the time being. "From what you've said so far, I take it you know the reason why Daughter Gernet sent me here?" I said, changing the subject.

"I believe I do," Finol said, looking relieved. "Gris explained it to me in detail. You are to lead a band of outlaws and terrorize the northlands, with the ultimate goal being to weaken Prince Tyrale's allies by appropriating their wealth so that we can use it to strengthen our position in the coming war." I nodded and Finol glanced toward the door with a look of disapproval. "Although, my lord, I do not recall any part of what I was told stating that whores would be involved in this noble endeavor."

I crossed my arms over my chest and looked at the steward harshly. "They are women first and whores second, Finol. Try to remember that." Finol just sniffed and stared at me with a blank expression, not saying anything. I knew at some point I'd have to get him to accept the women, but I decided that was a battle best fought another day. "As to why they're here with me," I said, "sometimes a man's line gets crossed by something unexpected and adjustments have to be made quickly. That's what happened in this case."

Finol shook his head. "I do not understand, my lord."

"That's all right, Finol," I replied as Sim appeared at the entrance to the great hall. "You don't need to."

"The horses have been taken care of," Sim said to me. He held up our saddlebags. "I've brought in what supplies we have left. What should I do with them?"

I gestured to the old steward that he should handle it and Finol stood, bowing slightly to me before approaching Sim. "Come with me, young man," he said, ushering Sim out of the great hall. "We'll take what you have to the kitchen and see if we have enough to make a passable meal."

I walked to the raised dais after they were gone and stared out one of the windows. The manor house was laid out on the length and I guessed the north and south-facing walls were about forty-feet wide and the east and west walls closer to eighty. A low stone wall covered in vines ran behind the house twenty yards away, with plots for four gardens laid out near the wall east of the manor house. All but one of the gardens was now completely entangled with weeds and grass, I saw, and the gardens were enclosed by weathered pole fences, some of which had fallen over.

Movement caught my eye as Flora and Margot appeared, walking along the back wall. The women paused to survey the plants growing in Finol's garden and even from where I stood, I recognized fennel, cabbage, lentils, parsnips, onions, peas, and beans. I felt a sudden feeling of nostalgia come over me as I thought of the garden my sister had tended zealously back on our farm in Corwick. I swallowed loudly, missing her terribly. I saw Flora laugh and say something to Margot. The older woman smiled and shrugged and then the two moved on out of my sight.

"This room is beautiful!"

I turned to see Aenor standing in the entrance to the great hall. "Yes, it is that," I agreed as I stepped down from the dais and approached her. "Finol has done an admirable job of maintaining it."

Aenor walked to the table and ran her hand admiringly across the wood surface. "No one has a house like this where I come from," she said wistfully.

"You don't have lords and ladies?" I asked.

Aenor shook her head and I was suddenly struck by how pretty she was. She had on the same blue cotton dress I'd first seen her wearing in Hillsfort. She'd let her hair down at some point and it now hung in lazy curls down to her breasts, fanning out to the sides fetchingly when she shook her head. "No, in Swailand, all but the chieftains live in *tuftstrands.*" I frowned at the unfamiliar word and she smiled. "Sorry, I don't know the word for it in your language." She made a face as she thought and then nodded to herself, using her hands to emphasize. "A house built in the ground," she said. "With dirt and grass walls and roofs."

"Oh," I said, having a hard time picturing the concept. "That's interesting. So where do your chieftains live?"

"*Aestrands,*" Aenor replied. Before I could say anything, she added, "Houses with legs." Aenor walked to the south windows and ran the material of the drapes through her fingers, sighing at the feel. "The *aestrand* sits in the center of our village," she explained. She lifted a hand high above her head. "The chieftain sits in the sky and is the eye of our people, watching out for danger." She shrugged. "I have never been inside an *aestrand*, but I am sure it cannot compare to anything that I have seen in this land since I was brought here."

"Maybe one day you can go back?" I suggested. "You're free now to do what you want."

Aenor shook her head again. "Oh no," she said. "There is nothing left for me in Swailand." She gestured out the windows where I could see Margot and Flora walking back the way they'd come along the wall. "My family are all dead and my friends are here now."

I nodded that I understood just as Finol reappeared in the great hall entrance. "The boy and I have managed to scrape together a meal, my lord," Finol said. "It's just a simple pottage, I'm afraid. I have it cooking over the fire right now. Do you wish to eat when it's ready or would you prefer to let it stew and wait until we're closer to mid-day?"

I glanced at Aenor with an eyebrow arched and she giggled charmingly. "I'm starving."

I grinned back at her and then gestured to the steward. "There you have it, Finol. It would seem that we'll eat when it's ready."

That night I found myself standing alone with a candle in my hand in Lord Canten's solar; which was a room built off the main house that I figured had to be about forty-feet long by thirty wide. I had initially told Finol to let the women use the solar and that I wanted to sleep out in the great hall, but the old steward had been incensed at the idea. The only way I could get him to calm down was to agree to use the solar myself. We compromised by having the women adjourn upstairs to the guestrooms, while Finol and Sim remained behind to sleep in the great hall. A massive, four-posted bed sitting on a high platform dominated one wall of the solar, with a tall, narrow table sitting beside it. Flames danced and twisted inside a fireplace of rounded stone that sat directly across from the bed on the opposite wall. A narrow alcove was set at the far end of the room where two carved, high-backed chairs sat in front of a rectangular window. The walls, I saw with distaste in the candlelight, were painted a garish green color, with bright gold stars added here and there for emphasis. I had no idea what the purpose of the stars was, but I have to admit that my first thought was that somehow Haverty the apothecary had snuck in when no one was looking and had painted the room in one of his moments of madness.

I noticed an arched doorway set within the alcove and I passed through it into a second, smaller room. Inside, I found a table with six chairs sitting around it and a tidy writing desk and bench against one wall. The walls in this room, I was relieved to see, were of finely carved wood and stained a dark, walnut color. Paintings covered all four of the walls starting from waist height and moving upward to the top of the twelve-foot-high ceiling. I took my time examining the paintings, and though I was no expert on the finer points of artistry, I suspected that most were of an exceptional quality. When I was done admiring the paintings, I returned to the main room and set the candle on the table near the bed. I moved to stand and stare into the fire, feeling surprisingly lonely in the silence that was broken only by the crackling of the flames. I slowly turned and walked around the room, not sure what I should do with myself and feeling completely out of place. The rooms were as immaculately clean as the great hall and I looked down with dismay to see that my heavy boots were leaving dirty footprints behind me with each step that I took on the plush red and yellow rug that lined the floor. I moved as carefully as I could to the alcove and sat and pulled my boots off. Then I just sat there and looked around, still finding it hard to believe how much my life had changed in only a few short days. Was it only a week ago that I'd been naked and starving, locked in a cage? I wondered. Now, here I was sitting in the room of a lord that was twice as big as the house I'd grown up in and worrying about leaving marks on the dead man's rug. The Mother and The Father sometimes work in mysterious ways, I thought to myself as I finally stood and stripped off my clothing.

I cautiously climbed up into Lord Canten's bed, marveling at the softness of the down-feathered mattress on my naked skin and the feathered bolster that I lay my head on. I pulled the oddly sweet-smelling bedclothes about me, then lay back and stared up at the carved ceiling. If only my father and Jeanna could see me now, I thought. I smiled when I realized they were probably sitting with Mother Above and looking down on me at that very moment. I said a silent prayer to The Mother, asking Her to watch out for them and I kissed the Pair Stone around my neck, feeling content for the first time in many days. I realized I wasn't tired enough to sleep just yet, so I reached for the scrolls that I'd set on the table near the bed and began to reread them in the light of the candle. I saw my father's name halfway down the first scroll and again I wondered why Daughter Gernet had used it. I shook my head, frustrated at not knowing the answer to that. To distract myself, I turned to the second scroll to study the names on it.

There were twelve names in all — none of which I recognized — along with each man's occupation and where they could be found. I knew each of the twelve men must be tied to Prince Tyrale somehow, and that they would be my first targets once I'd hired men to join me. Most of the men on Daughter Gernet's list were merchants, specializing in either salt, iron or textiles, while two others were noblemen, and one something called a moneylender. I'd known already without seeing the list that I wouldn't be able to go after Lord Corwick, but I had been hoping to get a chance at Lord Demay. I was still deeply disappointed that I'd have to turn my attention away from that bastard. I had a sudden vision of Shana on the last day I'd seen her and I felt a pang of loss. Even with my upgraded situation and my feelings for her, I knew I would always be just a peasant in her eyes. Shana had befriended me in

Gasterny, but I suspected that it was more out of gratitude for what Baine and I had done for her than anything else. I had little doubt that she'd forgotten about me long ago.

I was so engrossed in my thoughts that I didn't realize until at least the third sharp-sounding knock that someone was at the solar door asking for permission to enter. I frowned, getting a little tired of Finol's relentless deference to me. "You don't have to knock to come in, Finol!" I shouted at the door in irritation. "You've been living in this manor house for years now! It's more yours than mine!"

The door opened and I was surprised to see Aenor standing in the entrance, not Finol. "May I come in, Hadrack?" she asked, looking uncertain after my harsh tone a moment ago.

I began to get up, then thought better of it as I caught a glimpse of my nakedness beneath the bedclothes. "Of course," I said, motioning her in. "Sorry about that. I thought you were Finol come to bother me." Aenor smiled and closed the door, then stood at the entrance with her hands clasped together in front of her. She looked around the room, frowning slightly at the walls. "It's hideous, isn't it?" I said.

Aenor grinned and nodded. "Horrible," she agreed.

I pushed the feathered bolster back against the wall behind me, then sat up and set the scrolls down on my lap. "So," I said. "What can I do for you?"

Aenor was still wearing the blue dress, but her feet were bare and she walked across the rug, smiling with pleasure at the feel of it on her skin. She saw the fire was almost out and threw several pieces of wood on, then bent and used the poker to move the coals around the wood. Within moments the flames grew stronger, lighting up the room. She continued to poke and prod at the wood with her back to me while I just sat in silence and watched. I could see Aenor's naked silhouette clearly through the thin cotton material and I suddenly became very aware that we were alone.

"There," Aenor finally said with satisfaction as she set

the poker down and turned to face me. "That's better." She approached the bed and tilted her head to one side coyly as she stood on the rug. "You should see the look on your face," Aenor said with a pleasant laugh as she began to undo the lace of her dress.

"I'm not sure this is such a good idea," I said weakly.

"Why not?" Aenor asked. "The girls and I talked and we all agreed we owed you something for what you did for us." Aenor chuckled. "Since Flora thinks she is too fat and Margot thinks she is too old, I was the natural choice to show our appreciation."

"But I..." I started to protest.

Aenor held up a hand to stop me. "It's all right, Hadrack," she said. "I know there is another girl out there somewhere. I'm not looking to take her place."

"There isn't," I responded too quickly, automatically thinking of Shana.

"Uh-huh," Aenor said with a knowing grin. "I know that look in a man's eyes. That is the look of love." I opened my mouth to deny it, then I clamped it shut, knowing that there was no point in arguing with her. Aenor winked at me, then in one quick motion she let her dress drop to the floor. I stared with admiration at the naked woman across from me, mesmerized by her brown skin gleaming in the firelight and by her small, pert breasts and hard, dark nipples. I felt my pulse quicken with desire and I turned my mind away from all other thoughts, just accepting the moment for what it was. Without saying another word, I slowly pulled the bedclothes aside and made room for Aenor in my bed.

13: HANLEY OF LASKERLY

The next morning, Sim and I headed out for the village of Laskerly at first light. The day began just like the day before it, crisp and sharp, with a faint whisper of fall tainting the light breeze. For the first time since I'd left Halhaven, I was grateful for Malo's heavy cloak to pull about me to help ward off the cold. Sim was wearing one of Finol's worn purple cloaks and I had to suppress a laugh every time I looked at him. My companion was almost as big as I was and his great bulk was bursting out of the small garment in every direction imaginable. I strongly doubted the bright cloak was doing much to keep him warm, but despite that, Sim seemed pleased with it for some reason and insisted on wearing it.

"You look like you're in good spirits this morning," Sim noted.

We were guiding our horses up the rocky hill where we'd caught our first glimpse of Witbridge Manor the day before and I turned to look at him. "Do I?" I said, feigning surprise. "Must be something in the air, I suppose."

Sim snorted and shook his head. "More like something in your bed last night would be my guess." I grinned at Sim and shrugged my shoulders as we reached the top of the hill. What could I say? The entire manor probably knew about Aenor coming to me before it even happened. "I know exactly how you feel on that score," Sim added with a chuckle and a knowing wink.

I lifted one eyebrow in surprise. "Flora?"

Sim laughed and shook his head. "No. The other one, Margot. She's as thin as a hog's tail and makes noises like one too, but by The Mother that woman knows what she's doing."

"And what about Flora?" I asked as we headed west toward Laskerly. "Did she give Finol a ride at the same time?"

"That old bastard?" Sim said, making a face. "If she had he'd be dead right now. Mark my words."

I grinned at that and pulled my cloak tighter about me as the wind strengthened, trying to find the gaps in my clothing. We rode across fields of long grass and through small patches of forested areas for several hours as the sun slowly rose behind us. Sim and I talked now and again, but for the most part we rode in silence as I turned my thoughts inward, thinking about my next move. Our main purpose for going to Laskerly was to buy supplies for the manor, but I also had hopes of finding at least five or six men there to join my band. I felt with Sim already with me, and Baine and Jebido coming in the spring, that five or six more would be the ideal number. I was uncomfortable with the idea of bringing the type of men I expected to hire back to the manor, but Sim seemed unconcerned about it. He assured me more than once that I would have my pick of many eager applicants in Laskerly, and that some of them might even be decent men. I had my doubts about that, but all I could do was hope and try not to fret over it too much until we got there.

Before I'd retired to the solar the night before, I'd decided — against Finol's advice — to be honest, and open with Sim and the three women. It didn't seem right to me that they would be risking their lives just by being associated with me without knowing the reason for it beforehand. I felt I owed everyone the truth, and despite Finol's obvious displeasure, I'd sat them all down around the table in the great hall and told them what I was really doing in Witbridge Manor. The look on Sim's and the women's faces probably mirrored my own when I'd first heard about the coming war between the House and twin princes. But, all things considered, I have to say that they took it fairly well. After I was finished explaining what Daughter Gernet wanted of me, the women immediately pledged to serve along with Sim on the side of The Mother. To be honest, I don't know what I would have done if one or more of them had favored The Father instead. I hadn't thought that far ahead and I was greatly relieved that it turned out I didn't have to worry about it.

"Hadrack?" Sim said, cutting into my thoughts. "Can I ask you something?" I glanced over at him from beneath my hood and frowned with displeasure as Sim pursed his lips in apology. "Sorry," he muttered, looking slightly flustered. "I mean, Lord Alwin, can I ask you something?" I nodded in approval, having told all of them last night to get used to calling me Lord Alwin when we were outside the manor house. I motioned for him to proceed. "There's one thing about what you told us last night that's been bothering me," Sim said.

"Only one?" I asked with a sigh. "Because there's more than one thing about all this that bothers me, Sim. But in the end we have to trust in Daughter Gernet's leadership and that eventually both sides of the House will find some kind of peace."

"By killing each other?" Sim asked doubtfully.

I shrugged, grimacing as I thought of the civil war coming to Ganderland. "Sometimes the only path to peace is with a sword in your hand," I said, thinking suddenly of Einhard and the Piths. Where was my friend right now and what was he doing? I wondered. I'd asked Finol about the Piths the night before, but the old steward had heard nothing new about them since their defeat. He assumed — like everyone else in Ganderland it seemed — that the Piths were finished and that would be the end of it. Having lived with the Piths for over a year, I felt I understood them as well as anyone could. I knew the term 'defeat' and 'finished' didn't apply to them. They would be back. The only question was when.

"But what do I do if I get a Son in confession?" Sim asked, cutting into my thoughts. "That's what I don't understand. What do I say to him?"

I frowned at that, cursing my stupidity, knowing that

I'd overlooked this as well. The men I would soon be hiring—undoubtedly criminals and murderers all, despite what Sim thought — would still go to regular confession to try to keep their souls clean. So too would Finol, Sim, and the women. What would they do if a Son were to ask pointed questions of them? What would I do, for that matter? To lie inside the confessional was to virtually guarantee a long stay with Father Below. I involuntarily shuddered at the thought. A part of my mind also wondered what would happen to those of us who supported The Mother in the coming war, should we find ourselves kneeling at The Father's feet on judgment day? Would we be tainted in His eyes and be subjected to unknown horrors for our loyalty to The Mother? I shook my head, not wanting to think about it and I thrust that thought firmly from my mind.

"For now," I said, thinking fast. "Only confess to a Daughter. If you get a Son, make some excuse and don't go into confessional with him." I glared at Sim. "Do you understand me?"

Sim nodded, clearly unnerved by the look on my face. "Yes," he said. "I understand."

"Good," I grunted. I decided when we got back to the manor that I'd have Finol write a letter to Daughter Gernet, explaining our predicament. I was confident that she would know what to do about confessional. As for my concerns about The Father, the moment I was with the Daughter again I'd broach the subject to her privately. While I fully understood there were no guarantees in this life, it would go a long way to helping everyone's peace of mind if I had some kind of assurances from Daughter Gernet that I could offer the men, not to mention myself.

We were following a double trail of deep ruts left by carts through a forest of oak, alder and twisted beech trees. Sim, the women and I had already come this way on our journey to Witbridge Manor the day before and I remembered the area well. The trees grew thick and wide here, with branches hanging low over the trail, blocking the view of the sky for the next quarter mile. A massive rotted stump sat off the trail to my left and I glanced at it as we passed. I knew by seeing that stump that we were less than an hour away from the village of Laskerly. I decided it might be a good time to take a moment to rest the horses and my aching backside before we got there. I turned to Sim, about to tell him to stop when I saw a dark form drop silently from the branches directly above Sim's head. I barely had time to shout a warning before the figure collided with Sim and both men fell heavily to the ground. Sim's mare ran off through the trees in fright and I instinctively hauled sideways on Angry's reins. The big stallion turned just as I heard a shout of dismay above me and a dark form hurtled helplessly past me. I felt a desperate hand clutch at my shoulder, the man's grasping fingers sliding off my cloak before the figure hit the ground hard with an audible grunt. I started to draw Wolf's Head, then froze in place as men wearing dark cloaks appeared from the trees near the stump. Most of the men clutched rusted swords or twisted clubs, with one towering blond-haired fellow holding a bow that was aimed directly at me.

"Best put that fancy sword back where it belongs," said a tall man with a black beard showing beneath his hood. "Before my man makes a hole in you. Tyris can take the eye out of a squirrel at fifty paces."

I could feel rage welling up inside my chest, furious at myself for being caught unawares so easily. I jammed Wolf's Head back in its scabbard bitterly and lifted my hands to the sides, palms up. I was relieved to see Sim sitting up and rubbing his head, while his attacker rose to his feet as well, wobbling uncertainly as he moved to join his companions. I flicked my eyes down to the man who'd attempted to jump me and I felt a moment of satisfaction. The man's head was twisted at an odd angle and his eyes were fixed and staring at Angry's hooves.

"What do you want?" I barked as Angry snorted and

pawed at the ground in warning as the men spread out around us.

"What do we want?" the black-bearded man replied with a sharp laugh. He halted his men with a raised hand. "We want whatever you have. All of it." I ground my jaws in frustration as he pulled back his hood, revealing a young-looking face with close-set, brown eyes, a flat nose, and one of his top teeth missing. I guessed he couldn't be more than eighteen or nineteen-years-old. "You have the honor of meeting Black Thomin the outlaw," he said with a gap-toothed grin. "Now hand over your money, that lovely sword, and your horse."

I rolled my eyes at the irony of us being robbed by outlaws, feeling anger radiating outward as I dropped my hand to Wolf's Head. I glared at the men surrounding me. Whether Tyris was as good with a bow as Black Tomlin claimed or not, I knew that Angry and I could be on the outlaws in moments. These men were simple peasants and overconfident and weren't expecting me to do anything, simply because, in my place, they knew they wouldn't do anything either. I figured with the element of surprise on my side, it would be a simple matter to take down the bowman, then work on the rest. I tensed, gripping Wolf's Head tighter as I waited for the perfect moment to pounce.

"Don't forget why we're going to Laskerly, my lord!" Sim called out from behind me. "Remember the owl! The Mother is always with you!"

Sim's voice had a strange lilt to it, as though he were trying to tell me something and I paused, frowning as I thought about what he was saying. Or rather, what he was trying to say. I felt the anger begin to drain from me and I took my hand off Wolf's Head as I considered his words, trying to understand. It took me a moment, I must confess, but then something clicked in my mind and I slowly grinned. I looked back at Sim and nodded to let him know I now understood. These men hadn't happened on us by chance, which is what Sim was trying to tell me. I said a silent prayer of thanks to

Mother Above, knowing that it was She who had sent the outlaws here to me. My problem of finding men to join me had fallen into my lap, I realized, and it might be solved right here and now. That is, as long as I played things right.

"I don't think you'll be robbing anyone today," I finally said to Black Thomin. "I'll not give anything of mine to a sorry excuse for an outlaw like you."

Black Thomin's eyes bulged in his head in surprise and his face reddened. "What did you say to me?" he demanded.

I slowly dismounted, keeping my hands where the outlaws could see them. I noticed Tyris never took his eyes off me as he followed me with his bow. I was impressed to see his arms were steady and solid, with no sign of wavering from holding a drawn bow that long. I took two steps toward Black Thomin, skirting the dead man before I stopped with my hands on my hips. I could hear Sim moving behind me and then heard him whispering to Angry, trying to calm him. Good man, I thought, knowing Sim would keep the big black under control and out of my way. I'd insisted Sim wear Finol's sword before we left, but my companion had confessed to me he wasn't much use with it, so I knew I couldn't count on him to do much if things went wrong and it came down to a fight. If only Baine and Jebido were with me, I thought as I studied the men surrounding us, assessing the strengths and weaknesses in each of them. I counted seven men, most of whom were dressed in tattered cloaks and rags and looking half-starved to death. None of them on their own, other than Tyris, would be much of a threat, I knew, but together they would be formidable. I saw with surprise that a boy with his right arm hanging in a sling stood alone along the treeline and when I looked closer it dawned on me that I knew him. It was Hanley, the boy I'd let escape back over the wall in Gasterny. That's where I'd heard of Laskerly before, I realized. Would Hanley remember me? I wondered as I worked out my plan. Would it matter in the end if he did? We'd soon find out.

"I called you a sorry excuse for an outlaw," I said as I spit on the ground. "You think you're a leader of men, but all I see is a frightened boy." I took another step forward, holding Black Thomin's eyes with mine. "Look at you," I said with distaste. I glanced around. "All of you. You're not men. You're worse even than the beggars who line the streets of Halhaven. Living in the woods eating grubs and plants to stay alive. It's pathetic."

I could hear Sim moving Angry farther back behind me, but I remained focused on Black Thomin and his men, some of whom were muttering angrily at my words. I glanced again at Tyris, but he seemed unaffected by my insults. A good man to have under pressure, I thought. Hopefully Tyris had a good brain in his head to go along with his archery skill. Finol had told me yesterday that Daughter Gernet had begun sending operatives all across the countryside the moment I'd arrived in Halhaven, spreading rumors about the supposed exploits of the Outlaw of Corwick. I'd been somewhat miffed at the idea that she'd taken me for granted so easily, but now I dearly hoped that one of those operatives had reached Laskerly already. I would need Black Tomlin's men, and specifically Tyris and Hanley, to have heard of me if what I had in mind had any chance of working.

"You have a big mouth!" Black Tomlin growled. He pointed his rusty sword at me. "Give us your money or die. Choose now!"

I shrugged and reached inside my cloak, careful to draw out the smaller moneybag that I'd taken from Skind Kurko. I hefted the bag for the outlaws to see and their eyes lit up as the coins jingled musically inside. There were only four or five Jorqs left in it, I knew, and I threw the bag at Black Tomlin's feet. I waited as the outlaw pounced on it eagerly.

"I have a question I'd like to ask," I said once he'd grabbed it.

"I'm not interested in what you want," Black Tomlin grunted. He stood and opened the moneybag and rolled the Jorqs out onto his palm.

"Oh, I'm not talking to you," I said to the outlaw dis-

missively. I gestured around to his men. "I'm talking to them."
I glanced at Black Tomlin with disdain. "My opinion of you
hasn't changed from earlier. You're still as useless as a rat
turd." Black Tomlin's eyes flashed in rage and a hint of uncer-
tainty as I spread my arms and addressed his men. "Are you
enjoying your life so far?" I asked. "Fighting over scraps on a
bone like dogs?" No one answered me, many of them blinking
in confusion and looking at each other with blank looks. "The
reason I ask," I said, "is that I see men who have allowed themselves to become worse than animals under the leadership of
this bastard." I pointed to Black Tomlin. "What has he done for
any of you?" I demanded with a snort. "Look at you. Starving
and dirty. Hiding in the trees and barely able to scratch out a
living as you prey on hapless travelers and merchants." I gestured to the money in Black Tomlin's hand. "All for a few meager Jorqs, most of which this turd-sucker probably keeps for
himself."

"We don't have no choice," an outlaw with a ragged red
beard muttered. "We're wanted men. There's nowhere for us
to go."

"That's where you're wrong," I said with a quick shake
of my head. "There is a place for you."

"Yeah," Hanley said from the trees with a sarcastic
laugh. "Dancing at the end of a rope, you mean!"

Around him the other men laughed and I grinned.
"Well, that's the chance we all risk when we take this path," I
said. "But that's not what I meant."

"What do you mean by we?" Hanley asked. He stepped
out from the trees and stared at me suspiciously. Hanley was
holding a heavy club in his left hand and he waved it at the
other men. "We're simple men who didn't want to fight some
lord's war. Now we're outlaws with a price on our heads and
we have to steal to survive." He pointed the club at me. "You're
not one of us. You're just a rich man trying to talk your way
out of being robbed."

"That's where you're wrong," I said. I could see Black

Tomlin opening his mouth out of the corner of my eyes, clearly about to try to take back control of the situation. I pointed at him. "I can offer all of you everything this boy can't." I saw Tyris frown and ease up slightly on the bow and I hurried on, encouraged. "I need men," I explained. "Good men just like you to come work for me."

"Kill him!" Black Tomlin growled as he pointed his sword at me. He turned to glare at Tyris. "Kill that man right now!"

I knew that as long as Black Tomlin was still alive the other outlaws would be conflicted in their loyalty. While I didn't relish killing the man, I realized it was the only way to bring the others over to me. Black Tomlin had made a critical error by not demanding I throw down Wolf's Head immediately, and it was about to cost him dearly. I felt a moment of guilt at what I was about to do, but the fact of the matter was, the moment Black Tomlin had picked up a sword, he'd automatically accepted the consequences of what could happen to him. All men did. Today, I would be Black Tomlin's consequence. I shared a look with Tyris, hoping the indecision I thought I saw on his face was real. I drew Wolf's Head in a single fluid motion and lunged forward, gutting Black Tomlin neatly with the end of my sword before he could even react. The outlaw leader's mouth dropped open in surprise and he dropped his rusty sword as I quickly withdrew my blade from his stomach. I moved backward several paces and waited. Black Tomlin stared down at the red stain spreading across his filthy tunic in horrified fascination. He tried to speak, took two unsteady steps toward me, then gurgled up a mouthful of dark blood and fell. I glanced at Tyris, who still had his bow aimed at me, then at the other shocked outlaws.

"I can change all of your lives for the better if you let me," I said into the silence. I had promised Finol that I'd keep my hood up and my face hidden in Laskerly and let Sim do most of the talking. But Finol wasn't here now and my line had changed dramatically since that promise. I decided to change my plans along with my line and I slowly lowered my hood, revealing my scarred face. "My name is Hadrack," I said. "The Outlaw of Corwick, and I want you to join me."

Tyris slowly lowered his bow in indecision as Hanley pointed his club at me. "I know you!" he said, unable to hide the surprise in his voice.

"And I know you, Hanley of Laskerly," I replied. I gestured to his arm. "I guess you landed the wrong way when you jumped the wall."

"It was worth it," Hanley said with a shrug. He looked around at the other outlaws. "This is him," he said, pointing again at me. "The lord I told you about who let me go at Gasterny."

"I'm no lord," I said as I stooped to wipe Wolf's Head clean on the grass. I stood and sheathed the sword. "I told you, I'm a peasant just like the rest of you."

"You don't look like no peasant," the red-bearded man said.

"Nor will any of you," I said. "If you join me."

"You fought with the Piths at Gasterny?" Tyris asked, looking slightly perplexed. "Why?"

I laughed as Sim and Angry approached behind me. "That tale will take hours to tell," I said. "And now is not the time for it." I gestured with a thumb behind me in the direction Sim and I had come from. "I have a manor house several hours from here. Come work for me and there will be food, lodging and clothing for all of you."

"My lord," Sim said, offering me Angry's reins. "May I go find the mare? She's not used to being alone." I knew Sim loved that mare and that he'd be devastated to lose her, so I nodded and took the big black's reins from him. "Will you be all right, my lord?" Sim asked, glancing at the outlaws.

"Not to worry, Sim," I said, loud enough for all to hear. "These are good men. There's no need to fear, go find your horse." Sim took one more glance at the ragged men, then turned and hurried off into the trees, whistling for the mare.

I turned back to the outlaws with one eyebrow raised. "So, what do you say? Do you want to stay here, scrounging in the woods or come back with me and live like real men?"

It didn't take them very long to decide. After all, what sane man would say no considering their current situation in life? Once Sim had located the mare and returned to us, I sent him on into Laskerly alone to get the supplies by himself. I pulled Sim aside before he left and gave him twenty Jorqs, trusting in him implicitly, before I led the six outlaws back toward Witbridge Manor.

And that's how my little band, who would quickly become infamous from one end of the kingdom to the other riding alongside the Outlaw of Corwick, came to join me.

14: OLD FRIENDS

The biggest surprise once I returned to Witbridge Manor with my six new charges, was that Finol took an instant liking to the boy, Hanley. The old steward didn't seem to care much about the other outlaws, but Hanley struck a chord in him for some reason. Within minutes of our arrival back at the manor house, the two were off by themselves talking together like old friends. I'd listened to the stories of the men on the way back to Witbridge, not shocked in the least to learn that most of the tales were quite similar. All of them, except for Tyris — who had been a seasoned soldier — were simple peasants who'd been called to arms by their lord. Each had decided to run away from the fight; whether from cowardice or common sense, I still wasn't sure. I remembered how we'd stormed out of the gates of Gasterny that fateful morning and charged into the terrified peasants massed in front of us, crushing and maiming them. Many of those peasants had turned and run for their lives into the forest and I wondered if some of these men around me today had been among them. Had it been me in their place, would I have kept running too? I didn't have a good answer to that question, so I decided I'd reserve judgment until I came to know each of them better.

The red-bearded fellow was named Putt, and he and Anson, a great-shouldered man with a shaven head and missing ear, had both been drawn from the village of Hannum with many others to fight for Lord Corwick. Cain, Niko, and Hanley were all from a collection of small villages around Laskerly and had been lent to Lord Corwick to die against the walls of Gasterny by their liege lord, Lord Falmir. Tyris, on the other hand, was a twelve-year veteran of King Jorquin's archers and had been posted in more than a dozen different stations across the kingdom in his career.

After we'd settled in a little at Witbridge, I pulled Tyris aside to question him further. We walked together toward the stables and I motioned for him to follow me around the back to the paddock. He and I leaned on the fence for a time, saying nothing as we watched the horses graze and frolic. Jebido had told me once that most people would hang themselves with their own words if given half the chance, so I waited to see what the archer would say. The outlaws all had horses of their own — which they'd most likely stolen — and though I was no expert, I could tell that many of them were far from top quality stock. With Angry and the other horses we already had and the new animals we'd just added, the small paddock was quickly becoming crowded and barren of edible grass. The feed Sim would be bringing from Laskerly would help, but I knew we'd have to picket the horses somewhere else soon. I decided I'd send Hanley out in the morning to find a suitable grazing spot for them and then I thrust the problem from my mind. There were bigger issues to contend with. I could sense that my companion was becoming uncomfortable and possibly a little bit nervous, but he continued to remain silent as he waited for me to speak.

"So," I finally said, deciding I'd waited long enough. I examined Tyris' face carefully, trying to get a feel for what kind of man he was. I thought the archer could be close to thirty-years-old, judging by his eyes and the crinkles around them, but certainly no more than that. He looked competent and smart to me. I wondered how he would react to taking orders from a peasant, not to mention someone much younger than him. I was planning to talk with each of the men at some point, but since Tyris was the most experienced of them, I thought I'd start with him to try to get an idea of what the men were thinking. "You told me on the way here that you were with the king's archers," I said to begin.

"Yes," Tyris said cautiously. "Most recently I was stationed at Starmhold Garrison out west until we were ordered to Gasterny after the Piths captured it."

"And then you spent a year just sitting around and waiting for something to happen," I said.

"We did," Tyris muttered. "And a most boring and uninteresting year it was, too."

I nodded at that, knowing exactly how he felt. "Were you involved in the attack on the garrison?" I asked, feeling a momentary pang as I thought of Eriz and Ania and all the others who had died in Gasterny.

"No," Tyris said with a shake of his head. "Two days before that happened I got in a fight with a Cardian."

"Over money or a woman?" I asked with a wry grin, knowing that it was always one or the other.

Tyris looked slightly embarrassed. "A woman. When it was over, the man was dead and my choices were few. Stay and face the noose or run and live."

"An easy choice, then," I said. I was relieved to know that Tyris had not been on the other side of the walls that day. There was something about the man that I instantly liked and I was glad my feelings for him wouldn't be tainted by the knowledge of what he might have done against us.

"I spent about a week wandering the country after that," Tyris said. "I hadn't been on my own in a long time and I didn't know where to go or what to do. All I knew was I couldn't trust anyone not to turn me in as a deserter. I didn't even know about the fall of Gasterny until I came across Black Tomlin and the others." Tyris grimaced. "He wasn't much of a leader, that one, but it was either him or nothing, so I decided to join with him."

"Twelve years is a long time to spend in service," I said. "Do you miss it?"

"It is a long time," Tyris agreed solemnly. "And I do miss it, but I also know that part of my life is over now."

"You do understand that I'm no friend of Lord Corwick or the king?" I said. Tyris just nodded, his face expressionless. "If you stay here, they'll be your enemies. Does that bother you at all?"

Tyris shook his head without hesitation. "They care nothing for me, so why should I care for them? They would both just as soon stretch my neck with rope as look at me."

"You'll follow me, then?" I asked. "Even knowing that I'm not highborn?"

"I will," Tyris said, looking me in the eye. "But only if you hold to the vow you already pledged to us."

"I promised you food and lodging and I meant it," I assured him. "You have my word on that."

Tyris bowed his blond head and nodded. "Yes, those things too. But I meant you vowed to make us feel like men again." I was surprised by the momentary look of anguish simmering in the back of Tyris' eyes. The archer turned away and focused on the horses as he shrugged his shoulders. "Running seemed like the only thing to do at the time, but it didn't take me long before I realized I should have stayed and accepted the noose. It would have been more honorable than living like a common thief without any purpose." Tyris looked back at me. "Hold to your vow and give me that purpose back, and I swear by The Mother and The Father that I'll serve you faithfully. Highborn or not."

I thought about that for a moment, wondering how much I should say. Tyris seemed like a man to depend on, but I hadn't gotten a feel for the others yet. Until I did, I thought it would be wise to say as little as possible to him about the task Daughter Gernet had given me. Finol's caution, which I had initially brushed off as an old man's paranoia, was finally starting to rub off on me. There was too much at stake now and it suddenly dawned on me that it wasn't just my life that was at risk if word got out who I really was. The fate of all the lives in Witbridge was now firmly wrapped around my own. It was a sobering thought. I also knew that if it came right down to it, we could still accomplish our goal without telling the outlaws everything. The fact that they knew my name was something I now regretted, but what was done was done. I tried not to think about what also might have to be done if one or more of them could not be trusted. I decided to put my faith in The Mother and not worry about it, knowing that it was She who had sent these men to me in the first place.

"I'm not here by accident," I finally told Tyris, choosing my words carefully. "I can't tell you why yet, but there is a reason, and it's not to just rob innocent people. Serve me well and I promise you'll regain everything you lost and more."

Tyris studied me for a moment, searching my face, before finally he nodded and extended his hand. "That's good enough for me."

I locked forearms with Tyris, relieved at how well it had gone and hopeful that my talks with the others would go just as smoothly.

A week went by after that. A week that saw Sim and Putt heading back to Laskerly every other day for supplies, weapons, better horses for the men, and a hundred other things I never would have thought to buy. My funds were quickly becoming depleted under the steward's constant demands, but I'd never seen the man happier, though we did argue from time to time over how the money should be spent. Finol was forever trying to get me to buy materials to repair the manor, while I was more interested in outfitting my outlaws in preparation for the coming raids. Finol was a tough taskmaster and he quickly had the manor house running at top capacity. Everyone was fearful of getting one of his stinging reprimands and most of the time I just avoided the old steward, which seemed to suit him just fine. I knew Finol was angry with me for not spending more money on Witbridge, as well as for not listening to his advice about keeping my face concealed. The fact that in hindsight I secretly agreed with him that it had been a mistake, was something I had no intention of ever telling the old man.

Finol was followed everywhere by Hanley — who the steward had seemingly taken on as an apprentice — and the two of them delegated jobs to both the men and the women with almost religious fervor. During that week, the manor house slowly but surely began to regain some of its long lost glory, though it would take a lot more time and money than I was willing to spend to restore it properly. Cain, who was a short, brown-haired man with massive hands, had spent several years working as a stonemason's apprentice, and he began to rebuild the outer walls with the help of Tyris and myself. It felt good to do physical labor again, even if the others did show me deference that I didn't always want. There was a small limestone quarry on the other side of the woods about two miles from the manor house and Tyris and I would go there each morning and cut rough sections of stone that we'd drag back along the road by horse for Cain to sculpt. It was hard work, but pleasant just the same, and as Tyris and I broke off sections of rock with chisels and hammers, it constantly brought back memories of my years down in Father's Arse working with Jebido and Baine. I wondered from time to time how my friends were doing, hoping that they were healing well and that I'd see them soon.

My talks with each of the other outlaws had gone well, and I have to say I was fairly confident that I could trust them, if and when I decided to tell them what was really going on. I discussed that very concept with Sim, Finol, and the women on more than one occasion, but we all came to the same conclusion that it would be better to wait and see. The outlaws not knowing right now had little effect on their day-to-day lives, so there didn't seem any particular hurry. Later, once we were ready to start raiding, that might change. But until it did, I decided to just let things lie where they were.

The biggest surprise after I talked with all of the outlaws had been Hanley, who was the youngest son of a miller in Laskerly. Hanley had a bright and engaging personality and we'd mostly talked about his ideas for the manor; or rather, he'd talked and I'd listened. I quickly came to see why Finol liked the boy, as Hanley's enthusiasm for improving the manor house seemed to know no bounds. But, despite that enthusiasm, his ideas, like widening the stream and building a mill, among others, were not something I cared about getting involved in. I was just at Witbridge Manor to do the task required of me and then leave. I couldn't tell Hanley that, of course, and so I listened to him politely and let him dream. Rebuilding the walls of the manor was something I did agree with, however, as making the manor house more secure just made good practical sense. That practical work also gave Finol, Sim and I time to watch the men and gauge their ability to work and get along together, so I considered it time well spent. Hanley's right arm had healed badly and it was doubtful that he'd ever be able to lift a sword or use the arm effectively again. But despite this, the boy seemed completely unperturbed by it. I wasn't sure what use Hanley would be once we started raiding, but for now I just let Finol take charge of him. I figured I'd decide what to do with him later on.

The women worked mainly in the gardens and the kitchen, though occasionally Aenor would come with Tyris and I to the quarry, to 'just get away for a while', as she put it. She was surprisingly agile and strong for such a slight girl, reminding me somewhat of Ania that way.

Life at the manor became one of routine the first week, and everyone seemed happy enough, though an incident arose near the end of that week that I hadn't anticipated. In hindsight, I suppose I should have seen it coming, but in my defense, I did have quite a few other things on my mind. I was awoken in the dead of night by the sounds of a fearsome row coming from the guest rooms upstairs. Aenor was sleeping on her stomach in our bed, snoring softly and completely unaware, so I dressed quickly and climbed the stairs. I immediately saw Putt and Niko brawling outside Flora's room while Flora stood unashamedly naked in her doorway, blocking the entrance with her bulk. I took three steps toward the men, then grabbed each by the neck of their tunics and hauled them apart.

"What goes on here!?" I roared, annoyed at being

awakened for this. Both Putt and Niko started talking at once and I had to shout again for silence. I pointed to Putt. "You go first."

"This sneaky shit-eater knows it's my turn!" Putt said hotly, gesturing to Niko with a thumb. "He had her two nights ago and yet, here he is again with his prick in his hand trying to get in ahead of me."

"A bald-faced lie, you bastard!" Niko spat back. Niko was a thin youth of about seventeen, with wide ears, a long nose and thick black hair that hung down to his shoulders. "It was you who had her two nights ago, you goat-faced turd! It's my turn tonight!"

I rolled my eyes and glanced at Flora. "Care to step in and settle this?" I asked.

"They're both lying!" Flora said with a snort. She gestured behind her. "Tonight it's Tyris' turn." She jutted her chin at Putt. "You know the schedule. You're with Margot tonight and Niko is tomorrow night."

"I don't want her!" Putt proclaimed loudly. He glanced at me apologetically. "I'm sorry, but she's so skinny I'm always afraid it'll come out the other side."

"You wish," Niko grunted under his breath.

Despite myself, I started to grin at the image, then I caught myself and glowered at the two men. "Get back to the great hall and stay there," I ordered. "And if I hear you two fighting again, you'll have to deal with me from across swords. You understand me?" Both men reluctantly nodded and clomped dejectedly back down the stairs. I could hear them arguing in whispers as they left, but I chose to ignore it and I focused on Flora instead. "Maybe you should put something on," I said with an uncomfortable frown.

Flora jiggled her large breasts at me and laughed coyly. "Like what you see, Lord Alwin?"

I could feel my face reddening and I worked hard at staring her in the face. "This can't happen, Flora," I said, knowing once again I'd failed to anticipate something that should have been obvious.

The potential for trouble in a house full of rough men will always exist, but add women into the mix and all of a sudden that potential becomes a virtual guarantee. I knew unless I did something now to take care of it, sooner or later someone was going to get hurt badly.

"I can't help it if they prefer their women to be on the buxom side," Flora said with a shrug. "Besides, since everyone knows Aenor is your girl, and Margot is not as young as she used to be, it's understandable that the men would fight over me."

"I don't care!" I said firmly. "Our first raid will be soon and I need everyone focused on that, not on you."

Flora's face turned serious and she nodded. "I know, Hadrack. I'm sorry, I was just teasing you. I thought you'd be happy with what we're doing."

"Why would I be happy about my men beating on each other in the dead of night?" I asked.

Flora shook her head. "Not that. I mean Margot and me. In Hillsfort, Hape charged a half Jorq each for what your men are getting here for free." Her mouth twitched upward slightly. "I don't know a lot of things, Hadrack, but I do know men. Keep them well bounced and satisfied during the night and they'll work twice as hard for you during the day. This is just our way of helping."

I sighed and glanced at the ceiling. "I appreciate it, Flora. But I can't afford to have my men fighting amongst themselves."

"It won't happen again," Flora assured me. "In the morning, Margot and I will speak with the boys and make sure they understand. They either follow the schedule we set without argument or we start keeping our legs closed." She winked at me and headed back into her room. "That should solve the problem."

I nodded and headed back down the stairs, secretly agreeing with her that it would solve it. I knew the men would quickly realize that it was better to get something now and again, rather than get nothing at all, and if there were any more disagreements regarding the women after that, I never heard of it. Occasionally over the next few days, one of the men would appear with a scuffed face or bruised eye, but nothing serious enough for me to make an issue over it and I quickly turned my thoughts to other things.

I spent most of my time at night in my solar going over the list of targets Daughter Gernet had given me, memorizing everything I could about the twelve men. I remember reading a book about military tactics in Gasterny with a phrase in it that had stayed with me, and I repeated it over and over again to myself.

"Know your enemy even better than they know themselves," the passage had said, "and the battle is more than half won."

Each morning I took several hours away from the walls to work with the men individually on their swordsmanship. Putt and Cain were the most accomplished with the blade, with Niko and Anson showing reasonable competence, though they were both prone to making unforced errors. I didn't bother working with Hanley. With his arm bent permanently at a strange angle the way it was, there seemed no point. As for Sim, all I can say is he wasn't joking with me when he said he had no skill with a sword. Sim was a hopeless case, flat-footed and much too slow. I tried to imagine him going up against a Pith, man or woman, and I shuddered, knowing that he'd last less than a few seconds. I tried to instill patience and rhythm in his movements, but after a week of frustration where I lost my temper repeatedly, I finally gave up and just gave Sim an axe to wield. He was strong and fearsome-looking and I figured if nothing else he'd help to frighten people. It would have to do.

Tyris, on the other hand, was as formidable an archer as Black Thomin had claimed, and as the tall blond man displayed his skills to me, I couldn't help but be impressed. I believed he could give even the Piths a good challenge with the bow and I looked forward to Jebido and Baine coming in the spring even more now. I knew my younger friend would enjoy having another archer around as skilled as Tyris was and that the two would become instant friends.

Two weeks after we'd arrived at Witbridge Manor, I gathered Finol, Sim, and the women around the table in the extra room in my solar — which had become our unofficial meeting spot where we could talk without fear of being overheard — and I told them who I'd decided our first target would be.

"Alga the merchant!" I announced dramatically. Alga was fifth on Daughter Gernet's list and I held my index finger on his name as I looked at the faces sitting around the table. "He's from Gandertown but goes to Whitemill on the last Tuesday of every month."

"The last Tuesday of the month is next week," Aenor pointed out.

"It is," I nodded.

"Whitemill is near the coast," Finol added as he tugged thoughtfully at his beard. "Several days ride from here."

"So I understand," I agreed. "It seems the merchant has a mistress there."

"That's going to be a problem," Flora cut in. "Most men don't carry around sacks of gold with them when they're going to meet a whore behind their wife's back."

"I imagine that depends on the quality of the whore," I replied with a grin. Flora chuckled and bowed her head in acknowledgment and I sat back in my chair. "It's not the woman that interests me, anyway. Alga always stops in at the docks to collect the monies owed to him from his shipping businesses in Whitemill right after he sees her."

"Ah," Finol said in understanding as heads nodded around the table. "So you plan to visit him after he visits the whore."

"I do," I said.

"He's going to have guards," Sim warned.

I shrugged. "Probably. Hopefully we can deal with them without anyone getting hurt." No one said anything to that, probably because like me they had their doubts it could be done. I glanced at Finol. "How are our finances holding up?"

Finol frowned. "Not good. We only have seventeen Jorqs left, but there's still a lot that needs to be done before the manor is back in shape."

"You know that's not my biggest concern right now," I said, glancing back at the list.

"Well, I am the steward of Witbridge Manor!" Finol said crossly. "And it's my job to make it my concern!"

Finol had stressed the word 'my' twice for emphasis and I could see color quickly rising in his wrinkled cheeks. I sighed inwardly, knowing that we were heading for another row. My companions all looked down at the table uncomfortably in anticipation. Finol and I were always going to be at odds over this, I realized, unless I did something to change it right now. The old man loved the manor more than life itself, and it had crushed him to slowly watch it degrade over the years. I knew I was Finol's only chance at ever seeing Witbridge Manor restored to its former glory. I decided it would be far simpler just to give him what he wanted and save myself from the months of arguments and snide remarks yet to come.

I held my hand up, stalling the old steward before he said anything more. "How much do you need?" I asked.

"How much do I need for what?" Finol demanded, looking thrown off by my question.

"For the manor," I said. "How much do you need to fix it?"

"Which part?" Finol asked cautiously.

"All of it."

Finol's eyebrows rose in surprise. He turned his head and looked up at the ceiling and I could see his lips moving as he did arithmetic in his head. "Several hundred Jorqs should do nicely," he finally said with a straight face.

"Several hundred!" Sim gasped in shock. "But that's a fortune!"

Finol shrugged, ignoring Sim as he looked at me with a challenge in his eyes. "You asked what I need. Well, that's the answer."

"Then you shall have it!" I said, keeping the look of surprise I felt at the amount from my face. Daughter Gernet had instructed me to use whatever we needed to operate the manor from the money we stole from our enemies. I doubt she had considered a complete rebuild of Witbridge Manor when she'd told me that, but she wasn't around at the moment and I felt making peace with the old steward now was worth risking Daughter Gernet's ire later when she found out. "You'll get your Jorqs," I promised Finol with a grin. "And you'll have Alga the merchant to thank for it too!"

Alga the merchant was an enormously fat man, with a pointed beard, shiny bald head, and an odd, pigeon-toed walk that had most of the outlaws chuckling and making fun of him from the moment they saw him. Lanterns lit up a small area of a long dock that spanned the shoreline, pushing back the moonless night around the fat man as he got down from a carriage just like the ones I'd seen in Gasterny. He paused to look up at the three-story warehouse above him and then glanced toward three long ships with high prows and wide bellies filled with cargo that sat lashed together in the water twenty feet away from him. The thick oak hulls made a faint screeching sound as the boats rocked gently against each other on the light tide. A wide-shouldered man with a long sword on his hip, a short sword at the small of his back, and another long sword strapped over his shoulders, escorted Alga toward the warehouse. Two heavily-armed men stood near the front door and they greeted the merchant respectfully before one of them opened the door for the fat man to enter.

Sim, Tyris, Cain, Niko and I were standing in the shadows of a dark, abandoned building fifty yards further down the dock from Alga's warehouse.

"Where are they?" Sim finally muttered impatiently after we'd waited for several long minutes after the merchant had disappeared inside.

"There," Tyris said, pointing.

I saw with relief that Putt and Anson were making their way along the dock from the north. I could just hear the off-key notes of the song they were singing as they stumbled and clutched at each other to keep themselves from falling. Anson had a torch burning brightly in his right hand, which he waved around for emphasis as he sang, sending sparks flying in every direction.

"They sure look like they know what they're doing," I muttered, impressed despite myself at the performance. If I hadn't known better, I would have sworn the two men were dead drunk.

"From years of experience," Cain whispered beside me with a low laugh.

Putt and Anson reached the warehouse and they both bowed cheekily to the guards, then turned toward the boats, swaying precariously on the weathered planks that over-looked the water. Putt paused, said something to Anson, then undid his trousers and sent a thin stream of piss arcing out over the side of the dock. Anson swayed unsteadily while he waited for Putt to finish, then finally fell to his knees close to the moored boats.

I could feel the men around me tensing and I held up my hand in the darkness. "Wait until they move," I cautioned, glancing at the two guards at the warehouse door. "No killing if you can help it," I added.

"Get away from there you drunken louts!" one of the guards shouted as he took several threatening steps forward.

Anson looked over his shoulder at the man, then let out a high-pitched laugh and swung the burning torch over his head before he sent it hurtling toward the center boat. Both of the guards shouted in alarm at the same time as the heavy canvas covering the cargo erupted in flames.

"Now!" I said as the guards ran toward the fire. The five of us crossed the distance to the boats in seconds. We were making a lot of noise in our armor, but the guards never looked behind them, distracted as they were by the flames. Sim and Cain each clutched heavy clubs and they used them efficiently to silence the men from behind with a solid whack to each of their skulls. I could already feel the heat from the burning boats through my helmet and I pointed down at the prostrate bodies lying at the edge of the dock. "Get them back where it's safe!" I ordered Putt and Anson as I headed for the door of the warehouse.

I pushed open the door and then paused, peering through the eye slots of my wolf helmet at the two men seated at a table in the center of the room. Alga had his back to me and he was counting from a heaping stack of golden Jorqs, while a thin wisp of a man with a large goiter that jutted out from his neck obscenely sat opposite him. The guard with the three swords stood behind the merchant and he whirled in surprise when he heard me enter and reached for the long sword at his back.

"I wouldn't do that if I were you," I said as I took several steps into the room. Behind me my men entered and spread out with their weapons in their hands, looking formidable in the shiny new armor and helms that I'd purchased for them. Tyris held his drawn bow aimed at the guard and I gestured to the archer. "My friend can take the eye out of a squirrel from fifty paces," I said, grinning as I used the same words Black Tomlin had used on me. I figured the dead outlaw might appreciate the irony of it somehow, depending on where he landed after judgment day. The guard reluctantly let his hand drop to his side and I nodded to him in approval. I remembered the mistake Black Tomlin had made with me and I pointed to the floor. "Throw your weapons down and then move back,"

I ordered. The guard did as he was told, dropping both long swords and the short sword at his feet, then he took several steps backward.

"The knife in your boot, too," Tyris grunted, motioning with his bow.

The guard hesitated, then reached into his boot and pulled out a knife, which he angrily tossed aside.

"Watch him closely," I said to Sim, loud enough for the guard to hear. I pointed to the axe in Sim's hand. "If the bastard even blinks, cut him in half with that."

I moved closer to the table to tower over the merchant and the man with the goiter, who I saw was visibly sweating and shaking uncontrollably.

"Who are you?" Alga demanded as he stood up to face me, his giant belly quivering with indignation. I was impressed by the fat man's apparent lack of fear, though I was less impressed with his intelligence, since a fortune in gold sat in front of him and he was surrounded by hostile, armed men. "I am a representative of Prince Tyrale!" Alga snapped at me when I didn't respond. "Any attack on me is an attack on him! And I promise you it will be dealt with severely!"

I put my gauntleted hand over the merchant's face and pushed him roughly back into his chair. "I care nothing for your prince!" I growled down at him. I ran my fingers over the Jorqs on the table. "But I do care for these. My name is Hadrack, the Outlaw of Corwick." Alga's face registered his surprise and I saw fear finally creeping into his eyes. I smiled inside my helm. I picked up a Jorq, examined it, then threw it back in the pile. "I care for them so much that I think I'll take them with me to make sure that they stay safe."

Alga's eyes bugled and he started shaking his head back and forth. "You can't!" the merchant finally gasped in horror.

"Why not?" I asked, starting to enjoy myself. "What's to stop me?"

"You'll ruin me!" Alga protested as he put his pudgy, bejeweled fingers on my arm and tugged at me in desperation. "I have creditors! People I need to pay with this money!"

"That's not my concern," I said. I shrugged the merchant's hand off me, then motioned to Cain and Niko to come forward. The outlaws hurried to the table and began scooping the gold into canvas sacks we'd brought with us.

"I need this money!" Alga sobbed as he watched Cain and Niko work. He looked up at me with tear-filled eyes. "Please, have mercy on a poor businessman just trying to make an honest living!"

"Lord," I said with a grunt.

"What?" Alga said, pausing in his blubbering to look at me in confusion.

"Please, Lord Hadrack, have mercy," I said. "You forgot to be polite."

Alga blinked several times and then he nodded apologetically. "Of course. Of course. How rude of me. Please, Lord Hadrack, have mercy on a poor businessman."

I put my hand on Alga's shoulder, grimacing with distaste at the sponginess of his flesh. "Sorry friend, mercy is for the weak." I nodded to Cain and Niko, who'd finished gathering up the Jorqs, then motioned to the others that it was time to leave. I waited until my men had left the warehouse, then I paused in the doorway and looked back over my shoulder. "My men are firing the building as I speak, so if I were you, I'd considering getting out while you still can."

We took almost three hundred Jorqs from Alga the merchant that night. Not to mention burning his warehouse down to the ground and sinking all three of his ships and destroying their cargo. It would be some time, if ever, I figured, before the fat merchant recovered enough to be of any help financially to Prince Tyrale in the coming war.

Our return to Witbridge Manor was one of triumph and, as promised, I handed over two-hundred of the stolen Jorqs to a delighted Finol, with the understanding that he wouldn't bother me for money to repair the manor for a long time to come. The raid had gone off better than I could have ever hoped for. I was so impressed with the performance of my men that I decided, after talking it over with Finol, Sim, and the women first, that it was finally time to let the rest of the outlaws know what was really going on. We gathered in the great hall on the second night after our return and everyone sat on the benches around the table while I paced the room and talked. I told them my entire story, starting at the beginning with what had happened in Corwick, then my enslavement along with Baine and Jebido, until our eventual rescue by Einhard and the Piths.

"So that's why you were with them," Tyris said in wonder at that point.

"Yes," I nodded. "I warned you it would be a long story."

I talked for over an hour and explained in detail how we'd met Daughter Gernet in Gasterny, then about the prince's murder and Shana's abduction. I told them about Jebido, Baine's and my eventual capture by the Cardians after Gasterny fell, and how Malo had saved us from the king's executioner. Then, while they were still digesting that, I told them the real reason why we were all together in Witbridge Manor. After I was done, the room fell silent and I stood by the fireplace and waited, not knowing what to expect as I studied the faces around me.

Finally, Tyris stood and he came around the table to me and knelt at my feet. "You have upheld your vow and more," he said. "And because of this I pledge that I will be your sworn man in all things. I offer my skill with a bow and the loyalty in my heart to both you and The Mother in this quest, if you'll have me."

I blinked down in surprise at the blond archer, then finally nodded, feeling a lump rising in my throat. "I accept your service, Tyris of Witbridge," I said. "And I am honored to have you at my side."

Tyris stood and we locked forearms, then one by one, each of my companions rose and knelt and repeated the blond archer's words. Even the women joined in, and from that moment on, it wasn't just Finol who called me lord; they all did. The relationship we forged that night in the great hall of Witbridge Manor quickly became that of a close-knit family. The eleven of us were now united in a single cause, one which we considered to be bigger than any one of us. I would have gladly trusted any of them with my life and I knew that they felt the same way about me, and about each other.

For the rest of the fall and long into the winter, we raided all across the western and northern lands of Ganderland as tales of the Outlaw of Corwick continued to grow. Though I was not overly keen on it, we made sure to rob any of the rich we came across in our travels to ensure Prince Tyrale didn't become suspicious. I figured doing that, coupled with the outlandish rumors that Daughter Gernet's people were already spreading about us, would be more than enough to keep the prince off the scent. It got to the point that just seeing us was enough for hardened, well-armed men to throw down their weapons and submit, even though not one life had ever been taken by us in any of our raids. As the months went by and the names on Daughter Gernet's list were slowly crossed off one by one, the manor's coffers grew larger and larger. I wasn't sure what we were supposed to do with all the money we'd taken, as Daughter Gernet hadn't told me that part, so we just hoarded it and waited for instructions. Eventually there was so much money that I had to have Hanley design a secret chamber beneath the great hall to stow it all in.

I refused to let Hanley go on raids with the rest of us, which I think he was secretly relieved about. Instead, Finol gave Hanley his support to modify the manor and its holdings with the money I'd given him in any way the boy saw fit. After each raid, we'd return a week or two later to find something new in Witbridge, like a wooden watchtower, a bigger, thicker gate, a larger stable, a rebuilt well, or, much to the boy's obvious delight, a brand new mill built along the stream. Hanley and Finol hadn't done the work themselves, of course. The old steward had been right that first day, and not long after we'd begun raiding, people began to return to Witbridge. The old steward paid these people for their labor, which was a novel idea at the time, and as word got out, more and more people came seeking work. I can't say I was overly happy about that part, I must confess. I'd enjoyed my freedom greatly in the early days and had completely forgotten about who and what Lord Alwin was supposed to be. Now, much to my chagrin, whenever I went outside the manor walls, it was with bandages on my face, a bent back, and a twisted leg that I became quite skilled at dragging behind me like I'd seen my father do all his life.

Most of the existing houses along the road had already been reclaimed and rebuilt by the new arrivals, with more houses appearing almost daily. A great bear of a man dressed in wolf furs named Ermos arrived with his family in the middle of the winter and he took up residence in the smithy, to the delight of everyone in the manor. Anson had taken on the role of blacksmith for us, but truth be told, the bald man wasn't very good at it. I was forever fearful that Angry would throw a shoe at the worst possible moment.

Despite my role of invalid, life was good at Witbridge, and a cold, humorless winter slowly turned into a fine, dry spring. I was sitting in my solar reading a book that I'd gotten Sim to buy for me in Laskerly one sunny morning in early April, when suddenly the watchtower bell rang. I ran outside, strapping on my sword as my men began to gather in the courtyard.

"What is it?" I demanded, glancing up to see that Cain was on watch duty.

"Riders approaching, lord!" Cain called down.

"How many?" I asked.

"Looks like four!"

I nodded in relief, knowing that there were too few for them to be the king's men. I climbed up into the tower, shading my eyes to see better and then I grunted in surprise, realizing one of the riders was a woman. As the figures on horseback drew closer, I finally broke out into a wide grin and I laughed with delight as I slapped Cain heartily on the back.

"It's all right!" I called down to the courtyard. "They're friends!"

I scurried back down the ladder as fast as I could and ran to the new gate, swinging it open just as the riders reached it. I stepped back with my hands on my hips and a grin on my face as the horses trotted inside and halted in the courtyard.

"Shit, Hadrack!" Jebido grunted in surprise when he saw me. "You've grown a foot, you ugly bastard!"

I laughed as he and Baine dismounted while Jin and Malo watched us from atop their horses. My two friends and I embraced warmly, slapping each other soundly on the backs with all of us talking at once. Finally we broke apart still laughing like children as I stepped back to look at them. Jebido was thinner, I saw, and greyer than I remembered, but he looked healthy and happy, though there was still a shadow of the pain he'd been through lingering in his eyes. Baine was dressed in his usual black and had grown taller, with heavier shoulders and a thick, full beard that any man would be proud of. I felt my grin slowly falter at the dark look that suddenly crossed Baine's face.

"What is it?" I asked in apprehension. I'd only seen that look on Baine's face a few times in my life, and none of those times had been good. "What's wrong?"

"It's Shana," Baine replied almost reluctantly.

"Tell me," I said, feeling a deep thud in the pit of my stomach. "Is she dead?"

"No," Jebido answered, looking grim as he shook his head. "Not yet."

"Hadrack," Baine said. "Lord Demay plans to hang her a week from now!"

15: CHOICES

"Hanley!" I roared, turning to glare at the boy. "Fetch me my armor!" Hanley nodded, looking frightened as he turned and ran for the manor house. "Putt, Sim, saddle the horses!" I ordered. "The rest of you get ready to ride! We leave in ten minutes!"

My men broke and ran for the manor house to get their weapons while I stood in the courtyard staring up at the sky and willing myself to contain the rage I felt boiling up in my chest. The bastard! I thought, picturing my hands wrapped around Lord Demay's rat-like neck. I imagined Shana, alone, terrified and helpless and I closed my eyes, groaning at the image of her with a noose around her neck. No matter what happened or what the cost, I vowed, I would not allow that to happen.

"Hadrack!"

I opened my eyes to see Jebido standing before me. My friend had his fists bunched tightly in my tunic and he shook me for emphasis. "Are you listening to me?" he demanded.

"What?" I growled, putting my hands over his. I could feel the need to smash something welling up inside me and I fought to control it. I carefully took my friend's hands and lifted them away from my clothing. I was afraid with the anger that I could feel racing along my veins that I'd accidentally hurt Jebido. I tried hard to focus on what he was saying.

"You can't go," Jebido said, looking at me with a mixture of frustration and sadness on his face.

"What are you talking about?" I demanded as Hanley appeared clinging and clanging as he ran down the steps with my armor piled high in his arms. "Drop everything there," I growled at the boy as I pointed to the ground by my feet.

Hanley gently lowered the armor to the cobblestones and I grunted in annoyance. "You forgot my helmet." Hanley looked crestfallen, then took off running again as I shifted my gaze back to Jebido. "Tell me."

"It's a trap, Hadrack," Jebido said. "The entire castle will be waiting for you,"

"A trap?" I repeated as I began donning the armor. I paused as I thought it over. "Did Lord Demay plan this?"

"Not by himself," Baine said with a quick shake of his head. "That bastard Lord Corwick is involved too."

I nodded, hardly surprised. It made sense that Lord Corwick would have thought of something like this. Using Shana as bait seemed entirely too clever to be Lord Demay's handiwork. "Trap or not, I'm going," I said as I bent and fastened the gold buckles at the back of my greaves.

"Hadrack, we need to talk," Jin said as she dismounted and came to me.

I straightened and she put her hand on my chest, staring up at me with her big blue eyes.

"You shouldn't be here," I told her. "This is no place for a child."

I could see a sudden hurt rise in her eyes. "I'm almost fourteen-years-old!" she said crossly. "I'm no child. And if not for me, you would never have known about Lady Demay at all. My grandmother had no intention of letting you find out about it until it was too late."

I glanced at Jebido and he nodded that it was true. "Jin came to us at Haverty's and we set out the moment we heard. Baine and I were almost here when she and Malo caught up to us. It would seem your actions as the Outlaw of Corwick have not gone unnoticed by your enemies. Since no one can find you, it looks like they decided to try to get you to come to them instead."

"Jin never should have told them," Malo said from atop his horse. He glanced at the Daughter-In-Waiting and I could see the obvious annoyance on his face. "But what's done is done. I'm here to officially tell you that Daughter Gernet forbids you to go to Calban."

"Forbids me!" I snapped, incensed by the House Agent's arrogance. "If I want to go to Calban I will, and nobody can stop me!" I ignored Malo after that and instead I took Jin gently in my arms. "Thank you," I said. "If not for you I might never have known."

Jin pressed her face against me and I could tell that she was crying. "I didn't want to tell you at first," she said into my chest. "I'm terrified of what will happen if you go, but I couldn't live with myself if I didn't say anything." She finally sniffed and pushed herself away from me. "I don't ever want there to be secrets between us, Hadrack. That's why you had to know. But you also need to know that I came here with Malo to convince you not to go to Calban."

"Why?" I demanded, confused now.

Jin smiled sadly. "Because Malo is right and I knew you wouldn't listen to him." I frowned, about to protest and Jin shook her head, silencing me. "No, you have to listen. I know you don't believe it, but they'll kill you if you go there. I know they will." Jin looked up at me and I could see despair swirling in her eyes. "I'm so sorry, but you can't save her. You have to accept that."

"No, I don't," I said stubbornly. I imagined Shana sitting in some filth-covered cell somewhere while Lord Demay and Lord Corwick used her like a pawn on a chatrang board and I started to shake with fury. None of it made any sense. Lord Demay had gone to great lengths to get Shana out of Gasterny and now, less than six months later, it appeared he was willing to kill her. "Why would Lord Demay agree to execute his own wife just to get me?" I asked Malo. "It sounds like this is all just some kind of elaborate ruse, hoping I'll show up."

"It's not a ruse," Malo said with a sigh as he swung a leg over his horse and dropped to the ground. "He has a reason for executing her. A good one."

I glanced at Jin and she nodded in confirmation. "She

tried to kill him," she whispered.

"Lady Demay took his right eye with a sewing needle," Jebido added with admiration. "A half an inch deeper and she'd have killed the bastard and the world would have been a better place."

"The execution has been sanctioned by both sides of the House and by the king's regent," Malo said as he came to stand before me. "The attempt on Lord Demay's life was witnessed by more than ten people, so there was no choice but to approve the petition. There's nothing anyone can do to stop it now."

"You mean there's nothing anyone wants to do!" I grunted. I poked my finger for emphasis against Malo's chest armor. "Including you!"

"Calban Castle will be crawling with soldiers," Malo said in a flat voice. "At least three or four hundred if our information is correct. All you'd be doing by going there is throwing your life away for no good reason."

"No good reason!" I shouted in disbelief. I thrust my face an inch from Malo's and glared at him. "You think saving a woman's life isn't a good reason?"

"That's not what I meant and you know it," Malo said, meeting my angry gaze without blinking. "Lady Demay's execution will be tragic, but she had to know there would be repercussions for her actions. Sacrificing yourself will solve nothing, as they will kill her regardless of what you do. You're too important to our plans to waste on a hopeless cause."

I snorted and shook my head as I turned my back on the House Agent. "And what about you two?" I demanded, glaring at Baine and Jebido. "Where do you stand in all this?"

My friends shared an uneasy look. "I don't see that there's much of a choice, Hadrack," Jebido finally said, looking unhappy. "We didn't know it was a trap until Malo caught up to us and told us." Jebido sighed and removed his helmet, then ran his fingers through his silver hair. "You know I care for the girl, but we'd need an army to get her out of there. I just don't see what we can do."

"There might be a way," Finol interrupted. He took several steps forward and glanced at me. "If I may, my lord?" I saw Jebido's eyebrows rise in surprise at how the steward had addressed me and I nodded for Finol to proceed. "If we can get several men into the castle before the execution," he said, tugging at his beard. "Perhaps a day or two before? Then maybe we could get her out somehow before the trap is fully set."

"They'll be watching for that," Malo said in a dismissive voice. "They're no fools, those two lords. They'll have her under lock and key in a place where no one will ever find her. Not only that, but my spies tell me that anyone entering the castle right up until an hour before the execution is to be searched thoroughly. Hadrack will never get past the gates."

"You said up until an hour before," Baine said. "What happens after that?"

Malo shrugged. "The gates will be left unguarded and no one who enters will be searched."

"How inviting," Baine grunted bitterly.

"Indeed," Malo agreed. "They want Hadrack to get inside."

Lord Demay and Lord Corwick had thought of everything, I realized, supremely confident that no matter what I tried, their line would ensnare me. What I needed to do was not just break that line, I needed to turn it upside down in a way that they wouldn't see coming. I thought about what Finol had said, looking at it now from a different angle as an idea slowly began to form in my mind. Would they have thought of that? I wondered. I couldn't imagine that they would have. After all, who would risk such a thing and the potential repercussions on judgment day? Even if they hadn't thought of it, could I get the kind of support that I knew I would need from the House to even make the attempt? I glanced at Malo's dour face, knowing that I'd have to convince the House Agent to go along with it first. An unenviable task to say the least. Hanley came running back with my helmet as

I started pulling off the armor I'd just put on and he looked at me in obvious confusion.

"Take it all back," I said to the boy. "I'm not going to need it just yet." I turned to my companions. "I have an idea," I said. "It's just a seed right now, but if we're going to make it grow I'm going to need all of your help." I motioned to the manor house. "Let's go inside where we can talk."

We settled in the great hall, with Finol, Sim, Jebido, Baine, Malo and Jin all sitting around the table while I took my customary place standing by the fireplace. I always found I thought better standing up and pacing rather than sitting down. The rest of my men leaned against the walls or sat on the dais along with Flora, Margot and Aenor, listening intently. I saw both Jebido and Baine look at my men and the women with curiosity and I knew they were wondering why they were here at all. The four new arrivals to Witbridge Manor would quickly come to learn that I did things quite differently than most in Ganderland. Each of my outlaws' opinions and ideas mattered to me, which was something that I'd learned from my year living with Einhard and the Piths. And, as with the Piths, the opinions of the women were valued just as highly as those of the men. Any decision I made would be talked about beforehand by all of us, though I don't deny that in the end my word, just like Einhard's, was final. Everyone in Witbridge understood that fact completely, but I knew it meant a lot that I valued their opinion and weighed their thoughts before deciding what to do. It had meant the same thing to me when I was with the Piths.

"So," I said. "Before I begin, I think that introductions are in order." I introduced the women first, then quickly ran through the names of each of my men, indicating them one by one. The outlaws stood and nodded when they were singled out, but none of them spoke, clearly uncomfortable under the scrutiny of the House Agent.

"Hadrack," Malo finally said after I was finished introducing everyone.

"Lord Hadrack!" Aenor responded with an edge to her voice, surprising the room with her reprimand. My men were slowly nodding in agreement, emboldened by Aenor's nerve.

Malo paused, then inclined his head. "Lord Hadrack, then," he said, looking slightly amused. "Before we begin, there is something else you should know."

I put my hands behind my back. "Then by all means, let's hear what it is."

Malo looked again to my men, then he shook his head. "I think it would be better if you heard this alone." He looked at me meaningfully. "It's about that name Daughter Gernet promised you."

I took a deep breath, having forgotten in all the excitement that Daughter Gernet had said she'd send me another name from the surviving nine once spring had come. "You can speak freely here, Malo," I said. I gestured to the outlaws with my head. "My men know everything about Corwick and the nine. There are no secrets between us."

Malo's eyebrows rose in surprise and he shrugged. "Very well," he said. "Daughter Gernet is very pleased with what you've accomplished so far. You've set Prince Tyrale and his cause back a great deal."

"Speaking of that," I said with a frown, thinking of the fortune lying beneath our feet. "What about all the money we've taken? How do we get it to her?"

"I have a wagon on its way here for that," Malo said. "Six House Agents will escort the gold back to the Holy House in Halhaven. From there it will be shipped to Prince Tyden."

"Fair enough," I said, glad to have the issue cleared up.

"As for the name," Malo continued. He removed a roll of parchment from his clothing and offered it to me. "I believe you know a man named Hervi Desh?"

"Heavy Beard," I said so low I doubt anyone heard me.

I turned back ten years to the chase that had started it all. I remembered vividly how Heavy Beard had fallen off his horse after I'd frightened the animal. Desh had also been the one who'd gone to Corwick Castle to bring Lord Corwick back to our farm. If he hadn't done that, my father and everyone else in the village might have lived. I could feel my hands hurting from clenching my fists so hard and I slowly unclenched them as I took a deep breath.

"Tell me," I said tightly, ignoring the offered parchment.

"Desh is now an advisor to Prince Tyrale himself," Malo said. He threw the parchment on the table. "Getting to him is next to impossible these days."

"So, if I can't get to him, why are you telling me this at all?" I said, knowing there was more.

"Because next week he's going to be in a small village up north called Dellcliff. He's going there for his sister's wedding and, for the first time in many months, will be vulnerable. It's only for one day and might be the only chance you'll ever get to take him."

"Next week?" I said, looking at Malo suspiciously. I glanced at Sim. "Calban Castle is where from here?"

"Southwest, my lord," Sim replied immediately. "Four days hard ride."

"And Dellcliff is how far to the north?"

Sim shrugged. "At least five days, lord. Maybe more."

I grunted, not surprised as I turned to hold Malo's eyes. "That's convenient, don't you think?" I said to the House Agent.

Malo didn't say anything, but I saw Jin, who was sitting beside him, stare down at the table with a surprised look on her face. I knew the girl hadn't known about Desh and I started to pace, feeling angry at the obvious blackmail. I knew Malo was betting that my vow of vengeance against the nine would weigh more to me in the end than the life of a woman I'd only known for a few days. The bastard must have planned using Desh as a backup in case I refused to obey Daughter Gernet's wishes. I rubbed my hand over my eyes, feeling my pulse pounding in my temples as I fought to control myself. Finally

I paused beside a small stool that sat to one side of the fire-place and I cursed and kicked the stool hard. The stool was made of heavy oak and was well crafted and it flew through the air toward the dais like a hawk let loose from the tether. Putt had to duck quickly as the stool sailed over his head and then crashed through the window behind him, sending shards of glass spraying everywhere.

"My lord!" Finol protested, jumping up in alarm.

The steward immediately gestured to the women to start cleaning up the mess, while I strode to the table and leaned on it, peering down into Malo's face. "Do you think I'm stupid?" I growled.

"I think no such thing," Malo said calmly.

"Yet, you come into my manor!" I shouted, incensed even more by the blank look on the House Agent's face. "Dangling that murderous bastard in front of me like some kind of precious jewel! Hoping I'd be so dazzled by its gleam that I'd forget all about Shana!"

"Hadrack, please," Jin said as she stood. She wrung her hands together, looking ready to cry again. "Malo made a mistake. He should have known better."

"Yes, he should have!" I snapped. I turned my angry gaze on Jebido and Baine. "Did you know about this?"

"Not a chance!" Baine snorted, looking almost as angry as I felt. He gave Malo a baleful stare. "Neither of us would have ever tried to pull something as underhanded as this on you."

"Never!" Jebido agreed, his thin face red with anger. "We both know what that vow means to you, Hadrack." Jebido glared at Malo. "Some things are sacred and I've half a mind to take you outside and remind you of what the word honor means!"

Malo cleared his throat, ignoring my friends as he focused on me. "You need to understand, Hadrack…" The House Agent paused as shouts of protests immediately arose. Malo sighed and nodded, lifting his hands to silence my men. "Let me try this again, shall I?" He turned to me. "Lord Hadrack, you need to understand that this offer comes directly from Daughter Gernet, not me."

"Is that supposed to make me feel better?" I asked, standing up and crossing my arms over my chest. "They may be her words, but you both speak from the same mouth."

Malo stared at me and I could see a faint glint of anger in his eyes now as he gestured around the great hall. "You've risen high since the last time we saw each other. With a fancy manor, servants, and sworn men, all clearly loyal to you. But don't ever forget where you really come from, Lord Hadrack, and how quickly you can be returned there, should Daughter Gernet choose to do so." Malo put his hands on the table and leaned toward me. "All we care about is the mission you were sent here to accomplish. Nothing else matters. So it's time you pull your head out of your ass and accept that."

My men began to shout angrily again and I silenced them all with a glare before turning back to the House Agent. "And what if I don't accept it?" I said. "What if instead, I just walk away from this mission of yours right now? Then what will you do?"

I saw Jin's eyes widen in apprehension and I thought even Malo looked a little uncertain. "Then we'd find someone else to do it," he said unconvincingly.

I laughed, knowing he was bluffing. "No, you won't," I said. "Because there is no one else." I leaned forward on the table until we were less than a foot apart. "And we both know it."

"So you're telling me you'd walk away from The Mother right now?" Malo said softly. "Knowing how important the task is that She's set for you?"

"Not with any happiness," I conceded. I looked around at my men, my two friends, and the women, pausing as I caught Aenor's eye. She nodded to me in encouragement. The truth was, I didn't want this to end. We were family here at Witbridge and I knew that if it came right down to it, I couldn't walk away now. Despite the disgust I felt at how Malo had tried to manipulate me, I knew he'd only done so out of need, not malice. That didn't make me like the House Agent much at the moment, however, and I took a deep breath as I studied him thoughtfully. "What happens if I don't go after Desh?" I asked, skirting away from the subject of me leaving.

Malo sat back and shrugged. "The choice is yours. Daughter Gernet promised you a name. If you choose not to use it, then that's on you, not her."

"And I imagine if I don't use it, I'll have to wait a long time before I get another one," I said.

Malo and I locked eyes and he remained silent, which was a clear enough message as far as I was concerned. I thought about how many times I'd imagined killing Heavy Beard and I slowly nodded to myself, realizing that the man's time hadn't come yet. I'd get another chance, I knew. Be it six months from now, a year or five years. Sooner or later I'd find him and the others and I'd kill them all, with or without Daughter Gernet's help.

"I don't care about Hervi Desh right now," I finally said to a room hushed in anticipation. I felt a calmness come over me, knowing somehow that my father and sister and everyone else who'd died in Corwick would approve of my choice. The vow I'd made to them was unbreakable, and for the first time since I'd uttered it, I understood that the promise didn't have to have a time limit attached to it. Each of those men would pay eventually for their crimes, just like Hape, Calen and Merk already had. I'd dedicated my entire life to finding and killing the nine, but today I was choosing to set that aside for something else. Something that I could no longer deny to myself or anyone else. "The life of the woman I love is in jeopardy," I said, strangely relieved to have spoken it out loud. I stood straight and shrugged as I glanced around the room. "In the end, that's all that matters to me. Lady Demay has probably forgotten about me by now, and even if she hasn't, I know I'm nothing but a peasant to her. But peasant or not, I do intend to save her." I glanced at Malo, letting him see the resolve burning in my eyes. "You and Daughter Gernet need to understand that there's nothing you can say to me that will ever change my mind." I crossed my arms as I held the House Agent's eyes. "So, Malo, you can either choose to help me or you can get out of my way. Right now, I really don't care which."

Malo sat for a time, weighing my words, until finally he sighed in exasperation. "I guess the only thing left to do, then, is go with you and make sure you don't get yourself killed."

I smiled in satisfaction, nodding to the House Agent as the room erupted in cheers.

"But how will you do it?" Jin finally asked in a trembling voice as the cheers slowly faded. "Malo told me it's impossible."

"Nothing's impossible," I said, feeling confidence coming over me. I winked at Jin and grinned. "We'll save Lady Demay from the noose by giving those bastards exactly what they want."

16: THE WOLF
AND THE LAMB

Calban Castle was built on a kidney-shaped, rock-covered island that sat in a large bay almost three-hundred feet out from the mainland. A long bridge of heavy, sun-bleached planks stretched from the sand-covered shore below me, all the way across the water to the island. I knew there was a dock on the northern side of the castle somewhere that serviced Lord Demay's ships, but I couldn't see it from where I sat my horse. Malo had told me that a narrow road led upward from that dock to a second, smaller gate on the northern wall that was well guarded and usually kept locked. That second gate would be crucial to my plans.

It was ten o'clock in the morning and the tide coming in from the bay crashed heavily against the shore of the island with each powerful wave. Spray and white foam broke around the rocks of Calban, shooting skyward fifty feet or more before falling back with a resounding wet slap. White gulls with black-stained wingtips cawed and shrieked as they circled above the towering spires that flew Lord Demay's coiled-snake banner. I took a deep breath, wrinkling my nose at the fetid odor of decay coming from the shoreline as I scanned the bay for Lord Demay's ships. I couldn't see anything moving on the water and I felt a sudden pang of anxiety. Were they moored at the dock as we'd been told they would be? I wondered. Or were they even now out hunting for intruders among the many islands that I could see in the distance?

It was the day of the execution and I could feel a bone-deep weariness weighing me down. I stared at Calban through the heavy House Agent helmet that I wore and tried to shake off my fatigue. The helmet was rectangular and a little small for me, and it was forever pinching my forehead when I moved. But it was all we had, so it would have to do. My companions and I had ridden for two days and two nights to get to Calban in time, and we'd made it with about two hours to spare. I could see the same exhaustion that I felt reflected in the others' eyes and I prayed that each of us had enough strength left to see this through. The dappled grey and black mare that I rode shifted her weight beneath me, shaking her head as the wind whipping off the bay toyed with her long black mane. She was a good, solid mount, but even so, I was surprised at how much I missed Angry and his fickle moods. I knew the chances someone might recognize the horse the Outlaw of Corwick rode were slim, but I wasn't willing to take that chance, so I'd brought the mare instead. Besides, the big stallion was needed elsewhere this day.

"What now?" Tyris asked beside me in a tired-sounding voice.

I glanced at the blond archer, who was wearing flowing black robes and sitting an elegant-looking brown mare. I was hugely impressed at how natural and at ease he seemed in his priest's garb. "We wait for those merchants to pass through the gates," I said, gesturing to three carts laden with canvas bundles plodding across the bridge toward the castle. More people were marching silently in twos and threes behind the merchants, but it was the wagons I was most curious about. "I want to see how the guards deal with them before we move," I added.

Tyris simply nodded, looking surprisingly calm as we sat and watched. The execution was slated for mid-day, so I knew we still had plenty of time. Besides, the longer we remained outside the walls of Calban, the less the chances were that something could go wrong. I glanced at Tyris again. Had it been me impersonating a Son, I doubt I could have maintained the same composure he was showing. We all knew that what we were doing today was a sin against The Father. But

Tyris, more than any of us, had to know that by donning the black robes, his punishment, should it come to that, would be the most severe. Tyris and Jebido had both volunteered to play the role of the Son, but since Lord Demay had already seen Jebido's face at Gasterny, I had to go with the blond archer. I glanced behind me at Malo, Hanley, and the two women. Malo wore his bright red surcoat with the Blazing Sun emblem on it and his face was hidden by an identical helm to mine. The House Agent waited in stoic silence, while beside him Flora sat her horse dressed in regal yellow robes with her hair piled high and fanned at the top. Aenor was beside Flora on a frisky white stallion and looking small and vulnerable in her grey, Daughter-In-Waiting robes. Thankfully, Jin had known how to do the women's hair, though she'd refused to speak to me for several days once she'd realized I had no intention of letting her come with us to Calban. Hanley sat behind me on a tan-colored gelding wearing brown robes with his bald head gleaming in the sunlight. The boy had been truly dismayed when he'd learned he'd have to shave off his long black locks. But all Sons-In-Waiting shaved their heads, so there had been little choice.

"You're sure The Mother approves of this?" Flora asked, sounding nervous. She glanced at Malo when the House Agent failed to respond. "Well?"

Malo sighed loudly from inside his helmet. "The answer hasn't changed since you last asked it," he said sarcastically. "Which I believe was about ten minutes ago."

"Humor me!" Flora snapped, her eyes flashing. "Tell me again!"

Malo inclined his head, having learned over the last week that with Flora, it was easier, in the end, to just give her what she wanted. "Daughter Gernet has promised a special cleansing to each of us after this is over," he said. He turned his head and I knew his eyes were on me. "Assuming any of us are still alive to receive it, of course."

"But what about us?" Hanley asked, indicating Tyris

and himself. "Will her cleansing clear our souls with The Father too?"

Malo shrugged. "That I cannot say."

"Great!" Hanley muttered. "What are we supposed to do then?"

"Don't get yourself killed," I grunted. "If you don't die you won't end up at The Father's feet." I turned and grinned at Hanley through my helmet. "Problem solved."

Hanley said something under his breath but I ignored it as I watched the three guards standing in front of the towering barbican approach the merchants and begin searching them. One of the guards began a heated conversation with the merchants, while the other two drew their swords and began stabbing into the bundles of canvas.

"I'm glad we didn't try to get in that way," Tyris muttered as a guard rolled onto his back under the first wagon and began tapping underneath it with the hilt of his sword.

I thought of Gasterny and how Carbet had smuggled Shana out of the garrison with the false-bottomed carriage. Lord Demay was taking no chances, I realized. It took another ten minutes before the merchants were finally allowed in, and once they'd passed through the gates, I gestured that it was time to go. Flora and Tyris took the lead, riding side by side, with Aenor and Hanley riding behind them. Malo and I brought up the rear. A steady stream of people were making their way along the sandy shore, coming from both the east and the west. I could tell that most of them were just simple peasants and tradesmen from the surrounding villages and towns called to the castle by their lord. Having been one of them once, I knew that call was one that could not be ignored. We descended the hill and cut through a field of sparse grass that was slowly giving way to the sand from the shore. We finally reached the bridge as people moved aside to let us pass and many of them reached up to touch our feet or legs, praising The Mother and The Father and begging us for mercy for Lady Demay. Tyris and Flora responded to these pleas with fixed smiles on their faces and pious nods, touching hands and shoulders and offering kind words as we progressed.

We were about halfway across the bridge when Malo grunted to get my attention. He nodded his head silently toward the bay. A sail had appeared above a tree-covered island about a mile away, followed a moment later by a second one. I watched as the sleek ships maneuvered around the island, then steadied, heading for the dark mass of Calban Castle. The wind had shifted and strengthened in the last few minutes, coming now from the northwest as it whipped at our clothing with enthusiasm. I could hear faint shouts carried on the wind as the ships' captains ordered the sails lowered as they turned to the oars to fight the tide. The ships seemed to crawl over the water, coming in at a slight angle to the tide, until eventually they both disappeared from view behind the bulk of the castle. At least I knew where the ships were now, I thought, grateful that it was one less thing to worry about. I glanced again at the dozens of small islands rising in the hazy distance. If all had gone well, then somewhere among those islands waited my men and a ship to carry us away from Calban once we had rescued Shana. I tried not to think what might happen if Jebido and Baine had failed to lay their hands on that ship, and instead I concentrated on the rhythmic beat the horses' hooves made against the planks. Everything had to fall into place perfectly for my plan to work and I knew that after days of plotting, our fates now rested solely in the hands of Mother Above. We finally reached the far side of the bridge and Flora and Tyris guided us onto a road that had been chiseled directly out of the rock surface of the island. A minute later we halted in front of the gates as a guard with a pointed beard and bushy eyebrows strode toward us with a frown on his face.

"Son?" he said. "We were expecting you yesterday."

Flora and Tyris shared a look and I tried not to fidget in the saddle. We had intercepted the Son and Daughter heading to Calban for the execution more than a day ago. Catching up to them had been a near thing, and for a time I had been terrified that we'd missed them. Daughter Gernet had called away her House Agent guarding the Daughter, leaving only the Son's agent as protection. The hardest part of the ordeal had been convincing that man to throw down his weapons, as I had been adamant that I didn't want to kill him unless I had to. I knew my sins were piling up fast enough as it was without the blood of a House Agent on them as well. I figured at the rate I was going, I'd need more than one cleansing to save me from The Father. As it turned out, my reputation as an outlaw was enough to give even a House Agent pause. After some haggling and bluffing on my part, and a great deal of pleading by the Daughter — who was well aware of our mission — he'd reluctantly submitted. We'd taken all their clothing and then tied them up in an abandoned barn and left them in the care of a mute villager named Duin, who Finol had assured me could be trusted.

"We ran into some trouble along the way," Tyris said, managing to sound pompous and indignant at the same time. "That heathen outlaw from Corwick tried to rob us!" The guard's bushy eyebrows rose in surprise as Tyris gestured to Malo and me. "The House Agents chased the coward off, of course, but we decided it would be safer to wait a day before continuing. That's why we're late."

"You made the right decision, Son," the guard said. "I'm sorry to hear of your troubles. Son Oriell will be quite relieved to hear that you're safe."

"Son Oriell?" Tyris muttered, looking surprised. "He's here?"

"Yes. He's been quite anxious about your whereabouts. I understand you and he are good friends?"

The news that the ugly priest was in Calban hit me like a punch in the stomach. I was thankful for my helmet, as I knew the dismay I felt was written clearly across my face.

"Er, yes," Tyris said, somehow maintaining his composure. "How is my old friend?"

"He seems well," the guard responded. "I have yet to

confess with him, but I'm told his empathy knows no bounds."

"A well-known fact," Tyris said with a weak smile. "So, Son Oriell came here for the execution, did he?"

The guard nodded. "He and Lord Corwick arrived two days ago."

Another jolt of surprise. Why hadn't I considered that Lord Corwick would be here? After all, it had been his plan all along. Malo must have sensed my growing unease and he reached out and placed his hand on my arm to calm me. I took a deep breath and nodded to him, letting him know that I was fine.

"I haven't had the pleasure of meeting Lord Corwick," Tyris said as he examined a fingernail. "I look forward to rectifying that."

The guard shrugged. "That's going to be difficult, Son. He was called to Gandertown yesterday."

"Such are the ways of The Father," Tyris said, turning his hands palms up. "Perhaps another time." Tyris casually caught my eye, then turned back to the guard. "We would like to enter now, my good man, and have a few moments to stretch our legs before the main event begins."

"Oh, of course, Son!" the guard said, looking flustered. "Forgive me!" He bowed, then moved aside as he swept his arm forward. "Welcome to Calban Castle!"

Tyris and Flora both nodded and they urged their horses onward, guiding us into the stone barbican that rose at least five stories above our heads. I glanced up at the murder holes in the ceiling and then at the narrow arrow slots that ran along both sides of the walls. I could feel hidden eyes peering down at us and I looked away, staring straight ahead at an inflamed pimple on the back of Hanley's bald head. Lord Demay desperately wanted the Outlaw of Corwick alive, we'd learned, so I hoped there was nothing to fear from the archers when my plan finally took effect. We trotted through the gates past a long line of silent guards and many of them made the sign of The Mother or The Father as we passed. The castle was big, I realized. Much bigger even than Corwick Castle, with monstrous turrets jutting out all along the walls. Each turret flew Lord Demay's red and black coiled-snake banner from tall poles of stripped ash. The banners snapped and crackled loudly in the wind and I could see the ash poles bending as the strong gusts coming off the bay tried to tear them from their moorings. I grimaced with distaste as I saw that several of the towers were also flying Lord Corwick's yellow banner below that of the coiled snake. A second towering barbican sat above us at the top of a long grade, with another set of gates inside it that gave access to the heart of the castle where I knew the keep lay. The castle was formidable, I realized. Jebido had been right, we would have needed an army to take it. Fifty or sixty peasants and merchants waited obediently at the base of the grade as soldiers searched them again before they were finally sent upward.

"I think our Lord Demay maybe a little paranoid," I heard Hanley mutter to Tyris under his breath.

Tyris chuckled and we began to move forward again, then the archer paused his horse and I saw some of the color leave his face. Son Oriell had just strode through the gates above us and he paused and stared down at us with a look of surprise on his face. I noticed a wide-shouldered House Agent wearing the identical white Rock of Life surcoat to mine standing two paces behind the priest.

"Be calm, everyone," I whispered as the two men made their way toward us past the flow of people going up.

The black-robed priest paused five paces from our horses with his hands on his hips and I could feel my heartbeat pounding in my ears as he regarded us. A Rock of Life pendant hung around his neck and its dark surface gleamed brilliantly in the sunlight.

"Son?" Son Oriell said uncertainly to Tyris. The priest glanced at Flora and I could see doubt beginning to form in his eyes. "This is rather unexpected."

"By The Father!" Tyris exclaimed. "It really is you!" Son

Oriell's eyebrows rose in surprise as Tyris jumped from his horse and ran to embrace the ugly priest. "I had no idea you'd be here!" Tyris cried as he kissed the priest on each cheek. "This is such an honor, Son!" Tyris gushed. "A true honor!"

"Well," Son Oriell said, stepping back and looking slightly bewildered. He glanced at his House Agent, who stood to the side with his legs spread and his hand resting on the hilt of his sword. "Do I know you?"

"No, Son," Tyris said with a quick shake of his blond head. "But what Son or apprentice hasn't heard of the great Son Oriell?" He turned to Hanley for confirmation and the boy nodded automatically as Tyris turned back. "Please forgive my enthusiasm. It's just that I'm a little overwhelmed to finally meet you."

Son Oriell's lips pursed and I could see his eyes light with pleasure. "Then it would seem you have me at a disadvantage, Son...?"

"Son Tyris, newly of Halhaven," Tyris said, bowing. He gestured to Flora. "And this would be Daughter Flora," he added. "One of Daughter Gernet's best and brightest."

"An honor, Daughter," Son Oriell said, barely glancing at her. He turned his eyes back to Tyris. "I was expecting Son Tremure," the priest said. "I do hope my old acquaintance is well?"

Tyris glanced behind him, then gently guided Son Oriell several steps away out of earshot. The archer and priest talked animatedly for a moment, and at one point Son Oriell laughed loudly. Finally he clasped Tyris on the shoulder, then headed back through the crowds with the House Agent following.

Several stable boys appeared to take our horses and the rest of us dismounted and handed them the reins as Tyris returned to us with a grin on his face.

"What did you say to him?" I whispered to Tyris as our horses were led away.

Tyris chuckled. "I told him that his friend had come

down with the trots the morning he was set to leave," Tyris said. "And that I'd been asked to come in his stead."

"But why did he laugh like that?" I asked. "What's so funny about getting the trots?"

Tyris grinned. "I also told him that a magnificent stag had been bagged that very same morning. And, since it was well known that Son Tremure loves his stag, that perhaps the trots had only been in his head."

"But how could you have even known the Son loved stag?" Flora asked in obvious admiration.

"I didn't," Tyris said with a chuckle. "But it seemed a safe bet. I've never met a priest yet that would say no to a good stag." I had to contain myself from throwing my arms around the blond archer as he gestured to the gate above us. "Anyway, we're to meet Son Oriell and Lord Demay in the upper bailey." He glanced at me meaningfully. "I made sure to mention that we'd been delayed by that rascal, the Outlaw of Corwick. I have no doubt our friendly priest is informing Lord Demay of that fact even as we speak."

I grinned and clapped the archer on the shoulder as I glanced up at the gates above us. I knew from Malo that Calban was broken up into three sections, with a lower, a middle, and an upper bailey. Each bailey was built on a grade and sat higher than the next, with each one guarded by a heavy barbican and thick gate. Those gates were all open today and were set in a perfect straight line. Malo had told me that you could be standing in the upper bailey and look back down through all three gates and see the head of the bridge perfectly. I dearly hoped that he was right about that, as it was essential to my plans. The keep was situated in the middle bailey, but the execution, I knew, was set to occur in the upper bailey.

Tyris and Flora took the lead as people flowed upward in a steady stream around us, urged on by impatient soldiers. I was surprised at how quiet and reserved the people seemed as we finally passed into the shadows beneath the barbican and then back out into the sunlight. More soldiers waited for us in the middle bailey and they guided the crowd onward with sharp words, directing them past the monstrous keep and up the next slope to the third set of gates. A man dressed in rich clothing exited the keep just as we reached it and he called out to us to get our attention. We paused, waiting as he hurried down the ramp and pushed his way through the crowd with an obviously forced smile on his face.

"Son, Daughter," the man said with a formal bow. "I am Kylan, Lord Demay's steward. His Lordship and Son Oriell request that you join them in the promenade in the upper bailey."

Tyris glanced at the gates above us, then turned to study the magnificent Holy House that sat regally against the west-facing curtain wall. "And the others? Will they be joining us there as well?"

"Others, Son?" Kylan asked with a raised eyebrow.

"The wards of the castle House, of course," Tyris said, nodding to the Holy House. "Our brethren."

"Ah," Kylan said as he flicked his eyes to the building. For just a moment I thought I saw a shadow cross his face, then it was gone. "The castle's Son and Daughter choose to spend this day in prayer and contemplation, Son. They feel their time is better served in that endeavor right now."

"I see," Tyris said. "A noble gesture indeed." He swept one hand toward the steward. "Then by all means, Kylan, please lead the way."

Kylan nodded and Flora and Tyris fell into step beside him as the rest of us followed behind respectfully.

"Is the time almost upon us, Kylan?" Flora asked.

"We have perhaps twenty minutes," the steward said as we headed upward. I could hear music and laughter coming through the gates above us and I took a deep breath, trying to still my rapidly beating heart. A young boy chasing a wooden ball down the slope almost collided with Kylan and the steward had to step quickly aside to avoid him. Kylan took a swipe at the boy's rear end with his foot and cursed when he missed.

"I'll be glad when this is finally over!" Kylan muttered angrily as the boy stuck out his tongue before he darted away.

"You're looking forward to Lady Demay's death?" Tyris demanded, unable to hide his anger.

"Not at all, Son!" Kylan responded emphatically. His eyes turned cautious. "Forgive me. I spoke out of turn."

"Something clearly troubles you, my friend," Tyris said kindly. He placed his hand on the steward's arm and we paused as we reached the entrance to the upper bailey. "The Daughter and I are here to listen and advise, not to judge. You may speak freely to us without fear."

Kylan sighed and glanced around. "Believe me, Son, when I say I take no pleasure in what is about to happen. I would stop it in a heartbeat if I had the power to do so." The steward ushered us through the gates and he swept his arm around the courtyard. "All I meant was I'd be glad when all of this foolishness was over."

The upper bailey was packed and almost overflowing with people. Bards, pipers, jugglers and storytellers all competed for the attention of the crowd amid the deep rumble of hundreds of voices. I felt instant disgust wash over me at the sight. A woman's life was about to be ended and these people were treating it as some kind of festival. It was infuriating. I saw that a large platform of freshly-cut planks had been built at the far end of the bailey and several spry acrobats were tumbling and flipping across it to the delight of the crowd. A colorful promenade of raised benches was built in a U-shape around the back of the platform, with just enough space left in between the two structures for a man to walk. Heavy white canvas had been draped over the promenade, shading the audience from the harshness of the sun. The northern gate was behind that promenade, I knew, but from where we stood, it was completely hidden from our view by the heavy canvas. Brightly colored pennants flew from poles all along the promenade, which I could see was quickly filling up with richly-dressed people. Square-faced towers flying the coiled-snake banner rose all along the walls, with two round towers set on each side of where I assumed the north-facing gate lay. I could see Son Oriell and Lord Demay sitting with several older ladies in the center box of the promenade and I grimaced at the sight of the lord. The ugly priest noticed us and he stood and shouted over the din to get our attention, motioning that we should join him. Only a few guards were walking the ramparts now as we slowly made our way through the crowd, with perhaps ten or so walking in amongst us. I glanced over my shoulder to see that most of the soldiers at the gates had disappeared out of sight as well; presumably into the surrounding towers. Lord Demay's trap was set. Now all he needed was for the Outlaw of Corwick to ride into it. We were several paces away from the edge of the western wing of the promenade and I looked at Malo, nodding to him that it was time. The House Agent didn't say anything, but within the blink of an eye he was gone, disappearing around the canvas sheets.

"Hadrack," Aenor whispered. She touched my arm and gestured to the platform. "You said they were going to hang her. There's no gallows!"

The acrobats were gone now, I saw, and all that waited on the platform was a single, ominous block of wood. They had changed their plans, it would seem. I tried not to think about the chopping block and what it meant as Kylan led us around the back of the platform to a set of wide steps that led up to the benches in the promenade.

"Ah, Son Tyris," Son Oriell said as we entered Lord Demay's box. He stood and embraced Tyris warmly.

I ignored the priest and studied Lord Demay, who sat on the benches dressed in full armor. The lord still wore the same wolf-tail helmet that I remembered seeing at Gasterny, but now a thick leather eye patch covered his right eye. Good for you, Shana, I thought. Good for you.

"I would like to present to you, His Lordship, Lord Demay," Son Oriell was saying to Tyris and Flora.

"It's an honor, my lord," Tyris said with a formal bow.

Lord Demay grunted moodily, never taking his good eye from the platform and the chopping block. Tyris seemed unruffled by the lord's rudeness and he gestured to Flora. "And this is Daughter Flora."

Flora made the sign of The Mother and bowed. "Daughter Gernet sends her best wishes, my Lord," Flora said. "Along with her condolences for your coming loss."

Lord Demay flicked his eye at Flora for a moment and nodded woodenly in acknowledgment before he turned back to the platform.

Son Oriell shrugged apologetically and gestured to the bench that sat to Lord Demay's left. "Please, both of you sit here beside me," he said to Tyris and Flora. "Your apprentices and House Agents can sit behind us."

The priest didn't seem to have noticed that Malo was no longer with us and Hanley, Aenor and I took our seats behind Lord Demay. Kylan moved to sit beside the two older women who sat on the lord's right just as a shrill horn sounded from the ramparts. The courtyard quickly fell into silence as an old man appeared through a doorway that led from the tower closest to the platform.

"Larstin," I heard Son Oriell whisper below me to Tyris. "Lord Demay's closest advisor and confident."

Tyris nodded as Larstin walked slowly toward the platform dressed in long white robes that dragged heavily across the ground. His beard was bushy and dark silver and he used a carved walking stick to support himself as he carefully climbed the stairs to the platform. Larstin finally paused by the chopping block before he turned somewhat stiffly to look back at Lord Demay.

Lord Demay nodded and Larstin faced the crowd. "Today," he said in a surprisingly strong voice that boomed off the stone walls. "You have been summoned by your lord to witness justice being served. From this day forth, never let it be said that it's only the common man who pays for his crimes." Larstin spread his arms, holding up the walking stick.

"Under the eyes of your lord, all who lift a hand against him will pay the ultimate price! Regardless of their name or stature!"

Larstin hesitated, seeming to have lost his train of thought and I glanced at Kylan's profile, startled to see tears sliding down the steward's cheek. The two older women beside him were dabbing at their eyes as well, I noted. I studied the crowd closer, realizing many within it were weeping openly and it suddenly dawned on me that these people loved Shana. I saw more than one hateful glance being directed toward Lord Demay from the onlookers, and even some of the guards moving among the people appeared troubled. The bards, musicians and the other entertainers had all been an act, I realized. The laughter and amusement of the people that I'd witnessed earlier had been brought on by fear of their lord, not joy.

"Enough of this, Larstin!" Lord Demay growled as the old man stood uncertainly, clearly having forgotten his words. "We don't have all day for you to figure out how to talk!" He signaled to the ramparts with a mailed hand and another horn sounded immediately.

Larstin turned toward the tower he'd just come from, looking confused as the doors opened, revealing four stone-faced soldiers. The men marched smartly forward and my breath caught in my throat as Shana appeared, flanked by four more soldiers behind her. She was dressed in a shimmering, sleeveless white dress that was cinched at the waist by a thin gold chain. Her hands were bound behind her and her hair was pulled back and fell to her hips in a single thick braid. Simple sandals were all she wore on her feet and she strode forward with her head held high, looking aloof and in control of herself. I thought she looked like a beautiful queen and I'd never felt prouder of anyone in my life.

I glanced over the heads of the silent crowd, all of whom were struggling to get a glimpse of the doomed woman. Where was Sim? I wondered, feeling the first stirrings of panic as the soldiers reached the platform. The men paused, fanning out to either side of the steps, leaving Shana alone at their base. She hesitated there, letting her gaze run over the promenade, and for just a moment, those eyes that I'd come to know so well in Gasterny, paused on me. I felt a jolt of love for this slight woman rise in my breast and I stared back at her, willing her to see me through my helmet and know that help was only moments away. Shana finally looked away and she stared at Lord Demay with contempt on her face as he glowered back at her.

"Come, child," Larstin said. He nodded to the soldiers. "Bring her up. The time is upon us."

Two of the men put their hands on Shana's elbows to direct her up the stairs and she shrugged them off with a snort. She glided up the three steps on her own and then stopped beside the chopping block to stare out over the silent crowd.

"Is there anything that you'd like to say before we begin?" Larstin asked, sounding condescending to my ears.

"There is," Shana said, not bothering to look at him. She regarded the anxious-looking men, women and children pressed up close to the platform and I could see the look of affection on her face. "Remember, my people, that it's better to die free, than to live life forever trapped in a cage!"

Cries of support for Lady Demay and heated protests denouncing the execution immediately rose from the onlookers. I saw the lord's face redden with fury at the continued shouted objections as two soldiers fought their way into the crowd to prod with their spears at two burly, vocal villagers, who pushed back at the soldiers angrily, heedless of their weapons.

Larstin waved his walking stick in the air just as more soldiers began to converge on the area. "Is this how you act before your lord!?" he cried. He pointed the stick and waggled it at the crowd. "You will remain silent or it won't just be your lady's head that's taken today!" A sudden hush fell back over the courtyard at his words and Larstin turned to look at Shana with a frown on his face. "There is no need to incite violence, my lady," he said reproachfully.

"I never liked you, Larstin," Shana said scornfully. "You've always been my husband's boot-licking dog." She looked the old man up and down with contempt. "So lick away, dog. The sooner I'm gone from this world and away from you and that pig, the better!"

"As you wish, my lady," Larstin said with a wry grin. "As you wish."

Larstin turned and gestured to the tower and the door opened immediately. If not for Hanley and Aenor, who grabbed my arms, I have no doubt I would have thrown myself on the man who stood there without a second thought. It was Quant Ranes, and he held my father's axe in his hands. Ranes strode forward like a conquering hero and he tapped the axe slowly in his hand as he walked. I could tell by the smug look on his face that the bastard was enjoying himself as he crossed the distance to the platform and leaped nimbly up the stairs. Ranes paused in front of Shana and twirled my father's axe nonchalantly as he grinned yellow teeth down at her. Shana just stared back at him, looking unimpressed. Ranes was more than twice Shana's size, but even with his armor and weapons, it was clear to everyone who the stronger person was. I glanced again down the length of the castle and cursed under my breath as Tyris turned to look back at me with a worried frown. Where in the name of The Mother was Sim? I loosened my sword in its scabbard, feeling my muscles tensing as Ranes grunted and gestured to the chopping block with the axe. Shana turned without a word and knelt before it in a single motion, placing her head sideways on the wood. We'd run out of time, I knew, and I stood just as Ranes positioned himself several feet away from Shana's vulnerable neck. I placed my foot on the bench between Flora and Tyris, about to leap down to the platform when a powerful voice suddenly echoed across the castle.

"Hold your hand!"

Every head in the courtyard turned in surprise as an armored rider trotted through the unguarded gates down in the lower bailey. Sim had finally arrived!

"Let her go!" Sim cried. The castle had natural acoustics and his voice echoed out over and over again, rolling toward us along the walls like the vengeful voice of The Father Himself. Despite myself, I felt the hairs on my arms stand on end as Sim drew Wolf's Head and waved it in the air. "Let her go!" Sim repeated. "Or I swear by The Mother that the Outlaw of Corwick will bring this cursed castle down on all your heads!"

Sim was mounted on Angry and the big black reared back on his hind legs on cue, glistening with power in the sunlight as Sim continued to whirl Wolf's Head over his head wildly. I was hugely impressed with how fierce he appeared, dressed as he was in my armor and wolf helmet.

"Get ready!" I growled at Hanley and Aenor as the guards in the crowd began running toward Sim. "As soon as I move, head for the gates. Tyris and Flora will meet you there." I tapped Tyris on the shoulder and gestured behind me and he nodded in understanding.

Everyone in the promenade was standing to get a better view now and I could see a wolfish grin spreading across Lord Demay's face as he glared down at Sim. The lord finally motioned to the ramparts with his hand and a horn echoed out across the castle as soldiers began pouring out of the towers and the keep like angry wasps, converging on the lower bailey. Many of those soldiers, I noted with distaste, wore pointed black boots. I turned my attention away from the Cardians and focused on Shana, who was sitting up in bewilderment and looking around. Quant Ranes seemed frozen in place above her for a moment as he stared at Sim, then he pushed past Larstin with a growl and leaped from the platform and began running for the lower bailey. As much as I desired my axe back, the choice between it and Shana was an easy one to make, so I forgot about Ranes and leaned forward and pushed as hard as I could against the backs of Lord Demay and Son Oriell. The two men cried out in surprise and pitched forward and then flipped over the box railing onto the people below. There were older women and children down there, I knew, and I felt a moment of guilt at what I'd done as people began to scream in surprise, pain and confusion.

"Run!" Tyris cried, cupping his hands to his mouth. "The Outlaw of Corwick's men are loose in the castle! Run for your lives!"

I flung my leg onto Lord Demay's bench and hopped onto it as panic spread along the promenade like a grass fire. I saw Son Oriell struggling to rise below me, entangled with a woman wearing a flowing blue dress and spitting out words that would make even the crudest of whore's blush. The priest finally extricated himself just as I leaped onto his back, flattening him again and pinning him down. Son Oriell groaned and I put my full weight on him, then used his egg-shaped head as a steppingstone as I leaped across to the platform.

Shana was already on her feet and I paused in surprise. Larstin was lying on the ground near the platform not moving and she was looking down at him with an expression of satisfaction on her face. I hurried over to her as I drew my sword. "We have to move!" I said as I sliced the ropes that bound her wrists. "We don't have much time!"

"Who are you?" Shana demanded.

"Just a man who likes to read," I replied, smiling inside my helmet.

"Hadrack!?" Shana gasped.

"The very same," I said with a laugh.

We leaped from the platform and ran for the promenade as I glanced back over my shoulder. Sim was shaking my painted wolf shield at the soldiers bearing down on him in defiance and I felt my heart leap in my throat, thinking that he'd waited too long. But, just as the first soldiers reached him, Sim swung Angry around and galloped back out the gate toward the bridge. I prayed that the archers above him in the barbican would remember their orders and stall their hands long enough for him to get away. More Cardians on horses were streaming out of the stables along the curtain wall to give chase, but I knew with confidence that there wasn't a horse in the world that could catch the big black once he had open land in front of him. I thrust Sim from my mind. He had gladly taken on my role and his fate was now in the hands of The Mother. I hurried Shana around the promenade away from prying eyes and we ran to the gate where the others were waiting for us in the shadows of one of the towers.

Two of Lord Demay's guards lay twisted and bloodied near the gates and I frowned as I glanced around. "Where's Malo?" I demanded.

"I don't know," Tyris said calmly. He gestured to the bodies. "Obviously he was here, but the gates are still locked."

I cursed under my breath. The gates were made of one-inch thick, grated iron bars and even though I knew it was useless, I grabbed the heavy padlock that sealed us in and rattled it. Without the key there was no way out.

"Malo, is that you?" I heard a voice call softly from outside the walls.

"Jebido?" I whispered back, peering through the bars.

Jebido and Baine appeared from around the wall. "Where's Malo with the key!?" Jebido hissed, looking anxious.

"I don't know," I said with a shake of my head.

"Well you better find him fast!" Jebido grunted as he looked back over his shoulder. "We've got two ships heading this way."

"What?" I gasped in surprise. I knew Lord Demay only had two ships and they were already moored at the dock. "Who are they?"

"Cardians!" Jebido spat out with distaste.

I groaned out loud. The Mother might be on our side, I thought, but it seemed The Father had other plans for us this day. "How far away are they?"

"Not far enough," Baine replied.

"I'll find the key," I said. I turned and handed Tyris the short sword I'd taken from the real House Agent the day before. "Watch out for them."

"With my life," Tyris promised.

"Hadrack," Shana said. "How...?"

I put a finger to Shana's lips, silencing her. "Now's not the best time for questions," I said. "I'll be right back."

I turned and ran for the closest tower door and flung it open. Three men lay dead inside the alcove and I cursed as I saw Malo's cracked helmet lying on the floor near the corpses. Had Malo gotten the key? I wondered. If he had and still lived, I figured he'd have to be up on the ramparts, so I leaped over the bodies and headed up the stairs, taking them two at a time. The first faint sounds of battle came to me as I climbed and I almost stumbled over another dead man who lay crumpled on the second-floor landing. I skirted around him and barrelled up the next flight of stairs until I found myself out on the ramparts, where two more men lay dead at my feet. I saw Malo crouched against the battlements waving his sword defensively at three soldiers who surrounded him. I realized the man closest to me was Son Oriell's House Agent and I took a hurried, two-handed slice at his midriff, hoping for a quick kill. The House Agent must have sensed me somehow and he spun nimbly away while at the same time taking a vicious backhanded slash with his sword at my head. I was caught by surprise by his speed as his weapon clanged hard against the top of my helmet, rattling me. I took two steps back, stunned and wobbling as the House Agent turned on me and attacked. The man was fast and strong and it was all I could do to fend him off as he pressed me relentlessly, pushing me backward. Everything I tried my opponent brushed off easily, almost contemptuously, and I felt the first seeds of doubt rise in me. I was tired after the long ride and I knew I wasn't prepared for someone as well trained as this man. I felt my confidence slipping away as I gave more ground under the House Agent's attack. I could see him grinning behind his helmet in anticipation of victory just as I heard the words Jebido had drilled into Baine and me years ago down in Father's Arse.

"You must not just think that you can win," he had said. "You must know that you can win!"

I felt the familiar whiteness building inside me and I tore off my helmet and smiled at my opponent. We were so close now, and all that stood between us and success was this arrogant House Agent mocking me. I knew I might not be as experienced as he was, but whatever I lacked in training compared to him, I knew I more than made up for with sheer rage and strength. I decided to let that rage and strength have free rein and I roared a challenge. I leaped forward, clearly surprising the House Agent as I fell on him, hacking and slashing with renewed vigor. Now it was my opponent's turn to fall back in desperation as I cut at his knees, then his head, then his chest, always keeping the man off balance. Despite my rage, however, the House Agent was incredibly good and I couldn't break through his defenses. I was so focused on our battle that it came as a complete shock to me when the agent suddenly sagged and dropped silently to the stone floor. I hadn't touched him at all.

"Forgive me," Malo said as he stooped to wipe his short sword off on the House Agent's white surcoat. "I believe you would have beaten him eventually, but time is short."

I grunted in understanding, fighting to catch my breath as I glanced at the two dead men Malo had been fighting moments ago. "The key?" I managed to gasp out.

Malo pulled a heavy iron key out of his belt and held it up. "Here," he said as he gestured to the dead House Agent with his sword. "My apologies for the delay, but Olo saw my face and I couldn't let him live."

"You knew him?" I asked.

Malo grimaced. "For many years."

I nodded and grasped my Pair Stone and said a quick prayer for the fallen agent before Malo and I hurried back outside. I was relieved to see that Tyris and the others were still where I'd left them. Jebido and Baine and the rest of my men were waiting at the gates and they gestured to us urgently as Malo unlocked the padlock and swung the gates open. We ran along the narrow road that dipped dramatically toward the water, following Jebido as he led us toward a rocky outcrop that jutted out from the island, blocking our view of the dock.

"Almost there!" I grunted to Shana as she ran by my side.

We raced around the outcrop, then came to a halt in dismay, watching as the Cardian ships deftly maneuvered up to the dock. Armored men with pointed boots and red capes began leaping over the sides of the ships before they'd even been secured. I guessed there had to be at least forty or fifty men already massing on the dock and I felt my heart sink. We were ten men — one a cripple — and three women. To advance now would be madness. But to go back would be equal madness. I could taste the bitterness of defeat washing over me as I glanced at the flat-bottomed merchant ship that would have taken us to safety. The boat sat moored a hundred feet away along the dock, rocking wildly on the tide. It might as well have been moored on the moon for all the good it would do us now, I thought bitterly.

"Hadrack!" Jebido said urgently. "We have to go back!"

"What!?" Baine demanded as he unstrapped his bow. He gestured behind him at the castle. "Our deaths wait for us back there!"

"Well, what do you think that is!?" Jebido snapped, pointing to the dock.

The Cardians had seen us now and they howled as they started to run up the incline toward us.

"He's right!" I said, coming to a decision. I shoved Baine back up the way we'd come. "Get to the gates!" I glanced at Malo as we started to run. "Lock them as soon we're through. That'll slow the bastards down!"

We rushed back up the slope, then burst through the gates in a disorganized pack and then had to spend several anxious moments searching for the lock. Malo had tossed it aside earlier and it was Hanley who finally located it behind a barrel. The House Agent snatched the padlock from the boy and locked us in just as the first of the Cardians appeared running around the outcrop. We fell backward against the promenade wall as the soldiers crashed into the gates, cursing in frustration as they tried to stab at us with swords and spears. A Cardian threw a spear awkwardly through the bars and it wobbled over our heads, tearing through the canvas of the promenade behind us. Baine shot several arrows back, dropping the Cardian who'd thrown the spear and another man, and the rest turned and ran for the protection of the outcrop.

"Now what?" Baine asked.

I glanced up at the empty ramparts and the towers around us, then peered cautiously around the promenade. The benches and courtyard had emptied, I saw, with people massing in confusion down in the middle bailey in front of the keep. Men, women, and children pushed and screamed at each other in panic, while here and there I saw mounted men and soldiers trying to fight their way through the crowds. I could see Quant Ranes and Lord Demay standing together in the lower bailey, while Son Oriell sat on a stool beside them holding his head. Several dozen Cardians stood in front of the gates, blocking the exit, while more stood in a protective ring around the three men. I saw movement out of the corner of my eye and glanced at the tower where Shana had been held. The steward, Kylan, was standing in the doorway watching us and he put his finger to his lips.

"Lord Demay believes the Lady is locked back up in the tower," he said in a low voice. "I told him that I saw one of the House Agents carry her there to keep her safe from the outlaw. The lord and Son believe they were pushed by people trying to flee and know nothing of what you attempted." He glanced at Shana, who'd come to stand beside me and he bowed. "You have many friends here, my lady. Know that we have not abandoned you."

"Thank you, Kylan," Shana said softly. "I'm grateful."

"These are troubling times, my lady," the steward said. "But soon, perhaps, if the First Pair is willing, that will change." He looked to his right and frowned. "You must hurry," he said. "They won't be fooled for long."

"Hurry and go where?" I demanded. "We're trapped!"

"Make your way to the keep," Kylan said. He glanced meaningfully at Shana. "The cavern will be your salvation."

I heard Shana gasp in surprise and I turned to her. "What's he talking about?"

"There's a cavern beneath the castle that leads out onto the bay," Shana said. "My husband had it built years ago in case of a siege."

"Are there boats?" I asked, feeling sudden hope.

I saw Shana's eyes cloud over. "Just a single skiff."

"How many can it hold?" I asked, already knowing the answer.

"Three, maybe four people," Shana replied, looking dejected. "No more than that."

I sighed and touched the Pair Stone around my neck. There were thirteen of us. I thought for a moment, then turned back to the steward. "Kylan, can you distract Lord Demay for us so we can get to the keep?"

The steward didn't hesitate. "I'll do what I can." He glanced at Shana. "Good luck to you, my lady."

Kylan made his way toward the middle bailey as I turned to my men. "On my signal, we break for the keep," I said. "No matter what happens, keep running. Once we get inside, Hanley and the women will make their way down to the cavern. The rest of us will hold them off as long as we can."

"I'm staying," Hanley said, looking determined. He gestured to the House Agent. "Let Malo go with them. He can protect them much better than I can."

"I stay with Hadrack," Malo said with a shake of his head. He looked at me and grinned wryly. "We've come this far, you and me. I'd like to see how this story ends."

Tyris stood across from me and I raised an eyebrow to

him.

"Not a chance," Tyris said. He smiled and hefted his black robe. "You'll need spiritual guidance if we're all going to get out of this alive."

One by one I asked my men to leave with the women, and one by one they all refused. I felt a lump rise in my throat at their loyalty, but I knew time was running out and I had to choose someone now. "Cain," I finally said. "You'll go." Cain opened his mouth to protest and I raised a hand, stalling him. "There's no time for this!" I said gruffly. "Just do as you're told!"

Cain nodded reluctantly and I looked around the promenade again. I could see Kylan had reached the Cardians guarding Lord Demay and they parted to make room for him. The steward gestured emphatically several times toward the bridge, looking agitated. Both Lord Demay and Quant Ranes took several strides toward the gates to see what he was pointing at, and I noticed some of the Cardians and even the ugly priest were peering toward the bridge. It wasn't much of a distraction, I knew, but it was better than nothing.

"Now!" I whispered.

I grabbed Shana's hand and we started to run, heading at an angle for the curtain wall that separated the upper and middle baileys. I could hear my companions right behind me and surprisingly we made it to the wall unseen. I took a moment to let everyone catch their breath, then with Shana beside me, we ran into the barbican and through the gates. Women screamed in terror when they saw us and men shouted as we pushed our way through the milling crowd. A soldier appeared around a wagon heaped with hay in front of me and he swung his sword clumsily at my head. I blocked his blade with mine, then slashed the man savagely across the stomach and we kept running. I glanced behind me just as a big soldier grabbed Putt by the hair, dragging him backward before Anson hacked the soldier down from behind. More soldiers and Cardians were coming from the lower bailey, converging on us as they pushed terrified people out of their way. Malo was right behind me and he cut down a skinny blond-haired boy holding a spear, then paused to allow Flora and Aenor to catch up to him.

Two of Lord Demay's soldiers stood at the top of the ramp with lowered pikes as we approached the keep and I turned to Shana. "Stay here with Malo!" I ordered.

I snarled and barrelled up the ramp toward the soldiers, but before I was even ten paces away, one of them spun and fell with an arrow in his chest, followed a second later by the other. I looked back over my shoulder at Baine and Tyris, who both grinned at me. I had no idea where Tyris had gotten a bow, but I thrust it from my mind as I threw open the doors to the keep and dashed inside. No one was waiting for me on the other side, I was surprised to see, and all was quiet save for several terrified-sounding feminine sobs coming from the great hall.

"Hurry!" I called over my shoulder as Shana, Malo and the rest of my companions burst through the entrance. The moment everyone was inside, Niko and Anson slammed the doors shut and dropped the bar. I turned to Shana. "Which way?" I asked.

"There!" Shana said breathlessly, pointing down the corridor. "Through the kitchens!"

I could hear the soldiers on the other side beginning to pound on the heavy oak door and I knew they wouldn't hold for long. "Get going!" I ordered, nodding to Cain.

"Hadrack," Shana said, hesitating. "I..."

"There's no time!" I snarled. I glared at Cain. "Get the women out of here or all of this will have been for nothing!"

Cain nodded grimly and he guided Shana down the corridor by the elbow as Flora and Aenor followed closely behind.

"Hadrack!" Shana called over her shoulder. "Find a way out! Please!"

I barely heard her as I focused on the weakening doors. We had to buy them time to get to the cavern, I knew, regardless of the cost. "Stand back!" I growled to my men. "We'll show these turd-suckers what real warriors look like!"

Anson and Niko were bracing the bar with their shoulders and they moved back as we spread out and waited. The heavy wooden doors shook and trembled beneath each blow as the men outside fought to break in. I could tell someone was using an axe out there and I smiled to myself, pretty sure I knew who that someone was. At least there was that, I thought. A section of wood near the latch burst outward and Anson immediately shoved his sword through the opening, grinning yellow teeth at the howl of pain on the other side.

"That was stupid," the bald man grunted just as a spear was thrust back through the hole, puncturing him in the side.

Anson fell with a groan just as the bar snapped and the doors exploded inward as soldiers began pouring into the room.

"Kill them!" I roared. "Kill the bastards!"

I threw myself forward, hacking and thrusting my sword wildly, while around me men cursed and fought in a mad scramble. Baine and Tyris stood behind the rest of us, shooting arrows over our heads into our attackers' faces, while Jebido fought on my left, and Niko on my right. I could see Ranes standing back on the ramp, watching the battle with my father's axe on his shoulder and a mocking grin on his face. I bellowed in anger, cutting down a soldier with blood pouring from his nose with a two-handed slash. In the same motion, I reversed my sword to stab a boy with crooked teeth in the chest. The boy staggered and Jebido crashed the edge of his shield into his face, shattering those crooked teeth and sending them flying in all directions. More men were rushing up the ramp behind Ranes and I could see red-caped Cardian archers in the courtyard running toward the keep.

"We need to fall back!" I grunted at Jebido.

"To where?" Jebido gasped as he blocked a sword thrust.

The Cardian archers were at the ramp, I saw, and I grimaced. "Anywhere but here." Jebido saw the archers and he nodded as I glanced behind me at Baine. "We have to move. Find us somewhere!"

"Up or down?" Baine asked as he loosed an arrow into the mass of struggling soldiers.

I hesitated, absently blocking a sword thrust and sending back one of my own. I cursed as I missed the man's exposed arm. Shana was down and I needed to draw them away from her, so it seemed there was but one choice. "Up!" I shouted.

Baine nodded and disappeared down the corridor and I turned my attention back to the fight. The stone floor of the keep was getting slick now and I could feel my boots sliding on top of the foul mixture of blood, puke and piss. A great bull of a man with a long beard and a heavy spear appeared in front of me and he bellowed and thrust the spear point at my stomach. I twisted aside, then grabbed the man by his beard and tugged. The big man stumbled forward and Niko skewered him in the belly with his sword.

"Hadrack, this way!" Baine called from down the corridor.

I didn't bother to look behind me, trusting in my friend. "Fall back!" I shouted. "Follow Baine!"

My men and I turned and ran down the corridor as Baine led us though an arched doorway protected by a heavy door. Putt was the last man through and he slammed the door shut and dropped the bar while I looked around in desperation. The room we were in was rectangular, with three lines of benches sitting in the middle and a strange looking musical instrument sitting on a pedestal at the end.

I knew the thing was called a harp and I turned to Baine. "Where now?"

"This way," Baine said, leading us through another doorway into a small alcove with a set of stairs leading up and down.

"Up you go," I ordered, motioning my men ahead of me. Malo went first, followed by Niko, Putt and Tyris. I looked around in dismay. "Where's Hanley?" Both Baine and Jebido looked at me blankly and I grimaced, knowing the boy had fallen. I put my hand on Baine's back and shoved him toward the stairs. "Move!"

Baine scurried up the stairs, quickly followed by Jebido. I could hear Lord Demay's men pounding at the sealed door and I knew they'd be in the harp room in mere moments. I started up the stairs, then hesitated. Had that been a scream I'd just heard from below? I felt my heart lurch in my throat as I heard it a second time, certain now that it had been Aenor. I heard the unmistakable sound of wood shattering and I knew I only had seconds left to make a choice. I reversed direction and headed back down the stairs, then dashed down the next flight just as men burst into the room above me.

I waited, holding my breath as I listened to the heavy clomp of booted feet going up the stairs as Lord Demay's soldiers chased after my men. Finally, once they were gone, I let my breath out and glanced around. I was in a small, dimly-lit room that smelled strongly of mold, with empty bottles and barrels covered in dust and cobwebs stacked haphazardly along the stone walls. A closed-door sat across the room and I ran to it and opened it cautiously. I winced as the hinges squealed in protest, but after several heart-pounding seconds of nothing but silence, I cracked open the door further and stepped out into a wide corridor. Torches flickered on the walls around me and I hesitated, unsure of which way to go. Trust in The Mother, I thought as I turned right and began to run.

The corridor finally ended at a darkened stairwell and I hurried down it, hoping I'd found the way to the cavern. Instead, I found myself in an empty room that smelled a lot like Haverty's laboratory. Four cots striped of bedclothes sat in the middle of the room and I could see blood-encrusted bandages lying on the floor. I was in the castle infirmary, I realized with disappointment. An open doorway led off to my right and I rushed through it anxiously, knowing that I could spend an eternity wandering around down here and never find

Shana and the others. I had only a moment to realize a man was standing outside the infirmary door just as something whistled toward my head. I instinctively ducked and heard the harsh sound of metal crashing against stone above me as sparks rained down on my head. I rolled away and came up onto the balls of my feet with my sword up.

"I've always had a nose for finding rats!" Quant Ranes said with a sneer. He turned my father's axe in his hand and looked at the blade. "You took a chip out of my axe," he said reproachfully. "It'll take me half a day to smooth that out."

"You mean my axe, you bastard!" I said. "And I intend to have back."

"And just how are you going to do that, boy from the bog?"

"By prying it from your cold, dead hands!" I growled.

Ranes grinned. "Good luck with that."

I could feel a calm fury coming over me as I took a cautious step forward. I had to find Shana, but Mother Above had just given me a gift in Quant Ranes, and I knew I'd have to deal with that first. I just needed to do it quickly.

"You look a lot like your father," Ranes said smugly.

"So do you!" I retorted. "But then again, all swine look alike to me."

Ranes chuckled and twirled the axe in his hand. "Do you remember I told you that it was me who stuck his head on that board?" I stayed silent and Ranes shrugged. "Well, I forgot to mention that I also pissed on his face after I stuck it there."

I knew Ranes was trying to bait me, but even so, I could feel the white-hot rage beginning to take over me. "You talk an awful lot," I grunted. "Old men usually do. They're more about what they used to do, rather than what they're going to do."

Ranes chuckled. "I'm not too old to piss on your head once I take it. Just like I did your father."

"Then do it!" I shouted.

I leaped forward and swung for Ranes' stomach. The older man twirled away, moving fast and I had to dodge a vicious swing from the axe that just glanced off my hip. I took a step back, grimacing as pain shot down my leg.

"That wasn't half bad," Ranes said with a laugh. "But predictable." He shook his head. "I thought you'd be better than this. I'm disappointed in you."

I kept quiet, conserving my breath as we circled each other. Torches lit the corridor every ten feet or so and they danced as we moved; the flames the only witness to our struggle. Ranes was very good, I realized, and even if I beat him, the chances were I'd be injured doing it. Maybe too injured to help Shana. This had to end now! Ranes was wearing full body armor, but no helmet, and as the flames flickered on the torch near him, I suddenly had an idea. I took several swipes at Ranes, pushing him backward and away from the closest torch. The older man easily blocked my attacks and I could tell he was feeling confident as I moved in closer to the wall. I'd been studying Ranes' movements from the beginning, which was something Jebido had instilled in me years ago. Ranes was strong, fast, and good with either hand, and I knew he wouldn't hesitate to strike at me from any angle. But for my plan to work, I had to make sure he came at me from only one angle. Twice now Ranes had mentioned my father's severed head and I knew he wanted to take mine with one swing of the axe. I decided I'd give him that swing.

I attacked with everything that I had, driving Ranes back against the wall and less than a foot from one of the torches. I knew in another moment the older man would slip away from me, either to my right or to my left. I guessed he'd go left and I rushed at him, going for his head. Ranes immediately dodged to my left, trying for my stomach with the axe as he whirled away. I was expecting exactly that move and I timed it, allowing the axe head to strike my armor at just the right angle. The blade didn't penetrate the armor, just as I'd hoped, but the blow still hurt more than I thought it would. I gasped and dropped my sword, slowly sinking to my knees as I held both my hands over my stomach. I groaned loudly, looking down at my hands as Ranes moved to stand over me. Ranes kicked my sword away and then he chuckled as he lifted my chin with the axe head.

"I told you, boy from the bog," he said. "You're predictable."

Ranes drew the axe back and I waited, looking up at him with defeated eyes. I could hear the wind whistling over my father's blade as it came for my head and at the last moment, I ducked sideways. The axe head hurtled past me and then I was up on my feet. I snatched the torch from the wall above me and jammed it viciously into Ranes' eyes. The older man screamed in agony and my father's axe fell from his hands and landed with a clang on the floor near my feet. I pounced on it as Quant Ranes clawed at his eyes and I shoved him hard from behind into the wall. Ranes bounced heavily off the stone and then spun toward me, his hands up to ward off the blow he had to know was coming.

"For my father, you bastard!" I shouted. Then I took his head.

It took me another ten minutes of anxious searching before I finally found a darkened stairwell that I was certain led down to the cavern. I stood at the top of the stairs and listened to the ominous silence coming from below as I breathed in the stale, heady scent of the bay that drifted up to me. This was the place, I knew. There could be no doubt about it now. I began the descent as my pulse roared wildly in my ears. I knew that whatever I'd find down below, it wasn't going to be good. I had my father's axe in my right hand and a torch in the other and I moved cautiously, pausing to listen with every second or third step. The stairs were narrow and uneven, as though carved in a hurry, and twice I stumbled and almost fell. Finally I reached the bottom landing where my heavy boots crunched loudly across loose chunks of rock as I walked. A low corridor bored through solid rock lay ahead of me and I took perhaps six or seven steps into it before it took a sudden turn to the left. I followed the bend, then halted in dismay as the light from my torch revealed two figures lying crumpled together on the stone floor. It was Cain and Flora I realized with a sinking feeling. I hurried toward them and then cursed as I saw the gaping wound in Cain's neck. I didn't need to look any closer to know that he was dead. I knelt by Flora's side and winced as I saw that her blonde hair and face were smeared with blood. Flora's chest was still rising and falling beneath her stained robes, albeit it unsteadily, and I said a silent prayer of thanks to The Mother that she lived.

"Is someone there?" I heard Aenor call out weakly in that strange accent of hers from farther down the corridor.

I raised the torch, just able to see Aenor's slight figure lying propped up against the wall about forty feet away. Aenor had both her hands pressed tightly against her stomach and she started to sob when she saw that it was me as I knelt beside her. Thick dark blood and pink entrails were oozing out from between her fingers and I grimaced, knowing what that meant.

"I'm sorry, Hadrack!" Aenor whispered.

I put my hand on Aenor's cheek and stroked it gently. "What happened?" I asked, trying to hide the dread I felt inside.

"Lord Demay," Aenor said. She coughed and I pretended not to notice as blood sprayed down her chin and onto her robe. "He took her." She gestured weakly behind me with her head. "There's a hidden door somewhere near the stairs. He came from there." Aenor closed her eyes and coughed again, spitting up more blood. She shuddered and I thought I'd lost her, but then she opened her eyes and looked at me with tears rolling down her cheeks. "I'm sorry. We tried to run, but it all happened so fast."

"There's nothing to be sorry about," I whispered. I moved her hair from her eyes and glanced down the darkened corridor, then back the way I'd come. "Do you know where they went?" I asked softly. I didn't want to leave Aenor to die alone in this dark place, but I knew if I didn't go now, Shana might die too.

"Back through the door," Aenor said. She lifted a bloody hand away from her wound and placed it on my chest. "I lied to you, Hadrack."

"About what?" I asked in puzzlement as I took her hand in mine.

"I did want to come between you and your girl," Aenor said. She smiled sadly. "Not at first. But once I got to know you, I couldn't help myself. I guess it wasn't meant to be." Aenor leaned her head back against the stone and I could see the light slowly fading from her eyes. "Go get her, Hadrack," she whispered weakly. "Go get your girl."

Aenor's head slowly dropped to her chest as she died and I sat back on my haunches, feeling a tear slowly slide down my scarred face. Finally I stood and stalked back the way I'd come, feeling an over-whelming anger rippling across my entire body. The bastard would pay for Aenor, I vowed! Aenor, Cain and Flora! I paused to check on Flora on the way back, but she remained as before and I knew there was nothing I could do for her at the moment. I also knew that if she had a voice right now, that voice would be telling me to save Shana no matter what. I hefted my axe and made my way around the bend, heading back to the landing and the stairs. Aenor had said the door was somewhere near the stairs, so I held my torch close to the stone and searched the wall on either side. After about five minutes of frustration, I finally located the cracks of the hidden doorway about six feet away from the steps on the eastern wall. It took some effort, but by using the blade of my father's axe as a wedge, I was finally able to pry the door open. I stepped through the doorway, mindful of my experience with Quant Ranes, but there was no one around. I found myself standing in a circular shaft, with nothing in front of me but a spiraling staircase that disappeared upward into the darkness. I raised the torch over my head and peered above me, but it barely seemed to help, so I just grunted and started to climb.

It seemed like it took me hours to climb those cursed stairs, but in reality it must have only been minutes. I finally reached a wide stone landing and I took a precious moment to try to catch my breath. I could see an archway leading off to my right in the torchlight, and though I still felt winded, I headed that way. I passed through the archway to find myself in a narrow corridor with the ceiling so low that I had to crouch. My hair brushed the stone above me and my shoulders scrapped against both sides of the wall as I moved. I fought a sneeze as the air inside the corridor turned musty and dank, trying not to think about getting trapped as the corridor became even smaller as I progressed. Finally I stepped out into a small, circular room where I could thankfully straighten my back. I saw a doorway made of solid stone sitting directly in front of me and I hurried over to it. I set the torch down and gave the door an experimental push, but nothing happened. I tried pulling carefully at it with my fingers, trying to be silent, but it wouldn't move. I was hesitant to use the axe to pry it open, fearful the noise would alert Lord Demay. I could hear raised voices coming from the other side of the wall and then something crashed loudly. I began pushing and pulling on the door frantically, cursing softly under my breath as it still refused to budge. I was about to use the axe regardless of the noise it made when finally something clicked and the door swung open an inch toward me. The voices on the other side instantly got louder.

"All you had to do was make an effort!" I heard Lord Demay say angrily.

"You're despicable!" I heard Shana snort. "You should have just killed me down there like you did the others."

"I'm giving you a chance to live, you stupid bitch!" Lord Demay shouted. "Show some gratitude!"

"Gratitude!?" Shana shouted back. "If you want me to

be grateful, you ugly, impudent bastard, then take your sword and end this!"

I decided I'd heard enough and I swung the door wide open, not caring as the hinges screeched as I stepped through. We were in Lord Demay's bed-chamber, I realized as I quickly scanned the room. Shana was sitting with her back to me in a high-backed chair twenty feet away, while Lord Demay stood in front of her with his sword held over his shoulder. Lord Demay's mouth dropped open in surprise as I stepped into the room and Shana whirled around in her chair, gasping when she saw me. Lord Demay got over his surprise quickly and he shouted in fury, drawing back his sword to plunge it into Shana's back. I did the only thing I could think of and I threw my father's axe. The axe was ungainly with its double-sided blade and long, carved handle, and it had never been designed as a weapon to throw. I could have probably thrown it twenty times on any other day and missed all twenty. But I like to think that on that day my father was with me and it was he who guided the axe for me. Whatever the case, the axe twirled end over end once, then caught Lord Demay squarely down the middle of his face, slicing deep into his brain. I thought instantly of the reeve and how I'd killed him similarly years before as Lord Demay slowly dropped his sword and then fell backward with a clash of armor to the carpeted floor.

Shana and I paused for a long moment after that, both of us unable to move in the sudden silence as we stared at each other. Then she was up and running to me and I could see tears streaming down her face. I put my arms around her and hugged her tightly to my chest as she sobbed against my dented and soiled armor. I don't know how long we remained that way, but eventually it dawned on me that I could hear cheering coming from the courtyard below us. I frowned in puzzlement and broke the embrace as I moved to the closest window.

"Will you look at that!" I said to Shana in surprise as she came to stand beside me.

Villagers and merchants and castle soldiers were all celebrating as a steady stream of Cardians ran for the open gates in flight. Many of the villagers held pitchforks, clubs and even swords, and they waved them in the air deliriously. I could see Malo, Baine and Jebido and the rest my men in amongst the villagers, and I was relieved to see that young Hanley was with them as well.

"What happened?" Shana asked in obvious shock.

"They fought for you!" I said in wonder as I turned to her. "Don't you understand? Your people turned on the Cardians and fought for you!"

"But why?" Shana whispered. "Why risk so much just for me?"

"Because you told them to live free, not stay trapped in a cage," I said with a laugh. I gestured to the cheering crowd. "They took your words to heart."

"Kylan must have organized them," Shana said, shaking her head in disbelief as she stared out the window.

"Your steward is a good man," I said. "I have one just like him back home."

Shana looked at me strangely at that and we stared at each other in the sudden awkward silence, both of us unsure of what to say next. Neither of us moved apart, though, and we stood at the window with our heads almost touching. I felt a shadow cross my heart at the lives lost to get me here and I knew there would never be a better moment than this to tell Shana how I felt. The lives that had been sacrificed were owed that at the very least. But, truth be told, now that the time had come, I was more terrified of uttering those few simple words than I would have been throwing myself up against a thousand Cardians.

"What?" Shana asked as she saw the look on my face.

I fought to say the words, afraid of the scornful reaction I was certain I would get. Shana stared up at me with her huge, unblinking eyes and I glanced away from them uncertainly. Perhaps I should just keep my mouth closed, I thought, and save her the embarrassment of having to reject me. My gaze fell on Lord Demay's body and my father's axe embedded in his face. I had a sudden vision of my mother, still heavy with my little brother Renfry in her belly as she sat with my father at the table in our home. They were laughing together in contentment and Jeanna and Lallo were there as well, laughing right along with them. We were simple peasants with nothing ahead of us back then. Nothing but a life of back-breaking hard work, hardship and death. Yet, despite all that, we had been happy. And the reason we had been, I realized, was all because of love. My family might be gone now, but the love I felt for them was still with me and I knew that it was a constant source of strength for me. I realized hiding the love I felt for Shana after all that had happened would be foolish, regardless of what the return reply might be. I finally shrugged off all my doubts and turned back to her.

"I love you!" I blurted out.

Shana stared at me for a moment and then her face lit up with a smile. "I know, Hadrack," she said softly as she reached up to trace the scar on my face with her finger. "I love you too."

"Really?" I asked, hardly daring to believe it.

"Really," Shana said with a musical laugh. "From the moment you burst through that door in the abbey, I knew that I loved you." I stared at her in amazement and she grinned almost shyly. "Why do you think I went to Gasterny with you in the first place?"

I felt wonder and joy explode inside me and, giddy as a child, I swept Shana up in my arms and headed for Lord Demay's bed.

"No!" Shana cried, looking alarmed.

I felt my face reddening and I faltered. I'd been around whores and Piths for far too long, I realized, knowing what a fool I'd just been. Shana was a lady, not some wild Pith warrior eager for a rutting at a moments notice.

"I'm sorry," I said, starting to put her down. "Forgive

The Wolf At Large

me, I was just caught up in the moment."

Shana laughed and hugged my neck, not allowing me to release her. "You giant ninny! I just meant not in here. I hate this room! Mine is down the corridor."

I stared at Shana in shock, then I laughed and whirled her around in my arms before I cradled her like a babe as I almost ran out of the room. I stepped out into a richly carpeted hallway and hesitated, not sure where to go.

"That one," Shana said, pointing demurely to a doorway at the end of the hall.

I reached the door and tried to open it, but with Shana in my arms I couldn't work the handle. I looked to her for help, but Shana just stared back at me with a challenge in her eyes. I chuckled and shrugged, then kicked the door in with a heavy kick. Shana laughed with delight and I paused in the doorway as a boy sitting on the floor by the door with his hands over his head cried out in terror. The boy peered through his arms at me and I recognized him as the same boy who'd been chasing the ball down in the middle bailey earlier today. To this day I have no idea how he'd gotten in there.

"Get out!" I growled at him. "This isn't for your eyes."

The boy stared at me for a moment, then he jumped to his feet and ran out of the room wailing as though a thousand angry Piths were after him. Truth be told, I barely noticed as I kicked the door closed behind me.

I'd found my girl.

EPILOGUE

I think I can sleep now. Finally, after more than six months of writing, the words are down on paper for all to see. I feel very tired and very old sitting here at my table and, as I look at my bed, I see it for the first time in many months now as an old friend, rather than the enemy it's been to me recently. I have barely eaten or slept since I started writing these words, afraid, I think, that The Mother would decide to take me in the dead of night before I'd finished my tale. While it's true that Lady Shana — as she would now be known — and I were destined to marry, that time had not yet come. I was only nineteen-years-old when Calban fell, with a price on my head and, as it turned out, still much work left to do. With the death of Lord Demay, Lady Shana became ruler of Calban, denying Prince Tyrale and his people a strategic castle, not to mention the loss of one of his most powerful lords. A war was brewing on the horizon for Ganderland. A war that promised to be vicious and brutal and one that would eventually tear the kingdom and the Holy House itself apart, pitting Son against Daughter and brother against brother. But, unbeknownst to any of us, forces outside the kingdom were on the move as well, quite rightly sensing weakness. Where there's weakness, I've learned over the years, opportunity always exists for those ruthless enough to try to seize it.

I was still young and naive enough after Calban that I truly believed the worst was now over for Shana and me. Lord Demay was dead by my hand, as were four of the nine, and I foolishly believed that nothing could stop me now that I had her love. Arrogance can be just as deadly as a Pith cavalry charge; I would soon come to learn. I think back on that arrogance now and all I can do is shake my head at how innocent I had been once. I had known nothing but heartache and misery my entire life up until that point, and as ridiculous as it seems to me now, I believed then that things were about to change for the better. I have never been so wrong about anything in my life.

But that, my dear friends, is a story best left for another day. My bed calls my name loudly right now and, after so many months, I can no longer ignore it. Tomorrow, if the gods allows it, I will sit and write again. There is still so much more of this story left to tell.

THE END

AUTHOR'S NOTE

I'd like to thank everyone for their overwhelming support of The Nine. To say I'm shocked by its success would be a huge understatement. I began writing The Nine on a cold January morning in 2019 simply for the pure joy of writing. I sat down in my den near a roaring fire, plopped a laptop across my legs and just started clicking away. I don't think I have ever had as much fun as that first day, and if not for my three-year-old black lab, who eerily knows exactly when an hour has passed since the last time we played frisbee outside, I probably wouldn't have even moved at all that day.

Other than the first line of the book, which I'd had in my head for years, I didn't really know where I was going with the story. I knew I wanted to create a character in the mold of Uhtred of Bebbanburg, written by the always amazing Bernard Cornwell, but that was all. I've been asked more than once why, if I'm such a big fan of Mr. Cornwell,did I go the fantasy route with the story, rather than pick a time in real history to write about like he does. The long answer to that question would probably fill another book, but the short one is, quite simply, I didn't want to be tied down to history. I was writing a story for fun, and quite honestly, I didn't know at the time if I would even finish it, let alone publish it. I mentioned in The Nine that I wrote several fantasy novels many years ago, and while I'm very proud of them and hope to finish the series some day, they did not do well. I had written those books believing that they would become the golden goose for my family and me and all our financial worries would disappear. Sadly, that didn't happen and I'd be lying if I said I wasn't devastated at the time. Eventually I accepted the fact the books would not sell and I moved on to other things, which, in the end, turned out to have been the right thing to do.

Life can be funny sometimes. The success I so dearly yearned for back then has found me now, at least for the moment, and while my wife and I are enjoying it immensely, we know that can change in an instant and we're taking nothing for granted. The Wolf At Large was just as much fun to write as The Nine was and the story of Hadrack, The Wolf of Corwick will continue.

Thank you, once again, for your continued support. I truly hope you enjoyed reading this book.

Terry Cloutier
February 2020

Also By The Author

The Wolf of Corwick Castle Series

The Nine (2019)
The Wolf At Large (2020)
The Wolf On The Run (Fall-2020)

The Zone War Series

The Demon Inside (2006)
The Balance of Power (2008)
The Master Eye (Unknown)

Peter Pickler and the Cat That Talked Back (2008)

Made in the USA
Monee, IL
22 January 2021